Other characters in Dragonlance may belong
to various creators, but Margaret, from the
very outset, made it clear to all concerned
that Raistlin was hers and hers alone. We
never begrudged her the dark mage—she
seemed to be the only one who could comfort
his character and soothe his troubled mind.
—Tracy Hickman

I'm still learning about Raistlin. With every
book I write about him and his twin and their
adventures in the world, I discover something
new.
—Margaret Weis

Brothers in Arms

The Raistlin Chronicles,
Volume Two

Margaret Weis and Don Perrin

For Tracy Hickman

BROTHERS IN ARMS
©1999 TSR, Inc.
All Rights Reserved.

TSR, Inc., is a subsidiary of Wizards of the Coast, Inc.
All rights reserved. Made in the U.S.A.

Cover art by Daniel Horne
First Printing: August 1999
Library of Congress Catalog Card Number: 98-88148

9 8 7 6 5 4 3 2 1

ISBN: 0-7869-1429-7
T21429-620

U.S., CANADA, ASIA,
PACIFIC, & LATIN AMERICA
Wizards of the Coast, Inc.
P.O. Box 707
Renton, WA 98057-0707
+1-800-324-6496

EUROPEAN HEADQUARTERS
Wizards of the Coast, Belgium
P.B. 2031
2600 Berchem
Belgium
+32-70-23-32-77

Visit our website at **www.tsr.com**

"*Warp*: The threads which are extended lengthwise in the loom, usually twisted harder than the weft, or woof, with which these threads are crossed to form the web or piece.

"*Weft*: The threads that cross from side to side of a web, at right angles to the warp threads, with which they are interlaced."

—*Oxford English Dictionary* (Second Edition)

BOOK 1

"I don't care about your name, Red. I don't want to know your name. If you survive your first three or so battles, then maybe I'll learn your name. Not before. I used to learn the names, but it was a goddamned waste of time. Soon as I'd get to know a puke, he'd up and die on me. These days I don't bother."

—Horkin, Master-at-Wizardry

1

Mists shrouded the Tower of High Sorcery at Wayreth, and a light rain fell. The rain shimmered on the mullioned windows. Drops welled up on the thick stone ledges of the windows, overflowed to trickle down the black obsidian walls of the Tower, where the raindrops collected in puddles in the courtyard. In that courtyard stood a donkey and two horses loaded with blanket rolls and saddlebags, ready for travel.

The donkey's head was lowered, her back sagged, her ears drooped. She was a spoiled donkey, fond of dry oats, a snug stable, a sunlit road, and a slow and easy pace. Jenny knew of no reason why her master should travel on such a wet day and had stubbornly resisted all attempts to drag her from her stall. The burly human who had attempted to do so was now nursing a bruised thigh.

The donkey would still be in her warm stall, but she had fallen victim to a ruse, a foul trick played on her by the big human. The fragrant smell of carrot, the lush scent of apple—these had been her temptation and her downfall. Now she stood in the rain, feeling much put upon and determined to make the big human suffer, make them all suffer.

The head of the Conclave, the master of the Tower of Wayreth, Par-Salian, gazed down upon the donkey from the window of his chambers in the North Tower. He saw the donkey's ears twitch, and he winced involuntarily as her left hind hoof lashed out at Caramon Majere, who was endeavoring to secure a pack onto the donkey's saddle. Caramon had fallen victim to the donkey once this day and he was on the lookout. He, too, had seen the telltale ear twitch, understood its portent, and managed to dodge the kick. He stroked the donkey's neck and produced another apple, but the donkey lowered her head. By the look of her, Par-Salian thought—he knew something about donkeys, though few would have believed it—the ornery beast was contemplating rolling on the ground.

Blissfully unaware that all his careful packing was on the verge of being dislodged and squashed flat, not to mention soaked in a puddle, Caramon began loading the two horses. Unlike the donkey, the horses were glad to be away from the confinement and boredom of the stalls, were looking forward to a brisk canter and the chance to stretch their muscles, see new sights. The horses frisked and stamped and danced playfully on the flagstone, blowing and snuffling at the rain, and looking eagerly out the gates at the road beyond.

Par-Salian, too, looked at the road beyond. He could see where it led, could see the road far more clearly than others at that time on Krynn. He saw the trials and travails, he saw the danger. He saw hope, too, though its light was dim and wavering as the magical light cast by a crystal atop a young mage's staff. Par-Salian had purchased this hope, but at a terrible cost, and, at the moment, hope's light did little more than reveal to him more dangers. He must have faith, however. Faith in the gods, faith in himself, faith in the one he had chosen as his battle sword.

His "battle sword" stood in the courtyard, miserable in the rain, coughing fitfully, shivering and chilled as he watched his brother—limping slightly from his bruised thigh—ready the horses for their journey. A warrior such as the brother would have rejected such a sword outright, for it was, to all appearances, weak and brittle, liable to break at the first pass.

Par-Salian knew more about this sword than did the sword itself, perhaps. He knew that the iron will of the young mage's soul, having been tempered with blood, heated by fire, shaped by fate's hammer, and cooled with his own tears, was now finest steel, strong and sharp. Par-Salian had created a fine-honed weapon, but like all weapons, it had a double edge. It could be used to defend the weak and the innocent, or to attack them. He did not know yet which way the sword would cut. He doubted if the sword knew.

The young mage, wearing his new red robes—plain homespun robes without adornment, for he had no money to purchase better—stood huddled beneath a rose tree blooming in the courtyard, finding what shelter he could from the rain. The thin shoulders of the young man shook occasionally, he coughed into a handkerchief. At every cough, his brother, hale and robust, would pause in his work to glance back at his frail twin anxiously. Par-Salian could see the young man stiffen with irritation, could see his lips move and almost hear his curt admonition for his brother to get on with his task and leave him be.

Another person bustled out into the courtyard, just in time to prevent the donkey from spilling her load. A neat and dapper man of middle years, wearing gray robes— he would not spoil his white robes with the stains of travel—and a hooded cloak, Antimodes was a welcome sight. His cheerful air seemed to dispel the gloom of the day as he chided the donkey, all the while fondling her ears, and instructed the robust twin on some point of packing, to judge by the hand-waving and gesticulating. Par-Salian could not hear their conversation, but he smiled at the sight. Antimodes was old friend, mentor, and sponsor to the young mage.

Antimodes lifted his head and gazed at the North Tower, looking up at Par-Salian looking down. Though Antimodes could not see the Head of the Order from where he stood in the courtyard, he knew perfectly well that Par-Salian was there and that he was watching. Antimodes frowned and glowered, making certain that Par-Salian was aware of his ire and disapproval. The rain and the mist were Par-Salian's doing, of course. The Head of the Conclave controlled the weather around the Tower of High Sorcery. He could have sent his guests off in sunshine and springtime had he chosen to do so.

In truth, Antimodes was not that upset about the weather. It was merely an excuse. The real reason for Antimodes's ire was his disapproval of the way Par-Salian had handled the young mage's Test in the Tower of High Sorcery. Antimodes's disapproval was so strong that it had cast a cloud over the two men's long friendship.

The rain was Par-Salian's way of saying, "I understand your concern, my friend, but we cannot live all our days in sunshine. The rose tree needs the rain to survive, as well as the sun. And this gloom, this dreary darkness is nothing, my friend, nothing compared to what is yet to come!"

Antimodes shook his head, as if he had heard Par-Salian's thoughts, and turned grumpily away. A practical and pragmatic man, he didn't appreciate the symbolism, and he resented being forced to start out on his journey wet to the bone.

The young mage had been watching Antimodes closely. When Antimodes turned away and went back to placating his irate donkey, Raistlin Majere turned his own gaze to the North Tower, to the very window where stood Par-Salian. The archmage felt the gaze of those eyes—golden eyes, whose pupils were the shape of hourglasses—touch him, prick his flesh as though the tip of the sword's blade had sliced across his skin. The golden eyes, with their accursed vision, gave no hint of the thoughts behind them.

Raistlin did not understand fully what had happened to him. Par-Salian dreaded the day when Raistlin would come to understand. But that had been part of the price.

Was the young mage bitter, resentful? Par-Salian wondered. His body had been shattered, his health ruined. From now on, he would be sickly, easily fatigued, in pain, reliant on his stronger brother. Resentment would be natural, understandable. Or was Raistlin accepting? Did he believe that the fine steel of his blade had been worth the price? Probably not. He did not yet know his own strength. He would have time to learn, the gods willing. He was about to receive his first lesson.

All the archmages in the Conclave had either participated in Raistlin's Test or they had heard about what had occurred during the Test from their colleagues.[1] None of them would accept him as an apprentice.

"His soul is not his own," said Ladonna of the Black Robes, "and who knows when the buyer will come to claim his property."

The young mage needed instruction, needed training not only in magic, but in life. Par-Salian had done some discreet investigation and found a teacher whom he hoped would provide a suitable course of study. A rather unlikely instructor, but one in whom Par-Salian had a lot of faith, though this instructor would have been astounded to hear so.

Acting under Par-Salian's instructions, Antimodes inquired if the young mage and his brother would be interested in traveling east during the springtime, to train as mercenaries with the army of the renowned Baron Ivor of Langtree. Such training would be ideally suited to the young mage and his warrior brother, who needed to earn their bread and butter, all the while honing their martial skills.

Skills they would need later, unless Par-Salian was very much mistaken.

There was no need for hurry. The time of the year was early fall, the season when warriors begin to think of putting away their weapons, start searching for a comfortable place to spend the cold winter days by the fire, telling tales of their own valor. Summer was the season of war, spring the season of preparing for war. The young man would have all winter to heal. Or rather, he would have time to adapt to his handicap, for he would never heal.

[1] The story of Raistlin's Test in the Tower of High Sorcery is related in *The Soulforge*, TSR publisher, 1998.

Such legitimate work would prevent Raistlin from exhibiting his talents in the local fairs in exchange for money, something he'd done in the past, much to the shock of the Conclave. It was all very well for illusionists or unskilled practitioners of the art to make spectacles of themselves before the public, but not for those who had been accepted into the Conclave.

Par-Salian had yet another motive for sending Raistlin to the baron, a motive the young man would never—if he was lucky—come to know. Antimodes had his suspicions. His old friend Par-Salian never did anything just for the doing of it, all his means were aimed at a specific end. Antimodes had endeavored to find out, for he was man who loved secrets as a miser loves his coins, liked to count them over in the night, fondle them and gloat over them. But Par-Salian was closemouthed, would not fall victim to even the most cunningly laid snare.

The small group was at last ready to set out. Antimodes climbed upon his donkey. Raistlin mounted his horse with assistance from his brother, assistance that he accepted churlishly and with an ill grace, by the looks of it. Caramon, with exemplary patience, made certain his brother was settled and comfortable, and then he swung himself easily into the saddle of his own large-boned steed.

Antimodes took the lead. The three headed toward the gate. Caramon rode with his head down against the slashing rain. Antimodes left with a backward glare for the North Tower window, a glare expressive of his extreme discomfort and irritation. Raistlin halted his horse at the last moment, turned in the saddle to gaze at the Tower of High Sorcery. Par-Salian could guess what was going through the young man's mind. Much the same had gone through his mind, when he had been young.

How my life has changed in only a few short days! I entered this place strong and confident. I leave it weak and shattered, my vision cursed, my body frail. Yet, I leave this place triumphant. I leave with the magic. To gain that, I would have traded away my very soul. . . .

"Yes," Par-Salian said quietly, watching until the three had ridden into the magical Forest of Wayreth and there vanished from his mortal sight. His mind's eye kept them in view much longer. "Yes, you would have. You did. But you don't know that yet."

The rain fell harder. Antimodes would be cursing his friend heartily now. Par-Salian smiled. They would have sunshine when they left the forest. The sun's heat would bake them dry, they would not have to ride long in wet clothes. Antimodes was a wealthy man, fond of his comforts. He would see to it that they slept in a bed in a reputable inn. He would pay for it, too, if he could find a way to do so that would not offend the twins, who had only a few meager coins in their purses, but whose pride could have filled the royal coffers of Palanthas.

Par-Salian turned from the window. He had too much to do to stand there, staring out into a curtain of rain. He cast a wizard-lock spell upon the door, a strong spell that would keep out even the most powerful mages, mages such as Ladonna of the Black Robes. Admittedly, Ladonna had not visited the Tower in a long, long time, but she took great delight in arriving unexpectedly and at the most inopportune moments. It would never do for her to find him involved in these particular studies. Nor could he allow any of the other mages who lived in or frequented the Tower to find out what he was doing.

The time was not right to disclose what little he knew. He did not yet know enough. He had to learn more, to discover if what he had begun to suspect was true. He had to learn more, to ascertain if the information he had gleaned from his spies was accurate.

Certain that no one short of Solinari, God of White Magic, could break the spell cast upon the door, Par-Salian seated himself at his desk. On the desk—which was of dwarf-make, a present from one of the thanes of Thorbardin in return for services rendered—lay a book.

The book was old, very old. Old and forgotten. Par-Salian had found the book only by references made to it in other texts, else he himself would not have known of its existence. At that, he'd been forced to search for it for a great many hours, search through the library of the Tower of High Sorcery, a library of reference books and spellbooks and magical scrolls, a library so vast that it had never been catalogued. Nor would it ever be catalogued, except in Par-Salian's mind, for there were dangerous texts there, texts whose existence must be carefully guarded, texts known only to the Heads of the Three Orders, certain texts known only to the Master of the Tower himself. There were also texts of whose existence even he was not aware, as proven by the book in front of him, a book he had finally discovered in a corner of a storage room packed either mistakenly or by design in a box labeled "Child's Play."

Judging from the other artifacts to be found in the box, the box itself had come from the Tower of High Sorcery in Palanthas and dated back to the time of Huma. The box had undoubtedly been among those hastily packed when the mages had swallowed their pride and abandoned their Tower, rather than declare all-out war upon the people of Ansalon. The box marked "Child's Play" had been shoved into a corner and then forgotten in the chaos following the Cataclysm.

Par-Salian brushed his hand gently over the leather cover of the old book, the only book to be found in the box. He brushed away the dust and mouse-droppings and cobwebs that had partially obliterated the book's embossed title, a title whose letters he felt as bumps beneath his fingertips. A title that raised bumps on his flesh.

The Book of Dragons

2

The trees of Wayreth Forest, wayward and magical guardian of the Tower of High Sorcery, lined up like soldiers on parade duty, stood tall and silent and stern beneath the lowering clouds.

"Guards of honor," said Raistlin.

"For a funeral," muttered Caramon.

He did not like the forest, which was no natural forest but a wandering and unexpected forest, a forest that was nowhere in sight of a morning and all around you in the evening. A dangerous forest to those who entered it unawares. He was thankful when they finally left the forest, or perhaps it was the forest who finally left them.

Whichever way it was, the trees took the clouds with them. Caramon removed his hat and lifted his face to the sun, basking in the warmth and the radiance.

"I feel like I haven't seen the sun in months," he said in a low voice with a baleful, backward glance at the Wayreth Forest, now a formidable wall of wet, black-boled trees, shrouded in gray mist. "It's good to be away from that place. I never want to go back, not as long as I live."

"There's absolutely no reason you should, Caramon," Raistlin said. "Believe me, you will not be invited back. Nor," he added an undertone, "will I."

"That's good, then," Caramon said stoutly. "I don't know why you'd want to go back. Not after"—he glanced at his brother, saw his grim expression, the eyes glinting, and faltered—"not after . . . well . . . what they did to you."

Caramon's courage, which had been squashed flat in the Tower of High Sorcery, was reviving wonderfully in the warm sunshine, out from under the shadows of the watching, distrustful trees.

"It's not right what those mages did to you, Raist! I can say it now that we're away from that horrible place. Now that I'm sure no one's going to turn me into a beetle or an ant or something just for speaking my mind.

"I mean no offense, sir," Caramon added, shifting his attention to their traveling companion, the white-robed archmagus, Antimodes. "I appreciate all you've done for my brother in the past, sir, but I think you might have tried to stop your fiends from torturing him. There was no need for that. Raistlin could have died. He very nearly did die. And you didn't do a thing. Not a damn thing!"

"Enough, Caramon!" Raistlin admonished, shocked.

He glanced anxiously at Antimodes, who, fortunately, did not appear to have taken offense at Caramon's blunt statement. It almost appeared as if the archmagus agreed with what had been said. Still, Caramon was behaving like a buffoon, as usual.

"You forget yourself, my brother!" Raistlin stated angrily. "Apologize—"

Raistlin's throat constricted, he could not breathe. He let fall the reins to grip the pommel of the saddle, so weak and dizzy he feared he might fall from the horse. Leaning over the pommel, he tried desperately to clear his throat. His lungs burned, just as they had during the time years back when he'd been so sick, the time he'd collapsed in his mother's grave. He coughed and coughed but could not catch his breath. Blue flame flickered before his eyes.

This is the end! he thought in terror. I cannot survive this one!

The spasm eased suddenly and Raistlin drew in a shuddering breath, another, and another. His vision cleared. The burning pain subsided. He was able to sit upright. Fumbling for a handkerchief, he spit out the phlegm and the blood, used the handkerchief to wipe his lips. His hand closed over the handkerchief quickly, stuffed it back into the silken cord belt he wore around his waist, tucked the stained cloth in the folds of his red robes so that Caramon did not see it.

Caramon was off his horse, standing at Raistlin's side, regarding him with anxiety, arms outstretched, ready to catch him should he fall. Raistlin was angry at Caramon, but more angry at himself, angry at the momentary twinge of self-pity that wanted to sob out, "Why *did* they do this to me? Why?"

He gave his brother a scathing look. "I am quite capable of sitting a horse without assistance, my brother," he said caustically. "Make your apologies to the archmagus and then let us proceed. And put your hat back on! The sun will fry what few brains you have left."

"No need for you to apologize, Caramon," Antimodes said mildly, though his gaze, when it fell upon Raistlin, was grave. "You spoke your heart. No harm in that. Your care and concern for your brother are perfectly natural. Laudable, in fact."

And that is intended as a rebuke to me, Raistlin said to himself. You *know*, don't you, Master Antimodes? Did they let you watch? Did you watch me kill my twin? Or what turned out to be the illusion of my twin. Not that it matters. The knowledge that I have it within me to commit such a heinous act is the same as the deed. I horrify you, don't I? You don't treat me as you used to. I'm no longer the prize discovery, the young and gifted pupil you were so proud to exhibit. You admire me—grudgingly. You pity me. But you don't like me.

He said none of this aloud. Caramon remounted his horse in silence, and in silence the three rode off slowly. They had not traveled ten miles when Raistlin, weaker than he'd anticipated, stated that he could go no farther. The gods alone knew how he had pushed himself this far, for he was so weak that he was forced to allow Caramon to help ease him from the saddle, half-carry him inside.

Antimodes fussed over Raistlin, ordering the best room in the inn—though Caramon said many times over that the common room would do for them both—and

MARGARET WEIS AND DON PERRIN

recommending the broth of a boiled chicken to settle the stomach.

Caramon sat by Raistlin's bed, gazing at him helplessly, until Raistlin, annoyed beyond endurance, ordered his brother to go about his business and leave him to rest.

But he could not rest. He was not sleepy, his mind was active, if his body was not. He thought of Caramon—downstairs flirting with the barmaids and drinking too much ale. Antimodes would be down there, too, eavesdropping on conversations, picking up information. The fact that the white-robed wizard was one of Par-Salian's spies was an open secret among the denizens of the Tower, a secret not hard to deduce. A powerful archmagus, who could whisk himself from place to place with a few words of magic, did not travel the dusty roads of Ansalon on the back of a donkey unless he had good reason to want to dawdle in inns and gossip with the innkeepers, all the while keeping an eye on who came in and who went out.

Raistlin left his bed to sit at a small table next to a window, a window looking out onto a wheat field, bright gold against the green of the trees beneath a sun-filled blue sky. In his eyes—the cursed hourglass eyes of enchantment, first inflicted in ancient days as a lesson on the arrogant and dangerous renegade sorceress Relanna—Raistlin saw the wheat turning brown with the coming of autumn, drying up, its stalks stiff and brittle, to break beneath the snow. He saw the leaves on the trees wither and die, drift down to lie in the dust until they were blown away on cold winter winds.

He shifted his gaze from the dismal view. He would spend this precious time, this time alone, on study. He opened and laid out on the table the small quarto that contained information about the precious Staff of Magius, the magical artifact given to him by Par-Salian as . . . what? Compensation?

Raistlin knew better than that. Taking the Test had been his choice. He had known going into the Test that it would change him. All candidates are given that warn-

16

ing. Raistlin had been going to remind Caramon of this fact before the coughing fit seized him and wrung him like a dog wrings a knotted dishtowel. Mages had died during the Test before this, and the only compensation their families received was the mage's clothes sent home in a neat bundle with a letter of condolence from the Head of the Conclave. Raistlin was one of the fortunate ones. He had survived with his life, if not his health. He had survived with his sanity, although he sometimes feared his hold on that was tenuous.

He reached out to touch the staff, which was never far from his grasp. During their days in the Tower, Caramon had rigged a means of carrying the staff on horseback, lashing the staff on the back of the saddle, always near to Raistlin's hand. The smooth wood tingled with the lightning feel of magic beneath his fingers, acted as a tonic, easing his pain—pain of body, pain of mind, pain of soul.

He meant to read the book, but he found himself distracted, pondering this strange weakness with which he was afflicted. He had never been strong, not like his hale and robust twin. Fate had played him a cruel joke, had given his twin health and good looks and a guileless, winning nature; had given Raistlin a weak body, nondescript looks, native cunning, a quick mind, and a nature incapable of trust. But in compensation, Fate—or the gods— had given him the magic. The tingle of the feel of the magical staff seeped into his blood, warming it pleasantly, and he did not envy Caramon his ale or his barmaids.

But this weakness, this burning of fever in his body, this constant cough, this inability to draw a breath, as if his lungs were filled with dust, the blood on the handkerchief. The weakness would not kill him, at least so Par-Salian had assured him. Not that Raistlin believed everything Par-Salian told him—white-robed mages did not lie, but they did not necessarily tell you the truth either. Par-Salian had been extremely vague when it came to explaining to Raistlin just exactly what was wrong with him, what it was that had happened to him during the Test to have left him in such a weak and pitiful condition.

Raistlin remembered the Test clearly, most of it, at least. The magical Tests were designed to teach the mage something about himself, also to determine the color of the robes he wore, to which of the gods of the magic he pledged his allegiance. Raistlin had gone into the Test wearing white robes to honor his sponsor, Antimodes. Raistlin had come out wearing red, the robes of neutrality, honoring the goddess Lunitari. Raistlin did not walk the paths of light, nor did he walk the shadowed paths of darkness. He walked his own path, in his own way, of his own choosing.

Raistlin remembered fighting with a dark elf. He remembered—a terrible memory—the elf stabbing him with a poisoned dagger. Raistlin remembered pain, remembered his strength ebbing. He remembered dying, remembered being glad to die. And then Caramon had come to rescue him. Caramon had saved his twin with the use of his twin's one gift—the magic. It was then, in a jealous rage, that Raistlin had killed his brother. Except that it had only been an illusion of his brother.

And Caramon had seen his brother slay him.

Par-Salian had permitted Caramon to watch this part of the Test, the last part. Caramon now knew the darkness that twisted and writhed in his twin's soul. Caramon should, by rights, hate his twin for what he'd done to him. Raistlin wished Caramon would hate him. His brother's hatred would be so much easier to bear than his pity.

But Caramon did not hate Raistlin. Caramon "understood," or so he said.

"I wish I did," Raistlin said bitterly.

He remembered the Test, but not all of it. A part was missing. When he looked back on the Test in his mind, it was like looking at a painting that someone has deliberately marred. He saw people, but the faces were blotted out, smeared over with black ink. And ever since the Test, he had the oddest feeling; the feeling that someone was following him. He could almost feel a hand about to touch his shoulder, the whiff of a cold breath on the back of his neck. Raistlin had the impression that if he could just turn around quickly enough, he'd catch a glimpse of whatever it was that lurked behind him. He'd caught himself more than once whipping his head around, staring over his shoulder. But there was never anyone there. Only Caramon, with his sad and anxious eyes.

Raistlin sighed and banished the questions, which wearied him for no good reason, for they led him nowhere. He set himself to read the book, which had been written by a scribe attached to Huma's army, and which occasionally mentioned Magius and his wondrous staff. Magius—one of the greatest wizards ever to have lived, a friend to the legendary Knight Huma—Magius had assisted Huma in his battle against the Queen of Darkness and her evil dragons.

Magius had placed many enchantments on the staff, but he had left no record of them, a common practice among magi, particularly if the artifact was exceptionally powerful and they feared it might fall into the wrong hands. Generally the master passed the artifact and the knowledge of its power on to a trusted apprentice, who would hand it on in turn. But Magius had died before he could hand over the staff. Whoever used the staff now would have to puzzle out its abilities for himself.

After only a few days' study, Raistlin had already learned from his reading that the staff gave the possessor the ability to float in the air as lightly as thistledown and that, if used as a club, its magic would increase the force of a blow, so that even someone as weak as Raistlin could deal considerable harm to an enemy. These were useful functions, but Raistlin was quite certain the staff was far more powerful. The reading was slow going, for the language was a mixture of Solamnic, which he had learned from his friend Sturm Brightblade, and Common and a slang used by soldiers and mercenaries. It would often take Raistlin an hour to figure out the meaning of a single page. He read again a passage, which he was certain was important, but one that he had yet to understand the meaning of.

We knew the black dragon was nearby, for we could hear the hissing of solid rock dissolving in the deadly acid of the foul wrym's spittle. We could hear the creak of its wings and its claws scrape against the castle walls as it climbed over them in search of us. But we could see nothing, for the dragon had cast upon us some sort of evil magic, which quenched the sunshine and made all dark as the wrym's own heart. The dragon's plan was to come upon us in this darkness and slay us before we could battle it.

Huma called for torchlight, but no flame could we kindle in the thick air, which had been poisoned by the fumes from the dragon's deadly breath. We feared that all was lost and that we would die in this unholy darkness. But then Magius came forward, bearing light! I know not how he accomplished it, but the crystal of the staff he bore drove away the darkness and let us see the terrible monster. We had a target for our arrows and, by Huma's command, we launched our attack. . . .

Several pages detailed the killing of the dragon, which Raistlin skipped over impatiently as information he would probably never need to know. No dragon had been seen on Krynn since Huma's time, and there were those who were now saying that even then they were only creatures of myth. That Huma had made it all up in order to glorify himself, that he'd been nothing but a showman, a self-aggrandizing liar.

I asked a friend how Magius had caused his staff to shine with such a blessed light. The friend, who had been standing near the wizard at the time, said that Magius spoke but a single word of command. I asked what the word was, for I thought it might be of use to the rest of us. He maintained that the word was "shark," which is a type of monstrous fish that lives in the sea and bites men in twain, or so I have heard sailors tell. I do not think he is right, for I tried the word myself, secretly, one night when Magius had left his staff propped up in a corner, and I could not make the crystal light. I can only suppose that the word is a foreign one, perhaps elvish in nature, for Magius is known to have dealings with their kind.

Shark! Raistlin sniffed. Elvish! What a fool. The word was obviously spoken in the language of magic. Raistlin had spent a frustrating hour in the Tower trying every phrase that he could think of in the arcane tongue, every word that bore even a remote resemblance to "shark." He had about as much luck causing the crystal atop the staff to light as had that long-dead and unknown soldier.

A burst of laughter came from downstairs. Raistlin could distinguish Caramon's booming guffaw among the shriller voices of the women. At least his brother was pleasantly occupied and not likely to barge in and disturb him.

Raistlin turned to look at the staff. "*Elem shardish*," he said, which meant, "By my command," a standard phrase used to activate the magic in many an artifact.

But not this one. The crystal, held fast in a golden replica of a dragon's claw, remained dark.

Frowning, Raistlin looked down at the next phrase he'd noted on his list. *Sharcum pas edistus*, another common magical command, which meant roughly "Do as I say." The command did not work either. The crystal gleamed, but only with a beam of reflected sunlight. He continued on through the list, which included *omus sharpuk derli*, for "I will it to be so," to *shirkit muan*, which meant "Obey me."

Raistlin lost patience. "*Uh, Lunitari's idish, shirak, damen du!*"

The crystal atop the staff burst into brilliant, radiant light.

Raistlin stared, astonished, and tried to recall what he'd said, the exact words. His hand trembling, his gaze divided between the wondrous, magical light and his work, he wrote down the phrase, *Uh, Lunitari's idish, shirak, damen du!* and its translation, *Oh, for god's sake, light, damn you!*

And there was the answer.

Raistlin felt his skin burn in embarrassment and was extremely thankful he had not mentioned his puzzlement to anyone, especially Antimodes, as he'd considered doing.

"*I* am the fool," he said to himself. "Making something simple into something difficult. 'Shark.' '*Shirak*.' 'Light.'

That is the command. And to douse the light. '*Dulak*.' 'Dark.'"

The magical light in the crystal blinked out.

Triumphant, Raistlin unpacked his writing equipment, a small quill made of a trimmed goose feather and a sealed bottle of ink. He was entering his discovery in his own small journal when his throat seemed to thicken and swell, shutting off the windpipe. He dropped the quill, causing an inkblot upon the journal, and coughed and choked and struggled for breath. When the spasm passed, he was exhausted. He lacked the strength to lift the feather quill. Barely able to creep back to his bed, he lay down thankfully, resentfully, to wait for the dizziness, the weakness to pass.

Downstairs, another roar of laughter. Caramon was in rare form, apparently. Out in the hallway, Raistlin heard two pairs of footfalls and Antimodes's voice. "I have a map in my room, friend. If you could just be so good as to show me the location of that goblin army. Here is some steel for your trouble. . . ."

Raistlin lay in his bed and struggled to breathe while life went on around him. The sun moved across the sky, the shadows of the window frame slid across the ceiling. Raistlin watched them and wished for a cup of the tea he drank that would ease his pain and wondered fretfully that Caramon did not come to check up on him, to see if there was anything he needed.

But when Caramon did come, late in the afternoon, doing his best to creep into the room without making any noise, he knocked over a pack and woke Raistlin from the first peaceful sleep he'd had in days, for which mistake Caramon received a bitter tongue-lashing and was ordered out of the room.

Ten miles in a single day. Hundreds of miles to go to reach their destination.

The journey was going to be a long one.

3

Raistlin felt better, stronger the next few days. He was able to travel more hours during the day. They reached the outskirts of Qualinesti in good time. Although Antimodes assured them that there was no hurry, that the baron would not muster his army until springtime, the twins hoped to reach the baron's headquarters, a fortress built on an inlet of New Sea, far to the east of Solace, before winter set in. They hoped to be able to at least have their names entered upon the rolls, to perhaps find a way to earn some money in the baron's service, for the twins were now desperately short of coins. Their plans were thrown awry, however. A river crossing proved disastrous.

They were fording the Elfstream when Raistlin's horse slipped on a rock and went down, throwing his rider into the water. Fortunately, the river was slow and sluggish in mid-autumn, after the rushing of the snowmelt in the spring. The water broke his fall, and Raistlin received no greater injury than loss of dignity and a dunking. But a soaking rainstorm that night prevented him from drying off. A chill set in and struck through to the bone.

The next day, he rode shivering beneath a hot sun and by nightfall had fallen into feverish delirium. Antimodes, who had rarely been sick in his life, knew nothing about treating illness. Had Raistlin been conscious, he could have helped himself, for he was a skilled herbalist, but he wandered in dark dreams, horrifying dreams, to judge by his cries and his moans. Desperate with worry for his twin, Caramon risked entering the woods of the Qualinesti elves, hoping to be able to find some among them who would come to his brother's aid.

Arrows fell thick as wheat stalks at his feet, but that did not deter him. He shouted to the unseen archers, "Let me talk to Tanis Half-Elven! I am a friend of Tanis's! He will vouch for us! My brother is dying! I need your aid!"

Unfortunately, the mention of Tanis's name seemed to make matters worse, not better, for the next arrow pierced Caramon's hat, and another grazed his arm, drawing blood. Admitting defeat, he cursed all elves heartily (though under his breath) and retreated from the woods.

The next morning, Raistlin's fever had abated somewhat, enough to permit him to speak rationally. Clutching Caramon's arm, Raistlin whispered, "Haven! Take me to Haven! Our friend, Lemuel, will know what to do for me!"

They traveled to Haven with speed, Caramon holding his ill brother in his arm, propped up in front of him on his saddle, Antimodes galloping behind, leading Raistlin's horse by the reins.

Lemuel was a mage. He was an inept mage, a reluctant mage, but he was a mage, and he and Raistlin had developed an odd sort of friendship on an earlier, ill-fated trip to Haven. Lemuel still held a fondness for Raistlin and readily welcomed him and his brother and the archmagus to his house. Giving Raistlin the very best bedroom, Lemuel saw to it that Antimodes and Caramon were comfortable in other rooms of the large house, then set about doing what he could to help the gravely ill young man.

"He is very sick, there's no doubt about that," Lemuel told the distraught Caramon, "but I don't believe there is cause for alarm. A cold that flew to his chest. Here is a list of some herbs I need. You know where to find the herbalist shop? Excellent. Run along. And don't forget the ipecac."

Caramon left, almost staggering with fatigue but unable to sleep or rest until he was assured his twin was being treated.

Lemuel made certain that Raistlin was resting as comfortably as possible, then went to the kitchen to fetch some cool water, to lave the young man's skillet-hot body, make some attempt to reduce the fever. He encountered Antimodes, enjoying a cup of tea.

Antimodes was a middle-aged human, dapper in his dress, wearing fine, expensive robes. He was a powerful mage, though economic with his power. He didn't like to soil his clothes, as the saying went. By contrast, Lemuel was short, tubby, of a cheerful disposition. He liked nothing better than to work in his garden. As for magic, he had barely enough to boil water.

"Excellent brew this," said the archmagus, who had, in fact, boiled the water himself. "What is it?"

"Chamomile with a touch of mint," said Lemuel. "I picked the mint this morning."

"How is the young man?" Antimodes asked.

"Not good," said Lemuel, sighing. "I didn't like to say anything with his brother around, but he has pneumonia. Both lungs are filled with fluid."

"Can you help him?"

"I will do what I can for him. But he is very ill. I am afraid . . ." Lemuel's voice trailed off. He shook his head again.

Antimodes was silent a moment, sipping at his tea and frowning at the teapot. "Well, perhaps it is better this way," he said at last.

"My dear sir!" Lemuel exclaimed, shocked. "You can't mean that! He's so young!"

"You see how he has changed. You know that he took the Test."

"Yes, Archmagus. His brother told me. The change is . . . quite . . . remarkable." Lemuel shivered. He cast the archmagus a sidelong glance. "Still, I suppose the Order knows what it is doing."

He cocked an ear down the hallway, listening for his patient, whom he had left in a fitful, troubled sleep.

"You'd like to think so, wouldn't you," Antimodes muttered gloomily.

Lemuel was uncomfortable at this, not certain how to reply. Filling his basin with water, he started to leave.

"You knew Raistlin before, I believe," Antimodes stated abruptly.

"Yes, Archmagus," Lemuel said, turning back to his guest. "He has visited me several times."

"What do you think of him?"

"He performed a very great service for me, sir," Lemuel replied, flushing. "I am in his debt. Perhaps you have not heard that story? I was being driven out of my home by a cult of fanatics who worshiped a snake god. Belzor, I think his name was, or some such thing. Raistlin was able to prove that the magic the cultists claimed came from the gods was actually ordinary, run-of-the-mill magic. He very nearly died—"

Antimodes used the sugar spoon to wave away death and gratitude. "I know. I heard. Aside from that, what do you think of him?"

"I like him," said Lemuel. "Oh, he has his faults. I admit that. But then, which of us does not? He is ambitious. I was ambitious once myself at that age. He is completely and wholly dedicated to the art—"

"Some might say obsessed," Antimodes observed darkly.

"But then so was my father. I believe you knew him, sir?"

Antimodes bowed. "I had the honor. A fine man and an excellent wizard."

"Thank you. I myself was a sad disappointment to my father, as you can imagine," Lemuel said, with a self-deprecating smile. "When I first met Raistlin, I said to myself, 'This is the son my father wanted.' I felt a kind of brotherly feeling toward him."

"Brother! Be thankful you are *not* his brother!" Antimodes said sternly.

The archmagus frowned so darkly, spoke in such a solemn tone that Lemuel, who could make nothing of this strange statement, excused himself by saying that he had to go check on his patient and left the kitchen with haste.

Antimodes remained at the table, so absorbed in his thoughts that he forgot the tea in the cup. "Near to death, is he? I'll wager he doesn't die. You" —he glowered at the thin air, as if it held a disembodied spirit—"you won't let him die, will you? Not without exerting every effort to save him. For if he dies, you die. And who am I to judge him, after all? Who has foreseen the role he is destined to play in the terrible times that are fast approaching? Not I, that is for certain. And not Par-Salian, either, though he would like very much for us to think so!"

Antimodes looked gloomily into the teacup, as if he could read the future in the leaves.

"Well, well, young Raistlin," he said after a moment, "I am sorry for you, that much I can say. Sorry for you and sorry for your brother. The gods—if there be gods—help you both. Here's to your health."

Antimodes raised the teacup to his lips and took a sip. Finding the tea cold, he immediately spit it back out.

* * * * *

Raistlin did not die. Whether it was Lemuel's herbs, Caramon's patient nursing, Antimodes's prayer, or the watchful care of one on another plane of existence, one whose life-force was inextricably bound up with the life of the young mage, or whether it was none of these and Raistlin's will alone that saved him, no one could say. One night, after a week during which he hovered in a no-man's-land between life and death, life won the battle. The fever broke, he breathed easier, and sank into a restful sleep.

He was weak—incredibly weak, so weak that he could not lift his head from the pillow without his brother's strong arm to support him. Antimodes postponed his own journey, lingered in Haven long enough to see that the young man had pulled through. Certain that Raistlin would live, the archmagus left for his own home, hoping to reach Balifor before winter storms made the roads impassable. He gave Caramon a letter of introduction to be given to Baron Ivor in Anti-modes's absence.

"Don't kill yourselves getting there," said Antimodes on the day of his departure. "As I tried telling you before, the baron will not be happy to see you now anyway. He and his soldiers will sit idle all winter, and you two would be just two more mouths to feed. In the spring, he will begin receiving offers for his army's services. Never fear that you will lack work! The Baron of Langtree and his mercenaries are well known and well respected throughout this part of Ansalon. He and his soldiers are in high demand."

"Thank you very much, sir," said Caramon gratefully. He helped Antimodes mount the recalcitrant Jenny, who had taken quite a liking to Lemuel's sweet apples and was in no hurry to resume her journey. "Thank you for this and for everything that you have done for us." Caramon flushed. "About what I said back there, when we were riding out of the forest. I'm sorry. I didn't mean it. If it hadn't been for you, sir, Raist never would have fulfilled his dream."

"Ah, dear me, my young friend," Antimodes said with a sigh, resting his hand on Caramon's shoulder. "Don't lay that burden on me, as well."

He gave Jenny a flick of the riding crop on her broad rump, which did nothing to improve her temper, and the donkey trotted off, leaving Caramon standing in the middle of the road, scratching his head.

Raistlin's health mended slowly. Caramon worried that they were a burden to Lemuel and hinted more than once that he thought his brother could make the trip back to their home in Solace. But Raistlin had no desire to return to their home, not yet. Not while he was still weak, his appearance so terribly altered.

He could not bear the thought of any of their friends seeing him like this. He envisioned Tanis's concern, Flint's shock, Tasslehoff's prying questions, Sturm's disdain. He writhed at the thought and vowed by the gods of magic, by all three gods of magic, that he would never return to Solace until he could do so with pride in himself and with power in his hand.

In answer to Caramon's concerns, Lemuel invited the two young men to stay as long as they needed, to stay all winter if they wanted. The shy and diffident mage enjoyed the company of the two young men. He and Raistlin shared an interest in herbs and herb lore and, when Raistlin was stronger, the two of them spent the days quite pleasantly pounding up leaves with a mortar and pestle, experimenting with various ointments and salves, or exchanging notes on such topics as how best to rid roses of aphids and chrysanthemums of spider mites.

Raistlin was generally in a better humor when he was in Lemuel's company. He curbed his sarcastic tongue in Lemuel's presence, was much kinder and more patient with Lemuel than he was with his own brother. Prone to self-analysis, Raistlin wondered why this should be so. One obvious reason was that he genuinely liked the cheerful and unassuming mage. Unfortunately, he also found that part of his kindness stemmed from a vague sense of guilt in regard to Lemuel. Raistlin couldn't define his guilt or understand the reason for it. So far as he could remember, he had never done or said anything to Lemuel for which he need apologize. He had committed no ungenerous act. But he felt as if he had, and the feeling bothered him. Oddly enough, Raistlin discovered that he could not walk into Lemuel's kitchen without experiencing an overwhelming sense of dread, which always brought the image of a dark elf to mind. Raistlin could only assume that Lemuel had somehow been involved in his Test, but how or why he had no idea, and, search his mind as he might, he could not dredge up the memory.

Once assured that Raistlin was out of danger and that Lemuel really wanted them to stay, that he wasn't just being polite, Caramon settled down to enjoy the winter in Haven. He earned a few coins by doing odd jobs for people—chopping wood, repairing roofs damaged in the fall rains, helping bring in the harvest, for he and Raistlin insisted on helping with Lemuel's household expenses. Thus Caramon came to know a great many of the town's citizens, and it was not long before the big man was as popular and well liked in Haven as he had been in Solace.

Caramon had girl friends by the score. He fell in love several times a week and was always on the verge of marrying someone, but never did. The girls always ended up marrying someone else, someone richer, someone who did not have a wizard for a brother. Caramon's heart was never truly broken, although he swore it was often enough and would spend the afternoon telling Lemuel in dolorous tones that he was finished with women for good, only to be entwined in a pair of soft, warm arms that very night.

Caramon discovered a tavern, the Haven Arms, and made that his second home. The ale was almost as good as Otik's, and the scrapple, made with scraps of pork, stewed with meal and pressed into cakes, was much better than Otik's, although Caramon would have allowed himself to be stewed with meal before he admitted it. Caramon never went to the tavern, he never went out to work, never left the house before making certain that there was nothing he could do for his brother.

Relations between the two—strained almost to the breaking point after the terrible incident in the Tower—eased over the winter. Raistlin had forbidden Caramon ever to mention the occurrence, and the two never discussed it.

Gradually, after thinking it over, Caramon came to believe that his apparent murder at the hands of his twin was his fault, a belief that Raistlin did not dispute.

I deserved death at my brother's hands, was the thought lurking somewhere in the back of Caramon's mind. He did not blame his brother in the least. If somewhere deep inside him, some part of Caramon was grieved and unhappy, he took care to trample on that part until he had stomped it into the soil of his soul, covered it with guilt, and watered it generously with dwarf spirits. He was the strong twin, after all. His brother was frail and needed protection.

Deep inside himself, Raistlin felt shame for his jealous rage. He was appalled to learn that he had the capability within him to kill his brother. He, too, trampled on his emotions, smoothed out the soil, so that no one—least of all himself—would ever find out anything had been buried there. Raistlin comforted himself with the idea that he'd known all along the image of Caramon wasn't real, that he'd murdered nothing but an illusion.

By Yule time, the relationship between the twins was almost back to what it had once been before the infamous Test. Raistlin did not like the cold and snow. He never ventured out of Lemuel's comfortable house, and he enjoyed listening to Caramon's gossip. Raistlin enjoyed proving to his own satisfaction that his fellow mortals were fools and idiots, while Caramon took immense pleasure in bringing a smile—albeit it a sardonic smile—to his twin's lips, lips that were too often stained with blood.

Raistlin spent his winter months in study. He knew now at least some of the magic contained within the staff of Magius, and though he found it frustrating to know that there were more spells that he did not know, perhaps would never know, he reveled in the knowledge that he possessed the staff and others did not. He worked on his war wizard spells, as well, in preparation for the day soon coming when he and Caramon would join up with the mercenary army, there to make their fortunes—of that both young men were firmly convinced.

Raistlin read numerous texts on the subject—many of them left behind by Lemuel's father—and he practiced combining his magic with Caramon's swordsmanship. The two killed a great many imaginary foes and a tree or two (several of Raistlin's early fire-based spells having gone awry), and were soon confident that they were already as good as professionals. Congratulating themselves on their skill, they agreed between them that they could take on an army of hobgoblins all by themselves. They half hoped that such an army might attack Haven during the winter and when no hobgoblins ventured near, the twins expressed resentment against the entire race of hobgoblins, a soft race, who would apparently rather skulk about in warm caves than go to battle.

* * * * *

Spring came to Haven, returning with the robins, the kender, and other wayfarers, bringing proof that the roads were open and the traveling season had begun. It was time for the twins to head east, to find a ship to take them to Langtree Manor, located in the town of Langtree on the Green, the largest city in the barony of Langtree.

Caramon packed clothes and food for the trip. Raistlin packed his spell components, and the two made ready to leave. Lemuel was genuinely sorry to see them go and would have made Raistlin a present of every plant in the garden had Raistlin permitted it. The tavern Caramon frequented nearly shut down from sorrow, and the road out of Haven was literally paved with weeping women, or so it seemed to Raistlin.

His health had improved over the winter, either that or he was learning to cope. He sat his horse with confidence and with ease, enjoying the soft spring air, which seemed better for his lungs to breathe than the sharp, cold air of winter. The knowledge that Caramon was keeping a watchful eye on his twin caused Raistlin to make light of any weakness he felt. He felt so well that they were soon able to ride almost ten leagues in a day.

Much to Caramon's dismay, they skirted Solace, taking a little-known animal trail discovered when they were children.

"I can smell Otik's potatoes," said Caramon wistfully, sitting up in the saddle, sniffing. "We could stop at the Inn for dinner."

Raistlin could also smell the potatoes—or at least he imagined he could—and he was suddenly overwhelmed with homesickness. How easy it would be to return! How easy to relapse once more into that comfortable existence, to make his living tending colicky babies and treating old men's rheumatism. How easy to sink into that cozy, warm feather bed of a life. He hesitated. His horse, sensing its rider's indecision, slowed its pace. Caramon looked at his twin hopefully.

"We could spend the night at the Inn," he urged.

The Inn of the Last Home. Where Raistlin had first met Antimodes. Where he had first heard the mage tell him of the forging of a soul. The Inn of the Last Home. Where people would stare at him, would whisper about him . . .

Raistlin drove the heels of his boots hard into his horse's flanks, causing the animal—unaccustomed to such treatment—to break into a trot.

"Raist? The potatoes?" Caramon cried, his horse galloping to catch up.

"We don't have the money," Raistlin returned shortly, coldly. "Fish in Crystalmir Lake are free to eat. The woods charge nothing for us to sleep in them."

Caramon knew very well that Otik would not ask them to pay, and he sighed deeply. He brought his horse to a halt, turned to look back longingly at Solace. He couldn't see the town, which was hidden in the trees, except in his mind. The mental image was all the more vivid.

Raistlin checked his horse. "Caramon, if we went back to Solace now, we would never leave. You know that, as well as I."

Caramon didn't respond. His horse shuffled nervously.

"Is that the life you want?" Raistlin demanded, his voice rising. "Do you want to work for farmers all your life? With hay in your hair and your hands steeped in cow dung? Or do you want to come back to Solace with your pockets filled with steel, with tales of your prowess on your lips, displaying scars of your battles to adoring barmaids?"

"You're right, Raist," Caramon said, turning his horse's head. "That's what I want, of course. I felt a sort of tugging feeling, that's all. Like I was being pulled back. But that's silly. There's no one left in Solace anymore. None of our old friends, I mean. Sturm's gone north.

Tanis is with the elves, Flint with the dwarves. And who knows where Tasslehoff is?"

"Or cares," Raistlin added caustically.

"One person might be there, though," Caramon said. He glanced sidelong at his twin. Raistlin understood the unspoken thought.

"No," said Raistlin. "Kitiara is not in Solace."

"How do you know?" Caramon asked, astonished. His brother had spoken with unshaken conviction. "You're not . . . not having visions, are you? Like . . . well . . . like our mother."

"I am not suffering from second sight, my brother. Nor am I given to portents and premonitions. I base my statement on what I know of our sister. She will never come back to Solace," Raistlin said firmly. "She has more important friends now. More important concerns."

The trail between the trees narrowed, forcing the two to ride single file. Caramon took front, Raistlin fell in behind. The two rode in silence. Sunlight filtered through the tree limbs, casting barred shadows across Caramon's wide back, shadows that slid over him as he rode in and out of the sunshine. The scent of pine was sharp and crisp. The way was slow, the path overgrown.

"Maybe it's wrong to think this, Raist," Caramon said after a very long silence. "I mean, Kit's our sister and all. But . . . I don't much care if I ever see her again."

"I doubt we ever will, Caramon," Raistlin replied. "There is no reason why our paths should cross."

"Yeah, I guess you're right. Still, I get a funny feeling about her sometimes."

"A 'tugging' feeling?" Raistlin asked.

"No, more of a jabbing feeling." Caramon shivered. "Like she was poking at me with a knife."

Raistlin snorted. "You are probably just hungry."

"Of course I am." Caramon was complacent. "It's nearly dinnertime. But that's not the kind of feeling I mean. A hungry feeling is an empty feeling in the bottom of your stomach. It sort of gnaws at you. This other kind of feeling is like when all the hair on your arms stands up—"

"I was being sarcastic!" Raistlin snapped, glaring out from beneath the rim of his red hood, which he wore pulled up over his head in case they happened across someone they knew.

"Oh," Caramon returned meekly. He was quiet a moment, fearing to further irritate his brother. The thought of food was too much. "Say, how are you going to cook the fish tonight, Raist? My favorite way is when you put onions and butter on it and wrap it in lettuce leaves and put it on a really hot rock. . . ."

Raistlin let his twin ramble on about the various methods of cooking fish. He was quiet, thoughtful, and Caramon did not intrude on his thoughts. The two camped on the banks of Crystalmir Lake. Caramon caught the fish, fourteen or so small lake perch. Raistlin cooked the perch—not with lettuce leaves, the lettuce being mostly underground at this time of year. They shook out their bedrolls. Caramon, his stomach full, soon fell asleep, his face bathed in the warm, laughing light of the red moon, Lunitari.

Raistlin lay awake, watching the red light of the moon play upon the water, dancing on the wavelets, teasing him to come join in their revels. He smiled to see them but kept to the comfort of his blanket.

He truly believed what he had told Caramon. He would never see Kitiara again. The threads of their lives had once been a whole cloth, but the fabric of their youth had frayed, unraveled. Now he pictured the thread of his own life unwinding before him, running straight and true toward his goals.

Little did he think that at this moment the weft of his sister's life, advancing at right angles to his own, would cross the warp of his life and his brother's to form a web, strange and deadly.

4

It was springtime in Sanction. Or rather, it was springtime in the rest of Ansalon, almost a year to the date from the time the companions had come together in the Inn of the Last Home to say their good-byes and to pledge to meet again five years in the fall. Spring did not come to Sanction. Spring brought no budding trees, no daffodils yellow against the melting snow, no sweet breezes, no cheery birdsong.

The trees had been cut down to feed Sanction's forge-fires, the daffodils had died in the poisonous fumes of the belching mountains known as the Lords of Doom. And if there had ever been birds, they had long since been wrung, plucked, and eaten.

Spring in Sanction was Campaign Season, celebrated for the fact that the roads were now open and ready for marching. The troops under the command of General Ariakas had spent the winter in Sanction huddled in their tents, half-frozen, fighting each other for scraps of food tossed to them by their commanders, who wanted a lean and hungry army. To the soldiers, spring meant the chance to raid and loot and kill, steal food enough to fill their shriveled bellies, and capture slaves enough to do the menial work and warm their beds.

Warriors made up the bulk of the population of Sanction, and they were in good spirits, roaming the town, bullying the inhabitants, who got their revenge by charging exorbitant prices for their wares, while the abused innkeepers served up rotgut wine, watered-down ale, and dwarf spirits made of toadstools.

"What a god-awful place," said Kitiara to her companion, as the two walked the crowded, filthy streets. "But it does sort of grow on you."

"Like scum on a pond," said Balif with a laugh.

Kitiara grinned. She had certainly been in prettier places, but what she'd said was true—she found herself liking Sanction. Rough, coarse, and crude, the city was also exciting, interesting, entertaining. Excitement appealed to Kitiara, who had been laid up for the past few months, forced to lie abed and do nothing except hear rumors of great events taking shape, and fret and fume and curse her ill luck that she could not be part of them. She had since rid herself of the minor inconvenience that had momentarily incapacitated her. Free of entanglements, she was free to pursue her ambitions.

Before Kit was even out of the birthing bed, she had sent a message to a disreputable inn known as The Trough in Solace. The message was to a man named Balif, who passed through town every so often and who had been waiting months for a message from Kit.

Her missive was short: *How do I meet this general of yours?*

His reply was equally terse and to the point. *Come to Sanction.*

When she was able to travel, Kitiara had done just that.

"What is that foul smell?" she asked, wrinkling her nose. "Like rotten eggs!"

"The sulfur pits. You get used to it," Balif answered, shrugging. "After a day or two, you won't notice it. The best part of Sanction is that no one comes here who doesn't belong here. Or, if they do, they don't stay long. Sanction's safe, and it's secret. That's why the general chose it."

"The city is aptly named, though. Sanction—it's a punishment to live here!"

Kit was pleased with her own little joke. Balif laughed dutifully, glanced at her admiringly as she strode along the narrow streets at his side. She was thinner than she had been when he'd last seen her over a year ago, but her dark eyes were still as bright, her lips still as full, her body lithe and graceful. She wore her traveling clothes, for she'd only just arrived in Sanction—fine leather armor over a brown tunic, which came to mid-thigh, revealing shapely legs in green stockings, leather boots that came to her knees.

Kitiara saw Balif look, understood the proposition, and—shaking her short, dark curls—she returned a veiled promise with her eyes. She was looking for diversion, amusement, and Balif was handsome in a cold, sharp-edged sort of way. What was equally important, he was a high-ranking officer in General Ariakas's new-formed army, a most trusted spy and assassin. Balif had the general's ear and access to his presence, an honor that Kit could not hope to achieve on her own, not without wasting valuable time, requiring resources she did not possess. Kitiara was flat broke.

She'd been forced to pawn her sword to provide money enough to travel to Sanction, and most of that money had gone to pay her passage on the ship across New Sea. She had no money at all now and had been wondering where she would spend the night. That problem was now solved. Her smile, the crooked smile that she could make so charming, widened.

Balif had his answer. He licked his lips and moved a step closer, put his hand on her arm to steer her around a drunken goblin, stumbling down the street.

"I'll take you to the inn where I'm staying," Balif said, his grip on her tightening, his breath coming faster. "It's the best in Sanction, though I admit that's not saying a lot. Still, we can be alo—"

"Hey, Balif." A man wearing black leather armor halted in front of them, blocking their path along the cracked and broken street. Eyeing Kitiara, the man leered. "What have we here? A fine-looking wench. I trust you'll share with your friends?" He reached out to grab hold of Kitiara. "Come here, sweetheart. Give us a kiss. Balif won't mind.

He and I have slept three to a bed before—ugh!"

The man doubled over, groaning and clutching his crotch, his ardor deflated by the toe of Kitiara's boot. A swift chop to the back of his neck drove him to the broken stones of the street, where he lay unmoving. Kit nursed a cut hand—the bastard had been wearing a spiked leather collar around his neck—and snatched her knife from her boot.

"Come on," she said to the man's two friends, who had been about to back him up, but who were now reconsidering their options. "Come on. Who else wants to sleep three to a bed with me?"

Balif, who had seen Kit's work before, knew better than to interfere. He leaned against a crumbling wall, his arms folded, watching with amusement.

Kitiara balanced lightly on the balls of her feet. She held the knife with easy, practiced skill. The two men facing her liked women who shrank from them in fear and terror. There was no fear in the dark eyes that watched their every move. Those eyes gleamed with keen anticipation of the fight. Kit darted forward, lashing out with the knife, moving so fast that the blade was a flashing blur in the few rays of weak sunlight that managed to struggle through the smoke-laden air. One of the men stared stupidly at a bloody slash across his upper arm.

"I'd sooner bed a scorpion," he snarled, and putting his hand over the cut to try to stanch the flow of blood, he gave Kit a vicious look and slouched away, accompanied by his friend. They left their third companion in the street, where the unconscious man was immediately set upon by goblins, who stripped him of every valuable he owned.

Kit sheathed her knife in her boot and turned to Balif, regarded him with approval. "Thanks for not 'helping.' "

He applauded. "You're a joy to watch, Kit. I wouldn't have missed that for a bag of steel."

Kit put her wounded hand to her mouth.

"Where's this inn of yours?" she asked, slowly licking the blood from the cut, her eyes on Balif.

"Near here," he answered, his voice husky.

"Good. You're going to buy me dinner." Kit slid her hand through his arm, pressed close to him. "And then you're going to tell me all about General Ariakas."

* * * * *

"So where have you been all this time?" Balif asked. His pleasure sated, he lay next to her, tracing over the battle scars on her bare breast with his hand. "I expected to hear from you last summer or at least by fall. Nothing. Not a word."

"I had things to do," said Kit lazily. "Important things."

"They said you went north to Solamnia, in company with a boy knight. Brightsword, or some such name."

"Brightblade. Yes." Kitiara shrugged. "We traveled on the same errand, but we soon parted company. I could no longer stomach his prayers and vigils and sanctimonious prattling."

"He may have started on that trip a boy, but I'll wager he was a man by the time you were finished with him," Balif said with a salacious wink. "So where did you go after that?"

"I wandered around Solamnia for a while, looking for my father's family. They were landed noblemen, or so he always said. I figured they'd be glad to see their long-lost granddaughter. So glad they'd part with a few of the family jewels and a chest of steel. But I couldn't find them."

"You don't need some moldy old blue blood's money, Kit. You'll earn your own fortune. You've got brains and you've got talent. General Ariakas is looking for both. Who knows, someday you might rule Ansalon." He fondled the scars on her right breast. "So you finally left that half-elf lover you were so taken with."

"Yes, I left him," Kitiara said quietly. Drawing the sheet up around her, she rolled to the other side of the bed. "I'm sleepy," she said, her voice cold. "Blow out the candle."

Balif shrugged and did what he was told. He had her body, he didn't care what she did with her heart. He was soon fast asleep. Kitiara lay with her back to him, staring into the darkness. She hated Balif at that moment, hated him for reminding her of Tanis. She had worked hard to put the half-elf out her mind, and she had very nearly done so. She did not ache for his touch at night anymore. The touch of other men eased her longing, though she still saw his face whenever any other man loved her.

Her seduction of the boy Brightblade had been out of frustration and anger with Tanis for leaving her; she meant to punish him by taking his friend for her lover. And when she'd laughed at the boy, ridiculed him, tormented him, she was, in her mind, tormenting Tanis. But in the end, she had been the one punished.

Her tryst with Brightblade had left her with child, and too sick and weak to rid herself of the unwanted pregnancy. The labor was hard, she had very nearly died. In her pain, in her delirium, she had dreamed only of Tanis, dreamed of crawling to him, begging his forgiveness, dreamed of agreeing to be his wife, of finding peace and contentment in his arms. If only he had come to her then! How many times she had almost sent him a message!

Almost. And then she would remind herself that he had rebuffed her, he had turned down her proposal to head north to join up with "certain people who knew what they wanted from life and weren't afraid to take it." He had, in essence, sent her packing. She would never forgive him.

Love for Tanis was strong when she was weak and in low spirits. Anger returned with her strength. Anger and resolve. She'd be damned if she'd go crawling back to him. Let him stay with his pointed-eared kin. Let them snub him and make a mockery of him and sneer at him behind his back. Let him make love to some little elven bitch. He had mentioned a girl in Qualinesti. Kit could not recall her name, but the she-elf was welcome to him.

Kitiara lay in the darkness, her back to Balif, as far from him as she could get without falling out of bed, and cursed Tanis Half-Elven bitterly and with vehemence until she fell asleep. But in the morning, when she was only half-awake, drowsy with sleep, it was Tanis's shoulder that she caressed.

5

ou were going to tell me about General Ariakas," Kit reminded Balif.

The two had lingered in bed until the morning. Now they walked through the streets of Sanction, heading for the armed camp north of town where the general had established his headquarters.

"I meant to fill you in last night," Balif said. "You gave me other things to think about."

General Ariakas had never been far from Kit's mind, but she mixed business with pleasure only when absolutely necessary. Last night had been pleasure. Today was business. Balif was an agreeable companion, a skilled lover, and thankfully, he didn't make a nuisance of himself by wanting to walk with his arm around her or holding hands with her, claiming her as his own personal possession.

But Kitiara was far too hungry to be satisfied with the small fish she had lured to her net. When the time was right, she would toss him back and wait for a bigger catch. She was not worried about hurting Balif's feelings. For one, he had no feelings to hurt. For another, he was under no illusions. He knew where he stood with her. She had rewarded him for his efforts, and she guessed he would use her to gain a more valuable reward from General Ariakas. Kit knew Balif too well to believe that he had kept track of her out of the goodness of his heart.

"Shall I tell you what I know of Ariakas or what is rumored?" Balif asked, speaking to her but not looking at her. His watchful and distrustful gaze focused on each passing person as he came toward him, glanced at each as he passed behind him. You watched your front and your back in Sanction.

"Both," Kit replied, doing the same.

The soldiers she encountered regarded her with respect, stepping aside to allow her room to pass and regarding her with admiration.

"Looks like you're the talk of the town," Balif observed.

Kitiara was feeling especially good this morning, and she gave her admirers her crooked smile and a toss of her curls in reply.

"'If truth is the meat, rumor is the sauce,'" she said, quoting the old saying. "How old a man is Ariakas?"

"Oh, as to that, who knows?" Balif shrugged. "He's not young, that's for certain, but he's no grandfather, either. Somewhere in the middle. He's a brute of a man. A minotaur once accused General Ariakas of cheating at cards. Ariakas strangled the minotaur with his bare hands."

Kitiara arched her dark eyebrow skeptically. In this instance, rumor was a bit hard to swallow.

"The truth! I swear it by Her Dark Majesty!" Balif averred, raising his hand to the oath. "A friend of mine was there and saw the fight. Speaking of Her Majesty, our Queen is said to favor him." He lowered his voice. "Some say that he was her lover."

"And how did he manage that?" Kit asked mockingly. "Did he travel to the Abyss for this rendezvous? Which of her five heads did he kiss?"

"Hush!" Balif was scandalized, reproving. "Don't say such things, Kit. Not even in jest. Her Dark Majesty is everywhere. And if she is not, her priests are," he added, with a baleful glance at a black-robed figure, skulking among the crowd. "Our Queen has many forms. She came to him in his sleep."

Kit had heard other terms for encounters of this sort, but she refrained from mentioning them. She had little use for other women in general, and that included a so-called

Queen of Darkness. Kitiara had been raised in a world where the gods did not exist, a world where a man was on his own, to make of himself what he would. She had first heard rumors about this newly arrived Queen of Darkness years ago, on her various travels throughout Ansalon. She had discounted such rumors, figuring this Dark Queen to be another creation of some charlatan priest, out to swindle the gullible. Just like that foul priestess of the phony snake god Belzor, a priestess who had died by Kit's hand, with Kit's knife at her throat. To Kitiara's surprise, the worship of the Queen of Darkness had not petered out. Her cult had grown in numbers and in power, and now there was talk of this Takhisis trying to break free from the Abyss, where she had long been imprisoned, returning to conquer the world.

Kit was quite willing to conquer the world, but she intended to do it in her own name.

"Is this Ariakas a good-looking man?" she asked.

"What did you say?" Balif returned.

They were passing the slave market, and both of them put their hands over their noses to avoid the stench. They waited to resume their conversation until they were well away from the area.

"Phew!" said Kit. "And I thought the rotten-egg smell was bad. I asked if Ariakas was a good-looking man."

Balif appeared disgusted. "Only a woman would ask such a question. How the devil should I know? He's not my type, for certain. He's a magic-user," he added, as if one went along with the other.

Kit frowned. Her people were from Solamnia, her father had been a Knight of Solamnia before his misdeeds caused him to be cast out. Kitiara had inherited her family's distrust and dislike of wizards.

"That's no recommendation," she said shortly.

"What's the matter with him being a wizard?" Balif demanded. "Your own baby brother dabbled in the art. You were the one who got him started, as I recall."

"Raistlin was too weak to do anything else," Kit returned. "He had to have some way to survive in this world. I knew it wouldn't be by the sword. From what you've told me, this General Ariakas has no such excuse."

"He doesn't practice his magic that much," Balif said defensively. "He's a warrior through and through. But it never hurts to have another weapon at hand. Like you keeping a knife in your boot."

"I suppose," Kitiara said grudgingly. So far, she was not much impressed by what she'd heard of this General Ariakas.

Balif saw this, understood, and was just about to launch into another tale of his admired general, a tale he was sure Kit would appreciate—how Ariakas had risen to power by the murder of his own father. But he had lost Kit's attention. She had come to a halt outside a smithy, was gazing with rapt attention at a shining sword displayed on a wooden rack outside the shop.

"Look at that!" she said, reaching out her hand.

The sword was a bastard sword, also known as a hand and a half sword, for its blade was longer and narrower than that of a traditional bastard sword—a factor Kit appreciated, since male opponents tended to have longer arms. Such a sword would compensate for her shorter reach.

Kitiara had never seen such a marvelous sword, one that appeared to have been made for her and her alone. She removed it carefully from its stand, almost afraid of testing it, fearful of finding some imperfection. She tried her hand around the leather-wrapped grip. Most grips on bastard swords were made for a man's hand, were too thick for hers. Her fingers wrapped lovingly around this grip, it fit her perfectly.

She checked the balance, making certain that the blade was not too heavy, which would lead to an aching elbow, or too light, tested to see that the pommel balanced the weight of the blade. The balance was ideal; the sword seemed an extension of herself.

She was falling in love with this blade, but she had to be careful, cool, not rush into this blindly. She held the sword to the light, examined all the parts—tugging on them, shaking them—to make certain that nothing rattled or wobbled. This test passed, she checked to see how the swept hilt fit her hand. Kit checked the clearance between guard and hand, making small testing movements with her wrist. The guard bars were ornately carved and lovely to look at, but appearance counts for nothing if the bars dig into your hand or forearm.

She stepped into the street, took up her fighting stance. She held the blade out in front of her, taking note of the length and the feel of the sword when extended. She tried a couple of test swings, halting them abruptly in mid-swing to determine the momentum and to see whether a movement, once begun, could easily be changed.

Finally, she placed the sword tip against the ground. Holding the sword in both hands by the guard, she applied pressure until the blade curved in a shallow arc. You don't want a blade so brittle it will break or one that will bend and stay bent. The blade was supple as a lover's caress.

The smith was banging away at his work inside the shop. His assistant, who had been keeping an eye out for potential customers and to shoo away kender, hurried to the door.

"We have much finer blades inside the shop, sir," he said, bowing officiously and gesturing inside to the hot and smoky interior. "If you'd care to step inside, sir—I beg your pardon, madam—I can show you the master's work."

"Is this some of your master's work?" Kit asked, keeping a fast grip on the sword.

"No, no, madam," the assistant said, looking scornful. "Note these other blades. These are the master's work. Now, if you'll only step inside . . ." He tried again to lure her into the shop, where he would have her at his mercy.

"Who made this sword?" Kitiara asked, having duly noted the other blades, noted the poor quality of the steel and the shoddy workmanship.

"What was his name?" The assistant frowned, trying to recall such an unimportant detail. "Ironfeld, I believe. Theros Ironfeld."

"Where is *his* shop?" Kitiara asked.

"Burned down," the assistant said, rolling his eyes. "Not an accident, if you take my meaning. He was too high and mighty for the likes of some in Sanction. Thought too well of himself. He had to be taught a lesson. We would not normally carry such inferior work, but the poor fellow who sold it to us was down on his luck, and the master is a most generous man. You appear to be a woman of discriminating taste. We can do much better for you. Now, if you'll just step inside the shop . . ."

"I want this sword," Kit said. "How much?"

The assistant pursed his lips in disapproval, spent several more moments trying to dissuade her, then named a price.

Kit lifted her eyebrows. "That's a lot for a sword of such poor quality," she said.

"It's been taking up shelf space," the assistant said sullenly. "We paid too much for it, but the poor fellow was—"

"Down on his luck. Yes, you mentioned that." Kitiara haggled with the man. Eventually she agreed to pay the price he asked, if he threw in a leather sheath and belt for free.

"Pay him," she told Balif. "I'll pay you back when I have the money."

Balif brought forth his purse and counted out the coins, all of them steel and all marked with the likeness of General Ariakas.

"What a bargain!" Kit said, buckling the belt around her waist, adjusting the fit to where it was comfortable and the sword was in easy reach on her hip. Had she been an inch shorter, the long blade would have dragged the ground. "This sword is worth ten times the amount that fool wanted for it! I *will* pay you back," she added.

"No need," said Balif. "I'm doing well for myself these days."

"I won't be in debt to any man," Kitiara said with a flash of her dark eyes. "I pay my own way. Either you agree or you take back the sword." She put her hand to the buckle, as if she would strip it off then and there.

"All right!" Balif shrugged. "Have it your way. Here, we go this direction, across the lava flow. The general's headquarters is inside a great temple built to honor the Dark Queen. The Temple of Luerkhisis. Very impressive."

A long, wide natural bridge made of granite spanned the Lava River, as it was known by the few natives left in Sanction after the arrival of the Dark Queen's forces. The river flowed down from the Doom range of the Khalkist Mountains that surrounded Sanction on three sides to pour, hissing, into the New Sea. The city was isolated, well protected, for only two passes led through the mountains, and these were heavily guarded. Anyone caught walking those paths was captured and taken into Sanction, to a second temple built to honor the Dark Queen and her evil cohorts, the Temple of Huerzyd.

Here all those entering Sanction were questioned, and those who gave the right answers were free to go. For those who did not have the right answers, there were the prison cells, with the torture chamber located conveniently nearby, "just a hop, skip, and a jump" (a kender's last words) from the morgue.

Those leaving Sanction by more pleasant and less permanent means needed a pass signed by General Ariakas himself. All others were detained and either forced to remain in Sanction or were escorted to the dread Temple of Huerzyd.

Balif had provided Kitiara with a letter of safe passage and a password, so she had been permitted to enter Sanction without making any side trips. She had arrived by ship, the only other way in and out of Sanction.

Sanction's harbor was blockaded by ships of Ariakas's army, which watched the surface, and by fearsome sea monsters, which guarded the deep. All pleasure craft and small fishing vessels belonging to Sanction's inhabitants had been seized and burned so that people could not use them to sneak past the blockade. Thus General Ariakas kept his troop buildup secret from the rest of Ansalon, who probably would not have believed it anyway.

At this time, almost four years prior to the start of what would become known as the War of the Lance, General Ariakas was just starting to gather his forces. Agents such as Balif, wholly loyal and completely dedicated, traveled in secret throughout Ansalon, making contact with all those inclined to walk the paths of darkness, appealing to their greed, their hatreds, promising them loot, plunder, and the destruction of their enemies if they would sign their lives over to Ariakas and their souls to Queen Takhisis.

Bands of goblins and hobgoblins, harried for years by the Solamnic Knights, came to Sanction, vowing revenge. Ogres were lured out of the mountain strongholds by promises of slaughter. Minotaurs came to earn honor and glory in battle. Humans arrived, hoping for a share of the wealth to be won when the elves were driven from their ancient homelands and the rest of Ansalon ground beneath the heel of General Ariakas. Dark clerics reveled in their newfound clerical power—a power given to no one else on Ansalon, for Queen Takhisis had kept her return to the world a secret from the other gods, with the exception of one, her son, Nuitari, god of dark magic. In his name, black-robed wizards worked their arcane arts in secret and prepared for the glorious return of their Queen to the world.

Nuitari had two cousins, Solinari, the son of the god Paladine and goddess Mishakal, and Lunitari, the daughter of the god Gilean. Solinari was god of white magic, Lunitari daughter of red or neutral magic. The three gods of magic were close, bound by their love of magic. Their three moons—the white, the red, and the black—orbited Krynn, so it was difficult for one to keep something hidden from the others, even one as cold and dark and secret as Nuitari.

And so there were those on Ansalon who saw the shadows cast by dark wings and who had begun to make their own preparations. When the Dark Queen finally struck, four years hence, the forces of good would not be taken completely by surprise.

That day was not here yet, only foreseen.

The stone bridge spanned the Lava River, opened onto the grounds of the Temple of Luerkhisis. The bridge was guarded by Ariakas's own personal troops—at the time, the only well-trained force in Sanction. Kitiara and Balif waited in line behind a wretched merchant who was insisting that he had to talk with General Ariakas.

"His men wrecked my establishment!" he said, wringing his hands. "They smashed my furniture and drank my best wine. They insulted my wife, and when I ordered them to leave they threatened to burn down my inn! They told me General Ariakas would pay for the damage. I am here to see him."

At this, the guards laughed loudly. "Sure, General Ariakas will pay," said one. Removing a coin from his purse, he tossed it on the ground. "There's your payment. Pick it up."

The merchant hesitated. "That's not nearly enough. I want to see General Ariakas."

The guard frowned, said harshly, "Pick it up!"

The merchant gulped, then bent to pick up the steel coin. The guard kicked the man in the rear end, sent him sprawling in the dirt.

"Take your payment and be gone with you. General Ariakas has better things to do than listen to you snivel about a few pieces of broken furniture."

"Any more complaints from you," said the other guard, getting in a kick for himself, "and we'll find some other place to do our drinking."

The merchant struggled to his feet, clutching the coin, and limped off toward the town.

"A very good day to you, Lieutenant Lugash," said Balif, approaching the guard post. "It's good to see you again."

"Captain Balif." The lieutenant saluted, stared hard at Kitiara.

"My friend and I have an audience this afternoon with General Ariakas, Lieutenant."

"What's your friend's name?" asked Lugash.

"Kitiara uth Matar," Kit answered. "And if you have a question, ask me. I can speak for myself."

Lugash grunted, regarded her appraisingly. "Uth Matar. Sounds Solamnic."

"My father was a Knight of Solamnia," Kitiara said, lifting her chin, "but he wasn't a fool, if that's what you're implying."

"Thrown out of the knighthood," Balif said in an undertone. "Gambling, working for the wrong people."

"So she told you, sir." Lugash sneered. "The daughter of a Solamnic. She could be a spy."

Balif stepped between the lieutenant and Kitiara, who had drawn her new sword halfway from its sheath.

"Simmer down, Kit," Balif advised, laying a restraining hand on her arm. "These are Ariakas's own personal troops. They're not like that piss-pants who tried to manhandle you yesterday. They're veterans who've proven themselves in battle, earned his respect. You'll have to do that, too, Kit." Balif glanced sidelong at her. "It won't be easy."

He turned back to the lieutenant. "You know about the information I gave the general on Qualinesti. You were there when I related it to him."

"Yes, sir," said Lugash, his hand on his own sword, his gaze dark on Kit. "What of it?"

"She's the one who came by it," Balif said, nodding his head in Kit's direction. "The general was very impressed. He asked to meet her. As I said, Lieutenant, we have an audience with him. Let us cross—both of us—or I will report you to your superior."

The lieutenant was not to be bullied. "I have my orders, Captain. My orders state that no one is to be allowed across the river today unless they're part of the army. You can go across, sir, but I'm going to have to detain your friend."

"Damn your eyes!" Balif cursed, frustrated.

The lieutenant was implacable, unmoving.

Balif turned to Kit. "You wait here. I'll go find the general."

"I'm beginning to think it's not worth it," Kitiara said, glowering at the soldiers.

"It's worth it, Kit," Balif said quietly. "Be patient. There's just been some sort of mix-up. I won't be gone long."

He hastened across the bridge. The guards returned to their posts, both of them keeping their eyes on Kitiara. Taking care to appear uncaring, she sauntered over to the edge of the bridge, stared across the Lava River to the great Temple of Luerkhisis.

Balif had termed the temple impressive. Kitiara was forced to agree with him. The side of the mountain had been carved into the likeness of the head of an enormous dragon. The dragon's nostrils formed the entrance to the temple. Two huge incisors were observation towers, or so Balif had told her. The great audience hall was inside the dragon's mouth. Formerly the Queen's dark clerics had resided there, but they had been displaced by the arrival of the army. General Ariakas had taken over quarters for himself in the temple and established a barracks for his own personal bodyguard. The dark clerics remained, but they had had to make do with less sumptuous quarters.

What must it be like to hold *that* much power? Kitiara wondered. Leaning on the parapet of the stone bridge, she stared over the turgid red river of lava at the temple, feeling the heat radiate from the river, a heat the dark clerics did their best to disperse, but which could not be cooled entirely. Nor did Ariakas want it cooled. The heat would enter the blood of his soldiers, send them pouring into Ansalon, a red river of death.

Kitiara's hands clenched tightly in longing. Someday, I'll know the answer, she vowed silently to herself. Someday such power will be mine.

Realizing she was gaping at the temple like a country-born yokel, Kitiara began to amuse herself by tossing stones down into the lava flow. Though the river was far below the bridge, she was soon bathed in sweat. Balif was right, though. One did get used to the smell.

Balif returned, bringing with him one of Ariakas's aides.

"The general says that Uth Matar is to be allowed to pass," said the aide. "And the general wants to know why he is being bothered by this."

Lieutenant Lugash paled, but he answered stoutly, "I thought—"

"That was your first mistake," said the captain dryly. "Uth Matar, I greet you in the name of General Ariakas. The general is not holding audience in the temple this day. He is engaged in training this afternoon. He asked that I escort you to his command tent."

"Thank you, Captain," said Kitiara, with a charming smile. Accompanying the aide and Balif across the bridge, Kitiara glanced at the lieutenant, memorized every feature on his ugly face.

Someday he'd pay for that sneer.

6

A thousand men were assembled on the practice field in front of the Temple of Luerkhisis in ranks four deep and two hundred and fifty long. They stood at the guard position—left foot forward, right foot back, shield up and sword at the ready. The sun blazed down on the troops from a clear blue sky. The heat from the Lava River roiled over them. Sweat collected under their heavy steel helmets, dripped down their faces. Their bodies, encased in padding and practice armor, were soaked.

In front of the line stood a single officer, wearing ornate bronze armor, a polished bronze helm, and a blue cloak, attached by large golden hasps at the shoulders. The cloak was thrown back, leaving his muscular arms bare. He was a large man, large-boned, muscular. Black hair, wet with sweat, flowed from beneath his helmet. He wore a sword at his side but did not draw it.

"Prepare to thrust," he ordered. "Thrust!"

Every soldier took a pace forward and lunged with his sword, then froze in that position. A thousand voices shouted out the short attack yell. An uneasy silence fell. The officer was frowning, his brows lowering beneath his bronze helm. The men glanced sidelong at each other and panted in the glaring sun.

General Ariakas had noticed several men in the front rank who, either from nervousness or eagerness to please, jumped before he gave the order, thrust their swords out too far. They had been off by only a few seconds, but it showed a lack of discipline.

Ariakas pointed at one of the offending soldiers.

"Company Master Kholos, take that man in the front rank and have him flogged. Never anticipate the word of command until it is given."

A human with the sallow skin and slavering jaws that bespoke some sort of goblin ancestry—one of four officers who stood behind the regiment—escorted the offending soldier to the side of the practice field. At his gesture, two sergeants, armed with whips, took their places.

"Remove your armor," the company master ordered.

The soldier did so, stripping off his practice armor and the heavy padding beneath it.

"Stand at attention."

The soldier, his face set rigid, stood stiff and straight. The company master nodded. The sergeants raised their whips and, one after the other, each struck the man's bare back three lashes. The soldier tried to stifle his cries, but at the sixth, with the blood trickling down his back, he gave a strangled yell.

The sergeants, their duty done, coiled their whips and stepped back along the sidelines. The soldier gritted his teeth against the pain as the salt sweat ran into his fresh wounds. Moving as rapidly as he could under the baleful eye of Ariakas, the soldier replaced his padding, which was quickly soaked in blood, and put the armor back on over it.

The company master nodded again, and the soldier hastened to take up his position in the ranks, assuming the same stance as the other soldiers around him, who were still holding the thrust-forward stance. Arms and legs quivered with the strain.

"Prepare to recover," Ariakas commanded. "Recover!"

Each man pulled back on his sword, as if recovering it from the belly of some phantom enemy, returning to the guard position. Resting, they waited tensely for the next order.

"Better," Ariakas stated flatly. "Prepare to thrust. Thrust! Prepare to recover. Recover!"

The drill went on for nearly an hour. Twice more Ariakas paused to have men flogged. This time, he chose men in the rear ranks—a sign that he was watching more than just the front rank. At the end of an hour, he was almost satisfied. The soldiers were moving as a single unit, every man's foot placed correctly, every shield held in the proper position, every sword exactly where it should be.

"Prepare to thrust—" Ariakas began, then stopped. The words hung in the hot air.

One soldier had not obeyed. Stepping forward, moving out of the front rank of the formation, the soldier tossed his sword into the dirt. He yanked off his helmet, threw it into the ground in front of him.

"I didn't sign up for this shit," he said, loud enough for everyone to hear. "I quit!"

None of the other soldiers said a word. After one swift glance, they looked away, fearing that they might be taken for accomplices. Their faces stony, they kept their eyes forward.

Ariakas nodded once, coolly.

"Front rank, fourth company," he said, addressing the rebellious soldier's comrades. "Kill that man."

The doomed man turned to his friends, raised his hands.

"Boys, it's me! C'mon!"

They stared at him, through him.

The man turned to flee, but he stumbled over his own armor, fell to the ground. Sixty-one men moved at once. Three of them, the three nearest the doomed man, performed just as they had practiced.

Prepare to thrust. Thrust.

The man screamed as three swords pierced his body.

Prepare to recover. Recover.

The soldiers jerked their weapons from the bloody corpse, fell back into position. The man's screams ended abruptly.

"Very good," said Lord Ariakas. "That's the first time I've seen any sign of disciplined behavior in the lot of you. Company Masters, have your companies break for twenty minutes, and make sure that the men are given water."

General Ariakas was conscious that he now had an audience—a young woman stood on the edge of the parade field, watching. Her hands were on her hips, her head tilted slightly to one side, a crooked smile on her lips. Removing his helmet, wiping the sweat from his face, Ariakas strode from the field to his command tent, a large tent over which flew his flag bearing a black eagle with outstretched wings. Company masters hurried onto the grounds, ordering the men to break out of formation. The thirsty men surged for the horse troughs that stood at the side of the parade ground. Dipping their hands into the tepid, sulfurous-tasting water, the men gulped it down and then splashed it over their bodies. Then they sank to the ground, exhausted, to watch the sergeants drag the dead body off to another area of the camp. The camp dogs would eat well this night.

Inside his command tent, Ariakas took off the cloak, tossed it into a corner. An aide assisted him to remove the heavy bronze breastplate.

"Damn, that was hot work!" Ariakas groaned and massaged his tight back muscles.

A slave brought in a large gourd filled with water. Ariakas drank it, sent the slave back for another, drank part of that, and dumped the remainder over his head. He lay down on his bunk, ordered the slave to remove his boots.

The four company masters came to the tent, knocked on the center pole.

"Enter." Ariakas remained lying at ease on the bunk.

The company officers removed their helmets, saluted, and stood at attention, waiting. They were tense, wary.

Kholos, Fourth Company Master, spoke first. "Lord Ariakas, I apologize for the insubordination—"

Ariakus waved his hand. "No, don't worry about it. We're trying to beat buffoons and ruffians into some semblance of a decent fighting force. We've got to expect some setbacks. In fact, I commend you, Company Master.

Your men behaved very well. All the men are shaping up better than I had hoped. They're not to know that, though. The men should think I am disgusted with them. In fifteen minutes, go back out and commence company drill. The same thing—thrust and recover. Once they have that perfected, they can learn anything."

"Sir," said the Second Company Master. "Should we order the sergeants to flog the men if necessary?"

Ariakas shook his head. "No, Beren, flogging is my tool. I want them to fear me. With fear comes respect." He grinned. "Content yourselves with being hated, gentlemen. Make do with stern looks and a few choice words. If any of the men disobey, send them to me, and I will deal with them."

"Yes, sir. Any other orders, sir?"

"Yes. Drill for at least another hour and a half, then break for evening meal, let the men retire for the night. When it's good and dark and the men are sound asleep, rouse them out of bed and have them shift their tents from the north to the south side of the camp. They must learn to wake quickly when the alarm sounds, learn to work in the dark and to keep organized so that they can break camp any time in any weather."

The four officers turned to leave.

"One more thing," Ariakas called after them. "Kholos, you will be taking command of this regiment in two weeks' time. I will be forming a new regiment with all new recruits then. Beren, you will stay with me as my senior company master, and you other two will go with Kholos. I'll promote new officers to fill the rest of the positions. Clear?"

All four saluted and returned to their companies. Kholos looked particularly pleased. It was a good promotion and, after the unfortunate incident, showed that Ariakas still had confidence in him.

Ariakas shifted his position on the bunk, groaned again as he willed the muscles in his back to relax. He recalled the days of his youth, when he had marched ten miles wearing thirty pounds of chain mail and a heavy steel breastplate over that and still had energy enough to enjoy the clash of battle—to revel in the exhilarating love of life that comes only when you may be about to lose your life, to hear again the thunderous crash when the front ranks come together, to recall the fierce struggle to determine who would live and who would die. . . .

"Sir. Are you awake, sir?" His aide hovered at the tent pole.

"Am I some old man, to indulge in an afternoon nap?" Ariakas sat bolt upright, glared at the aide. "Well, what is it?"

"Captain Balif here, sir. As requested. And he has brought a visitor."

"Ah, yes." Ariakas recalled the comely young woman standing on the edge of the parade ground. By the gods, he *was* getting old to have forgotten about her! He was clad only in his boots and the short skirt made of strips of leather, which he wore beneath his chain mail, but if the stories he had heard about this woman were true, she would not be disturbed by the sight of a half-naked man. "Send them in."

The woman entered the tent first, followed by Balif, who saluted and stood at attention. The woman took in her surroundings at a glance, then her gaze fixed on Ariakas. Here was no shy maiden, with modest downcast lashes. Here was no brazen whore, either, whose fluttering lashes concealed the hard glint of greed. This woman's gaze was bold, unabashed, penetrating, and fearless. Ariakas, who had expected—naturally enough—to be the one doing the judging, found that he himself was being judged. She was sizing him up, appraising him, and if she didn't like what she saw, she'd leave.

At any other time, Ariakas might have been offended, even insulted, but he was pleased with the way the troops had performed today, and this woman with her curly hair, her well-formed figure, and her dark eyes intrigued him mightily.

"Sir," said Balif, "I present Kitiara uth Matar."

Solamnic. So that's where she came by that proud, defiant air, as if daring the world to do its damnedest. Someone had taught her to wear a sword, to wear it with ease, as if it were just one more part of her body, and such a fine body at that. Yet there was something fey about this Kitiara. That crooked smile was not born of a self-righteous Knight.

"Kitiara uth Matar," said Ariakas, clasping his hands over the girdle of his leather skirt, "welcome to Sanction." His gaze narrowed. "I have met you before, I believe."

"I cannot claim the honor, sir," said Kitiara. The crooked smile widened slightly. In the dark, smoky eyes was a flicker of fire. "I am certain I would have remembered."

"You have seen her, sir," interjected Balif, whose presence Ariakas had nearly forgotten. "You two did not meet. It was in Neraka. Last year, when you were there overseeing the construction of the great temple."

"Yes! I recall now. You'd been scouting out Qualinesti, as I recall. Commander Kholos was quite pleased with your report. You will be glad to know that we intend to put the information you gave us to good use against the heathen elves."

The crooked smile stiffened a moment, then hardened. The fire in the dark eyes flared, then was quickly quenched. Ariakas wondered what rock he'd struck his flint against, to cause such a spark.

"I am glad to have been of service to you, sir," was all she said, however, and her tone was cool, respectful.

"Please, be seated. Andros!" Clapping his hands, Ariakas summoned one of the slaves, a boy of about sixteen, captured during a raid on some unfortunate town, who bore the marks of his hard life and ill usage on his bruised face. "Bring in wine and meat for our guests. You will share my supper, will you not?"

"With pleasure, sir," said Kitiara.

Another slave was dispatched to find more folding camp chairs. Ariakas shoved a map of Abanasinia off a table onto the ground and the three took their seats.

"Forgive the crudeness of the repast." Ariakas spoke to both his guests, though his eyes were fixed on only one.

"When you come to visit me in my headquarters, I will serve you one of the finest meals in all of Ansalon. One of my slaves is a most excellent cook. Her cooking saved her life, and so she puts her heart into it."

"I look forward to that, sir," said Kitiara.

"Eat! Eat!" Ariakas said, waving to the haunch of freshly roasted venison, which slaves brought in on a sizzling platter and placed on the table. Drawing his knife from his belt, he cut off a hunk of meat. "Do not stand on ceremony. By Her Dark Majesty, I am hungry! We had hot work out there today."

He glanced at the woman, to see what she would say.

Kitiara, her own knife in her hand, cut off meat for herself.

"You are a strict disciplinarian, sir," she observed, eating the greasy meat with the relish of a longtime campaigner who is never certain when or where she will find her next meal. "And you have troops to spare, it would appear. Either that or you plan to raise another army of the dead."

"Those who join my army are well paid," Ariakas replied. "And I pay on time. Unlike some commanders, I don't lose half my troops in the spring so that they can go home to put in their crops. My soldiers are not required to live off the towns they capture and loot—that's a bonus. Regular pay gives a man pride; it's a reward for a job well done. But even then"—he shrugged his massive shoulders—"I still have malcontents, like any commander. Best to get rid of them right away. If I start to coddle them, cater to them, the rest will slack off. They'll lose respect for me and my officers and next they'll lose respect for themselves. And when an army loses respect for itself, it's finished."

Kitiara had stopped eating to listen to him, was giving him the compliment of her full attention. When he was finished, she paid him a further compliment by considering his words, then she nodded once, abruptly, in agreement.

"Tell me about yourself, Kitiara uth Matar," Ariakas said, gesturing to the slave to refill their wine cups. He noted that Kitiara drank hers neat and that she enjoyed it, but she could put the cup aside. Unlike Balif, who had drained his first and gulped his second and was now starting on a third.

"Not much to tell, sir," she said. "I was born and raised in Solace in Abanasinia. My father was Gregor uth Matar, a Solamnic of noble birth, a Knight. He was one of their best warriors," she added, a statement of fact, not bragging. "But he couldn't stomach their petty little rules, the way they try to run a man's life. He sold his sword and his talents where he chose to sell it. He took me to see my first battle when I was five and taught me to use a sword, taught me how to fight. He left home when I was young. I haven't seen him since."

"And you?" Ariakas asked.

Kitiara lifted her chin. "I'm my father's daughter, sir."

"Meaning you don't like rules?" He frowned. "You don't like to obey orders?"

She paused, thinking out her words carefully, shrewd enough to know her future depended on them, but with strength and pride and confidence enough to tell the truth.

"If I found a commander I admired, a commander in whom I could place my trust and my respect, a commander who had both common sense and intelligence, I would obey the orders given by such a commander. And . . ." She hesitated.

"And?" Ariakas repeated, urging her on with a smile.

She lowered her dark lashes, her eyes glimmered beneath them. "And, of course, such a commander must make it worth my while."

Ariakas leaned back from the table and laughed. He laughed long and loud, banging his cup on the table, laughed until one of his aides—defying all convention—peered inside the tent to see what had so captured his lordship's fancy. Ariakas was not generally celebrated for his good humor.

"I think I can promise you a commander who can satisfy all your requirements, Kitiara uth Matar. I have need of several more officers. I think you will fill the bill. You must prove yourself, of course. Prove your courage, your skill, your resourcefulness."

"I am ready, sir," Kitiara said coolly. "Name your task."

"Captain Balif, you have done well," said Lord Ariakas. "I will see to it that you are rewarded." Writing on a small scrap of paper, Ariakas yelled for his aide, who entered with alacrity. "Take Captain Balif to the counting room. Give the pursers this." He handed over the chit. "Come back to see me tomorrow, Captain. I have another assignment for you."

Balif rose somewhat unsteadily to his feet. He accepted his dismissal with good humor, having caught sight of the amount written down on the chit. He knew well enough that he'd lost Kitiara, that she'd moved to a higher level, a level where he could not follow. He also knew her well enough to guess that she was not likely to exert herself in the future on his behalf. He'd had his reward. He rested his hand on her shoulder as he passed. She shrugged off his touch, and so they parted.

Having rid himself of his aide and Captain Balif, Ariakas pulled shut the tent flaps. He came up behind Kitiara, grabbed hold of a handful of dark, crisp curls, pulled her head back, and kissed her on the lips, kissed her hard, roughly.

His passion was returned, returned with a force that startled him. She kissed him fiercely, her nails digging into the bare flesh of his arms. And then, when he would have taken more, she broke free of him.

"Is this how I am to prove myself, sir?" she asked. "In your bed?"

"No, damn it! Of course not," he said harshly. Grabbing hold of her around her waist, he pulled her body close to his. "But we might as well enjoy ourselves!"

She leaned away from him, arching her back, her hands on his chest. She was not being coy, she wasn't fighting him. Indeed, to judge by her glistening eyes and quickened breathing, she was fighting her own desires.

"Think, sir! You say you want to make me an officer?"

"I do. I will!"

"Then if you take me to your bed now, it will be whispered among the soldiers that you have made an officer of your toy, a plaything. You said yourself that the men should have respect for their officers. Will they have respect for me?"

Ariakas regarded her in silence. He had never before met a woman like this, a woman who could meet him—and best him—on his own ground. Still, he did not release her. He had never before met a woman who so tantalized him.

"Let me prove myself to you, sir," Kitiara continued, not drawing away from him, but nestling close, close enough that he could feel her warmth, the quivering tension in her body. "Let me make a name for myself in your army. Let your soldiers speak of my courage in battle. Then they will say that Lord Ariakas takes a warrior to his bed, not a whore."

Ariakas ran his hand through her curly hair, entangling his fingers. His hand clenched in her curls, pulling her hair painfully. He saw the involuntary tears start to her eyes. "Never before has any woman said 'no' to me and lived to tell of it," he said.

He gazed at her long, waiting to see a flicker of fear in those dark eyes. If he had seen it, he would have snapped her neck.

She regarded him calmly, steadfastly, with a hint of the crooked smile on her lips.

Ariakas laughed, somewhat ruefully, and released her. "Very well, Kitiara uth Matar. What you say makes sense. I will give you a chance to prove yourself. I have need of a messenger."

"I suppose you have plenty of message boys," Kitiara said, looking displeased. "I seek glory in battle."

"Let us say that I *had* plenty of message boys," Ariakas said with an unpleasant smile. He poured two cups of wine, to blunt the edge of their unfulfilled desire. "Their numbers are dwindling. I have sent four prior to this and not a single one has returned."

Kitiara's good humor returned. "This sounds more promising, sir. What is the message and to whom is it to be delivered?"

Ariakas's heavy black brows drew together, his expression stern and grim. His hand clenched over the wooden wine cup. "This is the message. You will say that I, Ariakas, general of the armies of Her Dark Majesty, command him, in the name of Her Dark Majesty, to report to me here in Sanction. You will tell him that I have need of him, that Her Dark Majesty has need of him. You will tell him that he defies me—and his Queen—at his peril."

"I will carry your message, sir," said Kitiara. She arched an eyebrow. "But the man may need persuading. Do I have your permission to do what I need to do in order to force his compliance?"

Ariakas smiled slyly. "You have my permission to *try* to force him to obey me, Kitiara uth Matar. Though you may not find that an easy task."

Kitiara tossed her head. "I have never met the man who said 'no' to me, sir, and lived to tell of it. What is his name? And where do I find him?"

"He lives in a cave in the mountains near Neraka. His name is Immolatus."

Kitiara frowned. "Immolatus. An odd name for a man."

"For a man, yes," said Ariakas, pouring out another cup of wine. He had the feeling she was going to need it. "But not for a dragon."

7

Kitiara lay beneath her blankets, her arms beneath her head, glowering up at the red moon, the laughing red moon. Kit knew very well why the moon laughed.

"Snipe hunt," Kitiara fumed aloud, with a vicious snap of her teeth over the words. "It's a goddam snipe hunt!"

Tossing off the blankets, for she could not sleep, she stomped around the small fire, drank some water, then, bored and frustrated, she sat back down, to poke at the red-glowing charred logs with a stick. Sending a shower of sparks into the night sky, she accidentally doused what remained of the small blaze. Kitiara was remembering a snipe hunt, remembered the prank, which had been played on the gullible Caramon.

All the companions were in on the prank, with the exception of Sturm Brightblade, who, if he had been told about it, would have lectured them interminably and ended by spoiling their fun. He would have let the snipe out of the bag, so to speak.

Whenever the friends came together, Kitiara, Tanis, Raistlin, Tasslehoff, and Flint spoke of the glories of the snipe hunt, of the excitement of the chase, the ferocity of the snipe when cornered, the tenderness of snipe meat, which was said to rival chicken in flavor. Caramon listened with round eyes, open mouth, and growling stomach.

"The snipe can only be caught by the light of Solinari," Tanis said.

"You must wait in the woods, quiet as a sleepwalking elf, with a bag in your hand," Flint counseled. "And you must call, 'Come to the bag for a treat, snipe! Come to the bag for a treat!' "

"For you see, Caramon," Kitiara told her brother, "snipes are so gullible that when they hear these words, they will hurry straight to you and run right into the bag."

"At that point, you must tie the ends of the sack together swiftly," Raistlin instructed, "and hold the bag fast, for once the snipe realizes he has been tricked, he will try to free himself and, if he does, he will tear apart his captor."

"How big are they?" Caramon asked, looking a little daunted.

"Oh, no larger than a squirrel," Tasslehoff assured him. "But they have teeth sharp as a wolf and claws sharp as a zombie's and a great spiked tail like a scorpion."

"Be sure to take a good strong sack, lad," Flint advised, and was then forced to muzzle the kender, who was suddenly overcome with a severe attack of the giggles.

"But aren't the rest of you coming?" Caramon asked, surprised.

"The snipe is sacred to elves," Tanis said solemnly. "I am forbidden to kill one."

"I'm too old," Flint said with a sigh. "My snipe hunting days are over. It is for you to uphold the honor of Solace."

"*I* killed *my* snipe when I was twelve," Kitiara said proudly.

"Gee!" Caramon was impressed, also downcast. He was already eighteen and had never heard of a snipe before now. He held up his head. "I won't let you down!"

"We know you won't, my brother," Raistlin said, laying his hand on his twin's broad shoulder. "We are all very proud of you."

How they laughed that night, all of them together in Flint's house, picturing Caramon standing out there all night, pale and quivering in the darkness, calling out, "Come to my bag for a treat, snipe!" And they laughed still more in the morning, when Caramon appeared, breathless with excitement, holding up a bag containing the elusive snipe, which was wriggling a great deal.

"Why's it giggling?" Caramon asked, peering at the sack.

"That's a sound made by all captured snipe," Raistlin said, barely able to speak for his suppressed laughter. "Tell us of your hunt, my brother."

Caramon told them how he had called and how the snipe had come rushing out of the darkness and jumped into his sack, how he—Caramon—had bravely pulled together the end of the sack and, after a struggle, subdued the vicious snipe.

"Should we hit it over the head before we let it out?" Caramon asked, brandishing a stick.

"No!" the snipe squeaked.

"Yes!" Flint roared, making an unsuccessful attempt to snatch the stick from Caramon.

At this, Tanis, feeling the prank had gone far enough, freed the snipe, who looked very much like Tasslehoff Burrfoot.

No one laughed louder than Caramon, once the joke was explained to him, all of them assuring him that they had fallen for it. All except Kit, who said that she, for one, had never been such a booby as to go on a snipe hunt.

At least not until now.

"I might as well be standing in these blasted mountains with a sack in my hand calling 'Here, dragon, here! I have a treat for you!'" She swore in disgust, kicked irritably at the charred remains of the log and wondered again as she had wondered for the past seven days—ever since she had left Sanction—why General Ariakas had sent her on this ridiculous mission. Kitiara believed in dragons about as much as she believed in snipes.

Dragons! She snorted in disgust. The people of Sanction talked of nothing else but dragons. People claimed to worship dragons, the Temple of the Dark Queen was formed in the image of a dragon, Balif had once asked Kit if she would be afraid to meet a dragon. Yet, to Kitiara's knowledge, none of these people had ever set eyes upon a dragon. A real fire-breathing, brimstone-eating dragon. The only dragon they knew was a dragon carved from the cold stone of a mountain.

When Ariakas had first told her she was meeting a dragon, Kit had laughed.

"It is no joke, uth Matar," General Ariakas had told her, but she had seen his dark eyes glint.

Then, still thinking it was a joke and he was making sport of her, she had been angry. The glint had disappeared from the general's dark eyes, cold and cruel and empty.

"I have given you a mission, uth Matar," General Ariakas had told her, his voice as cold and empty as his eyes. "Take it or leave it."

She had taken it—what choice did she have? She had requested an escort of soldiers. General Ariakas had refused brusquely. He could not, he said, afford to lose any more men on this mission. Did uth Matar feel incapable of handling this assignment on her own? Perhaps he would find someone else. Someone more interested in gaining his favor.

Kitiara had accepted General Ariakas's challenge to go into the Khalkist mountains, where this alleged dragon named Immolatus lived. The dragon had lived here for centuries, or so Ariakas told her, prior to being awakened by the Queen of Darkness. Kitiara had no choice but to accept.

Her first three days out of Sanction, Kitiara had been on her guard, watching for the ambush she was certain was coming, the ambush ordered by Ariakas, the ambush meant to test her fighting skills. She vowed that she would not be the one left holding the bag, or, if she was, that there would be heads inside.

But three days passed quietly. No one sprang at her out of the darkness, no one jumped her from behind a bush except an irate chipmunk, disturbed in his spring-time foraging.

Ariakas had provided her with a map showing her destination, a map he said came from the priests of the

Temple of Luerkhisis, a map revealing the location of the cavern of the supposed dragon. The nearer she drew to her destination, the more desolate became the countryside. Kitiara began to be uneasy. Certainly if she had chosen a location where one might find a dragon, this would be it. On the fourth day, even the few hopeful vultures that had been keeping a hungry eye on her since Sanction disappeared with ominous-sounding croaks as she climbed farther up the side of the mountain.

Not a bird, not an animal, not a bug did Kit see on her fifth day. No flies buzzed around her meal of dried trail beef. No ants came to drag off the crumbs of waybread. She had traveled far and fast. Sanction was out of sight behind the peaks of the second mountain, its peak hidden by the perpetual cloud of steam that hung over the Lords of Doom. Sometimes she could feel the ground tremble beneath her feet. She had put this down to the rumblings of the unquiet mountains, but now she wondered. Perhaps it was the rumbling of a great wyrm, turning and twisting in his dreams of treasure, dreams of death.

On the sixth day, Kitiara began to feel truly alarmed. The ground on which she walked was empty of life, barren. Admittedly she was up past the tree line and had left spring's warmth far below. But she should have found a few scraggly bushes clinging precariously to the rocks in the sunshine, patches of snow in the shadows. No snow remained, and she wondered what had caused it to melt. The one bush she did find on the trail was blackened, the rocks scorched, as if a forest fire had swept the side of the mountain. But there could not be a forest fire in an area where there were no trees.

She was puzzling over this phenomenon, had just about decided it must have been a lightning strike, when she rounded a gigantic granite boulder and stumbled upon the corpse.

Kit started and fell back a pace. She had seen plenty of dead men before, but none quite like this. The body had been consumed in fire, a blaze so hot that it had left behind only the larger bones of the body, such as the skull and the ribs, the spine and the legs. Smaller bones, those of the toes and fingers, were burned away.

The corpse lay facedown. He had been fleeing his enemy when the fire blasted him, searing the flesh from his body. Kitiara recognized the emblem on the blackened helm that still covered the head. The same emblem was on his sword, which lay several paces behind him. She guessed that if she turned over the corpse to look at the breastplate in which lay his bones, like a rib roast on a metal platter, she would see the same emblem yet again— the black-feathered eagle with outstretched wings, the emblem of General Ariakas.

Kitiara began to believe.

"You might have the last laugh after all, Caramon," she said ruefully, squinting in the sunlight to scan the top of the mountain.

She saw nothing except blue sky, but feeling exposed and vulnerable on the side of the steep mountain, she crouched behind the granite boulder, noted as she did so that where the boulder itself had been touched by the flames, the rock had started to melt.

"Damn it all to the Abyss and back," Kit said to herself, as she sat down on the ground in the boulder's shadow, with the charred corpse keeping her gloomy company. "A dragon. I'll be damned. A real, live dragon.

"Oh, stop it, Kit," she scolded herself. "It's impossible. You'll be believing in ghouls next. The poor bastard was hit by lightning."

But she was lying to herself. She could see the man clearly, fleeing from pursuit, flinging down his sword in his panicked flight, its blade of good solid steel, useless against such a terrible enemy.

Kitiara reached her hand into a leather pouch marked with the emblem of the black eagle and pulled out a small scroll—vellum rolled tight and thrust through a ring. She regarded the scroll with frowning thoughtfulness, chewing her nether lip. General Ariakas had given her the scroll, telling her that she was to deliver it to Immolatus.

Furious at the deceit being played upon her, Kit had taken the scroll without looking at it, thrust it angrily into her pouch. She had listened with barely concealed scorn to Ariakas telling her what he knew of dragons, just as she herself had told Caramon all she knew of snipes.

Kitiara examined the ring carefully. It was a signet ring. A signet in the shape of a five-headed dragon.

"Whew, boy," said Kitiara. She wiped the sweat from her brow. The five-headed dragon, ancient symbol for Queen Takhisis. Kit hesitated a moment, then slid the scroll from out the ring. Carefully, gingerly, she unrolled it, took a quick look at what it said.

Immolatus, I command you to obey the summons I send to you by this messenger. Four times before you have spurned my command. There will not be a fifth. I am losing patience. Take upon yourself human form and return to Sanction with the bearer of this, my ring, there to receive your orders from General Ariakas, soon to be general of my dragonarmies.

This order scribed by Wyrllish, High Cleric of the Black Robes, in the name of Takhisis, Queen of Darkness, Queen of the Five Dragons, Queen of the Abyss, and soon to be Queen of Krynn.

"Oh, damn!" said Kitiara. "Oh, damn it all."

Propping her elbows on her bent knees, she bowed her head in her hands. "I'm a dolt! An idiot! But who would have guessed? What have I done? How did I get myself into this?

"So much," she added, lifting her head to look at the corpse, her crooked smile straight and hard and bitter, "for all my hopes, all my ambitions. This is where it will end. On the side of a mountain, my bones fused to the rock. But who would have guessed Ariakas was telling the truth? A dragon. And I'm to be its goddam messenger!"

She sat for a long time on the summit of the desolate mountainside, gazing out into the empty blue sky that seemed so near, watched the sun slide from the sky, looking as if it were setting beneath her, so far was she above the horizon. The air was starting to cool off rapidly. She shivered, the gooseflesh raised on her arms beneath the finespun wool tunic she wore underneath her chain-mail corselet. She had brought with her a woolen cloak, lined with shaggy wool, but she did not unpack it.

"The air is liable to warm up soon," she said to herself, and a hint of the crooked smile returned. "Too soon and too warm for comfort."

Shaking off her lethargy, she pulled the cloak from her bag and, wrapping the sheepskin around her shoulders, she settled down to study—with more attention—the map given her by General Ariakas. She located all the landmarks: the mountain peak, which was split in twain, as if by some giant axe blade; a jutting crag, thrusting out of the side of the mountain, looking like a hooked nose.

Now that she knew where to look, she located the cave without too much difficulty. The opening to the dragon's lair was hidden beneath the overhang, not far from where she sat. A short walk over some rough terrain, but not difficult to reach. Solinari was waning this night, but would shed light enough for her to find her way among the rocks. Kit rose to her feet, looked down the side of the mountain. It had been in her mind to take the easy way out, to simply step off the edge and into the void below. The easy way out . . . the coward's way out.

"Lie, cheat, steal—the world winks at such faults," her father had once told her. "But the world despises a coward."

This might be her last battle, but she was determined it would be a glorious one. She turned her back on the sun and looked ahead, into the gathering darkness.

She had no plan of attack; she couldn't see that a plan would be of any great use. Nothing to do except barge in the front door. Placing her hand on the hilt of her sword, she set her jaw, gritted her teeth, and took a determined step forward.

An immense beast appeared at the edge of the lip beneath the overhang. Spreading its wings—massive wings, wings that dwarfed the eagle—the beast took flight, soaring into the air. Red scales caught the last of the afterglow, glinting and gleaming and sparking like cinders flying up from the blazing log or a gentlewoman's rubies, cast into the sunlight, or drops of blood. A snout; a tail, long and sinuous; a body so ponderous and heavy that it seemed impossible the wings could lift it; a spiked mane, black against the garish, dying light; enormous, powerful legs and feet with long, sharp claws; a seeking eye of flame.

For the first time in her twenty-eight years of life, Kit tasted fear. Her stomach clenched, sending hot bile surging into her dry mouth. Her leg muscles spasmed; she nearly collapsed. Her hand on her sword hilt went wet and nerveless. The only thought her brain could think was "run, hide, flee!" If there had been a hole nearby, she would have crawled into it. At that moment, even the leap into the void off the side of the mountain appeared to her to be a wise and prudent thing to do.

Kitiara crouched down in the shadow of the boulder and huddled there, shivering, the cold sweat beading on her forehead. Her chest was tight, her heart raced, she found it difficult to breathe. She could not take her eyes from the dragon, a sight that was awful, beautiful, appalling. He was forty feet long, at least. Stretched out end to end, he would have covered the parade ground and still lapped over into the temple.

She feared the dragon had seen her.

Immolatus had no idea she was there. She might have been a gnat plastered against the rock for all he knew or cared. He was flying out into the night to hunt. Several days had passed since his last meal, a meal that had, by great good fortune, come to him. After dining on the messenger, Immolatus had been too lazy to seek more food until hunger woke him from his pleasant dreams, dreams of plunder and fire and death. Feeling his shriveled stomach flapping against his ribs, he waited hopefully to see if another toothsome morsel might enter his cave.

None did. Immolatus fretted a bit, deeply regretted having indulged in sport with one of the soldiers, chasing the terror-stricken man down the cliff face, watching him burn like a living torch. If the dragon had been thinking ahead, he would have kept his captive alive until he was ready to dine again.

Ah, well, the dragon mused grumpily. No use crying over spilt blood. He took to the air, circled once around his peak to make certain all was well.

Kitiara held perfectly still, frozen like a rabbit when it sees the dogs. She ceased to breathe, willed her heart not to beat so loudly, for it seemed to echo around her like thunder. Kit willed the dragon to fly away, fly far away. It seemed he would do so, for he wheeled as if to catch the warm air currents rising up the mountainside. Kit was close to sobbing with relief, when suddenly her throat constricted.

The dragon shifted his flight. He sniffed the air, his huge head with its red eyes turning this way and that, looking for the scent that made his mouth water.

Sheep! This blasted sheepskin cloak! Kitiara knew as well as if she had been sitting between the dragon's shoulder blades that the beast smelled sheep, that he had an appetite for sheep for dinner, but would not be too disappointed to discover his mistake—a human in sheep's clothing.

The huge snout turned in her direction, and Kitiara could see the sharp fangs as the mouth opened in anticipation.

"Queen of Darkness," Kit prayed, asking for help for the first time in her life, "I am here by your command. I am your servant. If you want this mission to succeed, then you sure as hell better do something!"

The dragon drew nearer, darker than night, blotting out the first pale stars with its enormous wings. The deeper the darkness, the redder its baleful eyes. Helpless, unable to move, unable even to draw her sword, Kitiara watched death fly closer.

There came a frantic bleating, hooves beat against rock. The dragon dove. The wind of its passing flattened Kit against the boulder. The wings gave a single flap, a death cry echoed among the rocks. The dragon's tail twitched back and forth in violent pleasure. The dragon wheeled in the sky, flew back over her. Warm blood dripped onto Kitiara's upturned face. A freshly killed mountain goat dangled from the dragon's claws.

Immolatus was pleased with his catch and his luck—he had never before known a mountain goat to venture this near his cave. He hauled the bleeding carcass back into his cavern where he could dine at his leisure. He wondered a little about the strong scent of sheep he had detected on the mountainside, an odd scent, mingled with human, but he much preferred goat meat to mutton any day. Or human, for that matter. There was generally little meat on human bones and he had to work hard for what was there, ripping away the armor to get at it, armor that always left the taste of metal in his mouth. Back in his lair, he settled his large body onto the rocks, which should have been treasure—or so he always thought resentfully—and tore into the goat.

For the moment Kitiara was safe. Weak with relief, she huddled on the ground beneath the boulder, unable to move. Her muscles, tight with adrenaline, remained clenched. She could not loosen her hand from the hilt of her sword. By sheer effort of will, she forced herself to relax, calmed her racing heartbeat, caught her gasping breath.

First, she had a debt to pay. "Queen Takhisis," Kitiara said humbly, looking up into the night sky sacred to the goddess, "thank you! Stay with me, and I will not fail you!"

Her score settled, Kitiara pulled the sheepskin more closely around her and, lying in the starlit darkness, thought back on her talk with General Ariakas, a talk to which she had paid scant attention. She forced herself to try to remember what he had told her about dragons.

he goat had been a nice, plump one. Pleased with his meal and the fact that he hadn't had to work overly hard to catch it, Immolatus settled down upon his rocky bed. Imagining his rocks were piles of treasure, he went back to sleep, sought refuge once more in his dreams.

Most of the other dragons dedicated to the service of the Queen of Darkness had been pleased when Takhisis woke them from their long, enforced sleep. Not so Immolatus.

His dreams of the past century had been dreams of fire, of driving hapless humans and elves, dwarves and kender before him, of blasting their miserable dwellings to kindling, of scooping up their children in his great maw and crunching down on their tender flesh, of toppling castles and impaling screaming Knights upon his sharp claws, claws that could tear through the strongest armor. Dreams of sifting through the rubble, after it had cooled, picking up the sparkling jewels and silver chalices, magical swords and golden bracers, piling them onto the few wagons he had taken care not to set ablaze and then carrying the wagons in his claws back to his lair.

His cave had once been stuffed with treasure, so stuffed that he could hardly squeeze his own body inside. Huma—that wicked devil-Knight Huma and his accursed wizard Magius—had put an end to Immolatus's fun. They had nearly put an end to Immolatus.

The Dark Queen, curse her black heart, had called on Immolatus to join her in what was supposed to have been the war to end all wars. A war wherein the irritating scourge of Solamnic Knights would be obliterated, their foul kind wiped from the face of the long-suffering world. The Dark Queen had assured her dragons that they could not lose, that they were invincible. Immolatus had thought this sounded like fun—he was a young dragon then. He had left his treasure trove and gone to join his brethren: blue dragons, red and green, the white dragons of the snow-capped south, black dragons of the shadows.

The war had not gone as planned. The cunning humans had invented a weapon, a lance whose bright and magical silver metal was as painful to the dragon's eyes as its sharp tip was deadly to the dragon's heart. The horrid Knights carried this terrible weapon into battle. Immolatus and his kind fought valiantly, but, in the end, Huma and his dragonlance forced Queen Takhisis to retreat from this plane of existence, forced her to make a desperate pact. Her dragons would not be put to death but would sleep the centuries away and, so as not to upset the balance of the world, the good dragons, those of silver and of gold, would also sleep.

Immolatus's right wing had been torn by the cruel lance, his left hind leg ripped by the horrible lance, his stomach slashed by the infamous lance. The dragon limped back to his cave, his blood falling like rain on the ground, and there he found that, in his absence, thieves had stolen away his treasure!

His bellows of outrage split the mountain peak. He vowed, before he went to sleep, that he would never again have anything to do with humans, unless it was to rip off their heads and munch on their bones. He would have nothing more to do with the Queen of Darkness, either. The Queen who had betrayed her servants.

His wounds healed during his centuries-long sleep. His body regained its strength. He did not forget his vow. Seven years ago, the spirit of Queen Takhisis, now trapped in the Abyss, had come to her dragons, had called upon Immolatus to waken from his long sleep and join her once again in yet another war to end all wars.

The spirit of Queen Takhisis stood in his cave, his pitifully empty cave, and made her demands.

Immolatus tried to bite her. Unable to do so (it is difficult to sink one's teeth into a spirit), the dragon rolled over and went back to sleep, back to his lovely dreams of mangled humans and a cave filled with gold and pearls and sapphires.

But sleep wouldn't come or, if it did, he wasn't allowed to enjoy it. Takhisis was always about, annoying him, sending messengers with orders and dispatches. Why couldn't the woman just leave him alone? Hadn't he sacrificed enough for her cause? How many of her messengers did he have to torch to make his point?

He was recalling fondly the last human he had watched go up in smoke, was smiling over the memory of the scent of roasting human flesh, when Immolatus's pleasant dream shifted. He began to dream of fleas.

Dragons are not bothered by fleas. Lesser animals are bothered by fleas, animals not blessed with scales, animals with skin and fur. Yet Immolatus dreamed of fleas, dreamed of a flea biting him. The bite was not painful, but it was annoying, stinging. The dragon dreamed of the flea, dreamed of scratching the flea, and drowsily lifted a hind leg for the purpose. The flea ceased biting, and the dragon settled down, once more at peace, when that damnable stinging began again, this time in a different spot. The flea had jumped from one place to another.

Now seriously annoyed, Immolatus roused suddenly and angrily from his sleep. Early morning sunlight brightened his cavern, filtering through an air shaft that opened into the side of the mountain. Immolatus twisted his huge head, eyes glaring around to discover the pest, which was somewhere on his left shoulder, his jaws snapping to make short work of it. Immolatus was astounded to see, not a flea on his shoulder, but a human.

"Eh?" he roared, taken completely by surprise.

The human was clad in armor and a sheepskin cloak and sat perched upon Immolatus's great shoulder, sat there as coolly as one of those god-cursed Knights astride a war-horse. Immolatus glared, shocked beyond measure at such audacity, and the human jabbed the point of a sword painfully into the dragon's flesh.

"You have a loose scale here, my lord dragon," said the human, lifting the scale, which was the size of a large piece of flagstone and about as heavy. "Did you know that?"

His mind fuddled with his dream and the soporiferous effects of goat meat, Immolatus sucked in a deep breath, prepared to blast this irritating creature into the next plane of nonexistence. The brimstone breath caught in his throat, however, as his mind woke up a bit more and informed him that he would not only fry the unwelcome intruder but his left shoulder as well.

Immolatus gargled a bit, swallowed the flame that had been bubbling in his stomach. He had other weapons, a goodly number of magical spells, although these required effort to use on the dragon's part, and he was too lazy to bring to mind the complicated words required for their casting. His best and most effective weapon was fear. His enormous red eyes—their pupils were larger than the human's head—stared into the dark eyes of the human, and he brought into that small mind images of her own death. Death by fire, death by tooth and claw, death by rolling over on her and squashing her into a bloody pulp.

The human wavered beneath this assault, she shivered and grew pale, but, at the same time, the sword blade bit deeper.

"I don't suppose, my lord," said the human, with a slight quaver in her voice, a quaver she controlled and suppressed, "that you've ever cut up a chicken for a stew-pot. Am I right? I thought so. A pity. Because if you had cut up a chicken, my lord, you would know that this tendon, which runs right along here"—jab, jab, poke, poke with the sword blade—"controls your wing. If I were to cut this tendon"—the blade dug in a little deeper—"you could not fly."

Immolatus had never cut up a chicken—he generally ate them whole, several dozen at a time—but he was well acquainted with the construction of his own body. He was also well acquainted with injuries to his wings, injuries that left him a prisoner in his cave, unable to fly and to hunt, suffering the pangs of hunger and of thirst.

"You are powerful, my lord," said the human. "You are skilled in magic. You could kill me with a snap of your jaws. But not before I have inflicted a considerable amount of damage on you."

By now, Immolatus had lost his irritation. He had overcome his rage. He wasn't hungry, the goat had seen to that. The dragon was beginning to be fascinated.

The human was respectful, deferring to him as "my lord." Most appropriate and suitable. The human had been afraid, but she had conquered her fear. Immolatus applauded such courage. He was impressed with her intelligence, her ingenuity. He wanted to continue their conversation, which he found intriguing. He could always kill her later.

"Climb down off my shoulder," he said. "I'm getting a crick in my neck trying to see you."

"I am sorry for that, my lord," said the human. "But you must see that moving would put me at a considerable disadvantage. I will deliver my message from here."

"I won't harm you. For the time being, at least."

"And why would you spare me, my lord?"

"Let us say that I am curious. I want to know why in the name of our fickle Queen you are here! What do you want of me? What is so important that you risk death to speak to me?"

"I can tell you all that from where I sit, my lord," said the human.

"Confound it!" the dragon roared. "Come down at eye level! If I do decide to slay you, I will give you fair warning first. I will allow you to put up your pitiable defense, if for nothing else than for my own amusement. Agreed?"

The human considered the proposal, decided to accept it. She jumped lightly from the dragon's shoulder to land on the stone floor of his cave—the oh, so empty stone floor of his cave.

Immolatus regarded the emptiness with gloomy melancholy. "It cannot be the lure of my treasure that brought you. Not unless you have a burning desire to collect rocks." Sighing deeply, he rested his gigantic head upon a stone pillow, which placed the human level with his eyes. "That is better. More comfortable. Now, who are you and why have you come?"

"My name is Kitiara uth Matar—" she began.

Immolatus rumbled. "Uth Matar. It sounds Solamnic." He glowered, having second thoughts about slaying her later rather than sooner. "I have little love for Solamnics."

"Yet you respect us," said Kitiara proudly. "As we respect you, my lord." She bowed. "Not like the rest of the foolish world, who laugh when dragons are mentioned and claim that they are no more than kender tales."

"Kender tales!" Immolatus reared his head. "Is that what they say of us?"

"Indeed, my lord."

"No songs of conflagration, of holocaust? No tales of burning cities and scorched bodies, no stories of murdered babies and stolen treasure? We are . . . " Immolatus could barely speak for his indignation. "We are *kender* tales!"

"That is what you have become, my lord. Sadly," Kitiara added.

Immolatus knew that he and his brothers and sisters and cousins had been asleep for many decades—centuries, even—but he had thought that the awe in which dragons were held, the stories of their magnificent deeds, the fear and loathing they engendered would have been passed down through the ages.

"Think back to the old days," Kitiara continued. "Think back to the days of your youth. How many times did parties of Knights seek you out to slay you?"

"A great many," Immolatus said. "Ten or twenty at a time, arriving at least twice a year."

"And how many times did thieves enter your lair, bent on securing your treasure, my lord?"

"Monthly," said the dragon, his tail twitching at the memories. "More often than that if there happened to be a goodly number of dwarves in the area. Pesky creatures, dwarves."

"And how often, in this day and age, have thieves tried to sneak in and steal your treasure?"

"I have no treasure to steal!" Immolatus shouted in pain.

"But the thieves don't know that," Kitiara argued. "How many times have you been attacked in your cave? I would venture to guess the answer is none, my lord. And why is that? It is because no one believes in you anymore. No one knows of your existence. You are nothing but a myth, a legend, a story to be laughed at over a mug of cold ale."

Immolatus roared, a bellow that shook the walls and sent rivulets of rock dust cascading down from the cavern's ceiling, a bellow that caused the ground to quake and forced the human to cling to a handy stalactite for support.

"It is true!" The dragon gnashed his teeth savagely. "What you say is true! I never thought of it that way before. I sometimes wondered, but I had always supposed it was fear that kept them away. Not . . . not . . . obliviousness!"

"Queen Takhisis intends to see to it that they remember, my lord," Kitiara said coolly.

"Does she?" Immolatus muttered and shifted his great bulk. He scraped his claws across the stone floor, leaving gouge marks in the rock. "Perhaps I misjudged her. I thought . . . well, never mind. It is not important. And so she has sent you with a message for me?"

Kitiara bowed. "I am sent by General Ariakas, head of the Army of Queen Takhisis, with a message to Immolatus, greatest and most powerful of Her Majesty's dragons." Kitiara proffered the scroll. "Will it please your lordship to read it?"

Immolatus waved a claw. "You read it to me. I have difficulty deciphering the chicken scratches of humans."

Kitiara bowed again, unrolled the scroll, and read the words. When she came to, *"Four times before you have spurned my command. There will not be a fifth. I am losing patience,"* Immolatus cringed a bit, in spite of himself. He could hear quite distinctly his Queen's furious voice behind those words.

"But how was I supposed to know that the world had come to such a pass?" Immolatus muttered to himself. "Dragons forgotten! Or worse—laughed at, despised!"

"Take upon yourself human form and return to Sanction with the bearer of this, my ring, there to receive your orders from Ariakas, soon to be general of my dragonarmies."

"Human form!" Immolatus snorted a gout of flame from his nostrils. "I won't," he said grimly. "The world has forgotten dragons, has it? Then they will soon come to recognize their error. They will see me in my glory. I will fall upon them like a thunderbolt! They will come to know dragons then, by our Dark Queen! They will think that she has snatched the fiery sun from the heavens and hurled it into their midst!"

Kitiara pursed her lips.

Immolatus glared at her. "Well, what is it? If you think I am worried about disobeying the orders of Takhisis, I'm not," he said petulantly. "Who is she to name herself Queen over us? The world was given to *us* to do with as we liked. And then she came among us, making promises, a different promise with each of her five mouths. And where did those promises lead us? To the sharp end of some Knight's lance! Or worse—torn to pieces by some god-cursed gold dragon!"

"And that is precisely what will happen if you proceed with your plan, my lord," said Kitiara.

Immolatus growled and the mountain creaked. Smoke curled from between his fangs, his lips pulled back. "You are beginning to bore me, human. Take care. I find that I am starting to hunger."

"Go out there into the world and what will you do?" Kitiara asked, gesturing toward the exit hole of the dragon's cavern. "Destroy a few houses, burn some barns. You may even wreck a castle or two. A few hundred people die." She shrugged. "And what happens? You cannot kill everyone. The survivors band together. They come looking for you and they find you—alone, without support, abandoned by your brethren, forgotten by your Queen. The gold dragons come, too. And the silver. For there is nothing to stop them. You are mighty, Lord Immolatus, but you are one and they are many. You will fall."

Immolatus's tail lashed, and the mountain shuddered. The human was not daunted. She took a step forward, daring to come nearer the huge teeth that could have bitten her in twain with a single snap of the dragon's jaws. Though his anger burned like brimstone in his gut, Immolatus could not help but be impressed with the human's courage.

"Great lord, listen to me. Her Majesty has a plan." Kitiara explained, "She has wakened her dragons—*all* her dragons. When the time is right, she will call all her dragons to war. Nothing on Krynn will be able to withstand her fury. Krynn will fall to her might. You and your kind will rule the world in the Queen's name."

"And when will that glorious time come?" Immolatus demanded.

"I do not know, my lord," said Kitiara humbly. "I am only a messenger and therefore not privy to my commander's secrets. But if you come back with me to the camp of General Ariakas in human form, as Her Majesty recommends—for it is requisite that we keep all knowledge of your return secret—you will undoubtedly learn all there is to know."

"Look at me!" Immolatus snarled. "Look at my magnificence! And you have the audacity to ask me to diminish and demean myself by squeezing into a weak, soft, flabby, puny, squishy body such as the one you inhabit?"

"*I* do not ask such a sacrifice of you, my lord," said Kitiara, bowing. "Your Queen asks of you. I can tell you this, my lord Immolatus—you are Her Majesty's chosen. You alone have been asked to come forth into the world at this time to accept this difficult challenge. None of the others have been so honored. Her Majesty required the best, and she came to you."

"*None* of the others?" Immolatus asked, surprised.

"None, my lord. You are the only one of her dragons to be entrusted with this important task."

Immolatus heaved a deep sigh, a sigh that stirred up centuries of rock dust, enveloping the human in a cloud and setting her coughing and choking. Just another example of the pitiful nature of the form he was being asked to assume.

"Very well," said Immolatus. "I will take on human form. I will accompany you to the camp of this commander of yours. I will listen to what he has to say. Then I will decide whether or not to proceed."

The human attempted to make some response, but she was having difficulty catching her breath.

"Leave me," said the dragon. "Wait for me outside. Altering form is demeaning enough without having you standing there gawking at me."

The human bowed again. "Yes, my lord."

She laid her hand upon the end of a rope dangling down from the air shaft—a rope the dragon had not noticed until now. Grasping hold, she climbed it nimbly to the top of the cavern and crawled out the air shaft, hauling the rope up after her.

Immolatus watched this proceeding grimly. After the human had disappeared, he grasped a boulder in his red claw and jammed the boulder into the air shaft, wedging it in the hole tightly so that no other intruder could again sneak inside.

The cavern was now darker than he liked it and less airy; the sulfurous fumes of his own breath were starting to make the place stink. He'd have to open another air shaft, at considerable cost and trouble to himself. Humans! Blast them! Nuisances. They deserved to be burned. All of them.

He'd see to that later. In the meantime, it was only right and natural that Queen Takhisis should turn to him for aid. Though he considered her selfish and scheming, arrogant and demanding, Immolatus could not fault Her Majesty's intelligence.

* * * * *

Kitiara waited on the mountainside for the dragon to join her. The experience had been a grueling one; she freely admitted that she never wanted to undertake another like it so long as she lived. She was exhausted; the strain of controlling her fear, of trying to outwit the quick-thinking creature, had drained her almost past her endurance. She felt as weak as if she had marched twelve leagues in full plate armor and fought a prolonged battle in the process. Slumping down among the rocks, she gulped water from her flask, then rinsed her mouth, trying to rid herself of the taste of fire.

Tired though she was, she was pleased with herself, pleased with the success of her plan. Pleased, but not surprised. Kitiara had yet to meet the male of any species, dragon or otherwise, who was immune to flattery. And she would have to keep piling it on thick during the journey back to Sanction in order to keep her arrogant and potentially lethal companion tractable.

Kitiara slumped down on a boulder, rested her head in her arms. A man in armor came running toward her. His mouth open, screaming, his face contorted with fear and pain, but she knew him.

"Father!" Kitiara sprang to her feet.

He rushed straight for her. He was on fire, his clothes burning, his hair burning. He was being burned alive. His flesh sizzling and bubbling. . . .

"Father!" Kitiara screamed.

The touch of a hand woke her.

"Come along, worm," said a grating voice.

Kitiara rubbed the sleep from her eyes, wished she could rub its grit from her brain. She looked closely at the corpse, as she passed it. She was relieved to see that the man had been a foot shorter than Gregor uth Matar. Still, Kit could not repress a shudder. The dream had been very real.

The dragon poked her in the back with a long, sharp nail. "Keep moving, slug! I want to be done with this onerous task."

Kitiara wearily increased her pace. The next five days were going to be long. Very long indeed.

9

vor of Langtree was known throughout the surrounding countryside as the Mad Baron. His neighbors and tenants did truly think he was crazy. They loved him, they nearly worshiped him, but as they watched him ride his galloping steed through their villages, jumping hay carts and scattering chickens, waving his plumed hat as he dashed past, they would shake their heads when he was gone, clean up the debris, and say to themselves, "Aye, he's daft, is that one."

Ivor Langtree was in his late thirties, scion of a Solamnic Knight, Sir John of Langtree, who'd had the good sense to pack up his household and quietly leave Solamnia during the turmoil following the Cataclysm, traveling south with his family to an inlet on the New Sea. Finding a secluded valley, he'd built a wooden stockade and established his home. He worked the land, while his lady wife took in, fed, and clothed the poor exiles driven from their homelands when the fiery mountain fell upon Krynn. A great many of the exiles chose to live near the stockade and helped defend it against marauding goblins and savage ogres.

The years passed. The eldest Langtree son succeeded his father; the younger sons went off to war, fighting for causes that were just and honorable. If these causes happened to pay well, the sons brought their fortune home to the family coffers. If not, the sons had the satisfaction of knowing that they had acted nobly, and when they returned home, the family coffers supported them. The daughters worked among the people, easing poverty and helping the sick, until they married and went forth to spread the good work their lady mother had begun.

The land prospered. The fortress became a castle, surrounded by a small city, the city of Langtree. Several small towns and villages sprang up in the wide valley, more were established in a neighboring valley, all of their people swearing allegiance to the Langtree family. So prosperous did the Langtrees become that John III decided to call himself baron and deem his land holdings a barony. The villagers and city dwellers were proud to consider that they belonged to a barony and were more than willing to make their lord happy by so doing.

After the first baron of Langtree, sons came and sons went—mostly went, for the Langtrees loved nothing more than a thumping good battle and were always being carried back to the castle by their grieving comrades, half or wholly dead. The current baron was a second son. He had not expected to become baron, but had ascended to that title on the untimely death of his older brother, who had fallen while defending one of the outlying holdings against a tribe of hobgoblins.

As a younger son, Ivor had been expected to earn his living with his sword. This he had done, though not quite according to time-honored fashion. Having taken stock of his abilities and natural gifts, Ivor had come to the conclusion that he would do better hiring other men to fight with him than he would by hiring himself out to other men.

Ivor was an excellent leader, a good strategist, brave but not foolhardy and a firm believer in the Knight's Oath, "My honor is my life," if not the grinding and binding rules of the Measure. A small man—some mistook him for a kender, a mistake they did not make more than once—Ivor was slender and dark, with a swarthy complexion, long black hair, and large brown eyes. Men were wont to say of Ivor that though he was only five foot two, his courage stood six foot four.

Ivor was wiry and tough, clever in battle and deceptively strong. His plate armor and chain mail weighed more than some full-grown men. He rode one of the largest horses in the barony or out of it and rode it well. He loved to fight and he loved to gamble, he loved ale and he loved women, mostly in that order, which was the way he'd come by his nickname, the Mad Baron.

Having been most reluctantly made a baron by the death of his brother, Ivor had interviewed the stewards and the secretaries who undertook the daily running of the barony and, finding they were sound in their jobs and trustworthy, he placed them in charge and continued to do what he liked to do best—train men for battle and then find battles for them to fight.

Thus the barony thrived, and so did Ivor, whose exploits were the stuff of legend and whose mercenaries were much in demand. He had no need of money, he was offered more jobs than he could possibly accept and chose only those that suited him. The promise of steel had no power to sway him. He would turn his back on a sum large enough to build another castle if he deemed the cause unjust. He would spend money like water and his own blood in the same manner to fight for those who could pay only with their grateful blessings. Another reason he was called mad.

There was a third reason, too. Ivor, Baron of Langtree, worshiped an ancient god, a god known to have left Krynn long ago. This god was Kiri-Jolith, formerly a god of the Solamnic Knights. Sir John of Langtree had never lost faith in Kiri-Jolith. The Knight had carried his faith from Solamnia with him, and he and his family had kept that faith alive, a sacred fire in their hearts, a fire that was never permitted to die.

Ivor made no secret of his faith, though he was often ridiculed for it. He would laugh good-naturedly, and—just as good-naturedly—give the jokester a buffet on the head. Ivor would then pick up his detractor, brush him off, and, when the jokester's ears had ceased ringing, advise him to have respect for another's beliefs, if he could not respect those beliefs himself.

His men might not believe in Kiri-Jolith, but they believed in Ivor. They knew he was lucky, for they had seen him escape death in battle by a whisker more times than they could count. They watched their Mad Baron pray openly to Kiri-Jolith before he rode into battle, though never a sign or a word did he have that the god answered those prayers.

"It is not a general's business to take time to explain to every blasted foot soldier his plans for the battle," the Mad Baron used to say with a laugh. "So I don't suppose that it is the Immortal General's business to explain his plans to me, ha, ha, ha!"

Soldiers are a superstitious lot—anyone gambling on a daily basis with death tends to put his trust in luck-bringing objects, in rabbits' feet and charmed medallions and locks of ladies' hair. More than one, therefore, whispered a little prayer to Kiri-Jolith before the charge, more than one carried a bit of bison fur into the fray—the bison being an animal sacred to Kiri-Jolith. While it might not help, it could not hurt.

The Mad Baron was the nobleman to whom Caramon and Raistlin were going to present themselves. Caramon carried in a small leather pouch that he wore next to his skin the precious letter of introduction and recommendation written by Antimodes, addressed to Baron Ivor of Langtree. More valuable than steel to the brothers, the letter represented the hopes and plans of both the twins. This letter was their future.

Antimodes had not told them much about Ivor of Langtree (he had not told them his nickname, thinking that they might find this disquieting). The twins were considerably disconcerted, therefore, when they disembarked from their ship and asked for the way to the barony of Ivor of Langtree. They were met with wide grins and shaking heads and knowing looks and the pronouncements, "Ah, here's another couple of loonies come to join the Mad Baron."

"I do not like this, Caramon," said Raistlin one night, about two days' journey from the baron's castle where, according to one peasant, the Mad Baron was "making a mustard."

"I don't think the fellow meant 'mustard,' Raist," said Caramon. "I think he meant 'muster.' It's what you do when you recruit men for—"

"I know what the fool meant!" Raistlin interrupted impatiently. He paused a moment to give his complete attention to the rabbit simmering in the stewpot. "And that's not what I was talking about. What I don't like is the way we are met with winks and gibes whenever we mention Ivor of Langtree. What did you hear about him in town?"

Raistlin disliked entering towns, where he was certain to draw stares and gapes and gasps, to become the object of pointing fingers, hooting children, and barking dogs. The twins had taken to making their nightly camp off the road outside of villages, where Raistlin would either rest from the day's travels or, if he felt well enough, would roam the fields and the woods, searching for herbs that he used for spell components, healing, and cooking. Caramon walked into town for news, supplies, and to check to make certain they were traveling in the right direction.

At first, Caramon was reluctant to leave his twin alone, but Raistlin assured him that he was in very little danger, and this was true. More than one potential footpad, seeing the sun glisten on Raistlin's golden skin and glitter in the crystal ball atop the obviously magical staff, had skulked off to try his luck elsewhere. Indeed, the twins were rather disappointed that they had not had a chance to try their newfound martial talents on anyone during the long journey.

Caramon sniffed hungrily at the rabbit. The twins, short on money, were reduced to eating one meal a day and that was one they had to catch themselves. "Isn't it done, yet? I'm starving. It looks done to me."

"A hare sunning itself on a rock would look done to you," Raistlin returned. "The potatoes and onions are nowhere near cooked enough, and the meat must stew another half hour, at least."

Caramon sighed and tried to forget the rumblings in his stomach by answering his brother's earlier question.

"It is kind of odd," he admitted. "Whenever I ask about Ivor of Langtree, everyone laughs and makes cracks about the Mad Baron, but they don't seem to talk about him in a bad way, if you know what I mean."

"No, I do not," Raistlin said, glowering. He had a low opinion of his brother's powers of observation.

"The men smile, and the woman sigh and say he's a lovely gentlemen. And if he's mad, then some other parts of Ansalon we've been through could use his kind of madness. The roads here are maintained, the people are well fed, their houses are well built and kept in repair. No beggars in the streets. No bandits on the highways. Crops in the fields. Here's what I've been thinking—"

"You! Thinking!" Raistlin snorted.

Caramon didn't hear. He was concentrating on the pot, trying to hurry the rabbit.

"*What* were you thinking?" Raistlin asked at last.

"Huh? I dunno. Let me see . . . Yeah, I remember. I was thinking that maybe they called this Ivor the Mad Baron the same way we used to call Weird Meggin, Weird Meggin. I mean, *I* always thought the woman was cracked, but you said she wasn't and that she was malingered."

"Maligned," Raistlin corrected, casting a severe eye on his brother.

"That's it!" Caramon returned, nodding sagely. "That's what I meant to say. They mean the same thing, don't they?"

Raistlin gazed out to the road, where a steady stream of men, young and old, walked or rode, all headed for Langtree Castle, where the baron had his training grounds. Many of the men were obviously veterans, such as the two Raistlin was watching now. Both wore chain-mail corselets over leather tunics, lined with strips of leather at the bottom, which formed a short skirt. Swords rattled at their hips, their arms and faces and legs—bare beneath the tunic—were seamed with great ugly weals. The two veterans had come across a friend, apparently, for the three men flung their arms around each other, slapped each other on the back.

Caramon let out a wistful sigh. "Would you look at those battle scars! Someday—"

"Hush!" Raistlin ordered peremptorily. "I want to listen to what they're saying." He drew back his hood in order to hear better.

"So, it looks like you did well for yourself over the winter," said one of the men, eyeing his friend's broad stomach.

"Too well!" said the other, groaning. He wiped sweat from his forehead, though the sun was setting and the night air was cool. "Between Marria's cooking and the tavern's ale"—he shook his head gloomily—"and the fact that my chain mail shrank—"

"Shrank!" His friends hooted in derision.

"So it did," said the other, aggrieved. "You remember that time at the Munston siege when I had to stand guard duty in the pouring rain? The damn chain mail's pinched me ever since. My brother-in-law's a blacksmith, and he said he'd seen many a mail shirt shrink in the wet. Why do you think the smith dunks his swords in water when he's forging them, answer me that?" He glared at his comrades. "To make the metal tighten up, that's why."

"I see," said one of the men, winking at the other. "And I'll bet he also told you to throw out that old chain mail and order a whole new set."

"Well, sure," said the rotund soldier. "I couldn't be joining up with the Mad Baron wearing shrunken chain mail now, could I?"

"No, no!" said his friends, rolling their eyes and grinning out of the corners of their mouths.

"Besides," said the other, "there were the moth holes."

"Moth holes!" one said, about to burst from suppressed laughter. "Moth holes in your armor?"

"Iron moths," said the soldier with dignity. "When I found holes in my mail, I thought they were caused by defective links, but my brother-in-law said that no, the links were fine. It's just that there are these moths that eat iron. . . ."

This proved too much. One of the men collapsed in the road, wiping his streaming eyes. The other leaned weakly against a tree.

"Iron moths," said Caramon, deeply impressed. He glanced worriedly at his own brand-new, shiny chain-mail corselet, which he had purchased prior to leaving Haven and of which he was enormously proud. "Raist, take a look, will you? Are there any—"

"Hush!" Raistlin shot his brother a furious glance, and Caramon meekly subsided.

"Well, don't worry," said one of the men, slapping his chubby friend on the back. "Master Quesnelle will march that lard off you soon enough."

"Don't I know it!" The man sighed deeply. "What's in store for us this summer? Any jobs in the offing? Have either of you heard?"

"Naw." One of the men shrugged. "Who cares? The Mad Baron picks his fights well So long as the pay's good."

"Which it will be," said another. "Five steel a week, per man."

Caramon and Raistlin exchanged glances.

"Five steel!" said Caramon, awed. "That's more in a week than I earned in months working on the farm."

"I am beginning to think you are right, my brother," said Raistlin quietly. "If this baron is mad, there should be more lunatics like him."

Raistlin continued to watch the veterans. All this time, they had been standing in the road, laughing and exchanging the latest gossip. Eventually they fell into step— by force of habit—and marched down the road. No sleeping out-of-doors for these men, Raistlin reflected. No dining on scrawny rabbit and seed potatoes, which the twins had purchased with the last of their money from a farmer's wife. These men had steel in their purses, they would spend the night in a comfortable inn.

"Raist . . . can we eat yet?" Caramon asked.

"If you do not mind undercooked rabbit, I suppose we can. Watch out! Use the—"

"Ouch!" Caramon snatched back burned fingers, stuck them in his mouth. "Hot," he mumbled, sucking on them.

"It's one of the characteristics of boiling water," Raistlin observed caustically. "Here! Use the ladle! No, I don't want any meat. Just some of the broth and potatoes. And when you are finished, fix my tea for me."

"Sure, Raist," said Caramon between mouthfuls. "But you should eat some meat. Keep up your strength. You'll need it when it comes to fighting."

"I will not be involved in any actual physical fighting, Caramon." Raistlin smiled disdainfully at his brother's ignorance. "From what I have read, the war wizard stands off to the sidelines, a good distance from the battle, surrounded by soldiers to protect him. This enables him to cast spells in relative safety. Since spellcasting requires such intense concentration, the wizard cannot risk being distracted."

"I'll be there to watch out for you, Raist," Caramon said, when he could speak, having rendered himself momentarily speechless by shoving a whole potato in his mouth.

Raistlin sighed and thought back to the time when he had been so sick with pneumonia. He remembered his twin tiptoeing into the room in the night, drawing the blankets up around Raistlin's shoulders. There had been times when Raistlin was shivering with chills, when this attention had been most welcome. But there had been other times, when the fever burned hot, that Raistlin thought the blankets were meant to suffocate him.

In memory of his illness, he began to cough, coughed until his ribs ached and tears stood in his eyes. Caramon was all concern, watched him anxiously.

Raistlin cast aside the bowl containing his uneaten broth and wrapped himself, shivering, in his cloak. "My tea!" he croaked.

Caramon jumped to his feet, spilling the wooden dish with the remainder of his dinner onto the ground and hastened to fix the strange, ill-tasting and ill-smelling tisane, which eased his twin's cough, soothed his throat, and dulled the unceasing pain.

Huddled in his blanket, Raistlin cupped his hands over the wooden mug that held his tea, sipped it slowly.

"Is there anything else I can get for you, Raist?" Caramon inquired, regarding his brother in concern.

"Make yourself useful," Raistlin ordered peevishly. "You irritate me to death! Leave me in peace, and let me get some rest!"

"Sure, Raist," said Caramon softly. "I'll . . . I'll just clean up the dishes. . . ."

"Fine!" Raistlin said without a voice. He closed his eyes.

Caramon's footsteps thudded all around him. The stewpot clanged, the wooden bowls rattled. Wet wood, tossed on the fire, hissed and spat. Raistlin lay down, pulled his blanket up over his head. Caramon was actively working at being quiet.

Caramon is like this tea, Raistlin thought to himself as he drifted off to sleep. My feelings for him are mixed with guilt, tainted with jealousy. The flavor is bitter, it is hard to swallow. But once taken, a pleasant warmth pervades my system, my pain eases, and I can sleep, secure in the knowledge that he is there beside me in the night, watching over me.

10

The city of Langtree had sprouted up around the baron's castle, which afforded protection for the city's inhabitants and also, in the early days, a market for goods and services. The city was now prosperous with a small but burgeoning population that produced goods and services for itself as well as the castle and its inhabitants. Excitement and bustle were in the air, for it was spring muster and the city's population was swelling with the return of the veterans and the arrival of new volunteers.

Langtree was a peaceful place during the winter, when the chill winds blew down from the distant mountains, bringing sleet and snow. A peaceful city, but not a sleepy one. The blacksmith and his assistants spent the winter days working hard at the forge, making the swords and daggers, chain mail and plate armor, spurs and wagon wheels and horseshoes, which would be in high demand when the soldiers came back in the spring.

Farmers who could not see their fields for the snow covering them turned to a second craft. The winter was the time for fine leatherwork, and the hands that wielded the hoe in the summer now sewed belts, gloves, and tunics, fashioned sheaths for sword and knife. Most were plain and serviceable, but some were made with intricate, hand-tooled designs, which would command high prices. The farmers' wives pickled eggs and pigs' feet and laid up jams and jellies and jars of honeycomb to sell at the open-air markets. Millers ground flour and corn to make bread. Weavers worked at their looms, making cloth for blankets, cloaks, and shirts, all embroidered with the baron's crest—the bison.

Tavern owners and innkeepers spent the dull winter months cleaning and refurbishing and laying up quantities of ale and wine and mead, brewed cordials, and caught up on their sleep, which was always in short supply when the troops came to town. Jewelers and gold- and silversmiths fashioned objects of beauty to tempt the soldiers to spend their steel. Everyone in town looked forward to spring muster and summer campaign season. During this frantic, exciting time, they would make money enough to live on the remainder of the year.

Caramon and Raistlin had been to the Harvest Home Fair held at Haven every year—a gathering of people they both considered impressive. But they were not prepared for anything like spring muster in Langtree. The population of the town swelled fourfold. Soldiers filled the town—good-naturedly jostling each other in the streets, raising the roofs off the taverns with their laughter and their singing, thronging to the Street of Swords, haranguing the blacksmiths, teasing the barmaids, bargaining with the vendors, or cursing the kender, who were everywhere they didn't belong.

The baron's guards patrolled the streets, keeping a watchful eye on the soldiers, ready to intervene if there was trouble. Trouble was rare. The baron always had more volunteers than he needed. Anyone who made a misstep was out of his favor for good. The soldiers took care of each other, hustling drunken comrades out the back door, breaking up fights before they spilled out onto the street, and making certain that the tavern owners were well paid for any damages.

Reunions among friends happened on every street corner, with much laughter and reminiscing and the occasional sorrowful shake of the head remembering one who "ate his pay," which the twins discovered did not mean that he had gulped down steel coins for breakfast, but had taken a steel blade in the gut.

The language the mercenaries spoke was a jumble of Common, their own jargon, some Solamnic (spoken with a terrible accent that would have made it unrecognizable to a true resident of Solamnia), some dwarven—mainly to do with weapons—and even a bit of elven when it came to archery. The twins understood one word out of about five, and those words made little sense.

The twins had hoped to be able to slip into the city unnoticed, avoid attention. This proved difficult. Caramon stood head and shoulders above most of Langtree's population, while Raistlin's red robes, though stained with travel, caused him to stand out like a cardinal among sparrows in the more somberly dressed crowd.

Caramon was very proud of his shining new chain mail, his new sword, and its new sheath. He wore them ostentatiously and never failed to display them to what he assumed were admiring beholders. Now, he realized, to his deep chagrin, the very newness of which he'd been so proud marked him a raw recruit. He gazed with envy on the battered chain mail worn with such ease by the veterans and would have sold his new sword seven times over for one with a notched blade indicative of many hard-fought battles.

Though he could not understand the gist of most of the comments aimed his direction—many of which had to do with "pukes," which he couldn't fathom at all, even the occasionally obtuse Caramon could tell the remarks were not complimentary. He wouldn't have minded much on his own account—Caramon was used to being kidded and took teasing good-naturedly—but he was starting to grow angry over what they were saying about his twin.

Raistlin was accustomed to people regarding him with suspicion and dislike—people still distrusted wizards, in this day and age—but at least in the past they had viewed him with respect.

Not in Langtree. The soldiers appeared to dislike his calling as much as anyone and didn't have a particle of respect for him either. They certainly did not fear him, to judge by the gibes thrown his direction.

"Hey, witch boy, what you got under those fancy red robes?" called out one grizzled soldier.

"Not much, by the look of him!"

"The witch boy stole his mama's clothes. Maybe she'd pay to get them back!"

"The clothes, maybe. Not him!"

"Ooh, look out, Shorty. You're gonna make the witch boy mad. He's gonna turn you into a frog!"

"No, a lunkhead. That's what happened to the big guy with him." The soldiers laughed and hooted.

Caramon glanced at his brother uneasily. Raistlin's face was set and grim, the golden skin burnished with a sheen of red as the blood mounted to his cheeks.

"You want me to pound 'em, Raist?" Caramon asked in a low voice, glowering at their detractors.

"Keep walking, Caramon," Raistlin admonished. "Keep walking and pay them no mind."

"But, Raist, they said—"

"I know what they said!" Raistlin snapped. "They're trying to provoke us into starting a fight. Then *we'll* be the ones who get into trouble with the baron's guards."

"Yeah, I guess you're right," said Caramon unhappily. They were out of range of the teasing now, the soldiers having found something else to amuse them. But more soldiers filled the streets, and being in high spirits, they were looking for fun, and the young men were easy targets. They were forced to endure insults and derogatory remarks at every street corner.

"Maybe we should leave this place, Raist," Caramon said. He had entered the city proudly, filled with excitement. Now, completely crushed, he hung his head, hunched his shoulders, and tried to make himself as small as possible. "No one wants us here."

"We have not come this far to give up before we start," Raistlin returned with more confidence than he felt. "Look, my brother," he added quietly. "We're not alone."

A young man of indeterminate age, somewhere between fifteen and twenty, walked on the opposite of the street. Carrot-red hair, ragged and lanky, fell past his shoulders. His clothes were patched and too small for him; he had outgrown them but probably could not afford to purchase new. As he came near the twins, his attention fixed on Raistlin. The youngster stared at the mage with frank and open curiosity.

A soldier emerged from a tavern, his face flushed with drink. The long carrot-red hair proved too great a temptation. The soldier reached out, grabbed hold of a hank of hair and twisted, jerking the young man backward.

The youngster yelped and grabbed hold of his head. He must have felt as if his hair was being yanked out at the roots.

"What have we here?" the soldier demanded, chortling.

Wildcat was the answer.

Moving with marvelous agility, the youngster twisted in the man's grasp and lashed out at his molester, spitting and clawing and kicking. The attack was so savage and sudden, so completely unexpected, that the youngster landed four punches on the soldier's face and two kicks—one to the shin and one to the knee—before the man knew what had hit him.

"Look at that!" His drunken cohorts roared. "Rogar's been whipped by a baby!"

Furious, blood dribbling from a broken nose, the soldier landed a punch on the jaw that sent the youngster tumbling head over heels into the gutter.

Straddling his victim, the enraged soldier grabbed hold of the boy's shirt—tearing it—and yanked him, groggy and dazed and bleeding, out of the gutter. The soldier raised a meaty fist—his next blow might well kill the young man.

"I don't like this, Raist," said Caramon sternly. "I think we should do something."

"This time I agree with you, my brother." Raistlin was already opening one of the many small pouches that hung from his belt, pouches that held his spell components. "You take care of the bully. I will deal with his friends."

Rogar was intent on his prey, his friends were intent upon their wit. Rogar never saw Caramon, who loomed up from behind him, his large shadow falling over the man like a thundercloud passing before the sun, his fist landing on him like a bolt from the heavens. The soldier fell facefirst into the gutter. He would later waken with a ringing in his ears, swearing he'd been struck by lightning.

Rogar's two friends had their mouths open, laughing. Raistlin tossed a handful of sand into their faces, recited the words to a spell. The soldiers slumped to the street and lay there, snoring loudly.

"Fight!" screamed a barmaid, coming to the door with a tray of mugs, which she promptly dropped with a crash.

Soldiers clambered to their feet, jostling with each other to be first out the door, eager to join the fray. From down the street came whistles and shouts, and someone yelled that the guards were coming.

"Let's go!" Raistlin cried to his brother.

"Aw, c'mon, Raist! We can handle these bastards!" Caramon's face was flushed with pleasure. His fists clenched, he was ready to take on all comers.

"I said, we are going, Caramon!"

When Raistlin spoke in that tone, sharp and cold as a chunk of ice, Caramon knew better than to disobey. Reaching out, he caught hold of the youngster, who was swaying on his feet, and hauled him off as easily as if the young man had been a sack of potatoes.

Raistlin dashed off down the street, his red robes flapping around his ankles, clutching the Staff of Magius in his hand. He could hear Caramon thudding behind him and a parcel of drunken soldiers haring along after them.

"This way!" he yelled and, veering suddenly, made a sharp right turn and darted into a shadowy alley.

Caramon followed. The alley opened into another bustling street, but Raistlin halted about halfway down, in front of a wall made of wooden planks. The smell of horse and hay was strong. Raistlin tossed the Staff of

Magius over the wall. Caramon heaved the young man, arms and legs flying, over afterward.

"Give me a boost!" Raistlin ordered, reaching up his hands to catch hold of the top of the wall.

Caramon grabbed hold of his twin around his waist and boosted him with such energy that Raistlin missed his grasp and shot over the wall to land headfirst in a bale of straw. Caramon lifted himself by his hands, peered over the wall.

"You all right, Raist?"

"Yes! Yes! Hurry up before they see you!"

Caramon heaved himself up and over, tumbled into the straw.

"They went down the alley!" yelled a voice.

The clamor came their direction. The brothers crouched deeper into the straw. Raistlin put his finger to his lips, counseling silence. The young man Caramon had rescued lay in the straw beside them, gasping quietly for breath and watching them both with bright, dark eyes.

Booted feet stomped past the stable. Their pursuers ran by, burst into the street at the end of the alley, where someone shouted that the three had been seen heading toward the city gate.

Raistlin relaxed. By the time the soldiers realized they had lost their prey, they would have found another tavern. As for the guards, all they cared about was restoring order, not making arrests. They would not waste their time tracking down the participants in a bar fight.

"We are safe now," Raistlin was about to say, when dust from the dry straw flew into his mouth and set him coughing.

The spasm was a bad one, doubling him over in pain. He was thankful the attack had not struck him as he was fleeing, wondered vaguely that he had been able to run with such ease, run without even thinking about his infirmity.

Both Caramon and the young man they had rescued watched Raistlin anxiously.

"I am all right!" Raistlin gasped, striking away his brother's solicitous hand. "It's this blasted straw! Where's my staff?" he demanded suddenly, looking for it and not finding it. A pang of unreasoning terror constricted his heart.

"Here it is," said the young man, squirming and fishing for something beneath him. "I think I'm sitting on it."

"Don't touch it!" Raistlin demanded in a half-choked voice, lunging forward and thrusting out his hand.

Startled, recoiling from the mage as if he'd been a striking snake, the young man—wide-eyed—moved his hand away from the staff.

Raistlin clutched at it, and only when he had the staff safely in hand did he relax.

"I am sorry if I startled you," Raistlin said gruffly, clearing his throat. "The staff is quite valuable. We should leave here before someone comes. Are you all right?" he asked the young man curtly.

The young man glanced over his legs and arms, wiggled his fingers and his bare toes. "Nothing broken. Just a split lip. And I've had worse than this from Pa," he added cheerfully, wiping away blood.

Caramon peered out the front of the horse stall. A long line of stalls stretched off in both directions, another row stood across from them. About half the stalls were filled. Horses snorted and snuffled and shuffled their feet, munched hay. In the stall across from theirs, a big bay companionably rubbed heads with a chestnut. Sparrows flew in and out of the eaves, darting into the stalls to snitch a bit of straw for nest repair.

"No one around," Caramon reported.

"Excellent. Caramon, pick the hay out of your hair."

Raistlin brushed off his robes, the young man assisting him helpfully. After a brief inspection, Raistlin pronounced them in suitable condition to leave. Caramon took one more look, then the three emerged from the stall and walked along the row of horses.

"I really miss Nightsky," said Caramon, heaving a sigh. The sight and smell of horses brought back his loss. "He was a great horse."

"How did he die?" asked the young man in sympathetic tones.

"He didn't," Raistlin said. "We sold our horses to have money to buy our passage across New Sea. Ah," he added loudly, "thank you for allowing us to look around, sir!"

A stable hand clad in leather breeches and homespun shirt was leading two horses, saddled and bridled, out of their stalls. Two men, well dressed, waited in the stable yard. The stable hand came to a dead stop on seeing the odd-looking trio.

"Hey, what the—"

"We saw nothing we liked," Raistlin said, waving his hand. "I thank you all the same. Caramon, give the man something for his trouble."

With a courteous nod, Raistlin passed by the stable hand, who stared at them open-mouthed.

"Here you are, my good man," said Caramon, handing over one of their precious coins with as much nonchalance as if he scattered gold through the streets on a daily basis.

The three sauntered out of the stables. The stable hand glanced at his coin suspiciously and, finding it good, thrust it into a pocket with a grin.

"Come again!" he called out loudly. "Anytime!"

"There goes a night's lodging," Caramon said gloomily.

"Worth the price, my brother," Raistlin returned. "Otherwise we might have lodged in the baron's dungeons." He cast a sidelong glance from out his hood at the young man who walked alongside them.

In Raistlin's cursed vision, the young man seemed to wither and age and die as Raistlin watched. But as the flesh melted from the bones and the skin stretched taut, Raistlin detected some interesting features in the young man's face. A thin face, far too thin and older than the boy's years, which Raistlin guessed at about fifteen. He had a thin body, an oddly constructed body. The young man was short, he came to about Raistlin's shoulder.

Fine-boned hands hung from large wristbones, his bare feet were small for his height. His clothes were worn and ill assorted, but they were clean—at least they had been before he'd landed in a gutter and hidden in a stable. Now that he came to think of it, Raistlin noticed that all of them bore a distinct odor of manure and horse piss.

"Caramon," Raistlin announced, pausing at the door to a likely-looking tavern, "the unaccustomed exercise has made me hungry. I propose that we stop for supper."

Caramon stared, gaping, at his brother. Never in their twenty-one years together had he ever heard his twin—who didn't eat enough to keep a good-sized cricket alive—say that he was hungry. Admittedly, it had been a long time since Caramon had seen his twin run like that; in fact, he couldn't recall ever having seen Raistlin run anywhere. Caramon was about to say something expressive of his astonishment when he saw Raistlin's eyes narrow, a frown line crease his brow.

Caramon knew immediately that something was going on, something beyond his comprehension and that he was not to do or say anything that might imperil the situation.

"Uh, sure, Raist," Caramon said, gulping, adding weakly, "This seems like a decent enough place."

"I guess this is good-bye, then. Thanks for the help," said the young man, holding out his thin hand to each of them. He cast a wistful glance at the tavern. The smell of fresh-baked bread and smoked meats filled the air. "I'm here to join the army. Perhaps we'll see each other again." Shoving his hands in his pockets, his empty pockets, he stared down at his feet. "Well, good-bye. Thanks again."

"We are here to join the baron's army, as well," Raistlin said. "Since we are all strangers in town, we could dine together."

"No, thanks, I couldn't," said the young man. He stood straight, his head tossed back. Pride flushed his thin cheeks.

"You would be doing my brother and me a great favor," Raistlin said. "We have traveled a long distance, and we grow weary of each other's company."

"That's true enough!" said Caramon enthusiastically. A little too enthusiastically. "Raist and I, we sure do get tired of talking to each other. Why, only the other day—"

"That will do, Brother," Raistlin said coldly.

"C'mon," said Caramon, putting his arm around the young man's shoulders, the big man's arm practically swallowing him up. "Don't worry about money. You'll be our guest."

"No, please, really—" The young man stubbornly stood his ground. "I don't want charity. . . ."

"It's not charity!" Caramon said, looking shocked at the mere suggestion. "We're brothers-in-arms now. Men who've spilt blood together share everything. Didn't you know that? It's an old Solamnic tradition. Who knows? Maybe next time Raist and I won't have any money, and then it'll be your turn to take care of us."

The young man's face flushed again, this time with shy pleasure. "Do you mean that? Are we really brothers?"

"Sure we are. We'll take the oath. What's your name?"

"Scrounger," said the young man.

"That's an odd sort of name," Caramon said.

"It's my name, nonetheless," the young man returned cheerfully.

"Oh, well. Each to his own." Caramon drew his sword, lifted it solemnly, the hilt in the air. His voice was deep and reverent. "We have spilt blood together. By Solamnic tradition, we are bound closer than brothers. What you have is mine. What I have is yours."

"That may be truer than you know, Brother," Raistlin said wryly, plucking at Caramon's sleeve as the three entered the tavern with Scrounger in the lead. "In case you hadn't noticed, our new young friend is part kender."

II

The tavern, located on a side street, was known as the Swelling Ham and featured a pink and apoplectic-looking pig on its hinged sign. To judge by the smell, the Swelling Ham had only one thing to recommend it and that was the cheap prices, which were posted on a board in the window.

The Swelling Ham attracted a poorer crowd than the more prosperous taverns along the main street. There were few veterans, only those who had squandered their earnings, but many hungry hopefuls. Caramon looked over the crowd carefully before entering, saw no one who looked familiar, and pronounced it safe to enter.

The three found seats at a dirty table. Caramon was forced to appropriate a chair, first removing a slumbering drunk from it and depositing him on the floor. The barmaids, busy and distracted, let the drunk lie, stepping either on him or over him. One of the barmaids hurled three bowls of ham and beans in their direction and left to draw two ales for Caramon and Scrounger and a glass of wine for Raistlin.

"My mother was a kender," said Scrounger readily, talking between mouthfuls of white beans and ham and corn bread. "Or at least mostly kender. I think there was human blood in her somewhere, for she was like me, she looked more human than she did kender. If there was human blood in her, she didn't let it hinder her. She was kender through and through. Like everything else in her life, she had no idea how she came by me. That tasted really good." He shoved aside his empty bowl regretfully.

Raistlin passed his bowl, still full, to the young man.

"No, thank you." Scrounger shook his head.

"Take it. I am finished," Raistlin said. He had eaten only three mouthfuls. "It would go to waste otherwise."

"Well, if you're sure you don't want any more . . ." Scrounger seized the bowl, scooped up a large spoonful of beans, and chewed on it with a deep sigh of satisfaction. "I can't tell you when I've eaten anything that tastes this good!"

The beans were underdone, the ham rancid, the bread moldy. Raistlin cast an expressive glance at his brother, who was devouring his food with as much gusto as Scrounger. Caramon paused with the spoon to his mouth. Raistlin jerked his head at the young man.

Caramon looked stricken. "Ah, but, Raist . . ."

Raistlin's eyes narrowed.

Caramon sighed. "Here you go," he said, shoving his half-full bowl over to the young man. "I ate a big lunch."

"Are you sure?"

Caramon eyed the bowl sadly. "Yes, I'm sure."

"Gee, thanks!" Scrounger started in on his third bowl. "What were we talking about?"

"Your mother," Raistlin prompted, sipping at his wine.

"Oh, yeah. Mother had sort of a vague memory of a human having been kind to her once, but she couldn't remember where or when or even his name. She didn't know I was coming until one day I just popped out. She was never so surprised in her life. But she thought it was great fun, having a baby, and she took me with her, only sometimes she'd forget about me and leave me behind. But people would always find me and run after her to return me. She was glad to have me back, though I think that sometimes she didn't exactly remember who I was. When I got older, I used to return myself, which worked out fine.

"Then one day, when I was eight, I guess, she left me outside an herb shop to wait for her while she went in to try to sell the herbalist some mushrooms we'd found. We'd walked a long way that day. It was warm and sunny outside the shop, and I fell asleep. The next thing I knew, Mother was running out of the shop, with the shopkeeper yelling that they weren't mushrooms, they were toadstools and that she was going to poison him.

"I tried to keep up with her, but mother had a good head start, and I lost sight of her. The shopkeeper quit the chase and came back, cursing, for it seems that Mother had made off with a jar of cinnamon sticks in the bargain. I was going to follow her, but when the shopkeeper saw me, he was so mad that he knocked me down. I hit my head on a door stoop, and when I woke up it was night and Mother was long gone. I looked for her all along the road, but I never did find her."

"That's too bad," said Caramon sympathetically. "We lost our mother, too."

"Did you?" Scrounger was interested. "Did she leave you behind?"

"So to speak," said Raistlin with an angry glance for his twin. "You mentioned your 'pa,' " he added, changing the subject before Caramon could say any more. "Did you then find your father?"

"Oh, no." Scrounger shoved away the third empty bowl. Sitting back in the booth, he gave a contented belch. "That's just what he made us call him. He was a miller who took in stray kids to work in his shop. He said it was cheaper to feed us than it was to pay hired help. I was tired of roaming around, and he gave me a good meal at least once a day, so I stayed with him."

"Was he mean to you?" Caramon asked, frowning at this.

Scrounger thought this over. "No, not really. He'd hit me sometimes, but I guess I deserved it. And he saw to it that I could read and write Common, because he said stupid children made him look bad in front of the customers. I stayed with him until I was about nineteen. I thought I might be there forever. He was going to make me shop foreman.

"But then one day a really strange feeling came over me. My feet got real itchy, and I couldn't sit still, and I began to see the road in my dreams." Scrounger smiled, stared past them, out the window. "That road. Out there. I saw it stretch before me, and at the end I saw high mountains with snow on their peaks and green valleys covered with wildflowers and dark, spooky forests, cities with high walls and castles shining in the sun, vast seas with foam-flecked waves. The dreams were wonderful, and when I woke up and found myself surrounded by four walls, I was so sad I'd almost burst out crying.

"Then one day a new customer came into the shop. He was a very wealthy man who'd bought up several of the local farms and he wanted to sell us his grain. I started to talk to him and found out he'd been a soldier, a mercenary. That was how he'd earned his money. He told me exciting stories, all about his adventures, and that was when I made up my mind. I said that if he ever heard about anyone wanting to hire on soldiers, to let me know. He promised he would, and he was the one who told me about the Mad Baron. The baron was an excellent commander, so he told me, and a good soldier, and I could do worse than learn from him. So I left the mill and started out. That was last fall. I've been on the road about six months."

"Six months! Where do you come from then?" Caramon asked, amazed.

"Southern Ergoth," said Scrounger complacently. "The trip was fun, most of the time. I worked my way on board a ship across the New Sea, landed near Pax Tharkas, and walked the rest of the way from there."

"You said you are nineteen?" Raistlin found this hard to believe. "That would make you close to our age." He nodded at his twin.

"Give or take a year," said Scrounger. "Mother had no idea of the date when I was born. One day I asked her how old I was. Mother asked me how old I wanted to be. I thought it over and said it seemed to me that six sounded like a pretty good age, and she said six was fine with her, and so I was six. I began counting from there."

"And how did you come by your name?" Raistlin asked. "I have to assume that Scrounger is not your given name."

"It might be, for all I know," Scrounger replied with shrug. "Mother always called me whatever took her fancy at the time. The miller mostly called me 'kid' until I began to show a talent for acquiring things that he needed."

"Stealing?" said Caramon, looking severe.

"Not 'stealing,' " said Scrounger, shaking his head. "No, and not 'borrowing' either. It's like this. Everyone has something someone else wants. Everyone has something he doesn't need anymore. What I do is find out what those somethings are, and I make sure that everyone ends up with something he wants in exchange for something he doesn't."

Caramon scratched his head. "I dunno. It doesn't sound legal to me."

"It is. I'll show you."

"That'll be sixpence for the beans," said the barmaid, dragging her straggling hair out of her face in order to read the marks she'd chalked on their table. "Sixpence for the ale, and fourpence for the wine."

Caramon reached for the money purse. Scrounger's thin fingers closed over his arm, halting him.

"We don't have the money," said Scrounger brightly.

The barmaid glowered. "Ragis!" she called out ominously.

A big man standing behind the bar filling ale mugs looked her direction.

"But," Scrounger added hurriedly, "I see your fire is almost out." He gestured toward the large fireplace in which a charred log feebly sputtered.

"So? No one's got time to chop firewood, have they?" The barmaid returned defiantly. "And where do you come off complaining, scum? Ragis'll use you for firewood unless you hand over what you owe!"

Scrounger smiled at her. Even with his split lip, he had a most charming and disarming smile. "We'll pay with something worth more than money."

"There's nothin' worth more than money," said the barmaid sulkily, but she was intrigued.

"Yes, there is. Time and muscles and brains. Now, my friend here"—Scrounger rested his hand on Caramon's bulging arm—"is the fastest and best woodchopper in all of Ansalon. I am an expert at waiting tables. If you'll give us a bed for the night, my other friend—a wizard of great renown—has a magical spice that will make your beans a culinary masterpiece. Everyone will come to your tavern just to eat them."

"Our beans ain't culinary!" the barmaid said indignantly. "They ain't never made anyone sick!"

"No, no. I mean that this spice will make them taste as good as the beans eaten by the Lord of the City of Palanthas. Even better. When His Grace comes to hear of them—and I'll be sure to tell him—he'll journey all this way just to try them."

The barmaid smiled grudgingly. "Well, the customers *have* been complaining some. Not our fault, mind you. The cook got into the sherry, fell down the cellar stairs, and broke her ankle, which means Mabs and I've had to do the cooking *and* the cleaning *and* the table waiting. We're run off our feet, and Ragis can't leave the bar, not with this thirsty crowd."

She eyed Caramon, her gaze softening. "You *are* a strong one, ain't you? What's sixpence if we can't keep the fire going or bring up a new cask of ale from the cellar? All right. You chop the wood, and you, wizard"—she cast Raistlin a disparaging glance—"what have you got?"

Raistlin removed one of his pouches, reached in his hand, and brought out a bulbous white object with a strong and heady smell. "This is the magic ingredient," he said. "Peel it and chop it fine and put it into the beans. I guarantee you will bring customers in off the street."

"We're not suffering from lack of customers. But I grant you it'd be nice to serve a meal they don't throw back in my face." She sniffed at the white bulb. "That does smell good. You guarantee it won't poison no one?"

"My brother here will volunteer to eat the first bowlful," said Raistlin, and Caramon cast him a grateful glance.

"Well . . ."

"The Lord of Palanthas," Scrounger remarked dreamily. He took her red, work-worn hand and kissed it. "Vowing yours are the best beans he ever ate in his life."

The barmaid giggled and gave Scrounger's red hair a teasing yank. "Lord of Palanthas, my ass! You, wizard, go into the kitchen and add your magic spice."

She leaned over the table, showing a fine expanse of bosom framed by a dirty, frilly blouse, and erased the marks scrawled on the wood with her forearm.

"And there'll be a little something extra in this for you, my dear," said Caramon, resting his hand amorously over the barmaid's.

"Get along with you!" she cried, snatching back her hand, all the while bending over to whisper, "We close at midnight." With an arch look and a shake of her bedraggled hair, she flounced off in answer to a chorus of yells for more ale. "Yeah, yeah, I'm comin'! Keep your pants on!"

"For the time being," Caramon said beneath his breath, grinning. He went off, whistling, to the back lot to chop wood.

"Well done, Scrounger," said Raistlin, rising to his feet, preparatory to taking his "magic spice," otherwise known as garlic, to the kitchen. "You have saved us the price of a meal and a night's lodging. One question—how did you know what I had in my pouches?"

Scrounger's thin cheeks flushed, his eyes sparkled impishly. "I didn't forget everything my mother taught me," he said, slipping off to wait tables.

* * * * *

The next morning, the twins and Scrounger joined a long line of men forming a double column in the courtyard outside the baron's castle. A large plank of wood set on two trestles made a table. A piece of parchment had been nailed to the table, to keep the parchment from blowing away in the strong, offshore breeze. When the officers arrived, they would take the men's names, then send them off to the training camp.

Here the men would be fed and sheltered for a week at the baron's expense, undergoing rigorous training that was a test of their strength, their agility, and their ability to obey orders. Those who did not make the grade were weeded out during this week and sent packing with a small sum to thank them for their trouble. Those who survived the first week were given a week's pay. Those who survived after a month were accepted into the army. Of one hundred men who marked down their names on the list, eighty would be around after the first week. Fifty would be left by the time the army was ready to march.

The recruits had begun lining up at dawn. The day was going to be a hot one for spring. In the distance, clouds gathered on the horizon. There would be rain by afternoon. The hopefuls standing in line began to sweat before the morning was half over.

The twins arrived early. Caramon was so eager that he would have left before dawn, had not Raistlin, who foresaw a long day ahead of them, persuaded him to at least wait until the sun was up. Caramon had not spent the night with the barmaid after all—much to her disappointment. He had spent the night polishing his equipment, and by morning, clad in his new armor, he outshone the sun. He was too excited to eat more than one breakfast, sat fidgeting at the table, rattling his sword and asking every five minutes if they weren't going to be late. Finally Raistlin said that they could go, only because, as he said, Caramon was annoying him to the point of madness.

Scrounger was nearly as excited as Caramon. Raistlin doubted the baron would accept the thin and childlike youngster into the army, feared that Scrounger might be in for a severe disappointment. Such was the young man's ebullient nature that Raistlin guessed Scrounger would not be downcast for long.

The tavern owner was sorry to see them leave, particularly Raistlin. The garlic in the beans had proven quite magical, the smell luring customers in off the street. The owner had tried to prevail upon Raistlin to remain behind in the capacity of cook. Raistlin, though flattered, politely refused. The barmaid kissed Caramon. Scrounger kissed the barmaid, and they set off to the mustering grounds.

They took their places in line, waiting in the bright sunshine. About twenty-five men were already there ahead of them. They waited about an hour, during which some of those in line began to chat with their neighbors. Caramon and Scrounger were talking with the man behind them.

The man standing in front of Raistlin glanced at him, as if wanting to start a conversation. Raistlin pretended not to notice. He could already feel the dust from the road start to tickle his throat; he feared that he would suffer one of his coughing spasms, could imagine being cast out of the line in ignominy. He avoided the man's friendly gaze by studying the baron's fortifications with as much interest as if he intended to besiege them.

A sergeant, a cocky bantam of a man, bowlegged and missing one eye, arrived, escorted by five veteran soldiers. The sergeant cast a glance over the hundred or so men now in line. By the squint in his eye and the sardonic shake of his head, he wasn't impressed. He said something to his comrades, who laughed boisterously. Those in line fell suddenly and uncomfortably silent. The first man in line paled and shrank to almost nothing.

The sergeant took his place behind the table. The soldiers stood behind him, their arms crossed over their chests, wide grins on their faces. The sergeant's single eye was like a gimlet, boring through the first man in line to get a look at the second and so on until it seemed he was able to see through each recruit to the very last one. Pointing a grimy finger at the paper, he said to the first man in line, "Write yer name. If you can't write, mark your **X**. Take your place over there to my left."

The man, dressed in a farmer's smock and clutching a shapeless felt hat in his hand, shuffled forward. He humbly marked down his **X** and walked meekly over to stand where indicated. One of the veterans began to call out,"Here piggie, piggie, piggie." The others laughed appreciative. The farmer cringed and ducked his head, undoubtedly wishing the Abyss would open up and swallow him.

The next man in line hesitated before approaching. He seemed to be of two minds, one of which was telling him to run for his life. He took courage, however, and stepped forward.

"Write yer name," said the sergeant, already sounding bored. "If you can't write, mark your **X**. Take your place in line."

The litany continued. The sergeant said the same thing in the same tone to every man. The sergeant's comrades made comments about each recruit. The men took their places in line with their ears and cheeks burning. Most took it meekly enough, but the young man ahead of Raistlin grew angry. Flinging down the quill pen, he glowered at the veterans, fists clenched, and took a threatening step forward.

"Steady, son," said the sergeant coolly. "It's death to strike a superior officer. Take your place in line."

The young man, who was better dressed than most and who was one of the few to write his name, glared at the veterans, who grinned back at him. Lifting his head proudly, he stalked over and took his place in line.

"Fighting spirit," Raistlin heard one of them say, as he approached. "He'll be a good soldier."

"Can't control his temper," said another. "He'll be gone in a week."

"Bet?"

"Bet." The two clasped hands.

Raistlin's turn. He could see plainly enough that the object of this exercise was not only to enroll new recruits but to humiliate them, intimidate them. Having read up on training methods, he was aware that commanders used such means to tear a man apart, reduce him to nothing so that the officers could build him back up again into a good soldier, one who would obey orders without thinking, one who had confidence in himself and in his comrades.

"All very well for the common foot soldier," Raistlin thought disdainfully. "But it will be different with me."

As it happened, the sergeant had lowered his head to search for the name of the angry young recruit, thinking of taking a part of the bet. He was staring at the paper with his one good eye, trying to read the name upside down, when the name and the paper were obscured by a loose-flowing red sleeve and a hand and arm that gleamed with a golden sheen.

The men behind the sergeant give a low murmur, nudged each other with their elbows. The sergeant snapped his head up. The single eye focused on Raistlin, who said politely, "Where do *I* sign, sir? I am here to enroll as war wizard."

"Well, well," said the sergeant, squinting in the sun, "this is a new one. We ain't had one of your kind for quite a spell." He laughed and leered. "Spell. That's a joke."

"Where do I sign, sir?" Raistlin asked. The dust and heat were stifling. He could feel his throat starting to close, dreaded having a coughing fit now, before these grinning veterans. He pulled his hood low, keeping his face and eyes hidden. He did not want to give these men any more fodder for their jokes than was necessary. As it was, they already found him humorous enough.

"Where'd you get that gold skin, boy?" asked one of the veterans. "Maybe your mama was a snake, huh?"

"A lizard, most likely," said another, and they laughed. "Lizard-boy. That's his name, Sarge. Write that down for him."

"He'll be a cheap recruit," said the first. "All he eats is flies!"

"Bet he's got a long red tongue to catch 'em. Stick out your tongue for us, Lizard-boy."

Raistlin felt the cough seizing him. "Where do I sign?" he demanded, half-choked.

The sergeant, peering up, caught a sudden glimpse of the strange, hourglass eyes. "Go tell Horkin," he said over his shoulder to one of the men behind him.

"Where is he?"

"The usual."

The soldier nodded and left on his assignment.

Raistlin couldn't help himself. He began to cough. Fortunately, the spasm wasn't a bad one and passed quickly. But it was enough to set the sergeant frowning.

"What's the matter with you, boy? You sick? It ain't catchin,' is it?"

"My infirmity is not contagious," Raistlin said through gritted teeth. "Where do I sign?"

The man indicated the paper. "With all the rest," he said, his lip curling. He obviously didn't think much of this new recruit. "Go stand with the others."

"But I am here—"

"I know why you're here." The sergeant dismissed him from sight and mind. "Do as you're told."

His cheeks burning, Raistlin walked over to take his ignominious place with the other recruits, who were now all staring at him, as were most of those still waiting in line. Stoically, Raistlin ignored them all. His hope now was that Caramon wouldn't do or say anything to draw attention to himself. Knowing Caramon, that was a forlorn hope at best.

"Write yer name," said the sergeant, yawning. "If you can't write, mark your **X**. Take your place over there to my left."

"Sure thing, Sergeant," said Caramon cheerfully. He wrote his name with a flourish on the parchment.

"Big as an ox," said one of the veterans. "Probably about as bright, too."

"I like 'em big," said his comrade. "They stop more arrows that way. We'll put him in the front ranks."

"Thank you kindly, sir," said Caramon, pleased. "Oh, by the way," he added modestly, "I don't really need any training. I can just skip all that part."

"Oh, you can, can you?" said the sergeant.

Raistlin groaned. Shut up, Caramon! his twin said mentally. Shut up and walk away!

Caramon was charmed by the attention, however. "Yes, I know everything there is to know about fighting. Tanis taught me."

"Tanis taught you, did he?" said the sergeant, leaning forward. His friends covered their mouths with their hands, rocked back on their heels, enjoying the sport. "And who would this Tanis be?"

"Tanis Half-Elven," said Caramon.

"An elf. An elf taught you to fight."

"Well, really, it was mostly his friend, Flint. He's a dwarf."

"I see." The sergeant stroked his grizzled chin. "An elf *and* a dwarf taught you to fight."

"Me and my friend Sturm. He's a Solamnic Knight," Caramon added proudly.

Shut up, Caramon! Raistlin urged silently, desperately.

"And then there was Tasslehoff Burrfoot," Caramon went on, not heeding his twin's mental command. "He's a kender."

"A kender." The sergeant was awed. "An elf, a dwarf, *and* a kender taught you to fight." He turned to his fellows, who were red-faced with suppressed laughter. "Boys," he said solemnly, "tell the general to resign. We have his replacement."

At this, one of the men groaned and stomped his foot, trying desperately to contain his mirth. The other lost his composure and had to turn his back. His shoulders shook, he wiped away the tears streaming down his cheeks.

"Oh, that won't be necessary, sir," Caramon hastened to assure them. "I'm not that good yet."

"Oh, so the general can stay?" the sergeant asked. One corner of his mouth twitched.

"He can stay," said Caramon magnanimously.

Raistlin closed his eyes, unable to watch anymore.

"Thank you. We appreciate it," said the sergeant with deep gratitude. "And now"—the sergeant looked at the list—"Caramon Majere—" He paused. "Or would that be *Sir* Caramon Majere?"

"No, I'm not the Knight," said Caramon, anxious that there should be no misunderstanding. "That was Sturm."

"I see. Well, take your place in line with the others, Majere," said the sergeant.

"But, I told you, you really don't need to waste time training me," Caramon said.

The sergeant stood up, leaned forward and said softly, "I don't want to make the others feel bad. They might get discouraged and quit. So just play along, will you, Sir Caramon?"

"Sure. I can do that." Caramon was accommodating.

"Oh, and by the way, Majere," said the sergeant, as Caramon was walking over to join his chagrined twin, "if the drillmaster—that would be Master Quesnelle— makes any mistakes, you be sure and tell him. He'll appreciate the help."

"Yes, sir. I'll do that," said Caramon. Smiling, he joined Raistlin. "Gee, that sergeant's a nice guy."

"You are the world's biggest idiot," Raistlin said softly, furiously.

"Huh? Me? What'd I do?" Caramon demanded, amazed.

Raistlin refused to discuss it, however. He turned his back on his twin to watch as Scrounger approached the table.

The sergeant eyed him. "Look, kid, why don't you run along home. Come back in ten years when you've grown up."

"I'm grown up enough," Scrounger said confidently. "Besides, Sergeant, you need me."

The sergeant rubbed his forehead. "Oh, yeah. Give me one good reason."

"I'll give you several. I'm a scrounger and a good one. Whatever you need, I can get it. What's more, I can climb any wall standing. I can fit into tunnels mice would refuse to enter. I'm quick and I'm fast and I'm good with a knife in the dark. I can walk through the woods so quiet that compared to me caterpillars make the ground shake. I can slip into a three-story window and take the golden locket from around milady's throat and kiss her into the bargain, and she'll never hear me or see me. That's what I can do for you, Sergeant," said Scrounger. "And more."

The veterans had quit laughing. They were regarding Scrounger with interest. So was the sergeant.

"And you can talk the wings off a fly." The sergeant gazed at the young man intently. "All right. Put your name down. If you live through training, you might be of some use to the baron after all."

Feeling a touch on his shoulder, Raistlin turned.

"You the mage?" asked the soldier unnecessarily, since Raistlin was the only man in the compound wearing wizard's robes. "Come with me."

Raistlin nodded and stepped out of line. Caramon stepped out after him.

"You a mage, too?" the soldier asked, coming to a halt.

"No, I'm a soldier. I'm his brother. Where he goes, I go."

"Not now, Caramon!" Raistlin said in a low voice.

The soldier shook his head. "I have orders to bring the mage. Take your place back in line, Puke."

Caramon frowned. "We're never separated."

"Caramon!" Raistlin turned to his twin. "You have shamed me enough this day. Do as you are told. Get back in line!"

Caramon's face went red, then white. "Sure, Raist," he mumbled. "Sure. If that's what you want. . . ."

"That is what I want."

Caramon, hurt, returned to line, took his place beside Scrounger.

Raistlin accompanied the soldier through the gate and into the baron's castle.

12

he soldier led Raistlin into the courtyard, which was bustling with activity. Soldiers stood about in groups laughing and talking, or squatted on the ground, playing at knucklebones, a game involving tossing the foot bones of a sheep up in the air and catching them in a prescribed fashion, or pitching coins against the side of a wall.

Grooms led horses into or out of stalls, dogs were everywhere underfoot. A servant had hold of a yelping kender by the ear and was dragging him out of the main entryway. Some of the soldiers cast curious glances at Raistlin as he passed, others rudely stared. Coarse comments accompanied him through the castle gate and into the courtyard.

"Where are we going, sir?" Raistlin asked.

"The barracks," said his guide, indicating a row of low stone buildings lined with windows.

The soldier entered the main door to the barracks, led Raistlin down a cool, dark hallway off which were the rooms where the soldiers billeted. Raistlin was impressed with the neatness and cleanliness of the building. The stone floor was still wet from its morning scrub-down, fresh straw had been spread on the floors of the sleeping rooms, bedrolls were tightly wrapped and stowed in an orderly manner. Each man's personal possessions were wrapped in his bedroll.

At the end of the hall they came to a set of stone stairs spiraling downward. The soldier descended the stairs.

Raistlin followed along behind. At the end of the stairs stood a wooden door. Halting, the soldier gave a thunderous knock. There came a crash from inside, as of glass breaking.

"You whore's son!" yelled an irritated voice. "You've made me drop my potion! What in the Abyss do you want?"

The soldier grinned, winked at Raistlin. "I have the new mage, sir. You said I was to bring him here."

"Well, who the devil thought you'd be so blasted quick about it!" the voice grumbled.

"I can take him away, sir," said the soldier, speaking in respectful tones.

"Yes, do that. No, don't. He can clean up this mess, since he was the cause of it."

There came the sound of footsteps, a door bolt lifting with a clank. The door swung open.

"Meet Master Horkin," said the soldier.

Expecting a war wizard, Raistlin expected height, power, intelligence. He expected to be awe-inspired, or at least inspired. Lemuel's father had been a war wizard. Lemuel had often described his father, and Raistlin had discovered a portrait of him hanging in the Tower of High Sorcery—a tall man, with black hair streaked with white, a hawk nose and hawk eyes, and the long-fingered, slender-boned hands of the artist. That was his dream of what a war wizard would look like.

At the sight of the mage standing in the doorway, glaring at him, Raistlin's dream cracked down the center, spilling its contents in a flood of disappointment.

The mage was short, he came to about Raistlin's shoulder, but what he lacked in height he made up for in girth. He was relatively young, in his late forties, but there was not a hair on his head, not a hair anywhere, not an eyebrow or an eyelash. He was thick-necked, thick-shouldered, with ham-fisted hands—small wonder he had dropped the delicate potion bottle. He was red-faced, choleric, with fierce blue eyes whose blueness was emphasized by the redness of his face.

But it was not his odd looks that caused Raistlin to stiffen, caused his lip to curl. The mage—and to term him so was to pay him a compliment he likely did not deserve—wore brown robes. Brown robes—the mark of those who had never taken the Test in the Tower of High Sorcery, the mark of a mage who did not possess skill enough to pass or lacked the ambition to try to pass or was, perhaps, afraid. Whatever the reason, this mage had not committed himself to magic, had not given himself to it. Raistlin could have no respect for a man such as this.

He was consequently startled and piqued to see his own disdain reflected right back at him. The brown-robed mage was regarding Raistlin with no very amiable air.

"Oh, for Luni's sake, they've sent me a blasted Tower mage," Horkin growled.

To his deep chagrin, Raistlin was seized with a coughing fit. Fortunately it was short-lived, but it did nothing to impress Horkin.

"And a sickly one at that," he said in disgust. "What the hell are you good for, Red?"

Raistlin opened his mouth, proud to name his accomplishments.

"I'll bet you can cast a sleep spell," Horkin said, answering his own question. "A fine lot of good that'll do us. Give the enemy a nice little nap on the battlefield. They wake up refreshed and ready to slit our guts open. What the devil are you gawking at?" This to the soldier. "I assume you have work to do."

"Yes, sir, Master Horkin." The soldier saluted, turned, and departed.

Horkin grabbed hold of Raistlin's arm, yanked him inside the laboratory with a jerk that nearly took him off his feet, and slammed the door shut behind him. Raistlin looked around disparagingly, his worst fears realized. The so-called laboratory was a dark and shadowy subterranean room made of stone. A few battered spellbooks stood forlornly on a shelf. Various weapons hung on the wall—bludgeons, maces, a battered-looking sword, and some other wicked-looking implements Raistlin did not recognize. A beat-up, stained cabinet contained bottles filled with spices and herbs.

Horkin let go of the young mage, gazed at him speculatively, eyeing Raistlin as he might have eyed a carcass in the butcher's stall. He obviously did not think much of what he saw.

Raistlin stiffened beneath the insulting inspection.

Horkin put his meaty hands on his hips or at least in that general vicinity. He was built like a wedge, his shoulders and chest the most massive part.

"I am Horkin, *Master* Horkin to you, Red."

"My name is—" Raistlin began stiffly.

Horkin held up a warning hand. "I don't care about your name, Red. I don't want to know your name. If you survive your first three or so battles, then maybe I'll learn your name. Not before. I used to learn the names, but it was a goddamned waste of time. Soon as I'd get to know a puke, he'd up and die on me. These days I don't bother. Clutters up my mind with useless information."

His blue eyes shifted away from Raistlin.

"Now that is a damn fine staff," Horkin said, regarding the staff with far more interest and respect than he had regarded the young mage. Horkin reached out a thick-fingered hand.

Raistlin smiled to himself. The Staff of Magius knew its true and rightful owner, would not permit another to touch it. More than once, Raistlin had heard the crackle of the staff's magic, heard subsequent yelps and shrieks (mostly from kender) and seen the malefactor who had attempted to either touch the staff or make off with it wring a burned hand. Raistlin made no move to stop Horkin from seizing the staff, did not warn him.

Horkin took hold of the Staff of Magius, ran his hand up and down the wood, nodded approvingly at the feel. He held the crystal to his eye, examined it with one eye shut, peered through it. Holding the staff in two hands, he made a few passes with it, lunging out in a motion that stopped just short of cracking the amazed Raistlin in the ribs.

Horkin handed the staff back. "Well balanced. A fine weapon."

"This is the Staff of Magius," Raistlin said indignantly, holding the staff protectively.

"Oh, the Staff of *Magius*, is it?" Horkin grinned. He had a leering grin, thrusting out his lower jaw, with the result that his lower canines jutted up over his top lip. He moved closer to Raistlin to whisper. "I'll tell you what, Red. You can buy a dozen of those staves for two steel in any mageware shop in Palanthas."

Horkin shrugged. "Still, there is a mite of magic packed in that thing. I can feel it twizzle my hand. I don't suppose you have any idea of what the staff can do, do you, Red?"

Raistlin was too appalled to speak. Two steel in Palanthas! The magic—the powerful magic, the compensation given to Raistlin for his shattered body—dismissed as a "mite" that "twizzled"! True, Raistlin didn't yet know all the magic of which the staff was capable, but still—

"Thought not," said Horkin.

He turned his back, walked over to a stone table, and lowered his massive body onto a stool, which appeared incapable of supporting his weight. He placed a pudgy finger on the page of a leather-bound book that lay open on a stone table.

"I suppose there's no help for it. I'll have to start over again." Horkin motioned to a broken beaker that had spilled its contents over the stone floor. "Clean up the mess, Red. There's a mop and a bucket in the corner."

Anger seethed in Raistlin, bubbled over. "I will *not!*" he cried, thumping the toe of the staff into the stone floor to emphasize his ire. "I will *not* clean up your mess. I will not subordinate myself to a man who is beneath me. *I* took the Test in the Tower of High Sorcery! *I* risked my life for the magic! I was not afraid—"

"Afraid?" Horkin interrupted the torrent. He looked up from his perusal of the tome, grimly amused. "We'll see who's afraid, by Luni."

"When you are in my presence," said Raistlin coldly, nothing daunted, "you will refer to the goddess Lunitari with the respect she is due—"

Horkin could move rapidly for such a big man. One moment he was seated on the stool, the next he seemed to materialize right in front of Raistlin like some imp bursting up out of the Abyss.

"Listen to me, Red," Horkin said, jabbing his finger in Raistlin's thin chest. "First, you do not give me orders. I give you orders, and I expect you to obey those orders. Second, you will refer to me as Master Horkin or sir or master or master sir. Third, I can refer to the goddess any damn way I feel like. If I call her Luni it's because I have the right to call her Luni. Many's the night we've sat drinking together beneath the stars, passing the bottle, she and I. I wear her symbol over my heart."

He moved the finger from Raistlin's chest to his own, pointing at a badge with the symbol of Lunitari embroidered upon it, which he wore on his left breast, a badge Raistlin had not noticed. "And I wear her emblem around my neck."

Horkin drew forth a silver pendant from beneath his robes, held it up for Raistlin to see, shoving it in his face so that Raistln was forced to draw back to avoid having it jammed up his nose.

"Luni, the darling, gave me this with her own fair hands. I have seen her, I have talked to her." Horkins moved an impossible step closer, until he was practically standing on Raistlin's toes. The elder mage glared up at Raistlin, into him, through him.

"I may not wear her symbol," said Raistlin, standing his ground, refusing to fall back farther, "but I wear her color, which, as you have so astutely noted, is red. And she has spoken to me, as well."

Silence as charged as a thunderbolt crackled between them. Raistlin looked closely at the symbol of Lunitari. Made of solid silver, the symbol of the goddess was old, very old, and finely crafted, glimmered with latent power. He could almost believe that it had come from Lunitari.

Horkin looked closely at Raistlin, and perhaps the elder mage was thinking almost the very same thoughts as the younger.

"Lunitari herself has spoken to you?" Horkin asked, lifting the finger he'd been using to jab Raistlin, holding it in the air, pointing to the heavens. "This you swear?"

"Yes," said Raistlin calmly. "By the red moon, I swear."

Horkin grunted. He thrust his face another impossible inch nearer Raistlin. "Yes, *what*, soldier?"

Raistlin hesitated. He did not like this man, who was crude and uneducated, who probably did not possess a tenth of the magical power Raistlin possessed, and who would, nonetheless, force Raistlin to treat him as his superior. This man had belittled Raistlin, had insulted him. For a kender copper, Raistlin would have turned and stalked out of the laboratory. But in that last question, Raistlin detected a change of tone, a subtle note—not a tone of respect but of acceptance. Acceptance into a brotherhood, a hard brotherhood, a deadly brotherhood. A brotherhood that, if it accepted him in turn, would embrace him and hold to him with fierce, undying loyalty. The brotherhood of Magius and Huma.

"Yes . . . Master Horkin," Raistlin said. "Sir."

"Good." Horkin grunted again. "I might make something of you, after all. None of the others have ever even known who I was talking about when I mentioned Luni, dear Luni."

He raised what would have been his eyebrows, if he'd had any eyebrows to raise. "Now, Red" —Horkin pointed at the broken beaker— "clean up the mess."

13

Waiting in line with the other new recruits in the hot sunshine, Caramon watched his brother depart with considerable anxiety. In situations like this—new and unfamiliar—Caramon felt oppressed and uneasy when separated from his twin. Caramon had become accustomed to looking to his brother for guidance, was uncertain and unsure when Raistlin was not with him. Caramon was also concerned about his weaker twin's health and even ventured to ask one of the officers if he might go see if his brother was all right.

"Since all we're doing is standing in line," Caramon added, "I thought I could go see if Raistlin—"

"You want your mommy, too?" asked the soldier.

"No, sir," Caramon replied, flushing. "It's just that Raist's not very strong—"

"Not very strong!" the officer repeated, amazed. "What did he think he was joining? The Fine Ladies of Palanthas Embroidery and Hot Muffin Society?"

"I don't mean he's not strong," Caramon said, attempting to correct his mistake, hoping fervently his twin never came to hear what he'd said. "He's very strong in magic. . . ."

The officer's expression darkened.

"I think you should be quiet now," Scrounger whispered at Caramon's elbow.

Caramon considered this excellent advice. He fell silent, and the officer, shaking his head and muttering, walked off.

When the new recruits had all made their mark or signed the roll sheet, the sergeant ordered Caramon and the other recruits to march into the courtyard of the castle. Shuffling their feet and tripping over one another, they entered the courtyard and lined up in wavering, uneven rows. An officer brought them to what passed for attention, subjected them to a long list of rules and regulations, the infraction of any of which would bring about all sorts of dire occurrences.

"They say the gods dropped a fiery mountain on top of Krynn," said the officer, summing up. "Well, that ain't nothin' compared to what you'll get from me if you screw up. And now Baron Langtree would like to say a few words. Three cheers for the baron!"

The recruits shouted lustily. The Mad Baron took his place before them. He was jaunty, cocky, his tall leather boots, which came up over his thighs, would have swallowed him, but for his large plumed hat. Despite the heat, he wore a thick, padded doublet. His black beard and mustache emphasized his wide grin, his long black hair curled on his shoulders. He bore an immense sword, which seemed always on the verge of tripping him or becoming entangled in his legs, but, miraculously, it never did. Putting his hand on the sword's massive hilt, the Mad Baron made his customary welcoming speech, which had the advantage of being short and to the point.

"You're here to join an elite force of fighting men and women. The best in Krynn. You look like a pretty scabby group to me, but Master Quesnelle here will do his best to try to turn you into soldiers. Do your duty, obey orders, fight bravely. Good luck to you all, and let me know where to send your pay in the event that you don't survive to collect it! Ha, ha, ha!" The Mad Baron laughed uproariously and, still laughing, walked back to the castle.

After that, the new recruits were each handed a small loaf of bread, which, though heavy and hard to chew, was surprisingly good, and a hunk of cheese. Devouring his food, Caramon considered it a good beginning and wondered when the rest of the meal was going to be served. He and his stomach were doomed to disappointment. The men were permitted to drink their fill of water, then the sergeant marched the recruits off to the barracks—low buildings made of stone with large rooms, the same buildings through which Raistlin had passed. The recruits were given sleeping rolls and other equipment, including boots. All that they received was marked down against their names, the money for their equipment would be docked from their pay.

"This is your new home," the sergeant announced. "It will be your home for the next month. You will keep it clean and tidy at all times." The sergeant cast a disparaging glance at the well-swept floor and the new straw that covered it. "Right now," he announced, "it's worse than a pigsty. You will spend the rest of the afternoon cleaning up."

"Excuse me, sir," said Caramon, raising his hand in the air. He honestly thought the sergeant had made a mistake. Perhaps the man was nearsighted. "But the room is already clean, sir."

"You think that floor's clean, Majere?" the sergeant asked with deceptive solemnity.

"Yes, sir," said Caramon.

The sergeant reached out, grabbed a slop bucket from a corner, and dumped its foul contents onto the stone floor, soaking the straw that covered the floor.

"Now do you think the floor's clean, Majere?" the sergeant asked.

"No, but you—"

"No, what, Majere?" the sergeant roared.

"No, sir," said Caramon.

"Clean it up, Majere."

"Yes, sir," said Caramon, subdued. The other recruits were now mopping and scrubbing most industriously. "If I could have a mop, sir—"

"Mop?" The sergeant shook his head. "I wouldn't soil a good mop with this filth. A good mop's hard to come by. But you're different, Majere. You're expendable. Here's a rag. Get down on your hands and knees."

"But, sir—" Caramon grimaced. The smell was nauseating.

"Do it, Majere!" the sergeant shouted.

Trying to hold his breath to avoid the stench, Caramon took the rag and got down on his hands and his knees. He continued to hold his breath until he saw stars, then gulped in the quickest breath he could manage. The next moment he was reaching for the slop bucket, to deposit the contents of his stomach.

The floor was suddenly deluged with a flood of water, which effectively diluted the horrible smell, washed away much of the filth, and sloshed over the sergeant's boots.

"Sorry, sir," said Scrounger, looking apologetic.

"Let me wipe those off for you, sir," said Caramon, solicitously daubing at the toes of the wet boots with his rag.

The sergeant glared at the two of them, but there was a glint of laugher in his eyes and a hint of approval. Turning, he yelled at the other recruits, who were standing around, staring. "What the hell are you looking at? Get busy, the sorry lot of you! I want to be able to eat my dinner off this floor, and I want it clean before sundown!"

The recruits jumped to work. The sergeant strode out of the barracks, his face twitching in the grin he had worked hard to suppress. Discipline must be maintained.

The recruits removed the fresh straw, swept the floor with brooms made of rushes, poured water on the floor, mopped it until the stone was so clean that, as Caramon announced proudly on the sergeant's return, "You can see your face in it, sir!"

The sergeant grudgingly pronounced the work satisfactory. "At least until you're taught to do better," he added.

Caramon waited for the sergeant to announce that it was time to eat, either on the floor or off it, Caramon didn't care which, so long as he was given food and lots of it. The sergeant glanced at the setting sun, then glanced back thoughtfully at the men.

"Well, now, you're done early, so I'm going to give you a little reward."

Caramon smiled happily, anticipating extra rations.

"Pick up your bedrolls. Strap them to your back. Pick up your swords and your shields, put on your breastplates and your helmets, and"—he pointed to a hill in the distance—"run to the top."

"Why, sir?" Scrounger asked, interested. "What's up there?"

"Myself, with a whip," said the sergeant. Rounding on his heel, he caught hold of Scrounger's shirt and gave him a shake. "Listen to me, Puke. And this goes for all the rest of you." He glowered around at them, no hint of laughter in his eyes. "This is the first thing you will learn, and you will learn it now. When I give an order, you obey that order. You don't question it. We don't discuss it. We don't take a vote on it. You do it. Why? I'll tell you why. And this is the only time I will ever tell you why you are doing something.

"Because there will come a time when you're in battle, and the arrows are whistling around your ears, and the enemy is rushing down on you yelling and screaming like demons freed from the Abyss. The trumpets are shrieking, and hot, bloody metal slashes the air, and I'm going to give you an order. And if you take even one second to think about that order or to question that order or decide whether or not you're going to obey that order, you'll be dead. And not only will you be dead, but your buddies'll be dead. And not only will they be dead, but the battle will be lost.

"Now . . ." The sergeant let loose of Scrounger, dumped him on the stone floor. "Now, we'll start over again. Pick up your bedrolls. Strap them to your back. Pick up your swords and your shields, put on your breastplates and your helmets, and run to the top of that hill. You will notice," he added with a grin, "that I'm wearing my helm and my plate and carrying my sword and shield. Now, get those sorry asses moving!"

The order was obeyed, though with considerable confusion. None of the recruits had any idea how to fasten their bedrolls around their bodies. They fumbled at knots and, in several instances, watched in dismay as their bedrolls uncoiled out behind them. The sergeant went from man to man, bullying and shouting, but all the time instructing. Eventually, they were all more or less ready, with their helmets perched at odd angles on their heads, their swords clanking against their legs—occasionally tripping those unaccustomed to wearing a weapon—sweating under the heavy breastplates. Scrounger could not see from beneath his helmet, which was too large and fell down over his eyes, and he rattled around in the breastplate like a stick in an empty ale mug. The shield he carried dragged the ground.

Clad in his armor, his sword at this side, Caramon cast a longing, regretful glance in the direction of the eating hall, where he could hear the clatter of plates and smell the delicious odor of roast pig.

With a yell, the sergeant started his recruits on their way.

Night had fallen by the time they returned—at a run—from the hill. Six recruits had decided on the way that a military career was not for them, no matter how much it paid. They handed in their equipment—what they hadn't dropped on the trail—and limped, exhausted and footsore, back into town. The rest of the recruits staggered into the courtyard, where several collapsed and where several more learned why new recruits were termed "pukes."

The sergeant took a head count, discovered that two were missing. He shook his head and started out to see if he could find the bodies.

* * * * *

"What's this?" The Mad Baron paused on his way from touring the camp to look at an unusual sight.

Flaring torches and a huge bonfire lit the compound. Into the light came a very large and muscular young man with curly brownish-red hair and a handsome, open face. This young man carried, slung over his shoulder, a very thin and scrawny young man, who still clung gamely to a sword he had clutched in one hand and a shield, which he held in the other and which knocked the big man in the back of the legs whenever he took a step. The two were the last to make it down the hill.

Upon reaching the other recruits, who stood at sagging attention, the big man deposited the smaller man gently on the ground. The smaller man staggered, almost fell, but—digging the end of the shield into the ground—he used his shield to prop himself up and managed a triumphant, if exhausted, smile. The big man, who had carried his own shield and sword as well as his comrade, took his place in line. He did not look particularly worn out or winded. He just looked hungry.

"Who are those two?" the baron asked the sergeant.

"Two of the new recruits, sir," said sergeant. "Just back from a run up old Heave-Your-Guts. I saw the whole thing. The boy there collapsed about halfway up the hill. He wouldn't quit, though. Got to his feet and tried again. Made it a few steps and down he went. Damned if he didn't stand up and make another go at it. It was then that the big guy grabbed hold of him, slung him over his shoulder, and hauled him up the hill. Hauled him back down, too."

The baron peered closely at the pair. "There's something odd about that boy. Does he look like a kender to you?"

"The good Kiri-Jolith protect us! I hope not, sir!" the sergeant said fervently.

"No, he looks more human," said the baron on reflection. "He'll never make a soldier. He's too little."

"Yes, sir. Shall I muster him out, sir?"

"I suppose you better. Still," the baron added, "I like his pluck. And that big man. I like his loyalty. Let the skinny fellow stay. We'll see how he does in training. He may surprise us all."

"He may, at that, sir," said the sergeant, but he did not look convinced. The baron's comment about kender had shaken the officer badly. He made a mental note to count the metal plates and the wooden spoons, and if there was one missing, by the gods, the skinny fellow was gone, pluck or no pluck.

The recruits were sent to their dinners. They staggered into the mess hall, where several fell asleep over the meal, too tired to eat. Not liking to see food go to waste, Caramon took it upon himself to eat their dinners for them. But even Caramon had to admit that the stone floor felt as good to him as the softest feather bed when he was finally permitted to lie down to sleep.

He had closed his eyes for only a moment, or so it seemed, when he woke to a trumpet blast that brought him sitting bolt upright on the straw-covered floor, his heart thudding. His fuddled brain had no idea where he was or what was happening or why it should be happening to him at this ungodly hour. The barracks was pitch dark. Outside the windows—slits cut into the stone walls—he could still see the stars, though there might have been the faintest hint of dawn in the paling night sky.

"Huh? What? What?" Caramon mumbled and lay back down.

Flaring torches lit the barracks room. The torches glowed ruddily on the faces of those carrying them, faces that were grinning and jovial.

"Reveille! Up and at 'em, you lazy rotters!"

"No! It's still night!" Caramon groaned and piled straw over his head.

A booted toe slammed into Caramon's midriff. He woke wide awake this time, woke with a grunt and whoof.

"On your feet, you sons of gully dwarves!" the sergeant roared in his ear. "You're going to start earning that five steel!"

Caramon sighed deeply. He no longer considered the amount he was being paid generous.

*   *   *   *   *

The stars had disappeared by the time the recruits had dressed themselves in worn blue-and-gray tabards, gulped a hasty and highly inadequate breakfast, and marched to the training grounds—a large field located about a mile from the castle. Seemingly as sleepy as the men, the sun peeped above the horizon for a few moments, then, as if tired out by the effort, crawled under a blanket of heavy gray clouds and went back to sleep. A soft, soaking spring rain pattered down on the metal helmets of the sixty men, who had been bullied and cajoled into forming three ranks of twenty men each.

The sergeant and his staff handed out equipment—a practice shield and wooden sword.

"What's this, sir?" Caramon asked, eyeing the wooden sword with disdain. Lowering his voice, he said in confidential tones, so that the other recruits wouldn't feel bad, "I know how to use a real sword, sir."

"You do, do you?" the soldier said, grinning. "We'll see."

"No talking in the ranks!" snapped out the sergeant.

Caramon sighed. Hefting the wooden sword, he was astonished to find that it weighed twice as much as a good steel blade. The shield, also weighted, was extremely heavy. Scrounger could barely lift the shield off the ground. A second soldier passed among the ranks, handing out battered arm bracers. Caramon's arm bracer would not fit over his large forearm. Scrounger's slid off and fell into the mud.

Once every man was more or less accoutered, the sergeant saluted an older man who was standing on the sidelines.

"They're all yours, Master Quesnelle, sir," said the sergeant in the same dour and hopeless tones he might have used to announce that plague rats had sneaked into the castle.

Master Quesnelle grunted. Walking slowly and deliberately through the rain, the master-at-arms took his place in front of the troops.

He was sixty years old. His beard and hair, flowing beneath his helm, were iron-gray. His face was scarred from sword and knife wounds, deeply tanned from years of campaigning. He, too, was missing an eye—a patch covered the empty socket. The other eye was deep-set and glittered beneath the shadow of his helm. The eye seemed to shine more brightly than a normal eye, as if it sparked for two. The master held in his hand the same wooden sword and the same practice shield as the men. He had a voice that could carry over the din of battle, could probably be heard over a kender reunion at a mid-summer's fair.

Master Quesnelle studied the recruits, and his face grew grim.

"I'm told that some of you think you know how to use a sword." His single eye roved among them, and those it touched found it convenient to stare at their boots. Master Quesnelle sneered. "Yeah. You're all real tough bastards—every one of you. You remember one thing, and one thing only. You know *nothing!* You know *nothing,* and you know *nothing* until I tell you that you know something."

No one moved, no one spoke. The ranks, which had started relatively straight, now straggled all over the field. The men stood glumly, the heavy wooden swords in their sword hands, shields in the other, the rain dripping off the nose guards of their helms.

"I was introduced as Master Quesnelle. I am Master Quesnelle only to my friends and my comrades. You slugs will call me by my first name, which is Sir! Got that?"

Half the men in line, feeling the stinging eye upon them, said "Yes, sir" in despondent tones. The rest, not knowing that they were meant to answer, hastily threw in "Yes, sir" at the last moment, while one unfortunate made the mistake of saying, "Yes, Master Quesnelle."

Master Quesnelle was on him like a cat on a stinkbug. "You! What did you say?"

The poor fellow realized his error. "Yes, s-s-sir," he stammered.

Master Quesnelle nodded. "That's better. Just to impress that on your feeble mind, I want you to run around this field ten times, repeating to yourself, 'Sir, sir, sir.' Move!"

The recruit stared, his mouth opened. The sergeant loomed up in front of him, glaring. The recruit dropped his sword and shield to the ground and prepared to run.

The sergeant halted him, handed him his heavy sword and his very heavy shield. The recruit staggered off, began running around the perimeter of the training ground, yelling, "Sir, sir, sir" at intervals.

The master lowered his sword, the wooden blade dug into the ground.

"Did I make a mistake?" he asked, and he sounded almost plaintive. "I was under the impression you men were here because you wanted to be soldiers. Was I wrong?"

Master Quesnelle's eye ranged over the recruits, who shrank down behind their shields or tried to hide behind the men standing in front of them. The master frowned.

"When I ask a question, I want a battle roar back from you. Is that understood?"

Half the men caught on, responded with a growl. "Yes, sir."

"Is that understood?" the master bellowed.

This time the response was loud, unified, and direct. A great shout burst from the group. "Yes, sir!"

Master Quesnelle nodded briefly. "Well, it looks like we have some spirit here after all." He raised his wooden sword. "Do you know what to do with this?" he asked.

Several looked blank. A few, Caramon among them, remembered the drill and shouted back, "Yes, sir!"

Master Quesnelle appeared exasperated. "Do you know what to do with this?" he yelled, shaking his sword in the air.

The roar was near-deafening.

"No, you don't," he said calmly. "But you will by the time we're finished. Before you learn to use the weapon, you need to learn to use your body. Take your sword in your right hand. Place your right foot behind your left foot and put your weight on it. Bring your shield up like this." He lifted his shield in a defensive posture, held it to protect the vulnerable side of his body. "When I yell 'thrust,' you give me that roar, and you step forward and give the enemy in front of you a good running-through. You freeze in that position. When I yell 'recover,' you return to the ranks. Thrust!"

The master threw in the command on the heels of the word before it, tripping up all but the most attentive. Half the ranks thrust, and the others wavered, uncertain what to do. Scrounger was quick off the mark, and so was Caramon, whose blood was stirring and who was starting to enjoy himself. He stood in the second row on the end. His tabard hung on him like a dirty dishcloth, soaked through and chafing his arms. He gleefully thrust and yelled, and, after a moment, the rest of the ranks joined in.

"Freeze!" Master Quesnelle yelled. "Nobody move."

The recruits were poised at an awkward angle, holding their swords horizontal to the ground as if they had just made an attack. The master waited, looking them over complacently. Soon arm muscles began to burn, then to quiver trying to hold the weight of the heavy sword. Still no one moved. Caramon was starting to feel a bit of discomfort. He glanced at Scrounger, saw his friend's arm shaking, the sword wobbling. Sweat mingled with the rain. Scrounger clamped his teeth over his lower lip with the effort to hold the sword, whose tip was weaving and bobbing. Slowly the blade started to drop toward the ground. Scrounger watched in agony, helpless, his strength gone.

"Recover!" Master Quesnelle yelled.

Every man shouted in relief, the best battle yell any of them had made thus far.

"Thrust!"

Mercifully, the wait time before the recover was less.

"Recover!"

"Thrust!"

"Recover!"

Scrounger was gasping, but he held on to the sword grimly. Caramon was beginning to feel a bit worn. The man who had been running around yelling "sir" took his place back in line and began the exercise. After an hour, Quesnelle permitted the men to stand at the recover for a few moments, giving them time to catch their breath and ease their aching muscles.

"Now, do any of you slugs know why we fight in ranks?" the master asked.

Feeling that here was his chance to offer needed assistance to the master-at-arms, Caramon was the first to raise his sword in the air.

"So that the enemy can't break through and attack us from the side and rear, sir," Caramon replied, proud of his knowledge.

Master Quesnelle nodded, looked surprised. "Very good. Majere, isn't it?"

Caramon's chest swelled. "Yes, sir!"

Quesnelle extended his shield arm to one side, the arm holding his sword to the other. Keeping both arms fully extended—shield in one hand, sword in the other—he charged toward the front rank, who eyed him with trepidation, not knowing what to do, expecting him to halt when he reached them.

The master continued charging straight into the men. His shield flattened one recruit, who had not moved out of the way fast enough, the master's sword struck another full in the face. The master broke through the first rank and bore down on the second, who began ducking and dodging and trying to avoid being hit.

Master Quesnelle battered his way straight toward Caramon.

"You're in for it now," cried Scrounger, dropping down behind the huge shield.

"What'd I do?" Caramon demanded in dismay.

The master stood in front of Caramon, nose-to-nose, or rather, nose-to-breastbone. The master lowered his arms and glared up at Caramon, who had never been so frightened by anything in his life, not even a disembodied hand he had encountered at the Tower of High Sorcery at Wayreth.

"Tell me, Majere," the master shouted, "if these men are standing in ranks, how in the name of Kiri-Jolith did I just charge through them to get to you?"

"You're very good, sir?" was Caramon's weak reply.

Master Quesnelle held out his arms and turned. His shield whacked Caramon hard in the chest, knocked him backward. Quesnelle snorted and charged to the front, bashing and battering and scattering recruits as he went.

He turned to face the now disorganized company.

"I have just shown you why professional soldiers keep very tight ranks. *Tighten ranks! Move! Move! Move!*"

The men shuffled closer together until they stood shoulder to shoulder, the distance between shields only six inches at the maximum.

Master Quesnelle looked them over, grunted in satisfaction. "Thrust!" he shouted, and the exercise began again. "Recover! Thrust! Recover!"

The recruits kept this up for a good half-hour, then the master called a halt. The men stood at recover, bodies rigid. The rain had ceased, but there was no sign of the sun, which was apparently in no mood to rise any time soon.

Quesnelle extended his arms, sword and shield again, and hurled himself on the front rank. This time, the recruits were ready for him. The master's chest hit the center man's shield. He tried to go through, but the center man, exerting all his force, held the master-at-arms at a standstill. Quesnelle backed up a pace and tried to dodge between shields, but the men locked their shields in place.

The master retreated. Seemingly satisfied, he tossed his sword and shield onto the ground. The recruits relaxed, thinking the practice was at an end. Suddenly, without warning, the master turned on his heel, lurched forward and launched himself bodily straight into the front rank.

The front rank was startled but knew what to do. They brought their shields up to meet the master. He hit the front and fell back to stand before them. Quesnelle's single eye glinted.

"I think we may have some soldiers here after all."

Picking up his weapons, he took his place at the head of the company.

"Thrust!"

The men lunged forward in unison.

"Recover!"

The men fell back. Though tired, they were pleased with themselves, proud of the master's praise. It occurred to Caramon at that moment—and not before—to wonder what had become of his twin.

14

For a bent penny, Raistlin would have walked away, left this army, left this town. He had spent his first night staring into the bleak darkness, toying with the temptation. The situation was intolerable. He had come here hoping to learn battle magic, and what did he find? A crude and bullying man who knew less about magic than Raistlin did, yet who was not the least impressed by Raistlin's credentials.

Raistlin had cleaned up the broken beaker and its sticky contents, which had a strong smell of maple syrup and which Raistlin more than half suspected of being intended for Horkin's supper. After that, Horkin took him to view their quarters.

Raistlin was more fortunate than his twin, in that he and Horkin spent the night in the castle, not in the barracks. Admittedly, they were quartered in a small dungeonlike room below ground level, but they were given cots, were not forced to sleep on the stone floor. The cot was not in the least comfortable, but Raistlin came to appreciate it as he heard the rats skittering and screeching in the night.

"The Mad Baron likes mages," Horkin had told his new subordinate. "We get better food than the soldiers, we're treated better, too. 'Course, we deserve it. Our work's harder and more dangerous. I'm the only mage left in the baron's company. He started out with six of us. Some of them real corkers, too. Tower mages, like yourself, Red. Ironic, ain't it? Old Horkin, the stupidest of them all, the only one to survive."

Though exhausted, Raistlin could not sleep. Horkin snored so loudly that Raistlin half-expected the castle's other inhabitants to come running to see if a quake were shaking the castle walls.

By midnight, he had resolved to leave the next day. He would find Caramon and together they would depart, head back . . . where? Back to Solace? No, out of the question. To go back to Solace would be to go back in defeat. But there were other towns, other castles, other armies. His sister had spoken often of a great army forming in the north. Raistlin played with that idea for a while, eventually abandoned it. To go north was to run into Kitiara, and he had no desire to see her. They might try Solamnia. The Knights were reportedly looking for warriors and would probably be glad to take Caramon. But the Solamnics did not take kindly to magi of any sort.

Raistlin tossed and turned on his cot, which was barely wide enough to accommodate his slender frame. Horkin overlapped his cot by about six inches all around. Lying there, listening to what sounded like rats chewing on the cot legs, Raistlin realized suddenly that he'd suffered only one severe coughing spasm all day. Generally, he could count on having five or more.

He pondered this. "Can this hard life actually be beneficial to me?" he wondered. "The damp, the cold, the foul water, the putrid swill they term food . . . I should be half-dead by now. Yet, I have rarely felt more alive. My breath comes easier, the pain in my lungs is diminished. I have not drunk my tea all day."

He reached down to touch the Staff of Magius, which he kept lying beside the bed, always close to hand. He felt the slight tingle in the wood, the warmth of the magic spread through his body. "Perhaps it is because for the first time in many months, I am not dwelling on myself," he admitted. "I have other things to think about than if I am going to be able to draw the next breath."

By the advent of dawn, Raistlin had decided to stay. At the very least, he might be able to learn some new spells from the little-used spellbooks he had seen standing on the shelves. He fell asleep to the sound of Horkin's rumbling snore.

That morning, Raistlin was ordered to perform yet more menial tasks—sweeping the laboratory, washing empty beakers in a tub of soapy water, carefully wiping the dust from the books on the shelves. He enjoyed the dusting, mainly because he had a chance to study the spellbooks, and he was impressed by some of what he found. His hopes had been revived. If Horkin was able to utilize these books, he might not be the amateur he appeared.

Raistlin's hopes were dashed almost the next moment, when Horkin appeared at his elbow.

"Quite a few spellbooks here," Horkin said carelessly. "I've read only one, couldn't make much sense of it."

"Why do you keep them, then, sir?" Raistlin asked in frozen tones.

Horkin shrugged and winked. "They'll make good weapons if we're ever besieged." Lifting one of the larger, thicker books, he thumped it disrespectfully. "Put one of these tomes in a catapult and launch it, and it'll do some damage, by Luni."

Raistlin stared, appalled.

Horkin chuckled, gave Raistlin a painful nudge in the ribs with an elbow. "I'm joking, Red! I'd never do anything like that. These books are too valuable. I could probably get—oh, six or seven steel for the lot. They're not mine, you know. Most were captured during the Alubrey expedition six years ago.

"Now, you take this fancy black one." Horkin removed a book from the shelf, stood looking at it fondly. "I took it from a Black Robe last campaign season. He was running fast—to the rear, mind you—but I guess he thought he needed to run a bit faster, 'cause he flung aside the book, which must have been weighing him down. I picked it up and brought it back."

"What spells does it contain?" Raistlin asked, his hands itching to snatch the book from his master's hands.

"Beats the heck out of me," Horkin said cheerfully. "I can't even read the runes on the cover. I never looked inside. Why waste my time with a bunch of gobbledy-gook? Must have some choice spells though. Maybe someday you can take a look at it."

Raistlin would have given up half the years of his life to be able to read that book. He could not make out the runes either, but with study he was certain he could come to understand them. Just as, with study, he could come to understand the spells inside the book, a book Horkin could never read. A book that was nothing more to him than the price of a mug of ale.

"Perhaps if you let me take it back to my quarters—" Raistlin began.

"Not now, Red." Horkin tossed the book carelessly back on the shelf. "No time to waste puzzling out Black Robe spells that you, being a Red Robe, probably couldn't use anyway. We're running low on bat guano. Scout around the castle walls and pick up all you can find."

Raistlin had seen the bats leaving the castle's towers last evening in pursuit of insects. He left in pursuit of the bats' droppings, the runes on the spellbook burning in his mind.

"You can never have too much bat guano," Horkin remarked on his way out with a wink.

Raistlin spent two hours picking up the poisonous bat guano and putting it into a bag. He was careful to wash his hands well, then reported back to the laboratory, where he found Horkin eating supper.

"You're just in time, Red," Horkin mumbled, crumbs from the maize bread dribbling from the corners of his mouth. He mourned the loss of the syrup he usually poured over the hard, dry, yellow mass. "Eat up." He gestured to a second plate. "You're going to need your strength."

"I am not hungry, sir," Raistlin said diffidently.

Horkin did not stop chewing. "That's an order, Red. I can't have you passing out in the middle of a battle 'cause your belly's empty."

Raistlin pecked at the maize bread, was surprised to find that it actually tasted good to him. He must be hungrier than he imagined. He ate two large hunks and ended by conceding that maple syrup poured over the bread would have made a treat. Their meal finished, he cleaned up the dishes, while Horkin puttered around in a corner of the laboratory.

"Well," Horkin said, when Raistlin had completed his task, "are you ready to begin your training?"

Raistlin smiled scornfully. He could not imagine that Horkin had anything to teach him. Raistlin guessed that the session would probably end with Horkin begging Raistlin to teach him. As to Horkin's story of the six deceased Tower mages who had gone before him, Raistlin didn't believe a word of it. It was simply not possible that an unschooled, itinerant magic-user could have survived where skilled, trained magi could not.

"Let me get my equipment," said Horkin.

Raistlin expected the magic-user to bring along spell components, perhaps a scroll or two. Instead, Horkin picked up two wooden dowels, two inches in diameter and three feet long. Grabbing a bundle of rags from the table, he stuffed the rags in a pocket of his brown robes.

"Follow me." He led Raistlin out into the rain, which had started again, after a brief letup. "Oh, and leave your staff here. You won't be needing it today. Don't worry," he added, seeing Raistlin hesitate. "It'll be safe enough."

Raistlin had not let the staff out of sight—and barely out of touch—since the day he'd received it from Par-Salian's hand. He started to protest, but then he thought how silly he would look, fussing over the staff like a mother afraid of leaving her newborn babe in the care of others. Raistlin leaned the staff against a wall on which hung some of the weapons, with the rather absurd notion (he blushed to think of it) that Magius's staff would feel at home in such martial company.

Pulling his cowl over his head, Raistlin slogged through the mud. A mile's walk brought them to the training grounds, where a company of soldiers were practicing at the far end of the field. The soldiers all wore the same blue-and-gray tabard, but Raistlin recognized

Caramon, who stood head and shoulders above the rest. The soldiers didn't appear to be doing anything useful that Raistlin could see. Just yelling and jabbing with their swords and yelling some more.

The rain soaked through his robes. Soon he was shivering with the cold and was beginning to regret his decision to stay.

Horkin shook off the water like a dog. "All right, Red, let's see what they taught you in the mighty Tower of Wayreth."

He slashed the air with the two dowel rods, holding one in each hand, whipping them through the rain. Raistlin could not imagine what Horkin intended to do with the rods, which were not part of any spell that Raistlin could bring to mind. He was beginning to think that Horkin was slightly mad.

The war-mage turned and pointed to the opposite end of the field, a part far away from where the soldiers were lunging and yelling.

"Now, Red, what's one of your best spells, aside from sleep?" Horkin rolled his eyes.

Raistlin ignored the comment. "I am proficient in the launching of incendiary projectiles, sir."

"Incendi-whats?" Horkin looked bemused. He patted Raistlin on the shoulder. "You can speak Common, Red. We're all friends here."

Raistlin gave a deep sigh. "Magical bolts, sir."

"Ah, good." Horkin nodded. "Launch one of your bolts at the fence post on the far end of the field there. Do you see it?"

Raistlin put his left hand into the pouch he wore on the side of his belt, brought forth the small patch of fur—the spell component he would need to cast the spell. Locating the distant fence post, he withdrew into himself, seeking the words that would form the incantation necessary to produce a fiery bolt made of magic.

The next moment, he was on the ground, doubled over on his hands and knees, gasping for breath. Horkin stood over him with a dowel, which had just whacked Raistlin in the stomach.

Shocked by the painful and unexpected blow, Raistlin stared in blank astonishment, gasping for air and trying to calm his pounding heart.

Horkin stood over him, waiting, not offering to help. Eventually, Raistlin regained his feet.

"Why did you do that?" he demanded, shaking with anger. "Why did you strike me?"

"Why did you strike me, *sir?*" Horkin said sternly.

Raistlin, too furious to repeat the words, glared grimly at Horkin.

The war-mage lifted the dowel rod, used it this time as a pointer.

"Now you see the danger, Red. Do you think the enemy's going to stand there and wait while you go into a trance and sing 'la-de-da' and wiggle your fingers in the air and rub some fur on your cheek? Hell, no! You planned on casting the most powerful, the most perfect magical bolt that ever was, didn't you? You were gonna split that post in half, weren't you, Red? In reality, you cast nothing. In reality, you would have been dead, 'cause the enemy wouldn't be using a dowel rod. He'd be yanking his sword out of your scrawny belly.

"Lesson Number Two, Red—don't take too long to cast a spell. Speed is the name of the game. Oh, and Lesson Number Three—don't try to cast a complicated spell when there's an adversary breathing down your neck."

"I did not know you were an adversary, sir," Raistlin said coldly.

"Lesson Number Four, Red," Horkin said with a gape-toothed grin. "Get to know your comrades well before you trust your life to them."

Raistlin's stomach was sore, breathing was painful. He wondered if Horkin had cracked a rib, considered it likely.

"Try for the post again, Red," Horkin ordered. "Or if you can't manage to hit the post, somewhere in the general vicinity will be fine. Don't take all day."

Grimly, Raistlin clutched the bit of fur and tried to gather the words hastily in his mind.

Horkin lifted the other dowel rod, jabbed at Raistlin. The latter continued with his spell-casting, but then he saw, to his astonishment, a flicker of flame burst out of the base of the rod. The flame sizzled along the rod toward Raistlin, who tried desperately to ignore it. The flame neared the end of the rod.

His spell was almost complete. He was about to cast it when bright, blinding light flared. A loud bang nearly deafened him.

He flung up his arm to shield his face from the blast, only to see, out of the corner of his eye, Horkin swinging the other dowel rod. He struck Raistlin on the back, sent him sprawling facefirst into the mud.

Slowly, painfully, Raistlin picked himself up. His knees were scraped and bruised, his hands scratched. He wiped mud from his face and looked at Horkin, who was rocking back on his heels, mightily pleased with himself.

"Lesson Five, Red," said Horkin. "Never turn your back on an enemy."

Raistlin wiped mud and blood from his hands. He inspected the scratches, removed a small sharp pebble that had lodged beneath the skin.

"I believed that you skipped Lesson One, sir," Raistlin said, barely keeping his anger in check.

"Did I? Perhaps I did. Think about it," said Horkin.

Raistlin didn't want to think about it. He wanted to escape this crazed fool. There was no doubt in Raistlin's mind that Horkin was mentally deranged. Raistlin wanted to go back to a warm fire and dry clothes. He was certain he would catch his death out here in the wet. He would go find Caramon. Find Caramon and tell Caramon what this fiend had done to him. He had never seen Horkin cast the spell that blinded him.

Raistlin forgot his pain, forgot his discomfort. The spell! What was that spell? Raistlin didn't recognize it. He had no idea how it was cast. He had not seen Horkin reach for any spell components. He had not heard Horkin utter a word, recite any incantations.

"How did you do that spell, sir?" Raistlin asked.

Horkin's grin widened. "Well, now, so maybe there is a bit of magic you can learn from the sorry old mage who never took his Test. Stick with me this campaign season, Red, and I'll teach you all sorts of tricks. I'm not the last surviving mage in this gods-forsaken regiment because I was the best." He winked. "Just the smartest."

Raistlin had taken enough abuse. He started to turn away, when he felt Horkin's heavy hand upon his shoulder. Raistlin whipped around, anger cracking.

"By the gods, if you hit me again—"

"Simmer down, Red. I want you to look at something."

Horkin pointed to the training field. The recruits had been given leave to take a break, the men gathering around a water barrel. How they could possibly want more water was beyond Raistlin. The rain was falling harder. His robes were so wet that water ran in a steady trickle down his bare back. The recruits seemed to be in excellent humor, however, laughing and talking despite the rain.

Caramon demonstrated his sword technique, lunging out and falling back with such energy that he very nearly skewered Scrounger, who held his shield over his head, using it as a canopy to protect him from the rain. Horkin's expression altered, his bantering tone changed.

"We're an infantry regiment, Red. We fight. We die. Someday those men over there are going to be depending on you in battle. If you fail, you not only fail yourself, you fail your comrades. And if you fail them, they'll die. I'm here to teach you how to fight. If you're not here to learn how to fight, then just what the hell are you here for?"

Raistlin stood in silence, the rain thudding onto his wet robes, drumming on his head. Water dripped from his hair, hair that was prematurely white, a result of the terrors of the Test he'd undergone. Water ran down his hands, slender hands with long, nimble fingers, hands that shone with the sheen of gold, another mark of the Test. Yes, he had passed, but just barely. Though he could not remember all that had happened, he knew in his heart that he had come close to failing. He looked through the rain's gray curtain at Caramon, at Scrounger and the others whose names he did not know yet. His comrades.

Raistlin felt humbled. He regarded Horkin with new respect, realizing he had learned more from this man—this uneducated, low-level magic-user, whose kind is generally seen at fairs, pulling coins from their noses—than he had learned in all his years of schooling.

"I offer my apologies, sir," Raistlin said quietly. He lifted his head, blinked the rainwater from his eyes. "I believe that you have a great deal to teach me."

Horkin smiled, a warm smile. His hand exerted friendly pressure on Raistlin's shoulder, and Raistlin did not flinch away from the touch.

"We might make a soldier of you yet, Red. That was Lesson Number One. You ready to continue?"

Raistlin's gaze shifted to the dowel rods. He straightened his thin shoulders. "Yes, sir."

Horkin saw the look. Laughing, he tossed the dowel rods to the ground. "I don't think we'll be needing these anymore." He regarded Raistlin thoughtfully, then suddenly reached out and plucked the bit of fur, which Raistlin was still holding, from his hand.

"Now cast the spell."

"But I can't, sir," Raistlin protested. "I don't have another piece of fur, and that is the prescribed spell component."

Horkin shook his head. "Tsk, tsk. You're standing in the middle of a battle, being pushed and shoved from all directions, arrows whizzing over your head, men yelling and screaming. Someone jostles you, and down goes that bit of fur into the muck and blood, trampled beneath stomping feet. And you can't cast the spell without it." He shook his head again, sighed. "I guess you're dead."

Raistlin pondered. "I could try to find another bit of fur. Some soldier's fur cloak, perhaps."

Horkin pursed his lips. "The time is midsummer, you fight beneath the blazing sun. It's hot enough to roast a kender with your shield as a skillet. I don't think many soldiers are going to be wearing their fur cloaks into battle, Red."

"Then what do I do, sir?" Raistlin demanded, exasperated.

"You cast the spell without the fur," said Horkin.

"But it can't be done. . . ."

"It can, Red. I know because I've done it myself. I've always speculated," Horkin continued, musing, "that the old magi put that requirement in there as a bit of a wheeze. Or perhaps to give the fur trade in Palanthas a boost."

Raistlin was skeptical. "I've never seen the spell done without the component, sir."

"Well, now," said Horkin, "you're about to."

He lifted his right hand, muttered several words of magic, all the while twitching the fingers of his left hand in a complex pattern. Within seconds, a bolt of magic flame crackled from his fingers, flared across the field, and struck the fence post, setting it ablaze.

Raistlin gasped, amazed. "I did not think it possible! How did you manage to cast it without the fur?"

"I play a little trick on myself. That scene I described to you really happened to me once. An enemy arrow took the fur from my hand just as I was about to cast my spell." Horkin held out his hand, exhibited a long, jagged white scar, which ran across his palm. "I was scared and I was desperate and I was mad. 'It's just a stupid piece of fur,' I said to myself. 'I don't need it. By the gods, I can cast this spell without it!'" He shrugged. "And I did. Nothing has ever smelled quite so fine to me as burnt hobgoblin did that day. Now, you try it."

Raistlin peered across the field, and tried to mentally trick himself into believing that the fur was in his hand. He spoke the words, made the symbol.

Nothing happened.

"I don't know how you do it, sir," said Raistlin, chagrined, "but the rules of magic state—"

"Rules!" Horkin snorted. "Does the magic control you, Red? Or do you control the magic?"

Raistlin blinked, startled.

"Maybe I've misjudged you, Red," Horkin continued, a shrewd glint in his eyes, "but it's my guess that you've broken one or two rules before in your life." He tapped Raistlin's hand, tapped the golden skin that covered it. "If you never break rules, you're never punished. And it looks to me as if you've taken some punishment in your life."

Horkin nodded to himself, said softly, "Try it."

I control the magic, said Raistlin inwardly. *I* control the magic.

He raised his hand. Magic flared from his fingers, shot across the field. A second fence post burst into flame.

"That was fast!" Raistlin said, exhilarated.

Horkin nodded approvingly. "I've never seen it faster."

The recruits ended their practice for the day. They quick-marched down the road, chanting a cadence to keep in step.

"They're headed back for dinner," said Horkin. "We better go, too, otherwise there won't be any food left. You hungry, Red?"

To his vast astonishment, Raistlin—customarily a picky eater—was so hungry that even the thought of the tasteless stew served up by the camp cook was tantalizing. The two walked back across the muddy field, heading for the barracks.

"Begging your pardon, sir, but you didn't tell me the spell you used to distract me."

"You're right, Red," Horkin agreed. "I didn't."

Raistlin waited, but the mage just grinned to himself and said nothing.

"It must be a very complex spell," Raistlin observed. "The flame crawled along the wood rod, exploded when it reached the end. I've never heard of a spell like it. Is it one of your own magicks, sir?"

"You could say that, Red," said Horkin solemnly. He glanced sidelong at Raistlin. "I'm not sure you're ready for it."

Laughter, joyous laughter—laughter at himself of all things!—bubbled in Raistlin's throat. He forced himself to swallow the laugh, not wanting to disturb the mood, not just yet. He couldn't believe it, couldn't understand it. He had been beaten, mauled, mistreated, duped. He was covered with mud, soaked to the skin, and he'd never felt so good in his life.

"I believe that I am ready, sir," he said respectfully, and he meant it.

"Flash powder." Horkin cracked the two dowel rods together liked drumsticks, keeping his own cadence. "It wasn't a spell at all. You didn't know that, though, did you, Red? Fooled you completely, didn't I?"

"Yes, sir, you did," said Raistlin.

15

he rain fell in Sanction, fell on the hot lava flowing sluggishly and incessantly from the Lords of Doom, splashed with a hissing sound on the molten rock, and turned to steam. The steam coiled into the air, roiled around the ground; a thick fog hid the bridge guards from each other's sight, though they stood no more than ten paces from one another.

No training exercises this day. The men could not have seen their commanders, could not have seen each other. Ariakas had put them to work filling in the old latrines, digging new ones—a task where the less seen the better. The men would grumble, but it was a soldier's lot in life to grumble.

Ariakas sat in his command tent, writing out dispatches by the light burning from a wick set in a dish of tallow. Water leaked through the tent roof, dripped monotonously into an upended helm he'd placed under the drip to keep it from spreading over the tent floor. He wondered why he bothered. Due to the fog, his tent was almost as wet inside as out. The fog crept inside, licked its gray tongue over his armor, over the tent posts, over his chair and the table, left them glistening in the lamplight.

Everything was wet, damp, and gray. He could not tell what time of day it was, time had been swallowed up by the fog. Outside, he could hear the crunch of booted feet passing, men coming and going, cursing the rain and the fog and each other.

Ariakas paid them no attention, continued to work. He could have left this dripping tent, returned to the warmth of his office in the Temple of Luerkhisis. He might now be seated at his desk with a cup of hot mulled wine. He put the thought from his mind. Rarely did soldiers fight battles in warm, cozy rooms. They fought in the rain and the mud and the fog. Ariakas was training himself as much as his men, toughening himself to endure the rigors of campaign life.

"My lord." One of his aides knocked on the tent post.

"Yes, what is it?" Ariakas did not look up from his writing.

"That woman is back, my lord."

"What woman?" Ariakas was irritated at the interruption. These orders had to be clear and precise and detailed. He could not afford any mistakes. Not on this mission.

"The warrior woman, my lord," said his aide. "She asks to see you."

"Kitiara!" Ariakas looked up, laid down his pen. His work was not forgotten, but it could wait.

Kitiara. She had been on his mind ever since she'd left on her journey well over a month ago. He was pleased she had returned alive, though not particularly surprised, despite the fact that four others he'd sent to accomplish the same mission had either died or deserted. Kitiara was different, out of the ordinary. There was a sense of destiny about her, or so it seemed to him. He was gratified to find that he had been right.

Of course, she'd failed in her mission. That was only to be expected. The task on which he'd sent her had been impossible to achieve. He'd agreed to it merely to humor his Dark Queen. Perhaps now Takhisis would listen to him. Ariakas looked forward to hearing Kit's excuses. He considered it impressive that she'd had the courage to come back.

"Send her in at once," said Ariakas.

"Yes, my lord. She has a red-robed human magic-user with her, my lord," the aide added.

"She has *what*?" Ariakas was baffled. What would Kitiara be doing in the company of a red-robed wizard?

And how dare she bring one into his camp? Who could it be? That half-brother of hers? After their first meeting, Ariakas had questioned Balif about Kitiara. The general knew that she had twin half-brothers, one of whom was a dolt and the other a young wizard, a Red Robe at that.

"He's a strange-looking cove, that one, my lord," said the aide, lowering his voice. "Red from head to toe. And something dangerous about him. The guards would have never permitted him to enter camp—in fact they wanted to slay him on the spot—but the woman protected him, insisted that she was acting on your orders."

Red . . . from head to toe . . .

"By our Queen!" Ariakas exclaimed, rising to his feet as the truth hit him a stunning blow. "Send them both to me at once!"

"*Both* of them, my lord."

"Both! Immediately!"

The aide departed.

Some time passed—the guards must have been holding the two down by the bridge. Then Kitiara entered the tent, ducking beneath the dripping flap. She smiled to see him, a smile that was wider on one side of her mouth than the other, a smile that showed a flash of white teeth on only one side. A crooked smile, as he had noticed the first time he'd seen her. A mocking smile, as if she were laughing at fate, daring it to do its damnedest. Her dark eyes met his. She informed him of her triumph in that one single glance.

"General Ariakas." She saluted him. "I have brought Lord Immolatus, as ordered."

"Well done, uth Matar," said Ariakas. "Or should I say, Regimental Commander uth Matar."

Kitiara grinned. "Thank you, sir."

"Where is he?"

"Outside, sir. He waits to be properly introduced."

She rolled her eyes, quirked an eyebrow. Ariakas took the hint.

Kit turned toward the entrance to the tent and bowed low. "General Ariakas, I have the honor to present His Eminence, Immolatus."

Ariakas gazed with some impatience at the tent flap. "His Eminence!" Ariakas snorted. "What's he waiting for?"

"Sir!" Kit whispered urgently, "I respectfully suggest that you should bow when he enters. He expects nothing less."

Ariakas frowned, crossed his arms across his massive chest. "I bow to no one except my Queen."

"Sir," Kit returned in a harsh whisper, "how badly do you want the services of this dragon?"

Ariakas didn't want the dragon's services at all. Personally he could have done quite well without them. Queen Takhisis had decided that Ariakas wanted the dragon. Ariakas, rumbling a growl, bent his body a fraction of a degree.

A human male dressed in long robes the color of flame entered the tent. Everything about him was red. His hair was fiery red, his skin had an orangish tint to it, his eyes were red as sparking cinders. His features were elongated, sharp, pointed—pointed chin, pointed nose. His teeth were also sharp and pointed and rather more prominent than was quite comfortable to look upon. He walked with slow and stately step. His red-eyed gaze, noting everything, was bored by everything he noted.

He gave Ariakas a disdainful glance. "Be seated," said Immolatus.

Ariakas was not normally accustomed to receiving orders in his own command tent and he very nearly choked on the rage that surged up from his belly. Kitiara's hand, cool and strong, closed over his wrist, exerted gentle pressure. Even in this critical moment, her touch aroused him. Water droplets glittered in her dark hair, her wet shirt clung tantalizingly to her skin, her leather armor glistened.

Later, Ariakas thought, and, reminded by Kitiara's touch of the other woman in his life—Her Dark Majesty—he sat down in his chair. He eased himself slowly into the seat, however, slowly and deliberately, clearly implying that he sat down of his own volition, not because he was obeying Immolatus.

"Will you be seated, my lord?" Ariakas asked.

The dragon remained standing, which allowed him to look down his extraordinarily long nose at the mortals beneath him. "You humans have so many lords, so many dukes and barons, princes and kings. What are you, with your short and dreary lives, compared to me? Nothing. Less than nothing. Worm. Spelt with an 'o.' I am eminently superior. You will therefore refer to me as Eminence."

Ariakas's fingers curled in on themselves. He was fondly imagining those same strong fingers curling around His Eminence's neck. "My Queen, give me patience," he muttered and managed a dark-visaged smile. "Certainly, Your Eminence." He was wondering how he would explain the dragon's presence to his men. Rumor's black wings were probably already flapping around the campfires.

"And now," said Immolatus, folding his hands, "you will tell me this plan of yours."

Kitiara rose to her feet. "I am certain that you will excuse me, my lord—"

Ariakas caught hold of her forearm. "No, Commander uth Matar. You will remain."

Kitiara smiled on him, the crooked smile that was like fire in his blood, a fire that burned painfully in his groin.

"I am sending you on this mission, as well, uth Matar," Ariakas continued, relinquishing her reluctantly. "Close the tent flap. Tell the guards to form a perimeter around this tent, let no one pass." He cast a stern glance at both Kit and the dragon. "What I say in this tent goes no farther, on peril of your lives."

Immolatus was amused. "My life? Forfeit for a human secret? I should like to see you try!"

"The secret is not mine," said Ariakas. "The secret is Her Majesty's. Queen Takhisis. It is to Her Majesty you will be forced to answer if you permit the secret to escape."

Immolatus did not find this quite so amusing. His lip curled in a sneer, but he said nothing more, and he actually deigned to take a seat in a folding camp chair. The dragon leaned his elbow on General Ariakas's table, knocking the neat pile of dispatches onto the floor, and drummed his long, pointed fingers on the table, expressive of his extreme boredom.

Kitiara carried out her orders. He could hear her dismissing the guards, ordering them to form a perimeter around the tent some thirty paces away.

"Check to make certain there is no one outside," Ariakas commanded on her return.

Kitiara exited the tent again, made a complete circuit—he could hear her booted footfalls. She returned, shaking the water from her hair. "No one, my lord. You may proceed. I will keep watch."

"You can hear me from the tent flap, uth Matar?" Ariakas asked. "I do not want to raise my voice."

"My hearing is excellent, my lord," Kit replied.

"Very well." Ariakas was silent a moment. He frowned down at his disordered dispatches, sorting his thoughts.

Immolatus, his curiosity piqued by these precautions—as Ariakas had intended—was looking slightly less bored.

"Well, get on with it," the dragon growled. "The sooner I am able to abandon this weak and puny form I am forced to inhabit, the better."

"There is a city located in the very southernmost part of the Khalkist Mountains. The city is called by the somewhat prophetic name of Hope's End. It is inhabited by humans, and—"

"You want me to destroy it," said Immolatus with a flash of his sharp teeth.

"No, Your Eminence," said Ariakas. "Her Majesty's orders are quite specific. Only a few people, a very few, have been granted the knowledge that dragons have returned to Krynn. The day will come when Her Dark Majesty will permit you to unleash your fury upon the world, but that day is distant. Our armies are not yet trained, not yet prepared. The mission on which you are being sent is far more important than the mere destruction of a city. Your mission has to do"—Ariakas lowered his voice—"with the eggs of the dragons of Paladine."

The sound of that cursed name, the name of the god who reigned in heaven in opposition to Queen Takhisis, the name of the god of those who had done Immolatus so much damage, caused the dragon's flesh to twitch. He hissed in anger. "I do not permit that name to spoken in my presence, human! Speak it again and I will see to it that your tongue rots in your head!"

"Forgive me, Your Eminence," said Ariakas, undaunted. "I had need to speak it once, so that you could understand the gravity of the mission. I have no need to speak it again. According to reports from Her Majesty's clerics, the eggs of these dragons, which I shall henceforth refer to as 'metallic,' lie beneath the city of Hope's End."

Immolatus's red eyes narrowed. "What is this trickery, human? I have reason to know you are lying. Don't ask me to tell you how I know!" He raised a long-fingered hand. "Such knowledge is not for worms."

Ariakas was forced to exert all his self-control to keep from throttling his guest. "Your Eminence refers, no doubt, to the raid conducted by your kind upon the Isle of the Dragons in the year 287. A raid that did procure many eggs of the metallics. Many, but not all. It seems the metallics are not the fools we thought. They actually hid away some of the rarer, more precious eggs—those of gold and silver dragons."

"I am to destroy these eggs, then," said Immolatus. "It will be a pleasure."

"A pleasure deferred, I am sorry to say, Your Eminence," said Ariakas coolly. "Her Majesty has need of the eggs whole and intact."

"Why? For what purpose?" Immolatus demanded.

Ariakas smiled. "I suggest that you ask Her Majesty. If her *wyrms* require such information, I presume she will tell them."

Immolatus rose in anger, seeming to fill the tent with his swelling fury. Heat radiated from his body, warming the tent to such an extent that the water droplets on Kit's armor sizzled. Kitiara did not hesitate. Drawing her sword, she stepped between Ariakas and the dragon.

Confident, self-possessed, she stood ready to defend her commander with her blade and with her body.

"His lordship meant no insult, Great Immolatus," said Kitiara, though it was quite plain that his lordship had.

"Indeed, I did not, Your Eminence," said Ariakas, taking his cue from Kit. Even in human form, the dragon could cast any number of potent magical spells. Spells that could set ablaze Ariakas, reduce his camp and the city of Sanction itself to smoldering ashes.

He could never win a war against this powerful, arrogant monster, but Ariakas was pleased with his small victory. It put him in a conciliatory mood. He could afford to humble himself. "I am soldier, not a diplomat, Your Eminence. I am accustomed to speaking bluntly. If I have offended, I did not intend it. You have my apology."

Somewhat appeased, Immolatus resumed his seat. The heat in the tent returned to a more comfortable level. Ariakas wiped the sweat from his face. Kitiara sheathed her sword and resumed her place at the tent flap as though she had done nothing remarkable or out of the ordinary.

Ariakas followed her movements, as graceful as those of a stalking cat. Never had he known a woman like her! The lamplight glittered on her armor, cast dark shadows behind her, shadows that seemed to embrace her as he longed to embrace her. He ached to seize her, crush her to him, free himself of this pleasurable pain.

"Shall we get back to business?" Immolatus said. He was well aware of Ariakas's desire, scornful of the weakness of human flesh. "What does Her Dark Majesty require me to do with these eggs?"

Ariakas tamped down his lust. Anticipation would make the culmination that much more exciting.

"Her Majesty requests that you travel to Hope's End in company of one of my officers." Ariakas glanced at Kitiara, whose eyes flashed with pride and pleasure. "I am thinking of sending uth Matar, if you have no objections, Eminence."

"She is tolerable, for a human," said the dragon with a curl of his lip.

"Good. Once there, it will be your task to ascertain if the reports of the dragon eggs are true. It seems that though the clerics have strong evidence of the eggs' existence, the clerics cannot find them. The god whose name I may not pronounce has kept the knowledge of the whereabouts of these eggs concealed even from Her Majesty. Her Majesty believes that only another dragon can discover their whereabouts."

"And so she needs me to come in and do that which she cannot do herself," said Immolatus. A coil of smoke curled from one nostril, hung motionless in the thick and fetid air. "And what do I do once the eggs have been located?"

"You will return, inform me of the location and of the numbers and types of eggs you have found."

"And so I am to be Her Majesty's egg peddler!" Immolatus returned angrily. "A task any farm wench could perform!" He grumbled a bit, then added in growl, "I suppose there will be some fun. For, of course, you will want me to destroy the city and its inhabitants."

"Not exactly," said Ariakas. "True, no one must know about our search. No one must know the real reason you are in the city of Hope's End. But no one must know that dragons have returned to Krynn. The city will be destroyed, but it will be destroyed by other means, means less likely to draw attention to ourselves and to you, Eminence. We are therefore creating a diversion.

"Hope's End is just one city in the kingdom of Blödehelm. The king of Blödehelm, King Wilhelm, is now under the control of dark clerics. Acting on their 'advice,' he has imposed a tax upon the city of Hope's End, a completely unfair and ruinous tax, a tax that has the population rising up in revolt against him. King Wilhelm has requested that my armies aid him in quelling the revolt. We will be providing troops as requested. I will be sending in two of my newly formed regiments along with a mercenary force that King Wilhelm has hired—"

"Outsiders," said the dragon. "*Not* under your control."

"I am aware of that, Your Eminence," Ariakus returned testily, "but I do not yet have troops enough to obtain the objective. This is a training mission, as it is. I need the men blooded, and this war provides the perfect opportunity."

"And what is the objective? If we are not to destroy the city and butcher its inhabitants—"

"Ask yourself, Eminence. What purpose does a dead human serve? Nothing. He rots away, making a great stink and spreading contagion. Live humans, on the other hand, are extremely useful. The men work in the iron mines. The older children work in the fields. The young women provide my troops amusement. The very young and the very old obligingly die off, so one doesn't have to worry about them. Our objective, therefore, will be to capture the city and enslave its citizens. Once Hope's End is empty, Her Majesty may do what she will with the dragon eggs."

"And what of the mercenaries? Will they enslave or be enslaved? I should think they would be valuable to you, if you are, as *you* say, short on manpower."

The dragon was goading him, hoping to force him to lose his temper. Ariakas replied with deliberate calm, "The leader of these mercenaries is a Solamnic by ancestry. He knows King Wilhelm to be a man of honor and has been convinced that the cause for which he and his men fight is a good one. If this mercenary leader were to learn the truth, that he has been duped, he would be a threat to us. Yet, I need him. He is one of the best. He hires only the best soldiers—so my reports indicate. You see my predicament, Your Eminence."

"I do." Immolatus smiled, showing a vast number of sharp teeth, rather more teeth than was normal for a human.

"Once the city falls, these mercenaries are expendable." Ariakas waved a gracious hand. "I give them to you, Your Eminence. You may do with them what you wish . . . provided"—the hand became a warding hand—"that you do not reveal your true nature, your true form."

"You have taken most of the fun out of it," Immolatus complained petulantly. "Still, there is the challenge, the creative genius—"

"Precisely, Your Eminence."

"Very well." The dragon leaned back in his chair, crossed one leg over the other. "Now we can discuss my payment. I gather that this mission is of considerable importance. It must be worth a great deal to Her Majesty."

"You will be well rewarded for your time and trouble, Your Eminence," said Ariakas.

"How well?" Immolatus's eyes narrowed.

Ariakas paused, uncertain.

"If I may, my lord?" Kitiara intervened, her voice dark and sweet as chocolate.

"Yes, uth Matar?"

"His Eminence suffered a terrible loss during the last war. He was robbed of his treasure, while he was away fighting for Her Majesty's cause against the Solamnic Knights."

"The Solamnic Knights?" Ariakas frowned. He could not recall a war with the Solamnic Knights, who had fallen in disfavor and disrepute at the time of the Cataclysm and who had never really recovered their former glory. "What Solamnic Knights?"

"Huma, my lord," Kitiara said with a straight face.

"Ah!" Ariakas forced his mind to think more nearly along the lines of the long-lived dragon. Huma was a recent foe to Immolatus. "*That* Solamnic Knight."

"Perhaps Her Majesty might see fit to compensate His Eminence for at least some his loss—"

"*All* of his loss," Immolatus corrected. "I know the amount, down to the last silver chalice." Reaching into the sleeve of his robes, he withdrew a scroll, tossed it on the desk. "I have here an accounting. I want payment in kind, none of your steel coins. Filthy things, steel coins. Impossible to form into a really comfortable bed. And I don't trust steel to hold its value. Nothing is more reliable than gold. Nothing quite so suited to peaceful sleep as gold. Silver and precious gems are, of course, acceptable. Sign here." He indicated a line at the bottom of the document.

Ariakas frowned down at it.

"The city of Hope's End will undoubtedly have a considerable amount of treasure in its vaults, my lord," Kitiara hinted. "As well as what you will take from the merchants and the inhabitants."

"True," said Ariakas.

He had counted on that money for his treasury. Raising an army—an army capable of conquering all of Ansalon—was an expensive proposition. The wealth that would be handed over to this fool of an arrogant, greedy dragon would have forged a lot of swords, fed a lot of soldiers.

Provided he had a lot of soldiers to feed, which at the moment, he did not.

His Queen had promised him that more troops were coming. Ariakas was one of only a handful of people who knew of the secret experiments going on in the bowels of the mountains known as the Lords of Doom. He knew what the black-robed archmagus Drakart, the dark cleric Wyrllish, and the ancient red dragon Harkiel the Bender were attempting to create, perverting the eggs of the good dragons into creatures that would one day live to slay their unwitting parents.

Ariakas—a sometime magic-user himself—had his doubts as to the practicality of such an ambitious experiment. But if new troops, new and powerful and invincible troops, were to come from these dragon eggs, they would be worth the price of handing over a city's treasure.

Ariakas scrawled his name on the line. Rolling up the scroll, he handed it back to Immolatus. "My army is on the march. You and uth Matar will leave in the morning."

"I am prepared to depart immediately, sir," said Kitiara.

Ariakas frowned. "I said you would leave *in the morning*." He placed strong emphasis upon the words.

Kitiara was respectful but firm. "His Eminence and I should travel under the cover of darkness, sir. The fewer who see us the better. His Eminence attracts a considerable amount of attention."

"I can imagine," Ariakas muttered. He eyed Kitiara. He wanted her so badly, the pain was unendurable.

"Your Eminence, would you be so kind as to wait a moment outside. I want a word in private with uth Matar."

"My time is valuable," said the dragon. "I agree with the female. We should set out immediately."

He rose majestically to his feet. Gathering his robes in one hand, he swept out of the tent, paused at the entrance to glance behind. He raised the scroll, pointed it at Ariakas. "Do not test my patience, worm." He departed, leaving behind a faint smell of sulfur.

Ariakas seized Kitiara around the waist, pressed her body against his, nuzzled her neck.

"Immolatus is waiting, sir," said Kitiara, allowing herself to be kissed but again not yielding.

"Let him wait!" Ariakas breathed, his passion overtaking him.

"You will not like me like this, sir," Kit said softly, seductively, even as she fended off her seducer. "I will bring you victories. I will bring you power. No one and nothing will be able to withstand us. I will be the thunder to your lightning, the smoke to your devouring fire. Together, side by side, we will rule the world."

She put her hand over his questing lips. "I will serve you as my general. I will honor you as my leader. I will lay down my life for you, if you require it. But I am master of my love. No man takes by force what I do not choose to give. But know this, my lord. When I surrender to you at last, our pleasure on that night will be well worth the wait."

Ariakas kept firm and painful hold on her for another instant. Slowly he released her. He found pleasure in bed, but he found far more pleasure in battle. He enjoyed all aspects of war: the strategy, the tactics, the buildup, the clash of arms, the exhilaration of overcoming a foe, the final triumph. But the sweet feeling of victory came only when he fought a foe as skilled as himself, defeated an opponent worthy of his steel. He took no real pleasure in butchering unarmed civilians. Likewise, he found no real pleasure in making love to slaves, women who yielded to him out of terror, who lay shivering in his arms, limp and lifeless as corpses. In love as in war, he wanted—he needed—an equal.

"Go!" he said to Kitiara gruffly, turning aside, turning his back on her. "Go now! Leave while I am still master of myself!"

She did not leave immediately, did not flaunt her victory. She lingered. Her hand caressed his arm. Her touch sent fire through his veins.

"The night I return in victory, my lord, I am yours." She kissed his bare shoulder, then left him, opening the tent flap and slipping out into the rain to join the dragon.

That night, to the astonishment of his servants, Lord Ariakas took no woman to his bed. Nor did he, for many nights to come.

16

The twins' training continued without letup, week after week. The food was monotonous, the training monotonous, the same practice day after day, until Caramon could have performed the maneuvers while sleepwalking with a bag over his head.

He knew this because they were up so early every morning, he felt as if he were sleepwalking, and one day Master Quesnelle ordered bags to be put over their heads and told them to go through the same drill—thrust, recover, thrust, recover. Except by this time, they'd added pivot left, pivot right, lockstep, sidestep, retreat in formation, lock shields, and a whole host of other commands.

Not only did they drill every day, they cleaned their barracks every day, hauling off the straw from the day before, mopping the stone floor, shaking out their blankets, and replacing the straw. They bathed every day in a cold, rushing stream—a novelty to some of the men, who took baths once a year on Yule whether they needed it or not. One symptom of the Mad Baron's madness was that he insisted that cleanliness of the body and the living environs reduced the possibility of disease and the spread of fleas and lice—the soldier's customary companions.

The men marched up and down Heave Gut hill every day, carrying their heavy packs and weapons. Every man could make it now without difficulty, with the exception of Scrounger. His body was too light, and though he did as Caramon advised and ate twice as much of the tasteless, monotonous food as any other man in the ranks,

Scrounger did not gain in either height or bulk. He refused to admit defeat. Every day he collapsed in a gasping heap on the trail, half-buried beneath his shield, but Scrounger was always proud to point out that he'd gone "quite a bit farther today than yesterday, Master Quesnelle, sir."

The master-at-arms was impressed with Scrounger's spirit. Quesnelle confided to the Mad Baron in the weekly commanders' and officers' meeting that he wished to the gods the lad's body was as big as his heart.

"The men like him, and they cover for him, especially the big guy, Majere. He carries Scrounger's pack when he thinks I'm not looking. He holds back when they fight one on one or pretends that the little fellow's struck a blow that would have served an ogre proud. I've turned a blind eye to it so far. But there's no way he will make a foot soldier, my lord," said the master, shaking his head. "His friends are doing him no favors. He'll end up getting himself and the rest of us killed."

The other officers agreed, nodding their heads. The weekly meetings were held in the baron's castle, in an upper-level room that provided a fine view of the parade ground below, where the troops could be seen working on their equipment, oiling the leather straps to keep them supple, making certain that the sharp eyes of the sergeants could not detect a speck of rust on sword or knife.

"Don't muster him out yet," said the baron. "We'll find something for him to do. We just have to figure out what it is. Speaking of weaklings, how is our new mage shaping up, Master Horkin?"

"Better than expected for a Tower mage, Baron," Horkin replied, comfortably settling his bulk in his chair. "He seems a sickly chap. I passed through the mess hall the other night and heard him coughing until I thought he would hack up a lung. When I spoke to him about his illness, suggested that he was too weak to be part of my army, he gave me a look that shriveled me to ashes and swept me into the dustbin."

"The other men don't like him, my lord, and that's a fact," said Master Quesnelle, his expression dark. "I don't much blame them. Those eyes of his give me the creeps. He has a way of looking at you as if he sees you lying dead at his feet and he's about to throw dirt into the grave. The men say"—the master lowered his voice—"that he's bartered his soul in the marketplace of the Abyss."

Horkin laughed. Folding his hands calmly over his rotund belly, he shook his head.

"You may laugh, Horkin," said the master-at-arms dourly, "but I'm warning you that I think it likely one day we'll find your young mage lying dead in the forest with his head on backward."

"Well, what do you say, Horkin?" The baron turned to the master-at-wizardry. "I admit that I agree with Quesnelle. I do not much like this mage of yours."

Horkin sat up straight. His keen blue eyes boldly confronted each of the officers, not sparing the baron.

"What do I say, sir?" Horkin repeated. "I say that I never knew the army was a midsummer's picnic, my lord."

The baron was perplexed. "Explain yourself, Horkin."

Horkin coolly obliged. "If you're holding a contest to name the Queen of the May, my lord, then I admit that my young mage will not be a candidate. But I don't think you want the Queen of the May joining us in battle, do you, my lord?"

"That's all very well, Master Horkin, but his sickness—"

"Is not of the body, my lord. It is not catching," said Master Horkin, "nor is it curable. No, not even if the clerics of old were to return and place their healing hands upon him and call on the power of the gods could they restore Raistlin Majere to health."

"Is the sickness magical in nature?" The baron frowned. He would have been more comfortable with an ordinary, run-of-the-mill plague.

"It is my belief, my lord, that the young man's sickness *is* the magic!" Horkin nodded sagely.

The commanders and officers were dubious, they shook their heads and grumbled. Horkin's forehead furrowed in thought, furrowed so deeply that it seemed to draw his whole scalp into the process. He looked to the master-at-arms.

"Quesnelle, you wanted to be a soldier all your life?"

"Yes," said the master, wondering what this had to do with anything. "I guess you could say I've *been* a soldier all my life. My mother was a camp follower, my cradle was my father's shield."

"Just so." Horkin nodded again. "You wanted to be a soldier from childhood up. You, like our lord here, are a Solamnic by birth. Did you never think of becoming a Knight?"

"Naw!" Quesnelle appeared disgusted.

"Why not, if I may ask?" Horkin asked mildly.

Quesnelle considered. "Truth to tell, such a thing never crossed my mind. For one, I was not of noble birth—"

Horkin waved that aside. "There have been Knights in the past who were not of noble birth, who rose through the ranks. Legend says that the great Huma himself was one of these."

"What has this to do with the mage?" Quesnelle demanded irritably.

"You will see," said Horkin.

Quesnelle looked at the baron, who quirked a black eyebrow, as much as to say, "Humor him."

"Well"—Quesnelle's brow furrowed—"well, I guess that the main reason would be that when you're a Knight you have two commanders. One's a flesh-and-blood commander, and the other commander is a god. And you have to answer to both of them. If you're lucky, they both agree. If you're not . . ." Quesnelle shrugged. "Which do you obey? The torment of that question can rip a man's heart in two."

"True," murmured the baron, almost to himself. "Very true. I had never thought it about like that before."

"Me, I like my orders coming from only one place," said Quesnelle.

"I feel the same," said Horkin, "and that is why I am, in the ranks of magic, a humble infantryman. But our young mage, he's a Knight."

The baron's black eyebrows shot up into his thick curling black hair.

"Oh, I don't mean literally, my lord." Horkin chuckled. "No, no. The Solamnics would curl up and die first. I mean that he is a knight of magic. He hears two voices calling to him—the voice of man and the voice of the god. Which of them, in the end, will he choose to follow? I don't know. If, indeed, he chooses either of them," Horkin added, scratching his hairless chin. "I wouldn't be surprised to learn that he ends up turning his back on both, walking his own road."

"Yet, you've tipped a bottle with the goddess yourself from time to time, I believe," said the baron, with a smile.

"I am an acquaintance, my lord," Horkin replied gravely. "Raistlin Majere is her champion."

The baron was silent a moment, digesting this. "Let us return to our original discussion. Do you think it advisable for me to keep Raistlin Majere in my employ? Will he be of benefit to this company?"

"Yes and yes, my lord," said Horkin stoutly.

"Master-at-arms?" The baron looked to Quesnelle. "What do you say?"

"If Horkin vouches for the mage and will keep an eye on him, then I have no objection to his remaining," said Quesnelle. "I'm just as glad of it, in fact, for if the one twin left, we should lose the other. And Caramon Majere is shaping into a fine soldier. Far better than he gives himself credit for. I was thinking of transferring him to Flank Company."

He cast a glance at Master Senej, the commander of Flank Company, who nodded, interested.

"So be it," said the baron. He reached for the pitcher of cold ale that always ended the officers' meeting. "By the way, gentleman, we have our marching orders for our first battle."

"Where is that, my lord?" both officers asked eagerly. "And when?"

"We leave in two weeks' time." The baron poured the ale. "We are marching at the request of King Wilhelm of

Blödehelm, a fine king, a good king. A city under his rule has been taken over by hotheaded rebels, demanding that they be permitted to break away from Blödehelm and become an independent city-state. The rebels have, unfortunately, convinced most of the citizens to join them in their cause. King Wilhelm is gathering his own forces, he will be sending in two regiments to deal with the rebels. We will be there to assist. His hope is that once they see the force of our might arrayed against them, the rebels will realize that they cannot win and give up."

"A damn siege," said Quesnelle grumpily. "Nothing I hate worse than a boring old siege."

"There may be hot work for us yet, Master," said the Mad Baron soothingly. "According to my sources, the rebels are the type who would rather die fighting than be hung for traitors."

"Come now," said Quesnelle, brightening. "That's more like it! What do we know about these other two regiments?"

"Nothing." The baron shrugged. "Nothing at all. I guess we'll find out when we get there." He winked. "If they're not any good, we'll show them how to fight." He raised his ale mug. "Here's to Hope's End."

"What?" The commanders stared, dismayed.

"That's the name of the city, gentlemen," said the baron with a grin. "Hope's End for our enemies!"

The commanders drank the toast—and many more after that—with relish.

17

Good news, Red," said Horkin, entering the laboratory, more or less steady on his feet. He smelled very strongly of ale. "We have our marching orders. Two weeks we leave." He heaved a beery sigh. "That doesn't give us much time. Lots of work to do between now and then."

"Two weeks!" Raistlin repeated, feeling a little flutter in his stomach. He told himself the flutter was excitement and it was—partly. He looked up from the mortar and pestle he was wielding. His assigned duty this day was to grind up spices, which were to be used by the cook for their meals. Raistlin wondered why he bothered. Thus far the most exciting thing he'd found in his rabbit stew—which appeared to be cook's only known recipe—had been a cockroach. And it was dead. Probably of food poisoning.

"What is our objective, sir?" he asked, proudly using the military term he'd learned from the Magius book.

"Objective?" Horkin wiped the back of his hand across his mouth, mopping up the froth that still lingered on his lips. "Only one of us needs to know the objective, Red. And that's me. All you need to know is to go where you're told, do what you're told, when you're told to do it. Got that?"

"Yes, sir," Raistlin replied, swallowing his ire.

Horkin was perhaps hoping to set the young mage off so that he would have a chance to slap him down again. The knowledge helped Raistlin exert unusual self-control. He went back to pounding his spices, putting such effort into it that the cinnamon sticks smashed into bits, filling the air with their pungent scent.

"Pretending that's me in there, eh, Red?" Horkin asked, chuckling. "Want to see old Horkin smashed into a pulp, do you? Well, well. Put away the spices for today. Blasted cook! I don't know what he does with them anyway. Probably sells them. I know darn good and well he doesn't cook with them!"

Muttering, he waddled over to the shelf where the spellbooks stood, newly dusted, and reached up an unsteady hand to grasp the "fancy black one" as he termed it. "Speaking of selling things, I'm headed into town to the mageware shop to sell these books. Now that I have a Tower mage to read that black book for me, I want you to examine it and tell me how much you figure I should ask for it."

Raistlin clamped his teeth over his lips to keep his frustration from bursting out. The book was far more valuable for its spells than the piddling amount Horkin was likely to receive for it at the Langtree mageware shop. Shopkeepers generally paid little for spellbooks belonging to the followers of Nuitari, god of the Dark Moon, mainly because they were difficult to resell. Few black-robed wizards had the temerity to walk boldly into a shop and browse through the spellbooks belonging to their kind, spellbooks dealing with necromancy, curses, tortures, and other evils.

Like other wizards, Black Robes were well aware that truly powerful spellbooks were not likely to be found in mageware shops. Oh, you would hear tell now and then of a wizard who happened across a wondrous spellbook of old, lost to the ages, lying forgotten under a layer of dust on the shelf of some backwater shop in Flotsam. But such occurrences were rare. A wizard who wanted a powerful spellbook did not waste his time going from shop to shop, but traveled to the Tower of High Sorcery at Wayreth, where the selection was excellent and no questions were asked.

Horkin tossed the spellbook down upon the laboratory table and spent a moment admiring it—the spoils of battle—his bald head cocked to one side. Raistlin gazed at the book as well, but with a critical eye and a ravening curiosity to see what wonders it might contain. The thought occurred to him that perhaps he could buy it from Horkin himself, save up his pay until he was able to afford it.

There was small chance he would be able to read any of the spells yet, spells that were undoubtedly far too advanced for him. And most of the spells, especially the spells of evil, were spells he had no intention of casting. But he could always learn from the book. All spells—good, bad, and indifferent—were constructed using the same letters of the magical alphabet, which went together to form the same words. It was the way those words were spoken and arranged that affected the spellcasting.

He had another reason for wanting to study this spellbook. The book had been in possession of a Black Robe war wizard. Raistlin might have to someday defend against these very spells. Knowing how a spell was constructed was essential to knowing how to deconstruct it or how to protect oneself from its effects. All sound reasons. But, as Raistlin was forced to admit to himself, the true reason he was interested in this book was his passion for knowledge of his art. Any source—even an evil source—that would provide such knowledge was precious in his sight.

The book was quite new. The black leather of its binding was still shiny and showed few signs of wear. And the book's binding was fancy. Horkin's word was an apt description. The binding of most spellbooks was plain and unostentatious. Those who made them did not intend that they should attract the eye and hand of every curious kender. Far from it. Spellbooks were quiet, unassuming, glad to fade into the shadows, hoping to remain hidden, overlooked.

This book was different. The words, "Book of Arcane Lore and Power" were stamped in garish silver on the front in the Common language for anyone to read. The symbol of the Eye—a symbol sacred to magic-users—was embossed in each of the four corners, embellished with gold leaf. It was surrounded by the runes Raistlin had noted earlier, runes of magic. A red ribbon marker flowed from the closed tome like a rivulet of blood.

"If the inside's as pretty as the outside," said Horkin, reaching out his hand to open it, "perhaps I'll keep it just for the pictures."

"Wait, sir! What are you doing?" Raistlin demanded, putting out his own hand to stop Horkin's.

"I'm going to open the book, Red," said Horkin, impatiently shoving Raistlin's hand away.

"Sir," said Raistlin, speaking hurriedly and with the utmost respect, but also the utmost urgency, "I beg you to proceed cautiously. We are taught in the Tower," he added, in apologetic tones, "to test the magical emanations of any spellbook before attempting to open it."

Horkin snorted and shook his head, muttering beneath his breath about "highfalutin foolery," but seeing that Raistlin was adamant, the elder mage waved his approval. "Test away, Red. Mind you, just so you know, I picked the book up from the battlefield and carried it around for weeks, and it did no harm to me. No fiery jolts or anything like that."

"Yes, sir," said Raistlin. He smiled slyly. "Lesson Number Seven. It never hurts to err on the side of caution."

He stretched out his hand, held his hand over the book, about a finger's breadth from the surface, careful not to touch the binding. He held his hand there for a count of five indrawn and exhaled breaths, opening his mind, alert for the smallest sensation of magic. He had seen the magi in the Tower of High Sorcery at Wayreth practice this skill, but he had never had a chance to try it himself. Not only was he eager to see if this procedure worked, but there was something about this book he found disconcerting.

"How very odd," Raistlin murmured.

"What?" Horkin asked eagerly. "What? Do you feel anything?"

"No, sir," said Raistlin, frowning with puzzlement, "I don't. And that's what I find odd."

"You mean there's no magic at all in there?" Horkin scoffed. "That doesn't make any sense! Why would a Black Robe carry around a spellbook that had no spells in it!"

"Exactly, sir," Raistlin insisted. "That's why it's odd."

"C'mon, Red!" Horkin said, elbowing Raistlin out of the way. "Forget that Tower malarkey. The best way to find out what's inside the damn thing is to open it—"

"Sir, please!" Raistlin went so far as to close his gold-skinned, slender hand over Horkin's browned and pudgy wrist. Raistlin eyed the book warily, with increasing suspicion. "There is a great deal that I find disturbing about this book, Master Horkin."

"Such as?" Horkin was clearly dubious.

"Think about it, sir. Have you ever before known a war wizard to cast down his spellbook? His *spellbook*, sir—his only weapon! To let it fall into the hands of his enemy! Is that likely, sir? Would you do that yourself? It would be tantamount to . . . to a soldier throwing down his sword, leaving himself defenseless!"

Horkin appeared to consider this argument. He glanced askance at the book.

"And there is this, sir," Raistlin continued. "Have you ever seen a spellbook that so blatantly announces it is a spellbook! Have you ever seen a spellbook that advertises its mysteries to all and sundry."

Raistlin waited tensely. Horkin was staring at the book, intently now, scowling, his mind not so befuddled with ale that he could not follow his apprentice's reasoning. He removed his hand from book's binding.

"You're right about one thing, Red," said Horkin. "This blasted book *is* decked out fancier than a Palanthas whore."

"And for perhaps the same reason, sir," said Raistlin, trying hard to keep the proper note of humility in his tone. "Seduction. May I suggest that we practice a little experiment on the volume?"

Horkin was clearly disapproving. "More Tower magic?"

"No, sir," said Raistlin. "No magic at all. I will need a skein of silken thread, sir, if you have some handy."

Horkin shook his head. He seemed on the verge of opening the book just to prove that he was not going to be counseled by some upstart young pup. But, as he had told Raistlin, he had not survived in this outfit by being stupid. He was willing to concede that Raistlin had advanced some cogent arguments.

"Confound it!" Horkin grumbled. "Now you've got me curious. Carry on with your 'experiment,' Red. Though where you'll find silk thread around an army barracks is past my understanding!"

Raistlin already knew where to look for silk thread, however. Where there were embroidered insignia, there had to be silk embroidery thread.

He went to the castle, begged a skein from one of the housemaids, who gave it to him readily, asking him, with a simper and a giggle, if the rumors were true, was he really twin to the handsome young soldier she'd seen on parade and, if he was, would he would please tell his brother that she had a night off every second week.

"Got your thread? Now what?" Horkin asked on Raistlin's return. The elder mage was clearly beginning to enjoy himself—perhaps with the thought of the young mage's eventual discomfiture. "Maybe you're thinking of taking the book into a field and flying it, like one of those kender kites."

"No, sir," Raistlin said. "I am not going to 'fly' it. However, the suggestion of a field is an excellent idea. We should conduct this experiment in a secluded place. The training ground where we practice our magic would be ideal."

Horkin heaved an exaggerated sigh and shook his head. He started to reach for the book, halted. "I guess it'll be safe enough to carry it? Or should I fetch the fire tongs?"

"The fire tongs will not be necessary, sir," said Raistlin, ignoring the sarcasm. "You have carried the book before now without harm. However, I would suggest that you put the book into a conveyance of some sort. Perhaps this basket? Just to prevent its being opened accidentally."

Chuckling, Horkin lifted the book—handling it gingerly, Raistlin noted—and placed it gently into a straw basket. But Raistlin heard the elder mage mutter as they were leaving, "I hope no one sees us! Proper fools we must look, walking about with a book in a basket."

Due to the officers' meeting, the troops were not practicing this day. They had spent the morning cleaning their equipment. Now they were scrubbing down and whitewashing the outside walls of the barracks. Raistlin saw Caramon, but he pretended not to see Caramon's waving hand or hear his cheerful yell, "Hey, there, Raist! Where you going? On a picnic?"

"That your brother?" Horkin asked.

"Yes, sir," Raistlin answered, staring straight ahead.

Horkin swiveled his thick neck to take another glance. "Someone told me you two were twins."

"Yes, sir," Raistlin said evenly.

"Well, well," said Horkin, glancing at the young mage. "Well, well," he said again.

Arriving at the training ground, the mages discovered to their disappointment that the field was not deserted as they had anticipated. The Mad Baron was in the field practicing.

Mounted on his horse, a lance in his hand, the baron had leveled his lance and was riding straight at an odd-looking contraption consisting of a wooden crosspiece mounted on a base in such a way that it would swivel when hit. A battered shield had been nailed to one of the arms of the crosspiece. A large sandbag swung from the opposite end.

"What is this, sir?" Raistlin asked.

"The quintain," said Horkin, watching with pleasure. "The lance must strike the shield just so or— Ah, there, Red. That's what happens."

The baron missed his aim, struck the shield a glancing blow, and was now picking himself up off the ground.

"You see, Red, if you miss hitting the shield squarely, the off-center blow causes the sandbag to whip around and hit you squarely between the shoulder blades," said Horkin, when he could speak for laughter.

The baron uttered some of the most colorful and original expletives Raistlin had ever been favored to hear and stood rubbing his rump. His horse gave a low whinny that sounded very much like a snicker.

The baron fished a sodden pulpy mass from his pocket, a mass that had once been an apple, but which his fall had squashed flat. "You will suffer as I do, my friend," he said to the horse. "This would have been yours had we hit the mark."

The horse eyed the mashed fruit with distaste, but was not too proud to accept it.

"That machine will be the death of you, yet, my lord!" Horkin called out.

The Mad Baron turned, not at all disconcerted to find that he had an audience. He left his horse to munch on the maltreated apple and limped over to converse.

"By the gods, I smell like a cider press!" Baron Ivor looked back at the quintain, shook his head ruefully. "My father could hit dead center every time. Instead, it hits me dead center every time!" He laughed heartily at himself and his failure. "All that talk about knights put me in mind of him. I thought I would come out and set up the old machine, give it a tilt."

Raistlin would have died of shame had he been caught in such an undignified position by underlings. He was beginning to understand how the Mad Baron came by his appellation.

"But what are you up to, Horkin? What's in the basket? Something good, I hope! A little wine, maybe, some bread and cheese! Good!" The Baron rubbed his hands. "I'm starving." He peered into the basket, raised an eyebrow. "Doesn't look very appetizing, Horkin. Cook's given you worse than usual."

"Don't touch it, sir," Horkin was quick to warn. At the baron's querying glance, the warmage's face flushed. "Red here thinks that maybe there's more to this Black Robe's spellbook than meets the eye. He's"—Horkin jerked a thumb at Raistlin—"going to conduct a little experiment on it."

"Are you?" The baron was intrigued. "Mind if I watch? It's not any sort of wizardly secret stuff, is it?"

"No, sir," said Raistlin.

He had been plagued by self-doubt ever since they left the castle grounds, had been on the verge of admitting that he'd been mistaken. The book looked so very innocent riding along in the basket. He had no reason to suspect it was anything other than what it purported to be. Horkin had lugged it around and nothing untoward had happened to him. Raistlin was going to look a fool, not only in front of his commander—who already had very little use for him—but now in front of the baron, who might be mad but whose respect Raistlin was suddenly fiercely desirous of earning. He was about to humbly admit he'd been mistaken and to retreat with what dignity he had remaining, when his gaze fell once again on the book.

The spellbook with its gaudy cover and gilt-leaf edges and blood red ribbon . . . a Palanthas whore . . .

Raistlin seized hold of the basket. "Sir," he said to Horkin, "what I am about to do might be dangerous. I respectfully suggest that you and His Lordship remove yourselves to that stand of trees. . . ."

"An excellent idea, my lord," said Horkin, planting his feet firmly and crossing his arms over his chest. "I'll join you there myself in a moment."

The baron's black eyes sparked, his grin widened, his teeth gleamed stark white against his black beard. "Let me move my horse," he said and dashed away, stiffness and soreness forgotten in the prospect of action.

He led the horse at a running trot to the grove of trees, tied the animal to a branch and ran back, his face aglow with excitement. "Now what, Majere?"

Raistlin looked up, surprised and gratified that the baron had actually remembered his name. He hoped fervently that the baron would remember that name after all this was over, remember with something other than laughter.

Seeing that neither Horkin nor the baron was going to take his advice and retreat to a place of safety, Raistlin reached with extreme care into the basket, lifted the spellbook. For just an instant, he felt a tingle in the nerve endings of his fingers. The tingle dissipated rapidly, leaving him to doubt that he had felt it at all. He paused a moment, concentrating, but the tingle did not return, and he was forced to conclude, with an inward sigh, that he had felt it only because he wanted so desperately to feel it.

He laid the book down on the ground. Removing the skein of silk thread from a pocket, Raistlin formed a loop in the end of the thread. Moving with extreme caution, trying to refrain from lifting the book's cover, he prepared to pass the loop around the upper right-hand corner of the binding. The work was delicate. If what he suspected was right, the least false move might be his last.

He was alarmed to notice his fingers trembling, and he forced himself to calm down, to clear his mind of fear, to concentrate on the task at hand. Holding the loop of thread around his thumb and the first and second finger of his right hand, Raistlin slowly, slowly, slowly slipped the thread between the cover and the first page. He held his breath.

A rivulet of sweat trickled down the back of his neck. To his horror, he felt his chest close, felt a hacking cough rise up, ready to seize him by the throat. He choked it back, half-strangling, and, exerting all the control he possessed, held the thread steady. He slid the thread over the corner, secured it, and quickly drew back his hand.

The tightness eased, the need to cough passed. Looking up, he saw Horkin and the baron watching in tense anticipation.

"Now what, Majere?" the baron asked, his voice hushed.

Raistlin drew in a shaky breath, tried to speak, but found his voice was gone. He cleared his throat, rose trembling to his feet.

"We must go back to the trees," Raistlin said. Reaching down, he very gently lifted the skein of thread, began to carefully unroll it. "Once we have reached safety, I will open the book."

"Here, let me unroll the thread, Majere," the baron offered. "You look about done in. Don't worry, I'll be careful. By Kiri-Jolith," he said, backing up, allowing the thread to slide through his fingers, "I didn't know you wizards led such exciting lives. I thought it was all bat shit and rose petals."

The three reached the stand of trees, where the horse stood grazing and rolling its eyes as if it thought every one of them deserved to bear the baron's moniker. "We should be safe enough. What do you think might happen, Horkin?" The baron put his hand to his sword hilt. "Shall we be fighting a flock of demons from the Abyss?"

"I have no idea, my lord," Horkin replied, reaching into his pouch for a spell component. "This is Red's show."

Raistlin had no breath left to comment. Kneeling down, so that he was level with the book, he slowly and carefully tugged on the thread until it was taut in his hand. Raistlin looked around, motioned with his hand for the officers to crouch down. They did so, their mouths agape with wonder and excitement and expectation, their weapons ready in their hands.

Holding his breath, Raistlin said to himself, "Now or never" and pulled on the silk thread. The loop tightened around the corner of the book, held it fast. Working carefully, so as not to dislodge the thread, Raistlin tugged on the silk. The book's cover began to rise.

Nothing happened.

Raistlin continued to pull on the thread. The cover opened. He held the cover upright. The cover remained in that position, wavering a moment, and then fell. The silk thread slipped off the corner. The spellbook was open, its flyleaf, with large letters done in gold and red and blue inks, as gaudy as the front cover, winked derisively in the slanting sunlight.

Raistlin lowered his head so that the two men could not see his shame-filled face. He looked back at the book—sitting there so calmly, so benignly—with hatred.

Behind him, he heard Horkin give an embarrassed cough. The baron, heaving a sigh, started to stand up.

A slight breeze ruffled the pages of the book . . .

The force of the blast knocked Raistlin backward into Horkin and flattened the baron against a tree. The horse neighed in terror, jerked loose his tether, and galloped off for the safety of his stall. He was a battle-trained horse, but he was used to screams and shouts and blood and clashing swords. He could not be expected to put up with exploding books. Or if he was, he deserved something a damn sight better than mashed apple.

"Lunitari take me," said Horkin in awe. "Are you hurt, Red?"

"No, sir," said Raistlin, his head ringing from the blast. He picked himself up. "Just a little shaken."

Horkin staggered to his feet. His normally ruddy face was gray and moist as clay on the potter's wheel, his eyes wide and staring. "To think I carried that . . . that thing around with me . . . for days!"

He looked at the gigantic hole blown in the ground and sat down again quite suddenly.

Raistlin went to assist the baron, who was trying to extricate himself from the smashed branches of the young tree he had taken down in his fall.

"Are you all right, my lord?" Raistlin asked.

"Yes, yes, I'm fine. Damn!" The baron drew in a breath, heaved it out in a gusty sigh. He stared out across the field. Wisps of smoke from the blackened grass drifted past on the breeze. "What in the name of all that is holy and all that is not holy was that?"

"As I suspected, my lord, the book was trapped," Raistlin said, trying, but not succeeding, in keeping the triumphant tone out of his voice. "The Black Robe placed the deadly spell inside the book, then surrounded the lethal spell with another spell that effectively shielded the first. That's why neither Master Horkin nor myself"— Raistlin felt he could be generous in victory—"could sense the magic emanating from it. I guessed that it must take the opening of the book to activate the spell.

"What I didn't realize," he admitted, his pride deflating a bit, "was that lifting the cover itself would not activate the spell. Pages had to be turned as well, probably a certain number of pages. Of course, now that I think about it, that would be only logical."

Raistlin gazed out at the blackened grass, at the bits of ash, all that was left of the book, floating in the air. "A very elegant weapon," he said. "Simple, subtle. Ingenious."

"Humpf!" Horkin growled. Recovering from his shock, he walked out with the baron and Raistlin to inspect the damage. "What's so blamed ingenious about it?"

"The very fact that you carried the book away, sir. The Black Robe could have arranged for the spell to go off the moment you picked it up, but he didn't. He wanted you to take the book back to camp, take it among your own troops. Then, when you opened it . . ."

"By Luni, Red! If what you say is true"—Horkin passed a trembling hand over a brow now daubed in cold sweat—"we've all had a narrow escape!"

"It would have killed a lot of men," the baron agreed, peering into the deep hole. He clapped his arm affectionately around Horkin. "Not to mention my best mage."

"One of your best mages, my lord," said Horkin, giving Raistlin a nod and an expansive grin. "One of them."

"True," said the baron, and he reached out to shake Raistlin by the hand. "You've more than earned a place among us, Majere. Or perhaps"—he looked at Horkin and winked—"I should say 'Sir Majere.' "

The baron straightened, turned to see his horse disappearing down the road. "Poor old Jet. Books exploding under his nose. He'll be halfway to Sancrist by now. I best go see if I can find him and calm him down. A pleasant evening to you, gentleman."

"And to you, my lord," said Horkin and Raistlin, both bowing.

"Red, I've got to hand it to you, ," said Horkin, draping his arm companionably around Raistlin's shoulders. "You saved old Horkin's bacon. I'm grateful. I want you to know that."

"Thank you, sir," said Raistlin, adding modestly, "I have a name, you know, sir."

"Sure you do, Red," said Horkin, giving him a slap on the shoulder that nearly bowled him over. "Sure you do."

Whistling a merry tune, Horkin lumbered off after the baron.

18

ake up, little boys!" came a lilting, mocking falsetto voice. "Up, little boys, and greet the new day!" The voice altered to a gravelly shout, "I'm your mamma now, lads, and mamma says it's time to wake up!"

Well aware that a swift kick to his behind was the sergeant's gentle means of prodding his recruits to action, Caramon rolled out of his bedding, scattering straw left and right, and jumped to a standing position. Around him, men scrambled to obey. The barracks was still dark, but birds were up already—the fools—which meant that dawn was not far off.

Caramon was used to waking early. Many and many were the days of his youth when he'd rolled out of bed before even the birds were awake to trudge to the farm fields, timing his arrival just as dawn was breaking in order to lose none of the precious daylight. But Caramon never left his bedroll, never left his mound of straw, without deep regret.

Caramon loved sleep. He savored it. He craved it. Caramon had come to the conclusion long ago that a person spent more time sleeping than doing anything else in this life and therefore, Caramon decided, he should be good at it. He practiced at it all he could.

Not so his twin. Raistlin actually seemed to resent sleep. Sleep was some wicked thief, sneaking up on him before he was ready, stealing the hours of his life from him. Raistlin was always up early in the morning, even on holidays, a phenomenon Caramon couldn't understand. And many were the nights Caramon had found his twin slumped over his books, too tired to remain awake, yet refusing to deliver up his precious time to the stealthy robber, forcing sleep to wrestle him into submission.

Rubbing his eyes, trying to goad his mind, still relishing a pleasant dream, into wakefulness, Caramon thought sadly that for a man who enjoyed sleeping, he'd picked the wrong career. When he was a general himself someday, he'd sleep until noon, and anyone who would dare wake him would get a poke in the ribs . . . a poke in the ribs . . .

"Caramon!" Scrounger was poking him in the ribs.

"Huh?" Caramon blinked.

"You were sleeping standing up," Scrounger said, regarding his friend with admiration. "Like a horse. Sleeping standing up!"

"Was I?" Caramon asked with pride. "I didn't know a person could do that. I'll have to tell Raist."

"Helmets, shields, and weapons!" the sergeant bawled. "Outside in ten minutes."

Scrounger yawned a huge yawn.

It didn't seem possible a fellow that skinny could open his mouth that wide. "You're going to split your head in half if you do that too much," Caramon said worriedly.

"Majere," said the sergeant in a nasty tone, "are you going to favor us with your presence today? Or do you plan to spend the day filling in the latrines!"

Caramon dressed quickly, then donned his helmet, strapped on his sword belt, and hefted his shield.

The recruits dashed outside just as the first rays of light straggled past some low-lying clouds on the horizon. They lined up on the road in front of the barracks, forming three ranks. They'd done the same every morning since they had arrived, and by now they were good at it.

Master Quesnelle strode out to take his place in front of the assembled soldiers. Caramon waited expectantly for the order to march. The order did not come.

"Today, men, we are dividing you into companies," the master-at-arms announced. "Most of you will remain with me, but some of you have been chosen to join Company C, the skirmishers, under the leadership of Master Senej. When I call out your name, take two steps forward. Ander Cobbler. Rav Hammersmith. Darley Wildwood." The list continued. Caramon stood in semiwakefulness, letting the sun warm muscles stiff from sleeping on the stone floor. He wasn't expecting to be called. Company C was where they sent the very best men. Caramon started to drift off.

"Caramon Majere."

Caramon woke with a start. His feet took two practiced and precisè steps forward, acting in advance of his sleep-fuddled brain. He glanced sidelong at Scrounger, smiled, and waited for them to call his friend's name.

Master Quesnelle rolled up the list with a snap. "Those men whose names I have just called, fall out and report to Sergeant Nemiss over there." The master pointed to a lone soldier standing in the middle of the road.

The other recruits wheeled expertly and marched off. Caramon remained where he was. He looked unhappily back at Scrounger, whose name had not been called.

"Go on!" Scrounger urged him, not daring to speak aloud but mouthing the words. "What are you doing, you big idiot? Go!"

"Majere!" Master Quesnelle's voice grated. "Have you gone deaf? I gave you an order! Move that big ass of yours, Majere!"

"Yes, sir!" Caramon shouted. He wheeled, stepped out, and with his left hand grabbed hold of Scrounger by the collar of his shirt. Lifting the young man off his feet, Caramon brought Scrounger along with him.

"Caramon, what— Caramon, stop it! Caramon, lemme go!" Scrounger twisted and pulled, trying desperately to break Caramon's hold, but he could not free himself of the big man's firm grasp.

Master Quesnelle was just about to come down on Caramon with the cold force and fury of an avalanche, when he caught sight of the Mad Baron, standing in the background, watching with interest. The Mad Baron

made a small sign with his hand. Master Quesnelle, turning red in the face, snapped his mouth shut.

Caramon marched double-quick time. "You forgot to
call his name out, sir," he said in meek, apologetic tones
as he hastened past the irate master-at-arms.

"Yes, I guess I did," Quesnelle said, grumbling.

The rest of the company carried on with the normal
routine: morning run, breakfast, basic maneuver practice.
The twelve recruits whose names had been called stood
rigidly at attention in front of their new officer.

Sergeant Nemiss was a medium-sized woman with
the dusky black complexion of those who came from
Northern Ergoth. She had luminous brown eyes and a
sweet, pretty face, which, as the new recruits were about
to discover, had nothing whatsoever to do with her true
personality. Sergeant Nemiss was, in fact, a mean drunk
with a fiery temper, continually getting into brawls—one
reason she was a sergeant and would remain a sergeant
for the rest of her days.

Sergeant Nemiss stood and stared at the twelve—thirteen, counting Scrounger—for a good long time. Her gaze
fixed on poor Scrounger, who withered beneath it. The
sergeant's expression didn't alter, except perhaps to grow
rather sorrowful. "You," she said, pointing, "stand over
there."

Scrounger gave Caramon a look and a smile, which
said, "Well, we tried." He marched out to stand by himself at the side of the road.

Sergeant Nemiss shook her head and turned back to
face the rest.

"You men have been chosen to join my company. Master Senej commands the company. I am his second-in-
command. It is my job to train any new recruits in Master
Senej's company. Do I make myself clear?"

The twelve yelled out, "Yes, sir!" in unison. Scrounger
started to say, "Yes, sir," from force of habit but dried up
when the sergeant glared at him.

"Good. You men have been chosen not because you're
better than the rest but because you're not as bad as the

rest." Sergeant Nemiss scowled. "Don't get it into your fat heads that this means you're good. You're not good until I tell you you're good, and just standing here looking at you reprobates, I can tell right away that you're not even good enough to lick the boots of good soldiers."

The recruits stood sweating in the sun, not saying a word.

"Majere, fall out. The rest of you, go back to the barracks, gather up your things, and meet me here in five minutes. You're all moving to Master Senej's company barracks. Questions? Good, now move! Move! Move! Majere, over here."

The sergeant motioned Caramon to come stand beside Scrounger, who smiled hesitantly, ingratiatingly, and hopefully at the officer.

Sergeant Nemiss was not impressed. She eyed them both, particularly Scrounger, taking in his slender build, his quick, long-fingered hands, his unfortunately slightly pointed ears. Sergeant Nemiss's frown deepened.

"Just what the hell am I supposed to do with you— what's your name?"

"Scrounger, sir," said Scrounger in respectful tones.

"Scrounger? That's not a name!" The sergeant glowered.

"It's my name, sir," said Scrounger cheerfully.

"And that's what you can do with him, sir," said Caramon. "Scrounger here's an expert at scrounging."

"Stealing, you mean," said the sergeant. "I'll have no thieves in my outfit."

"No, sir," said Scrounger, shaking his head emphatically, keeping his eyes straight ahead as he'd been taught. "I don't steal."

The sergeant stared meaningfully at Scrounger's ears. Scrounger shifted his glance sideways, focused on the sergeant for an instant. "I don't 'borrow' things, either, sir."

"He's a scrounger, sir," said Caramon helpfully.

"You'll forgive me, Majere," said the sergeant, looking exasperated, "if I don't understand just what that term means or how the devil it's going to be of any use to me!"

"It's really pretty simple, sir," said Scrounger. "I find things for people that they want and they're willing to trade other things in return. It's a gift, sir," he added modestly.

"Is it?" The sergeant's lip curled. She paused, considering. "All right. I'll give you one chance. You bring me something I can use for the outfit—something of value, mind you—by this time tomorrow morning and I'll let you remain with this company. If you fail, you're out of here. Fair enough?"

"Yes, sir," said Scrounger, his face flushed with pleasure.

"Since this was your idea, Majere, you're detailed to go with him." The sergeant held up a warning finger. "No thievery involved. If I found out you've stolen anything, soldier, I'll string you up to that apple tree you see standing over there. We don't tolerate thieves in this army. The baron's worked hard to develop good relations with the townsfolk, and we intend to keep it that way. Majere, I'm holding you responsible. That means that if he steals, the same thing happens to you that will happen to him. If he so much as heists a peanut, you'll both swing for it."

"Yes, sir. I understand, sir," said Caramon, though he gulped a little when the sergeant wasn't looking.

"May we leave now on our assignment, sir?" asked Scrounger eagerly.

"Hell, no, you may not leave!" the sergeant snapped. "I have only two weeks to whip you clods into shape, and I'm going to need every second. The new recruits are going to be given leave tonight to go into town—"

"We are, sir?" Caramon interrupted, overjoyed.

"All but you two," said the sergeant coolly. "You two can carry out your assignment tonight."

"Yes, sir." Caramon sighed deeply. He'd been looking forward to going back to the Swelling Ham.

"Now go get your things, and report back here on the double!"

"I'm sorry you have to miss leave time, Caramon," said Scrounger, shaking straw out of his blanket.

"Bah! That's all right." Caramon shrugged off the thought of cold ale and warm, accommodating women. "Do you think you can pull this off?" he asked anxiously.

"It'll be tough," Scrounger admitted. "Usually when I do a trade, I know what I'm trading for." He gave the matter thoughtful, serious consideration. "But, yes, I think I can do it."

"I hope so," Caramon said to himself. He gave the apple tree a nervous glance.

Sergeant Nemiss led the men to a building located on the far side of the compound, halted them in front of the barracks.

An officer mounted on a coal-black stallion came from around the corner of the barracks. He was a tall man with dark hair and a jaw that looked as if it had been sawed off square, planed, and sanded.

He reined in his steed, looked over the men lined up in front of him. "My name is Master Senej. Sergeant Nemiss tells me you're not as bad as all the other recruits. What I want to know is this—are you good enough to join Company C?"

He roared out the name of the company, was answered by a deep-throated savage yell that came from inside the barracks. Soldiers dashed out, each man wearing a breastplate, helmet, tabard, carrying shield and sword. Caramon braced himself, thinking that the soldiers were about to attack. Instead, acting without any orders that Caramon had heard, the men of Company C came to a halt, forming into perfectly straight and orderly ranks. Their polished metal armor shone in the sunlight.

In less than one minute, the entire company of ninety men was in battle formation. All stood at the ready, shields up.

Senej turned back to the thirteen recruits. "As I said, I want to know if you're good enough to join my company. My company is the best company in the regiment, and I intend to keep it that way. If you're no good, you're going back to the training company. If you're good, you've got a home for as long as you live."

Caramon thought that he had never wanted anything so much in his life as to join this force of proud, confident soldiers. His chest swelled with pride to think he had been chosen to try for it, but his pride got lodged in his throat as he considered that he might not be good enough to make the cut.

"Fall out, men. Sergeant Nemiss will show you where you bunk."

The recruits had been assigned to wooden cots with at least twice the distance between sleeping areas as in their old quarters. Each man had a barracks box at the foot of his bunk in which to store personal items. Caramon thought he'd never seen such luxury.

After breakfast, Sergeant Nemiss ordered the thirteen new recruits off to the side.

"Now, you're doing well so far. A word of advice. Don't get friendly with the other lads just yet. They don't like new boys until you've proven yourselves. Don't take it personal. Once you've been through a campaign season with them, you'll be getting invitations to weddings for the rest of your life."

One of the men raised his hand.

"Yes, Manto, what is it?" the sergeant asked.

"I was wondering, sir, what does Master Senej's company do that makes it so special?"

"Oddly enough," said the sergeant, "that question isn't as stupid as it sounds. Our company is special because we're given all the special duties. We're the flank company. When the baron asks for skirmishers to advance out in front of the line, we're the ones. When there's an enemy to find, and he's playing slippery with us, we're the soldiers who go and find him. We fight in the line when we're ordered, but we do all the other dirty jobs that come up, too.

"Today, you're going to be issued a new weapon to go along with your sword. Now don't get all excited. It's just a spear. Nothing glamorous." The sergeant reached out, hefted a spear that had been leaning against a wall, and held it out in front of her. "Where you go the spear goes until your training's done."

Caramon held up his hand. "Uh, Sergeant. When's our training done?"

"You're done when I say you're done, Majere," said the sergeant. "You'll be done or washed out before we begin to march, and that's only a couple of weeks away. You've got lots to do and lots to learn in the meantime. Stick close to me and do as I tell you, and you'll come through just fine."

Nemiss took the thirteen out to the practice field, all carrying their new spears, all of the spears double-weight, just like their other practice equipment. Caramon hefted the spear with ease, but Scrounger could barely lift his. The butt end of Scrounger's spear dragged the ground, forming a long furrow behind him all the way to the training ground. Sergeant Nemiss just looked at him and rolled her eyes.

The rest of that day, they practiced with shield and spear. In the afternoon, they practiced throwing the spears. By day's end, Caramon's arm was so weak and trembly from the unaccustomed exertion that he doubted if he'd be able to lift a spoon to eat his dinner.

Scrounger had gamely tried to throw the spear, but after hurling himself right along with it a couple of times—landing flat on his face the first time and nearly spearing Caramon the second—he'd been excused from duty. Sergeant Nemiss employed him in fetching and carrying buckets of water for the men. It was plain to see that she didn't expect to have to deal with the young man in the future.

The thought of leave, of being able to spend a few hours in town, cheered the recruits considerably. Of their own accord, they ran back to the barracks, carrying their spears with them, singing a lively, bawdy marching song Sergeant Nemiss taught them.

The men gulped down their dinner and then left to scrub themselves raw, comb their hair, trim their beards, and put on their best clothes. Caramon started to follow their example—he was hoping to snatch a quick pint of ale before starting his scrounging—but he noted that Scrounger was lying down on his bunk, his hands beneath his head.

"Aren't we going into town with the rest of them?" Caramon asked.

"Nope." Scrounger shook his head.

"But . . . how are you going to scrounge for anything?"

"You'll see," Scrounger promised.

Caramon heaved a sigh that came from his toes. He put down the comb he'd been dragging painfully through his curly hair and, sitting disconsolately on his bunk, watched the rest of the men set off joyfully for town. Nearly all the soldiers who were off duty had been given leave this night. Only those standing guard or who had other assignments stayed behind. Caramon saw his brother leave in the company of Master Horkin. He overheard the two of them talking about visiting a mageware shop, then Horkin telling Raistlin that he knew of a tavern that served the finest ale in all of Ansalon.

Caramon had never felt so low-spirited in his life.

"We can at least get a couple of hours sleep," said Scrounger, once the barracks was silent. So very silent.

Which only goes to prove, Caramon thought, closing his eyes and snuggling into the straw mattress on the bunk, that things were never as bad as they seemed.

19

Caramon!"

Someone, it seemed, was always waking him.

"Huh?"

"It's time!"

Caramon sat up. Forgetting he was now sleeping on a bunk and not a bed of straw, he rolled over as usual. The next thing he knew, he was lying on the floor with no very clear notion of how he'd arrived there. Scrounger bent over him anxiously, shining a dark lantern full into his eyes.

"Are you hurt, Caramon?"

"Naw! And shut the cover on that damn thing!" Caramon growled, half-blinded.

"Sorry." Scrounger slid shut the cover, and the light vanished.

Caramon rubbed his bruised hip, his heart pounded. "'Sall right," he mumbled incomprehensibly. "What time's it?"

"Close to midnight. Hurry up! No, no armor. It makes too much noise. Besides, it's intimidating. Here, I'll shine the light."

Caramon dressed rapidly, eyeing his friend all the while.

"You've been somewhere. Where've you been?" Caramon asked.

"To town," said Scrounger. He was in high spirits. His eyes sparkled, and he was grinning from pointed ear to pointed ear. His glee had the unfortunate tendency to emphasize his kender heritage. Caramon, looking at his friend, thought of the apple tree, and quaked.

"We're in luck tonight, Caramon. Absolute, positive luck," Scrounger said. "But then, I've always been lucky. Kender generally are. Have you ever noticed that? Mother used to say it was because once upon a time the kender were the favorites of some old god named Whizbang or something like that. Of course, he's not around anymore. According to her, this god got mad at some uppity priest and threw a rock at his head and had to leave town in a hurry before the guards came after him. But the luck he gave the kender rubbed off, and so they still have it."

"Really?" Caramon was owl-eyed. "Is that so? I'll have to tell that to Raist. He collects stories about the old gods. I don't think he ever heard of one called Whizbang. He'll likely be interested."

"Here, let me help you with that boot. What was I saying? Oh, yes. Luck. There are two trading caravans in town! Think of that! One dwarven and one human. They're here to sell supplies to the baron. I've just been to pay a visit to each of them."

"So you have a plan?" Caramon felt relief wash over him.

"No, not exactly." Scrounger hedged. "Trading is like bread dough. You have to give the yeast a chance to work."

"What does that mean?" Caramon asked, suspicious.

"I know how to start it out, but the trade has to grow all on its own. C'mon."

"Where to?"

"Hush, not so loud! Our first stop's the stables."

So they were going to ride into town. Caramon thought that a good idea. His arm was stiff and sore from spear chucking, and now his rump hurt from the tumble he'd taken. The less exercise he had this night the better.

The two crept out of the barracks. Solinari and Lunitari were both out, one full and one waning. Thin, high clouds draped across the moons like silken scarves, so that neither gave much light, smudging the stars.

Guards walked the walls of the baron's castle, stopping now and then to grouse good-naturedly about missing the fun in town. Their watch was outside the castle courtyard, not inside, and so they didn't notice the two figures slipping from shadow to shadow, heading for the stables. Caramon wondered how Scrounger had managed to convince someone to give them horses, but every time he started to ask, Scrounger shushed him.

"Wait here! Keep a lookout," Scrounger ordered and, leaving Caramon at the stable door, the half-kender slipped inside.

Caramon waited nervously. He could hear sounds from inside the stable, but he couldn't place them. One of them was a loud thud, accompanied by the jingling of metal. Then the sound of something heavy scraping across a floor. Finally Scrounger emerged, panting but triumphant, hauling a leather saddle with him.

Caramon eyed the saddle, conscious that something was missing. "Where's the horse?"

"Just take this, will you?" Scrounger said, dumping the heavy object at Caramon's feet. "Whew! I didn't think it would be that heavy. The saddle was up on a post. I had to haul it off, and it was a struggle. You can carry that, though, can't you?"

"Well, sure, I can," said Caramon. He looked at it more intently. "You know, this looks like the saddle Master Senej uses on his horse."

"It is," said Scrounger.

Caramon grunted, pleased that he'd recognized it. He lifted the saddle without a great deal of effort. A thought occurred to him. "Carry it where?" he asked.

"Into town. This way." Scrounger started off.

"No, sir!" Caramon flung the saddle down on the ground. "No, sir. Sergeant Nemiss said no stealing, and she said I was responsible, and while I really don't think that the apple tree would bear my weight if they were to hang me from it, there's probably an oak around that would."

"It's not stealing, Caramon," Scrounger argued. "It's not borrowing either. It's *trading*."

Caramon remained skeptical. He shook his head. "No, sir."

"Look, Caramon, I guarantee that the company commander will sit on his horse on a saddle tomorrow, just like he sat on his horse on a saddle today. I guarantee it. You have my word. I don't like the looks of that apple tree any more than you do."

"Well . . ." Caramon hesitated.

"Caramon, I have to make this trade," said Scrounger. "If I don't, they'll throw me out of the army. The only reason I've lasted this long is because the baron thinks I'm a novelty. But that won't last once we go campaigning. Then I'll have to earn my keep. I have to prove to them that I can be a valuable member of the company, Caramon. I have to!"

The glee had gone from Scrounger's face. He was serious, in desperate earnest.

"It's against my better judgment"—Caramon heaved a sigh and picked up the saddle, grunting at the strain on his sore arm—"but all right. How do we get out of here?"

"The front gate," said Scrounger unconcernedly.

"But the guards—"

"Let me do the talking."

Caramon groaned but said nothing. Hoisting the saddle onto his head, he accompanied Scrounger to the gate.

"Where do you two think you're going?" asked the gate guard, looking considerably amazed at what appeared to be a giant sprouting a saddle for a head.

"Master Senej sent us, sir," said Scrounger, saluting. "This stirrup's loose. He told us to take it into town first thing in the morning."

"But it's night," the guard protested.

"*After* midnight, sir," said Scrounger. "Morning now. We're only obeying orders, sir." He lowered his voice. "You know what a stickler Master Senej can be."

"Yes, and I know he thinks the world of that saddle," said the guard. "Go along then."

"Yes, sir. Thank you, sir."

Scrounger marched out the gate. Caramon plodded

dolefully after him. The guard's last statement—about the master thinking the world of this saddle—had caused his heart to get tangled up with his socks.

"Scrounger," he began.

"Yeast, Caramon," said Scrounger, shining the lantern on the road. "Just think of yeast."

Caramon tried to think of yeast, he truly did. But that only reminded him that he was hungry.

* * * * *

"There are the caravans," said Scrounger, sliding the cover over the dark lantern.

Bonfires blazed in both camps. Tall humans passed back and forth in front of one fire; short, stout dwarves walked past the other.

Caramon dropped the saddle, glad for a chance to rest. One camp was made up of a circle of large covered wagons with horses tethered off to one side. The other camp was a circle of smaller wagons, none of them covered, all with ponies standing beside them, tethered to their respective wagons.

As the two watched, a tall man left the first camp and crossed over to the second.

"Reynard!" he shouted, speaking Common. "I need to talk to you!"

A dwarf stood up from the fire and clumped out to meet the human.

"Are you ready to meet my price?"

"Look, Reynard, you know I don't have that much steel on me."

"So what's the baron paying you in—wood?"

"I have to buy supplies," the man whined. "It's a long way back to Southlund."

"And it'll be longer riding bareback. Take my offer or leave it!" the dwarf said crossly. He started to walk off.

"Are you sure we can't come to some other arrangement?" the man asked, halting him. "You can make it for me! I don't mind waiting."

"I do," the dwarf returned. "I can't spare ten days lolly-gagging around here losing money just to make you a saddle, and you not wanting to meet my price for the one I do have. No. Come back when you have something to offer." The dwarf returned to his fire and his ale and his companions.

Caramon looked down at the saddle. "You're not thinking—"

"It's fermenting, my friend," Scrounger whispered. "It's fermenting. Let's go."

Caramon hefted the saddle, followed Scrounger to the human camp.

"Who goes there?" A man peered at them from one of the wagons.

"A friend," Scrounger called out.

"It's a big guy and a little guy," the lookout reported. "And the big guy's got a saddle. The boss might be interested."

"A saddle!" A middle-aged man with grizzled hair and beard jumped to his feet, eyed them warily. "Seems a funny time of night for saddles to come walking into camp. What do you two want?"

"We heard from some friends of ours that you were looking for a good saddle, sir," said Scrounger politely. "We also heard that you were a little short of steel at the moment. We have a saddle—a fine one, as you can see. Caramon, put the saddle there in the firelight where these gentlemen can get a close look at it. Now, we're willing to barter. What have you got to trade me for this fine saddle?"

"Sorry," the man said. "The boss is the one who needs the saddle, and he's in his wagon. Come back tomorrow."

Scrounger shook his head sadly. "We would like to, sir, we really would. But we go on long-range patrol tomorrow. We're with the baron's army, you see. Caramon, pick up the saddle. I guess our friends were mistaken. Good evening to you, gentlemen."

Caramon reached down, picked up the saddle, and heaved it back up on his head again.

"Wait a moment!" A tall man—the same one they'd seen talking to the dwarf—jumped down out of one of the wagons. "I overheard what you said to Smitfee here. Let me have a look at that saddle."

"Caramon," said Scrounger, "put down the saddle."

Caramon sighed. He had no idea that trading was this strenuous. It was far less trouble to work for a living. He plunked down the saddle in the dirt.

The human examined it, ran his hand over the leather, peered closely at the stitching.

"Looks a little worn," he said disparagingly. "What do you want for it?"

The man's tone was cold and offhanded, but Caramon had seen the way the man's hand lingered on the fine leather, and he was certain that the sharp-eyed Scrounger had seen it, too. The master's saddle was a good one, the second finest in the company, next to the baron's own.

"Well, now," Scrounger said, scratching his head. "What are you hauling?"

The man looked surprised. "Beef."

"Do you have a lot?"

"Barrels of it."

Scrounger thought this over. "All right, I'll take my payment in beef. The saddle in exchange."

The man was wary. This seemed too easy. "How much do you want?"

"All of it," said Scrounger.

The man laughed. "I've got sixteen hundred pounds of aging prime-grade beef! I only sold the baron a couple of barrels. No saddle in Krynn is worth that."

"You drive a hard bargain, sir." Scrounger appeared disconsolate. "Very well, my friend and I will take one hundred pounds of beef, but they have to be the choicest cuts. I'll show you what we want."

The man thought it over, then nodded and thrust out his hand. "You have a deal! Smitfee, get the two their beef."

"But, Scrounger," Caramon said worriedly in a loud whisper, "The master's saddle! He's going to be—"

"Hush!" Scrounger elbowed his friend. "I know what I'm doing."

Caramon shook his head. He had just watched his friend trade away the master's saddle, the master's highly prized saddle, for a barrel of beef. His arm and his rump were sore, and he was convinced that most of the hair on top of his head had been rubbed off by the saddle. To make matters worse, between the talk of bread and beef, his stomach was sounding hollow as a drum. He had the feeling he should call a halt to this dealing right now, grab the saddle, and march back to camp. He didn't do it for two reasons: one, to do so would be to show disloyalty to his friend and two, if he never picked up that blasted saddle again, it would be too soon.

The middle-aged hand led them to one of the far wagons. Hoisting out a barrel, he manhandled it to the ground.

"Here you go, gentlemen," he said. "One hundred pounds of high-grade beef. You won't find anything better between here and the Khalkists."

Scrounger inspected the barrel closely, leaning down to peer through the slats. He stood up, put his hands on his hips, pursed his lips and looked over all the other barrels on the wagon.

"No, this won't do." He pointed. "I want the barrel there, the one near the front. The one with the white mark on the side."

Smitfee looked over toward the caravan leader, who was standing protectively, legs straddled, over the saddle, just in case the two dealers had some idea of trying a doublecross. The caravan leader nodded.

Smitfee eased down the second barrel to the ground.

"All yours, lad." Smitfee grinned and walked off.

Caramon had the terrible feeling he knew what was coming, but he made a hopeful try. "I guess we'll just leave this for the baron's men to collect tomorrow with the wagon."

Scrounger gave him an ingratiating smile, shook his head. "No, we have to take this to the dwarven camp."

"What do the dwarves want with a hundred pounds of beef?" Caramon demanded.

"Nothing, right now," Scrounger said. "I think you could roll the barrel," he added. "You don't have to carry it."

Caramon walked up to the barrel, flipped it over on its side, and began to roll it over the bumpy and uneven ground. The task wasn't as easy as one might think. The barrel wobbled and jounced, veering off in odd directions when least expected. Scrounger ran alongside, guiding as best he could. They nearly lost it once. Rolling down a slight hill, the barrel got going too fast. Caramon's heart leaped into his throat when Scrounger hurled himself bodily at the barrel in order to stop it. By the time they reached the dwarven camp, both were hot and sweating and exhausted.

They rolled the barrel into the dwarven camp, startling one of the ponies, who let out a shrill whinny. Dwarves appeared from everywhere at once. One, Caramon could have sworn, popped up from right beneath his nose, alarming him almost as much as he'd alarmed the pony.

"Good evening, good sirs," said Scrounger brightly, bowing to the dwarves. He laid his hand on the barrel, which Caramon was holding steady with his foot.

"What's in the barrel?" asked one of the dwarves, viewing it with suspicion.

"Exactly what you're looking for, sir!" Scrounger said, slapping his hand down on top of it.

"And what would that be now?" the dwarf asked. Judging by the length of his whiskers, he was the leader of the caravan. "Ale, maybe?" His eyes brightened.

"No, sir," said Scrounger disparagingly. "Griffon's meat."

"Griffon's meat!" The dwarf was clearly taken aback.

So was Caramon. He opened his mouth, shut it when Scrounger trod hard on his foot.

"One hundred pounds of the finest griffon's meat a person could ever hope to see roasting nice and juicy over a fire. Have you ever tasted griffon's meat before, sir?

Some say it tastes like chicken, but they're wrong. Mouth-watering. That's the only way to describe it."

"I'll take ten pounds." The dwarf reached for his purse. "What do I owe you?"

"Sorry, sir, but I can't split up the lot." Scrounger was apologetic.

The dwarf snorted. "And what am I going to do with one hundred pounds of any kind of meat, griffon or no? The boys and I eat plain on the road. I don't have room in the wagons to waste hauling around fancy wittles."

"Not even to celebrate the Feast of the Life Tree," said Scrounger, looking shocked. "The most holy of the dwarven holidays! A day devoted to the honoring of Reorx."

"What? Eh?" The dwarf's shaggy eyebrows rose. "What feast is this?"

"Why, it's the biggest festival of the year in Thorbardin. Ah." Scrounger appeared embarrassed. "But I guess that you—being *hill* dwarves—wouldn't know anything about that."

"Who says we wouldn't?" the dwarf demanded indignantly. "I . . . I was a bit confused as to the dates, you know. All this traveling. A dwarf gets mixed up. So next week is the Festival of the . . . uh . . ."

"Life Tree," said Scrounger helpfully.

"Of course, it is," said the dwarf, glowering. He took on a cunning look. "Mind you, I know how we hill dwarves celebrate this great feast, but I don't know how they do it in Thorbardin. Not that I care particularly," he added offhandedly, "what those snooty louts do in Thorbardin. It's just that I'm curious."

"Well," said Scrounger slowly, "there's drinking and dancing."

The dwarves all nodded. That was standard.

"And they break open a fresh cask of dwarf spirits—"

The dwarves were starting to look bored.

"But the most important part of the entire feast is the Eating of the Griffon. It's well known that Reorx himself was a great lover of griffon."

"Well known," the dwarves agreed solemnly, though they shot sidelong glances at one another.

"He was said once to have downed an entire standing rib roast in one sitting, complete with potatoes and gravy, and was heard to ask for dessert," Scrounger continued.

The dwarves whipped off their hats, held them over their chests, and bowed their heads in respect.

"So, in honor of Reorx, every dwarf must eat as much griffon meat as he can possibly consume. The rest," Scrounger added piously, "he gives to the poor in Reorx's name."

One of the dwarves mopped his eyes with the tip of his beard.

"Well, now, lad," said the leader in husky tones, "since you've called our attention to the date, we will be wanting this barrel of griffon's meat after all. I'm a bit short on steel just now. What will you take in exchange?"

Scrounger thought for a moment. "What do you have that is unique? That you have only one of?"

The dwarf was caught off-guard. "Well," he began, "we have—"

"Nope." Scrounger said flatly. "Couldn't possibly."

"How about—"

Scrounger shook his head. "Won't do, I'm afraid."

"You're a hard bargainer, sir," the dwarf said, frowning. "Very well. You've driven me against the wall. I have"—he looked around, careful to see that they weren't overheard—"a suit of plate that was made in Pax Tharkas by the best dwarven metalsmiths for the renowned Sir Jeffrey of Palanthas."

The dwarf laced his hands over his belly, gazed at the two, expecting them to be impressed.

Scrounger lifted his eyebrows. "Don't you think that Sir Jeffrey might *need* his armor?"

"Not where he's going, I'm afraid." The dwarf pointed to the heavens. "Tragic accident. Slipped in the latrine."

Scrounger considered. "I assume the armor comes with the shield and saddle?"

Caramon held his breath.

"Shield yes, saddle no."

Caramon sighed deeply.

"The saddle is promised already," the dwarf added.

Scrounger mulled over the matter a good long minute before answering. "Very well, we'll take the armor and shield."

He thrust out his hand. The dwarf did the same, and they shook on the deal over the upturned barrel of sacred griffon.

The lead dwarf tromped to another wagon, returned dragging a wooden crate behind him. On top of the crate was a shield with the embossed emblem of a kingfisher on the front. Puffing, he dropped the crate at Scrounger's feet. "There you are, lad. Much obliged. That'll make room for the meat."

Scrounger thanked the dwarves and looked at Caramon, who reached down and, with much groaning, lifted the crate onto his shoulder.

"Why did you tell them it was griffon meat?" Caramon demanded.

"Because they wouldn't have been interested in plain old beef," Scrounger replied.

"Won't they know that they've been tricked when they open it?"

"If they do, they'll never admit it to themselves," Scrounger said. "They'll swear that it's the best griffon's meat they've ever eaten."

Caramon digested this for a moment, as they headed back down the road in the direction of the baron's castle.

"Do you think this armor will make up to the master for the loss of his saddle?" Caramon asked doubtfully.

"No, I shouldn't think so," Scrounger said. "That's why we're taking it back to the human camp."

"But the human's camp is back that way!" Caramon pointed out.

"Yes, but I want to get a look at the armor first."

"We can look at it here."

"No, we can't. Is that crate awfully heavy?"

"Yes," Caramon growled.

"Must be good solid armor then," Scrounger concluded.

"Lucky that you knew all about that feast in Thorbardin," Caramon said, bending double under the weight of the crate.

"What feast?" Scrounger asked. His mind had been on something else.

Caramon stared at him. "You mean—"

"Oh, that?" Scrounger grinned and winked. "We may have just started an entirely new dwarven tradition." He looked back to see how far they'd come. When the fires from the camps were only small orange dots in the darkness, he called a halt. "Come here, behind these rocks," he said, beckoning mysteriously. "Put the crate down. Can you open it?"

Caramon pried open the crate lid with his hunting knife. Scrounger shone the light from the dark lantern on the armor.

"That's the most beautiful thing I ever saw!" Caramon said, awed. "I wish Sturm could see this. Look at the kingfisher etched on the breastplate. And the roses on the beaver. And the fine leatherwork. It's perfect! Just perfect!"

"Too damn perfect," said Scrounger, chewing his lip. He glanced around, picked up a large rock, and handed the rock to Caramon. "Here, bash it a few times."

"What?" Caramon's jaw dropped. "Are you crazy? That will dent it!"

"Yes, yes!" Scrounger said impatiently. "Hurry up, now!"

Caramon bashed the armor with the rock, though he winced at every dent he put into the beautiful breastplate, feeling each almost as much if he'd been on the receiving end. "There," he said at last, breathing hard. "That should—" He stopped, stared at Scrounger, who had taken Caramon's knife and was now proceeding to make a cut on his forearm. "What the—"

"It was a desperate fight," murmured Scrounger, holding his arm over the armor, watching the blood drip onto it. "But it's comforting to know that poor Sir Jeffrey died a hero."

* * * * *

Smitfee stopped the two at the edge of the wagons. "What now?" he demanded.

"I have a trade to propose, sir," Scrounger said politely.

Smitfee looked at Scrounger closely. "I wondered where I'd seen ears like that before. Now I remember. You're part kender, aren't you, boy? We don't take kindly to kender, diluted or no. The boss is asleep. So go away—"

The boss walked around the side of the wagon.

"I saw Barsteel Firebrand hauling that barrel of beef into his wagon. He wouldn't buy so much as a rump roast off me. How did you do it?"

"Sorry, sir," said Scrounger, cheeks flushed. "Professional secrets. But he gave me something in return. Something I think you might find interesting."

"Yeah. What's that?" The men looked at the crate curiously.

"Open it up, Caramon."

"Old beaten-up armor," said Smitfee.

Scrounger's voice took on a funereal tone. "Not just any armor, gentleman. It is the magical armor of the valiant Solamnic Knight, Sir Jeffrey of Palanthas, along with his shield. The *last* armor of the gallant Sir Jeffrey," he said with sad emphasis. "Describe the battle, Caramon."

"Oh, uh, sure," said Caramon, startled at his new role of storyteller. "Well, there were . . . uh . . . six goblins . . ."

"Twenty-six," Scrounger cut in. "And don't you mean hobgoblins?"

"Yeah, that's it. Twenty-six hobgoblins. They had him surrounded."

"There was a little golden-haired child involved, I believe," Scrounger prompted. "A princess's child. And her pet griffon cub."

"That's right. The goblins were trying to carry off the princess's child—"

"And the griffon cub—"

"And the cub. Sir Jeffrey snatched the golden-haired griffon—"

"And the child—"

"And the child from the hobgoblins and handed the child back to his mother the princess and told her to run for it. He put his back against a tree and he drew his sword"—Caramon drew his sword, to illustrate the story better—"and he slashed to the left, and he slashed to the right, and hobgoblins fell at every blow. But at last they were too much for him. It was a cursed goblin mace hit him here"—Caramon pointed—"disrupted the magic, stove in his armor, and gave him his death blow. They found him the next day with twenty-five dead hobgoblins lying all about him. And he managed to wound the last one with his dying stroke."

Caramon sheathed his sword, looking noble.

"And the golden-haired child was safe?" asked Smitfee. "And the griffon cub?"

"The princess named the cub 'Jeffrey,'" said Scrounger in tremulous tones.

There was a moment of respectful silence.

Smitfee knelt down, gingerly touched the armor. "Name of the Abyss!" he said, astonished. "The blood's still fresh!"

"We said it was magic," Caramon replied.

"This famous battle relic's wasted on the dwarves," said Scrounger. "But it occurred to me that a caravan that happened to be traveling north to Palanthas might take this armor and the tale that goes with it to the High Clerist's Tower—"

"Our route does happen to lie north," said the leader. "I'll give you another hundred pounds of beef for the armor."

"No, sir. I can't use any more of your beef, I'm afraid." Scrounger said. "What else do you have?"

"Pig's feet pickled in brine. A couple of large cheeses. Fifty pounds of hops—"

"Hops!" said Scrounger. "What kind of hops?"

"Ergothian Prost hops. Magically enhanced by the Kagonesti elves to make the best beer ever."

" 'Scuse me. Conference." He motioned Caramon off to one side.

"Dwarves don't travel much to Ergoth these days, do they?" Scrounger whispered.

Caramon shook his head. "Not if they have to go by boat. My friend Flint couldn't abide boats. Why once—"

Scrounger walked off, leaving Caramon in midstory. Scrounger thrust out his hand. "Very good, sir. I believe we have a deal."

Smitfee hauled away the armor, treating it with great respect, and returned some time later with a large crate over his shoulder. He tossed the crate on the ground in front of him and bade them both good night.

Caramon looked down at the crate, then he looked up at Scrounger.

"That was a wonderful story, Caramon," Scrounger said. "I very nearly wept."

Caramon leaned down, picked up the crate, and heaved it onto his back.

* * * * *

"So, what have you brought me this time?" asked the dwarf.

"Hops. Fifty pounds of hops," said Scrounger triumphantly.

The dwarf appeared disgusted. "You evidently haven't met dwarves before, have you, lad? It's well known that we make the best beer in all of Krynn! We raise our own hops—"

"Not like these," said Scrounger. "Not *Ergothian* hops!"

The dwarf sucked in a deep breath. "Ergothian! Are you sure?"

"Take a whiff for yourself," said Scrounger.

The dwarf sniffed the air. He exchanged glances with his compatriots. "Ten steel coins for that crate!"

"Sorry," said Scrounger. "C'mon, Caramon. There's a tavern in town that will give us—"

"Wait!" the dwarf yelled. "What about two sets of Hylar chinaware with matching goblets. I'll throw in gold utensils!"

"I'm a military man," said Scrounger over his shoulder. "What do I need with china plates and gold spoons?"

"Military. Very well. What about eight enchanted elven longbows, handcrafted by the Qualinesti rangers themselves? An arrow fired from one of these bows will never miss its mark."

Scrounger stopped walking. Caramon lowered the crate to the ground.

"The enchanted longbows *and* Sir Jeffrey's saddle," he countered.

The dwarf shook his head. "I can't do it. I promised the saddle to another customer."

"Caramon, pick up the crate."

Scrounger resumed walking. The dwarf sniffed the air again.

"Wait! All right!" the dwarf burst out. "The saddle, too!"

Scrounger let out his breath. "Very well, sir. We have a deal."

* * * * *

Caramon was deep in a dream, battling twenty-six golden-haired children who had been tormenting a blubbering hobgoblin. Consequently, the sound of metal clashing against metal appeared to be part of his dream, and he did not bother to wake. Not until Sergeant Nemiss held the iron pot she was banging over his head.

"Get up, you lazy bum! Flank Company's first to fight! Up I say!"

He and Scrounger had returned to camp within an hour of day's dawning. Groggy from lack of sleep, Caramon stumbled out after the others to take his place in the ranks of men lined up in front of the barracks.

The sergeant brought the company to attention and was just forming them into a marching column when the sound of galloping hooves and a voice shouting in anger brought the marching to a halt.

Master Senej reined in his excited horse, jumped from the saddle. His face was red as the morning sun, a flaming, fiery red. He glared around at the entire company, recruits and veterans. All of them shriveled away to nothing in the heat of his anger.

"Damn it! One of you bastards switched my saddle with the baron's saddle again. I'm sick and tired of this stupid prank. The baron nearly had my head on a stick the last time this happened. Now, which one of you is responsible?" Master Senej thrust his square jaw out, marched up and down the ranks, glaring each man in the face. "C'mon. 'Fess up!"

No one moved. No one spoke. If the Abyss had opened wide at his feet, Caramon would have been the first to dive in.

"No one admits it?" Master Senej snarled. "Very well. The whole company's on half rations for two days!"

The soldiers groaned, Caramon among them. This hit him where it hurt.

"Don't punish the others, sir," said a voice from the back of the orderly lines. "I did it."

"Who the hell's that?" the master demanded, peering over heads, trying to see.

Scrounger stepped out of ranks. "I'm the one responsible, sir."

"What's your name, soldier?"

"Scrounger, sir."

"This man's about to be mustered out, sir," said Sergeant Nemiss quickly. "He's leaving today, in fact."

"That doesn't excuse what he did, Sergeant. First he's going to explain to the baron—"

"Permission to speak, sir?" said Scrounger respectfully.

The master was grim. "Permission granted. What do you have to say for yourself, Puke?"

"The saddle doesn't belong to the baron, sir." Scrounger replied meekly. "If you'll check, you'll see that the baron's saddle is still in the stables. This saddle is yours, sir. Compliments of C Company."

The soldiers glanced at each other. Sergeant Nemiss snapped out a command, and they all turned eyes front again.

The master studied the new saddle closely. "By Kiri-Jolith. You're right. This *isn't* the baron's saddle. But it's in the Solamnic style—"

"The very newest style, sir," said Scrounger.

"I . . . I don't know what to say." Master Senej was touched, the red flush of anger giving way to the warm flush of pleasure. "This must have cost a small fortune. To think you men . . . went together . . ." The master could not speak for the choke in his throat.

"Three cheers for Master Senej!" shouted the sergeant, who had no idea what was going on but was more than willing to take the credit.

The soldiers responded lustily.

Mounting his horse, seating himself proudly in his new saddle, the master responded to the cheers with a flourish of his hat, then galloped up the road.

Sergeant Nemiss turned around, lightning in her eye and thunder on her face. She fixed that eye upon Scrounger, sent the bolt flashing through him.

"All right, Puke. What the devil's going on? I know darn good and well that none of us bought Master Senej a new saddle. Did *you* buy it for him, Puke?"

"No, sir," said Scrounger quietly. "I did not buy it, sir."

Sergeant Nemiss motioned. "One of you men, bring me a rope. I said what I'd do if I caught you stealing, kender. Now, march!"

Scrounger, his face set, marched over to the apple tree. Caramon stood stock still in line, controlling his face with difficulty. He only hoped that Scrounger didn't carry the joke too far.

One of the soldiers returned with a stout rope, which he handed to the sergeant. Scrounger positioned himself beneath the apple tree. The soldiers continued to stand at attention.

Swinging the rope in her hand, Sergeant Nemiss looked up into the tree, seeking a suitable branch. She stopped, stared. "What the—"

Scrounger smiled, looked down modestly at his feet.

Reaching up into the apple tree, Sergeant Nemiss grabbed hold of something, lowered it carefully. The men did not dare break formation, but all tried desperately to see what it was she held in her hands. One of the veterans forgot himself and gave a low whistle. Sergeant Nemiss was so stunned that she never noticed this breach of discipline.

In her hands, she held an elven longbow. Gazing up into the tree, she counted seven more.

Sergeant Nemiss smoothed her hand over the fine wood. "These are the best bows in all of Ansalon. They're said to be magical! The elves won't sell them to humans—at any price. Do you have any idea what these are worth?"

"Yes, sir," said Scrounger. "One hundred pounds of beef, some dented Solamnic armor, and a crate of hops."

"Huh?" Sergeant Nemiss blinked.

Caramon took a step forward. "It's true, Sergeant. Scrounger didn't steal them. There's some humans and some dwarves camped out in town who'll vouch for that. He traded for everything, fair and square."

The last was a bit of a stretch, but what the Sergeant didn't know wouldn't hurt her.

Sergeant Nemiss's face went soft, gentle, lovely. She rubbed her cheek with deep affection against the smooth, supple wood of the elven bow.

"Welcome to C Company, Scrounger," she said with tears in her eyes. "Three cheers for Scrounger!"

The men gave the cheers with a will.

"And," added Sergeant Nemiss, "three cheers for the thirteen new members of C Company."

It seemed that the cheering, once started, would never stop.

20

Ariakas's troops were on the march. Not his own personal guard. Those men were too highly trained, too valuable to expend on this expedition. His troops had seen battle. His soldiers had captured Sanction and Neraka, plus all the surrounding lands. The men he was sending south to Blödehelm were the best of his new forces, men who had performed well during training. This was their blooding.

The mission was secret, so secret that not even the highest-ranking commanders knew the name of the objective. They received their orders for the next day's march the night before, orders delivered to them by wyverns. The troops marched at night, under the cover of darkness. They marched in silence, their boots muffled in cloth, the rings of their chain mail padded so that no one would hear the jingle. The wheels of the supply wagons were greased, the horses' harness covered with rags. Anyone unfortunate enough to stumble across the army's path was killed swiftly and without mercy. No one must be left alive to report that he had seen an army of darkness marching from the north.

Kitiara and Immolatus did not ride with the army. The two of them could travel faster than the monstrous military monster crawling across the land. Ariakas wanted them in Hope's End prior to the army's arrival, intending that they should discover the location of the eggs before the start of the battle. Their orders were to reach the city prior to the battle, enter the city in disguise, conduct their search, and leave before things got too hot.

Kitiara was glad they were on their own, away from the troops. Immolatus aroused too much curiosity, occasioned too much comment. In vain, Kit had endeavored to persuade the dragon that the garb of a red-robed wizard was not a suitable disguise for traveling in company with Her Dark Majesty's forces. Black, Kitiara hinted, was a far more attractive color.

Immolatus would not be persuaded. Red he was and red he would remain. Eventually, finding all her arguments useless, Kitiara gave up. She foresaw fights with the arrogant dragon and decided that this was a minor fray of no great consequence. She would save her strength for the battles that counted.

Kitiara wondered at the choice of the dragon—with his scathing disdain for all people regardless of race, creed, or color—for such a mission. It was not her place to question her orders, however. Particularly her last order, which had been delivered to her in secret prior to their departure from Sanction. At least she assumed the missive was an order. She supposed it could be a love letter, but Ariakas did not seem the type.

She kept that order—a hastily scrawled note from Ariakas—rolled into a small tight scroll, tucked in a pouch stowed in her saddlebag. She had not yet had a chance to read it. Immolatus demanded her constant attention. He had spent the day of their swift ride regaling her with stories of his various raids and slaughters, ransackings and lootings. When he wasn't reliving his days of glory, he was complaining bitterly about the food he was forced to eat while in his human form and how humiliating he found it to plod along on horseback when he could be soaring among the clouds.

They stopped to rest at night, and despite the fact that he was not sleeping on a bed of gold, Immolatus finally fell asleep. Fortunately, the dragon slept deeply. Much like a dog, he twitched and jerked in his dreams, snapped his teeth and ground his jaws. After watching his restless slumbers closely for long moments, Kit went so far as to shake Immolatus by the shoulder and call out his name.

He mumbled and growled but did not waken.

Satisfied that she could read her letter in private, Kitiara retrieved the scroll, read the missive by the firelight.

Commander Kitiara uth Matar

Should any circumstance arise in which it is the considered opinion of Commander uth Matar that Her Majesty's plans for the eventual conquest of Ansalon would be endangered, Commander uth Matar is hereby expressly commanded to handle the situation in any manner the commander deems suitable.

The order was signed *Ariakas, General of the Dragonarmies of Queen Takhisis.*

"Cunning bastard," Kitiara muttered with a grudging half-smile. After reading over the deliberately vague and unspecific order twice more, she shook her head, shrugged, and tucked it into her boot.

So this was the lash of the whip. She had been expecting some sort of punishment for her refusal. One did not say no to General Ariakas with impunity. But she had not expected anything so diabolically creative. Her opinion of the man rose a notch.

Ariakas had just placed responsibility for the success—or failure—of the mission on her. Should she succeed, she would be given a hero's welcome. Promotion. His lordship's favors—both in bed and out. Should she fail . . .

Ariakas was intrigued by her, fascinated by her. But he was not a man to remain intrigued or fascinated by anything long. Ruthless, power-hungry, he would sacrifice her to his ambition without a backward glance to see if her body still twitched.

Kitiara sat down near the fire, stared into the dancing flames. Slumbering near her, Immolatus snarled and snorted. The smell of sulfur was strong in the air. He must be setting fire to a city about now. She envisioned the flames devouring houses, shops. People enveloped in fire, living torches. Charred corpses, blackened ruins. The horrid smell of burning hair, seared flesh. Armies marching victorious, the ashes of the dead coating their boots.

The cleansing fire would sweep throughout Ansalon, clearing out the elven deadwood that lay rotting in the forests, burning away the tangled undergrowth of inferior races that impeded human progress, setting the spark to old-fashioned ideas such as those held by the decaying, tinder-dry knighthood. A new order would arise, phoenixlike, from the charred remains of the old.

"I will sit astride that new order," Kitiara said to the flames. "The leveling fire will burn bright in my blade. I will return to you victorious, General Ariakas.

"Or I will not return at all."

Resting her chin on her knees, Kitiara wrapped her arms around her legs and watched the flames consume the wood until all that was left were the cinders, winking at her in the darkness like the dragon's red eyes.

BOOK 2

"*Nothing ever happens by chance. Everything happens for a reason. Your brain may not know the reason. Your brain may never figure it out. But your heart knows. Your heart always knows.*"

—Horkin, Master-at-Wizardry

I

The citizens of Hope's End never meant to go to war. What had started as a peaceful protest over an unfair tax had escalated into full-scale rebellion, and none of the people of Hope's End quite knew how it had all gone so terribly wrong.

Rolling a pebble down a hill, they had inadvertently started a rockslide. Tossing a stick into a pond, they had created a tidal wave, a wall of water that might well drown them all. The cart of their lives, which had once been rolling so smoothly along the main road, had suddenly lost a wheel, toppled sideways, and was now careening down the cliff face.

The unfair tax was a gate tax, and it was having a ruinous effect on the businesses of Hope's End. The edict had come down from King Wilhelm (formerly known as Good King Wilhelm, now known as something not nearly as flattering). The edict required that all goods entering the city of Hope's End should be subject to a twenty-five percent tax and, in addition, all goods leaving Hope's End should be subject to the same tax. This meant that any raw materials entering the city, everything from iron ore for armor to cotton for lace petticoats, were taxed. The same armor and petticoats that left the city were also taxed.

In consequence, the price of goods from the city of Hope's End shot up higher than the latest gnome invention (a steam-powered butter churn). If the merchants did have money enough to pay for the raw materials, they had to charge so much for the finished goods that people could not afford to buy them. This meant that merchants could no longer afford to pay their workers, who no longer had money to pay for bread for their children, let alone lace petticoats.

Good King Wilhelm sent his tax collectors—hulking thuggish brutes—to see to it that the tax was levied. Those merchants who rebelled against paying the gate tax were intimidated, threatened, harassed, and sometimes physically assaulted. One enterprising entrepreneur had the idea of moving his business outside the city walls, in order to avoid the tax altogether. The thugs summarily shut down his operations, broke up his booth, set fire to his stock, and socked the enterprising citizen on the jaw.

Soon the entire economy of Hope's End was teetering on the verge of collapse.

To add insult to injury, the citizens of Hope's End discovered that their city was the only city in the realm to be so mistreated. The loathsome gate tax was levied on them alone. No other city had to pay it. The citizens sent a delegation to Good King Wilhelm requesting to know why they were being punished with this unfair tax. His Majesty refused to see the delegation, sent one of his ministers to relay his answer.

"It is the king's will."

In vain, the lord mayor sent envoys bearing letters to King Wilhelm pleading to lift the unfair tax. The envoys were turned away without ever being given audience with His Majesty. The envoys took no comfort in the rumor running through the royal city of Vantal that King Wilhelm was mad. A mad king is still king, and this one was apparently sane enough to see to it that his mad decrees were obeyed.

The situation grew steadily worse. Shops closed. The marketplace remained open, but the goods sold there were meager and few. Guild meetings—once little more than an excuse for the merchants to come together in good fellowship, share good food and drink—were now shouting matches, with each merchant demanding that something be done. Since each merchant had his own views on what that something was, each merchant was ready to heave an ale mug—now sadly filled with water—at the head of anyone who opposed him.

The Merchants Guild of Hope's End was the most powerful organization in the city. The guild held a virtual monopoly over all industry and commerce of the city. The guild supervised the smaller guilds, setting standards for crafts and seeing to it that these standards were upheld. The merchants felt, and rightly so, that shoddy workmanship reflected badly on the entire community. Any merchant caught cheating his customers was cast out of the guild and thereby lost his ability to make a living.

The Merchants Guild of Hope's End sought to improve the lot of all working men and women in the town, from seamstress and weaver to silversmith and brewer. The guild set fair wages, established the terms under which young men and women were apprenticed to trades, and arbitrated disputes between merchants. Guild members were not rabble-rousers. Their demands for better conditions for their people were not unreasonable. The guild had a cordial relationship with the lord mayor and with the high sheriff. The guild was respected throughout the city, its reputation for fairness and honesty so good that the work of craftsmen in other cities was judged by the accolade, "Good enough to be sold in Hope's End." Thus, when the edict concerning the reprehensible new tax was heralded throughout the city, the people confidently turned to the Merchants Guild to handle the situation.

In response, the guild leader, after much agonized deliberation, called a secret meeting of the guild members, a meeting held in a partially torn-down temple to a forgotten god located on the outskirts of the city.

Here, in the darkness lit by flaring torches, surrounded by his pale, determined, and resolute neighbors, associates, and friends, the guild leader made the suggestion that Hope's End secede from the realm of Blödehelm, become an independent city-state, a city-state with the ability to govern itself, pass its own laws, throw out the thugs, and end the ruinous tax.

In short—revolution.

The vote to secede had been unanimous.

The first order of business was to remove the lord mayor, replace him with a revolutionary council, which immediately elected the lord mayor as their leader. The next order of business was to drive out the thugs. Fortunately, the thugs made this simple by gathering together of an evening in their favorite tavern and drinking themselves into swinish insensibility. Most were hauled off in a drunken stupor, deposited outside the walls. Those who were sober enough to fight were subdued with ease by the city militia.

Once the thugs were gone, the gates of Hope's End were locked and barred. Messengers were sent to Good King Wilhelm informing him that the city of Hope's End had no wish to take the action it had taken but that its people had been driven to rebel. The Revolutionary Council of Hope's End offered the king one last chance to lift the heinous and unfair tax. If he did so, they would put down their arms, unlock the gates, and swear allegiance to Blödehelm and Good King Wilhelm for the rest of their days.

Figuring it would take the messenger four days of hard riding to reach the royal city of Vantal, a day to gain audience with the king, and another four days of hard riding to return, the Revolutionary Council didn't start to worry until the tenth day arrived with no sign of their messenger. Eleven days passed; worry became anxiety. On the twelfth day, anxiety flared into anger. On the thirteenth day, anger gave way to horror.

A kender arrived in the rebellious town (which only goes to show that locked and barred gates guarded by an army really *can't* keep them out!) telling the tale of a most interesting execution she'd recently witnessed in the royal city of Vantal.

"Honestly, I never saw anyone impaled in the public square before! Such a quantity of blood! I never heard such heartrending screams. I never knew a man could take so long to die. I never before saw a victim's head tossed in a cart, a cart being driven in this direction, now that I come to think of it. I never saw the sort of sign that was thrust into the victim's gaping mouth, a sign written in the victim's own blood. A sign that read . . . just give me a moment . . . I'm not all that good at reading myself, someone told me what it said . . . if only I could remember . . . oh, yes! The sign said: 'The fate of all rebels.' "

But they'd have a chance to see it for themselves, the kender added brightly. The cart was on its way to Hope's End.

Anger gave way to despair. Despair caved in to panic when scouts posted atop the city walls reported the sight of an enormous cloud of dust obscuring the northeastern horizon. Scouts, riding from Hope's End, returned with devastating news. An army, a large army, was within a day's march of their city.

The time for secrecy had passed. Ariakas's troops marched in the daylight now.

The people of Hope's End ran from house to house or stood on street corners or lined up in front of the home of the lord mayor or blocked the entrances to the Guild Hall. The people found it impossible to believe that this was happening to them and so they found it impossible to know what to do. Neighbor asked neighbor, apprentice asked master, mistress asked servant, soldier asked commander, commander asked his superiors, the lord mayor asked the guild members, who were busy asking each other: What do we do? Do we stay? Do we go? If we go, where do we go? What becomes of our homes, our jobs, our friends, our relatives?

The dust cloud grew and grew until the entire eastern sky was red at noontime, as if day were breaking with a new and bloody dawn. Some of the people decided to flee, particularly those who were new to the city, those whose roots were shallow and easily transplanted. They packed up what belongings they could carry onto carts or wrapped them in bundles and, bidding their friends farewell, trudged out the city gates and headed down the road in a direction opposite that of what everyone knew now was an approaching army. But most of the citizens of Hope's End stayed.

Like the giant oaks, their roots were sunk deep into the mountains. Generations of them had lived and died in Hope's End. This city, whose origins dated back—or so legend had it—to the Last Dragon War, had withstood the Cataclysm.

My great-grandparents are buried here. My children were born here. I am too young to start out on my own. I am too old to start afresh somewhere else. This is the house of my youth. This is the business my grandmother started. Must I give it all up and flee? Must I kill to protect it?

A terrible choice, a bitter choice.

After the last of the refugees had fled, the gates to the city rumbled closed. Heavy wagons trundled into place behind the gates, wagons loaded with boulders and rocks to form a barricade that would halt the enemy should the gates be forced open. Every available container was filled with water to fight fires. Merchants turned soldier and spent the day at target practice. Older children were taught to retrieve spent arrows.

The citizens expected the best and prepared for the worst—at least what they considered the worst. They still had faith in their king. At best, they imagined the army marching in orderly manner down the road, setting up camp. They pictured the commander riding out politely to parley, pictured their own representatives walking out under a flag of truce to meet with the commander. He'd make threats, they would react with dignity and stand their ground. Eventually he would give some, they would give some. Finally, after maybe a day of hard and difficult negotiating, they would come to an agreement and everyone would go home to supper.

The worst, the very worst they imagined could happen, was that perhaps it would be necessary to send a few arrows over the heads of the soldiers, arrows carefully aimed, of course, so that no one was hurt. Just to show that they were serious. After that, the army commander—undoubtedly a reasonable man—would see that besieging the city was a waste of time and manpower. And after that they would negotiate.

Horns sounded the alarm throughout the city. The army of Good King Wilhelm had come into view. Everyone who could walk clambered up atop the walls.

The city of Hope's End butted up against the mountains on three sides, looked out over a fertile valley on the fourth. Small farm holdings dotted the valley. The first small seedlings of the spring planting were starting to push through the fresh-tilled ground, a silken scarf of green spread across the valley. A road cut through a mountain pass, led into the valley and from there into Hope's End. Generally, at this time of day, one might stand upon the wall and see a farmer with his oxcart driving down the road, or a party of kender, or a tinker with his wagon filled with pots and kettles or some weary traveler looking gladly at the city walls and thinking of a meal and a warm bed.

Now came pouring down the road a river of steel, whose occasional ripples and eddies, tipped by metal that flashed in the sunlight, engulfed the small farms. The steel river flowed into the valley like a fall of rushing water, booted feet shaking the ground, a cascade of drum rolls marking their advance. Soon the flicker of flames could be seen, thin wisps of smoke rising from house and barn, as the soldiers looted the granaries, butchered the animals, and either killed or enslaved the farmers and their families.

The river of steel gathered in the valley, swirled into whirlpools of activity—soldiers setting up camp, pitching tents in the fields, trampling the seedlings, chopping down trees, plundering and looting the farms. They paid scant attention to the city and the people lining its walls, people who watched with pale faces and fast-beating hearts. At length, one small knot of soldiers separated themselves from the main body and rode toward the city gates. They rode under a flag of truce, a white banner nearly hidden by the smoke of the burning fields. The soldiers halted within hailing distance of the wall. One of the soldiers, wearing heavy armor, rode forward three paces.

"City of Hope's End," shouted the commander in a deep voice. "I am Kholos, commander of the army of Blödehelm. You have two choices: surrender or die."

The citizens on the walls looked at each other in astonishment and consternation. This was certainly not what they had expected. After some jostling, the lord mayor came forward to reply.

"We . . . we want to negotiate," he cried.

"What?" the commander bawled.

"Negotiate!" the mayor yelled desperately.

"All right." Kholos sat back more comfortably on his horse. "I'll negotiate. Do you surrender?"

"No," said the lord mayor, drawing himself up with dignity. "We do not."

"Then you die." The commander shrugged. "There, we negotiated."

"What happens if we surrender?" a voice shouted from the crowd.

Kholos laughed, sneered. "I'll tell you what happens if you surrender. You make my life a whole lot easier. Here are your terms. First, all able-bodied men will put down their arms, leave the city, and form a line, so that my slave-masters may take a good look at you. Second, all young and comely women will form a line so that I may take my pick. Third, the remainder of the citizens of Hope's End will haul out their treasure and stack it up here, at my feet. Those are your terms for surrender."

"This is . . . this is unconscionable!" the lord mayor gasped. "Such terms are outrageous! We would never accept!"

Commander Kholos turned his horse's head and galloped back to his camp, his guards following him.

The people of Hope's End prepared for battle, prepared for killing, prepared to die.

They believed they defended a cause. They believed they fought against an injustice. They had no idea that the war wasn't about them, that they were nothing more than small disposable pieces in a greater cosmic game, that the dread general who had ordered this attack hadn't even known the name of the city until he looked it up on a map, that the commanders of the newly formed dragon-armies viewed this as a training exercise.

The people of Hope's End believed that at least their deaths might count for something, when in reality, the smoke rising from the ashes of the city's funeral pyres would form a single dark cloud in an otherwise lovely blue sky, a single dark cloud that would be torn to shreds in the chill wind of the waning day, vanish, and be forgotten.

Dear Reader:

We want to know more about you! Please answer the following questions and drop the card in the mailbox; you don't even need a stamp! You will be entered into a random drawing for an autographed copy of *The Annotated Dragonlance® Chronicles*. Five winners will be chosen.

1) How many hours per month do you currently play paper-based roleplaying games (such as the Dungeons & Dragons® game)?
- ☐ 0—I don't play them at all
- ☐ 1-3 ☐ 4-7 ☐ 9-12 ☐ 13+

2) Have you ever played a paper-based roleplaying game? ☐ Yes ☐ No

3) Do you currently play computer roleplaying games (such as Baldur's Gate™ or Diablo)? ☐ Yes ☐ No

4) If you no longer play paper-based roleplaying games, why did you quit?
- ☐ N/A—I never played
- ☐ N/A—I still play
- ☐ Takes too much time
- ☐ Couldn't find players
- ☐ Other interests
- ☐ Switched to computer RPGs
- ☐ Money
- ☐ No interest
- ☐ Other _____

5) If you play the Dungeons & Dragons game, what campaign settings do you use? (Check all that apply.)
- ☐ N/A (I don't play Dungeons & Dragons)
- ☐ Dragonlance® campaign setting
- ☐ Forgotten Realms® campaign setting
- ☐ Greyhawk® campaign setting
- ☐ Ravenloft® campaign setting

- ☐ Planescape® campaign setting
- ☐ I make up my own
- ☐ I play without a campaign setting
- ☐ Other _____

6) How much money do you spend on paper-based roleplaying game products each month?
- ☐ $0-5 ☐ $6-15 ☐ $16-25 ☐ $26-35 ☐ $36+

7) How many hours do you spend per month playing any kind of game?
- ☐ 0—I don't really play any games
- ☐ 1-3 ☐ 4-7 ☐ 8-12 ☐ 13+

8) Age: _____

9) Gender: ☐ Male ☐ Female

10) Please agree or disagree with the following statements. When I look for new games, I look for games that:

	Agree	Disagree
I can learn quickly	☐	☐
I can play with my family	☐	☐
Require memory or knowledge	☐	☐
Involve strategies	☐	☐
Let me use my imagination	☐	☐
Present mental challenges	☐	☐
Are competitive	☐	☐
Let me learn while I play	☐	☐

	Agree	Disagree
Have beating my opponent as their object	☐	☐
Require little concentration	☐	☐
Are the newest and coolest, even if they're expensive	☐	☐

11) My favorite types of games are: (Check all that apply)
- ☐ Traditional card games (poker, bridge)
- ☐ Classic board games (chess)
- ☐ Modern board games (Monopoly)
- ☐ Standalone computer games (**Baldur's Gate**)
- ☐ Platform video games (PlayStation, N64)
- ☐ Internet (networked) games (StarCraft, Quake)
- ☐ Trading card games (**Magic**® game, Star Wars)
- ☐ Roleplaying games (**AD&D**® game, Vampire)
- ☐ Miniatures (Warhammer)
- ☐ Word/Knowledge games (Scrabble, Trivial Pursuit)

Name _____

Address _____

City _____

State, Zip Code _____

Email address _____

TSR 21429

BUSINESS REPLY MAIL

FIRST CLASS MAIL   PERMIT NO. 609   RENTON, WA

POSTAGE WILL BE PAID BY ADDRESEE

ATTN CONSUMER RESPONSE
WIZARDS OF THE COAST
PO BOX 980
RENTON WA   98057-9910

2

At about the time Good King Wilhelm was disemboweling the rebellious city's ambassador, the army of the Mad Baron began its march toward that doomed metropolis. Led by the baron waving his plumed hat and laughing heartily for no good reason other than his pleasure at the prospect of action, the baron's soldiers paraded down the road amidst cheers and well-wishes from Langtree's assembled townsfolk. After the last heavily laden supply wagon had rolled out the gates, the townsfolk returned to their homes and businesses, grateful for the peace and quiet, sad for the lost revenue.

The baron gave his troops plenty of time to reach their objective. The soldiers marched no more than fifteen miles per day. He wanted his troops fresh and ready to fight, not falling over from exhaustion. Wagons carried their armor, their shields and rations, so they did not have to stop for anything along the route, except for a brief rest at midday. Anyone who dropped out of the march from exhaustion, illness, or injury was teased unmercifully but was permitted to ride in the wagons alongside the drivers.

The men were in good spirits, eager for battle and glory and the pay at the finish. They sang songs as they marched, songs led by the baron's rich baritone. They played tricks and jokes upon the new recruits. Each man knew that this battle might be his last, for every soldier knows that somewhere is an arrowhead marked with his blood or a sword with his name etched on the blade. But such knowledge makes the life he is living at the moment that much sweeter.

The only person who was not enjoying the march was Raistlin. His weak body could not withstand even a moderate walking pace for very long. He grew weary and footsore after the first five miles.

"You should ride in the supply wagons, Raist," Caramon told him helpfully. "Along with the other—" He went red in the face and bit his tongue.

"Along with the rest of the weak and infirm," Raistlin finished the sentence.

"I-I didn't mean that, Raist," Caramon stammered. "You're a lot stronger now than you used to be. Not that you were weak or anything, but—"

"Just be quiet, Caramon," Raistlin said irritably. "I know perfectly well what you meant."

He limped off in high dudgeon, leaving Caramon to look after him and shake his head with a sigh.

Raistlin pictured the scornful looks of the other soldiers as they marched past him, lying recumbent on a sack of dried beans. He pictured his brother helping him out of the wagon every night, solicitous and patronizing. Raistlin resolved then and there that he would march with the rest of the army if it killed him—which it likely would. Dropping dead on the trail was preferable to being pitied.

Raistlin had lost track of Horkin during the march, supposed that the robust mage was in the front ranks, setting the pace. When the word came that Raistlin was to report to the master-at-wizardry, he was considerably astonished to find Horkin back with the supply wagons.

"I heard you were walking, Red," Horkin said.

"Like the rest of the soldiers, sir," said Raistlin, prepared to be affronted. "You needn't worry, sir. I am a little tired now, that's all. I will be better in the morning—"

"Bah! Here's your mount, Red."

Horkin indicated a donkey, tied to one of the wagons. The donkey seemed a placid sort, stood chewing hay, paying no attention to the organized confusion of making camp. "This is Lillie. She's very tractable, so long as you keep your pockets filled with apples." Horkin scratched the donkey between her ears.

"I thank you for your concern, sir," said Raistlin stiffly, "but I will continue to march on foot."

"Suit yourself, Red," said Horkin, shrugging. "But you'll have a devil of time keeping up with me that way."

He nodded toward another donkey who might have been Lillie's twin, so much did they resemble each other, even down to a black streak that ran from shoulder to rump.

"Do you ride, sir?" Raistlin asked, astonished.

Horkin was a thoroughgoing soldier, as the saying went. He had once by his own account force-marched seventy miles in one day carrying a full pack. Thirty miles per day was a stroll in the garden, according to Horkin.

"You are riding this time for my sake, aren't you, sir?" the young mage asked coldly.

Horkin placed a kindly hand on Raistlin's thin shoulder. "Red, you're my apprentice. And I'm honest when I say this. I really don't give a damn about you. I'm riding because I have a reason for riding, a reason you'll see in the morning. You could be of some assistance to me, but if you choose to march—"

"I'll ride, sir," Raistlin said, smiling.

Horkin left for the comfort of his bedroll. Raistlin remained behind, making friends with Lillie and wondering what perverse twist in his nature made him resent Caramon for caring and respect Horkin for not caring.

If Raistlin thought he was going to have an easy time of it, he learned his mistake the very next day. The two mages rode at the rear of the long column, alongside the supply wagons. Raistlin was enjoying the ride, enjoying the warm sunshine, when suddenly Horkin gave a wild shout and jerked on the reins, turned his donkey's head so violently that the animal brayed in protest. Kicking the donkey in the flanks, Horkin plunged recklessly off the trail, shouting for Raistlin to follow.

Raistlin did not have much say in the matter for Lillie did not like to be parted from her stablemate. The donkey trotted after Horkin and carried Raistlin with her. The two donkeys crashed through brush, stumbled down a steep gully, and dashed off across a meadow of clover.

"What is it, sir?" Raistlin cried.

He jounced uncomfortably on the donkey, whose gait was far different from that of a horse, his robes flapping around him, his hair streaming out behind. He was certain that Horkin was on the trail of nothing less than an army of goblins, and that his master intended on taking them on single-handed. Raistlin glanced back over his shoulder, hoping to see the rest of the army come racing along behind.

The rest of the army was, by now, out of sight.

"Sir! Where are you going?" Raistlin demanded.

He finally caught up, not through his own doing but because Lillie, apparently a most competitive animal, could not tolerate being left behind.

"Daisies!" Horkin shouted triumphantly, pointing to a field of white. He spurred his donkey on to greater efforts.

"Daisies!" Raistlin muttered, but he didn't have time for wonderment. Lillie had once again entered the race.

Horkin halted his donkey in the very midst of the field of white and yellow flowers, jumped from the saddle.

"C'mon, Red! Get off your ass!" Horkin grinned at his little joke. Grabbing an empty gunnysack from his saddle roll, he tossed it to Raistlin, took another for himself. "No time to waste. Pick the flowers and the leaves. We'll use both."

"I know that the daisy is good for easing coughs," Raistlin said, plucking flowers most industriously. "But none of the soldiers are currently suffering—"

"The daisy is what's known as a battlefield herb, Red," Horkin explained. "Grind it up, make an ointment from it, spread it on wounds, and it keeps them from putrefying."

"I didn't know this, sir," said Raistlin, gratified at learning something new.

They gathered the daisies and also some of the clover, which was good for wounds and other complaints. On the way back, Horkin again veered from the road, galloped off in search of brambles, which he said he used to cure the soldier's most common complaint—dysentery. Now Raistlin understood the need for the donkeys. By the time the two mages had completed their foraging, the army was miles ahead of them. They rode all afternoon just to catch up.

Their work did not end at night, for after a day spent in backbreaking labor harvesting the plants, Horkin ordered Raistlin to pluck the petals from the flowers or boil the leaves or pound roots into pulp. Tired as he was—and Raistlin could not remember ever feeling so exhausted— he took care each night before he slept to write down in a small book all that he had learned that day.

He had no rest on those days when their herbal work was done, for if he was not picking flowers, he was practicing his spell-casting. Prior to this time, Raistlin had always been fussily particular about his spells. He did not say the words until he was certain he could correctly pronounce each one. He did not cast the spell until he knew he could cast it perfectly. Speed was what counted now. He had to cast his spell fast, without taking time to think whether an "a" was pronounced "aaa" or "ah." He had to know the spell so well that he could recite the words rapidly, without thinking, without making a mistake. Trying to speak the words rapidly, Raistlin stammered and stuttered as badly as he had when he was eight years old. In fact, he told himself morosely, he'd said the words better at eight!

One might imagine that such practice was easy, a simple matter of repeating the words over and over as an actor memorizes his script. But an actor has the advantage of being able to rehearse his lines aloud no matter where he is, whereas the mage cannot, for fear of inadvertently casting the spell.

Raistlin was galled by the fact that Horkin—a mage of far less skill and learning—could say a spell so swiftly that Raistlin had a difficult time understanding him, cast the spell with never a miss. Raistlin persisted in his own practicing with grim determination. Whenever he had a free moment, he took himself off into the woods where he wouldn't hurt anyone if he did manage to cast an "incendiary projectile" in less than three seconds, which at this juncture did not appear likely.

His days taken up with backbreaking labor, his nights with concocting medicines and potions, writing, and studying, Raistlin was amazed that he had not collapsed from fatigue. But, in fact, he had never felt so well, so alive and interested in life. Long accustomed to holding himself up for self-evaluation, Raistlin came to the conclusion that he thrived on activity, both physical and mental; that without something to keep him occupied, his brain and body both stagnated. He coughed less frequently, though when the spasms came, they were unusually painful.

He even found Caramon less doltish than usual. Every night Raistlin joined his brother and his friend Scrounger for a supper of stewed chicken and hardtack. He actually enjoyed himself and found that he looked forward to their company.

As for Caramon, he was delighted at the change in his brother and, with his usual easygoing nature, did not spend time wondering at or questioning it. The night when Raistlin actually did manage to cast a fiery bolt, not once, but three times in rapid succession, he was so jovial during supper that Caramon secretly suspected his twin of imbibing dwarf spirits.

The march to Hope's End proceeded without incident. Company C, riding as advance scouts for the army, arrived within sight of the city on the appointed day to find the army of Good King Wilhelm camped outside the walls. The air was gray with the stench of burning, the sounds of shrieks and screams sounded eerily out of the smoke.

"Is the battle over, sir?" Caramon asked in dismay, thinking he'd missed it.

Sergeant Nemiss stood in the shadow of a large maple tree, blinking away the stinging smoke, trying to see through the pall that hung over the valley to determine what was happening. Her men gathered around her, keeping themselves concealed at the edge of the tree line.

Sergeant Nemiss shook her head. "No, we haven't missed the fight, Majere. Pah! The stuff gets in your mouth!" She swigged water from her canteen, spit on the ground.

"What's on fire, sir?" Scrounger peered into the smoke and falling ash. "What's burning?"

"They're looting the countryside," Sergeant Nemiss replied, after another drink of water. "Looting the homes and barns and setting fire to what they can't carry off. Those screams you hear—those are the women they've captured."

"Bastards!" Caramon said, his face pale. He licked dry lips, felt as though he might be sick. He had never before heard the cries of a person in torment. He gripped his sword hilt, rattled the blade in its sheath. "We'll make them pay!"

Sergeant Nemiss fixed him with an ironic eye. "Afraid not, Majere," she said dryly. "Those are our gallant allies."

* * * * *

The baron's army established camp with disciplined efficiency, under the critical eye of the baron's second-in-command, Commander Morgon. Caramon and his company stood guard duty around the camp's perimeter. Danger would presumably come from the direction of the city, but the guards' gaze shifted constantly between the city and the camp of their allies.

"What did the baron say?" Caramon asked Scrounger, who was making the rounds of the guard posts with the waterskin.

Scrounger had yet another talent besides deal making. He was a remarkable eavesdropper, a talent that amazed everyone, since eavesdropping is perhaps the one and only fault not generally consigned to kender.

A kender overhearing a conversation feels compelled to join that conversation, deeming that he has valuable information to share on the subject under discussion, no matter how personal or private that subject may be. Whereas a good eavesdropper must be silent, circumspect. When asked how he managed to come by such skills, Scrounger said that he thought it came from deal making, wherein it is always more profitable to keep the ears open and the mouth closed.

A good eavesdropper must also be in the right place at the right time in order to see and hear to best advantage. How Scrounger managed to be in all the places he managed to be in to hear all the information he managed to hear was a marvel and a wonder to his comrades. They soon ceased to question how he came to know, however, and relied on him for information.

Scrounger reported on the conversation he'd overheard while Caramon drank the warm and brackish water thirstily. "Sergeant Nemiss told the baron that the soldiers of King Wilhelm were looting and burning the countryside. The baron said to Sergeant Nemiss, 'This is their country. Their people. They know best how to deal with the situation. The city is in rebellion. It must be taught a lesson, a hard lesson and a swift one, or the other cities in the kingdom will see that they can flout authority with imp . . . impunity. As for us, we've been hired to do a job and by the gods we're going to do it.'"

"Huh." Caramon grunted. "And what did Sergeant Nemiss say?"

"'Yes, my lord.'" Scrounger grinned.

"I mean *after* she left the baron's tent."

"You know I never use language like that," Scrounger said mockingly and, hefting the heavy waterskin, he trudged off to the next guard post.

Raistlin had no leisure to sit and ponder the odd ways of their allies. He was kept busy the moment the army arrived, assisting Horkin in setting up the war wizard's tent, which was a smaller and cruder version of Horkin's laboratory. In addition to concocting the components they used for spells, the two mages also worked with the baron's surgeon, or "leech" as he was fondly known among the troops, to provide medicines and ointments.

Currently empty, the surgeon's tent would soon be used to shelter the wounded. Raistlin had brought with him several jars of ointment, along with instructions for their use. The surgeon was busy arranging his tools, however, and curtly bade Raistlin to wait.

The tent was neat and clean and lined with cots, so that the wounded would not be forced to sleep on the ground. Raistlin examined the tools—the saw for amputating shattered limbs, the sharp knife used to cut out arrow points. He looked at the beds and suddenly he saw Caramon lying there. His brother was white-faced, beads of sweat on his forehead. They had tied his arms to the bed with leather cord and two strong men, the surgeon's assistants, were holding him down. His leg bone was shattered below the knee, broken bone protruded from the torn flesh, blood covered the bed. Caramon, breathing harshly, was begging his brother for help.

"Raist! Don't let them!" Caramon cried through teeth clenched against the pain. "Don't let them cut off my leg!"

"Hold him tight, boys," the surgeon said and lifted his saw. . . .

"You all right, Wizard? Here, you better lie down."

The surgeon's assistant hovered near him, his hand on Raistlin's arm.

Raistlin cast a glance at the cot and shuddered. "I am perfectly all right, thank you," he said.

The blood-tinged mists cleared from his eyes, the bursting stars vanished, the sick feeling passed. He pushed aside the assistant's solicitous hand and left the tent, forcing himself to walk calmly and slowly, with no unseemly show of haste. Once outside, he drew in a deep breath of smoke-tinged air and almost immediately began to cough. Still, even tainted air was preferable to the stifling atmosphere inside that tent.

"It must have been the stuffiness that overcame me," Raistlin told himself, ashamed and scornful of his weakness. "That and an overactive imagination."

He tried to banish the picture from his mind, but the image of Caramon's suffering had been extremely vivid.

Since the picture would not fade, Raistlin made himself look at it long and hard. He watched in his mind's eye as the surgeon took off Caramon's leg, watched his brother linger for days in terrible agony, healing slowly. He watched his brother being carried back to the baron's castle in a wagon with other wounded. Watched his brother living the rest of his life as a cripple, his hale body wasting away beneath the pitying stares of their friends. . . .

"You would know how I feel then, my brother," Raistlin said grimly.

Realizing what he'd said and what he'd meant by saying it, he shivered.

"By the gods!" he murmured, appalled. "What am I thinking? Have I sunk so low? Am I so mean-spirited? Do I hate him that much?

"No." Raistlin thought back to those few terrible moments in the tent. "No, I am not quite such a monster as that." His mouth twisted in a rueful smile. "I cannot imagine him in pain without feeling anguish. And yet at the same time, I cannot imagine him in pain without feeling vengeful satisfaction. What black spot on my soul—"

"Red!"

Horkin's voice boomed behind him, startling him like a sudden and unexpected drum roll. Raistlin blinked. He had been so preoccupied with his thoughts that he'd walked into the war wizard's tent without even being aware of it.

Horkin stood glaring.

"What's the matter with the ointment? Wasn't it what he wanted?" Horkin demanded. "Didn't you tell him what it was for?"

Raistlin looked down at his hands to discover he was clutching a jar of ointment with a grip Death might have envied. "I . . . That is . . . yes, he was quite pleased. He wants more, in fact," Raistlin stammered, adding, "I'll make it up myself, sir. I know how busy you are."

"Why in the name of Luni did you bring this one back?" Horkin grumbled. "Why not just leave it there for him to use until you can make up the other?"

"I'm sorry, sir," Raistlin said contritely. "I guess I didn't think of that."

Horkin eyed him. "You think too goddam much, Red. That's your trouble. You're not being paid to think. *I'm* being paid to think. You're being paid to do whatever it is I think up. Now just quit thinking and we'll get along much better."

"Yes, sir," Raistlin said with more obedience than he usually showed to his master. He found it suddenly refreshing to let go all his tormenting thoughts, watch them drift away on the air currents like so much thistledown.

"I'll bring in the rest of the supplies. You start on that ointment." Horkin paused at the tent flap, gazed loweringly at the city. "The Leech must figure it's going to be a bloody battle if he's stocking up on war-flower cream." Shaking his head, he left the tent.

Raistlin, as ordered, refused to let himself think. Reaching for the mortar and pestle, he began to crush daisies.

3

There were many alehouses in the city of Hope's End. The name of this particular alehouse, an alehouse discovered by Kitiara on her arrival to the doomed city, was the Gibbous Moon.

The tavern's signage featured a picture of a man hanging from a rope, a picture done in lurid colors—the man's face was particularly gruesome—set against the backdrop of a bright yellow moon. What the hanging had to do with the alehouse's name was anybody's guess. Popular opinion held that the owner had mixed up the word "gibbous" with the word "gibbet," but this the owner always vehemently denied, though he could give no reason for the noose's presence, other than that "it attracted notice."

Swinging in the breeze very like the noose it portrayed, the sign brought many a passerby up short, caused many to stare in wide-eyed wonder, but whether or not it induced those same passersby to taste the food or sample the ale of a place denoted by a dangling corpse was another matter. The tavern was not exactly overwhelmed with customers.

The owner complained that this was due to the fact that the other tavern owners in town were "out to get him." It should be noted that this was not necessarily true. In addition to being cursed with the stomach-turning sign, the Gibbous Moon was situated in the oldest part of the city, located at the very end of a crooked street lined with abandoned, tumbledown buildings, far away from the marketplace, the merchant streets, and

Tavern Row.

The tavern was not prepossessing in appearance, being a mass of ill-assorted wooden planks topped by a wood shingle roof and not a single window, unless you counted the hole in the front of the alehouse where two of the planks were not on speaking terms and refused to have anything to do with one another. The building looked as if had been washed down the street in a flash flood, coming to rest smashed up against the side of the retaining wall. According to local legend, this was precisely what had occurred.

Kitiara liked the Gibbous Moon. She had searched all over the city for a place like this, something "out of the way" where a "body could find some peace and quiet," where a "person wasn't pestered to death by barmaids wanting to know if you wanted another ale."

The few customers of the Gibbous Moon did not have to put up with this inconvenience. The Gibbous Moon employed no barmaids. The tavern's owner, who was his own best customer, was generally in such a sodden stupor that the guests ended up serving themselves. One would think that this would be an open invitation to the unscrupulous to drink up their ale and leave without paying. The owner cleverly thwarted this practice by making the ale undrinkable, so that even though it might be free, it was still considered a bad bargain.

"You could not have found a more wretched pesthouse if you had searched the length and breadth of the Abyss," Immolatus complained.

He sat on the very edge of a chair, having already removed one splinter from his soft, squishy, and easily damaged human flesh. He deeply regretted the loss of his own steel-hard, shining red scales. "A demon who has spent tortured eternity roasting over hot coals would turn up his nose at the offer of a mug of that liquid, which has undoubtedly come from a horse who died of kidney disease."

"You don't have to drink it, Your Eminence," Kitiara returned testily. She was highly irritated with her companion. "Due to your 'disguise,' this is the only place in town where we can talk without having the people in the city staring at us and breathing down our necks."

She lifted the cracked mug. Ale slowly dribbled onto the floor. Kit tasted it, spit it out, and hastened the process by upending the mug. This done, she reached into her boot, removed a flask of brandy purchased from a more reputable tavern, and drank a swig. She returned the flask to her boot, not offering any to her companion, a mark of her displeasure.

"Well, Eminence," she demanded, "have you found anything? Any trace? Any hint? Any *eggs?*"

"No, I have not," Immolatus replied coolly. "I have searched every cavern I could find in these godforsaken mountains, and I can state categorically that there are no dragon eggs hidden anywhere there."

"You've searched *every* cavern?" Kitiara was skeptical.

"That I could find," Immolatus replied.

Kit was grim. "You know how important this is to Her Majesty—"

"The eggs are not hidden in any of the caverns I searched," said Immolatus.

"Her Majesty's information—" Kit began.

"Is accurate. There are eggs of the metallics hidden in the mountains. I can feel them, smell them. Gaining access to them—that's the trick. The location of the entrance to the cave is well hidden, cleverly concealed."

"Good! Now we're getting somewhere. Where is this entrance?"

"Here," said Immolatus. "In the city itself."

"Bah!" Kit snorted. "I admit that I know nothing about these so-called metallic dragons, but I can't picture them calmly laying their eggs in the middle of the town square!"

"You are right," Immolatus replied. "You know nothing about dragons. Period. May I remind you, worm, that this city is ancient, that this city was here when Huma the Accursed crawled, sluglike, upon the land. This city was here in an age and time when dragons—all dragons, chromatic and metallic—were revered, honored, feared.

Perhaps I even flew over this city once in my youth," the dragon said, gazing dreamily into the distant past. "Perhaps I considered attacking it. The presence of the metallics would explain why I did not. . . ."

Kit drummed her fingers upon the table. "So what are you saying, Eminence? That gold dragons perched on the rooftops like storks? That silver dragons cackled in coops?"

Immolatus rose to his feet, fire-eyed and quivering. "You will learn to speak of even my enemies with respect—"

"Listen to me, Eminence!" Kit returned, rising to face him, her fingers curling over the hilt of her sword, "The army of Lord Ariakas has this city surrounded. Commander Kholos is preparing to attack. I'm not sure when, but it's going to be soon. I've seen what the fools in this city term their defenses. I have a pretty good idea how long this wretched place can hold out. I also know some of Commander Kholos's plans for the assault. Believe me, we don't want to be caught inside this city when that happens."

"The dragon eggs are in the mountains," said Immolatus. He grimaced, wrinkled his nose. "Somewhere. I can sense them, the way one senses a fungus beneath one's scales. It starts with an itching that you can't quite locate. Sometimes you don't feel it for days, and then one night you wake up in torment. Every time I left the city, the itch faded away. When I returned, it was strong, overpowering."

He began to absentmindedly scratch at the back of his palm. "The eggs are near here. And I will find them."

Kitiara dug her nails into her palms so that she wouldn't dig them into the dragon's throat. He'd wasted precious time on some fool kender chase! And now, when time was critical . . . Well, there was no help for it. What can't be cured must be endured, as the gnome said when he got his head stuck in his revolutionary new steampowered grape press.

Having mastered her anger, or at least tamped it down into her belly, Kitiara muttered in no very good humor, "Well, what now, Eminence?"

They were the only customers in the alehouse. The owner had drunk himself into oblivion by suppertime and now lay sprawled upon the bar, his head on his arms. A dust-covered ray of sunshine filtered through the quarreling planks, wavered, and vanished as if appalled to find it had accidentally ventured inside.

"We have a day or two at the most remaining to us," Kitiara said. "We have to be out of here before the first assault."

Immolatus stood by the bar, frowning down at a rivulet of ale leaking from a sprung cask, forming a small pool on the hard-packed dirt floor. "Where is the old part of the city, Worm?"

Kitiara was growing extremely tired of being called that. The next time he did so, she was tempted to shove that word down his throat.

"What do you take me for, Eminence? Some ink-smeared historian from the Great Library? How should I know?"

"You've been here long enough," the dragon stated. "You might have noticed such things."

"And so should you, you arrogant—"

Kitiara washed down the next few highly descriptive adjectives with another gulp of brandy from the boot flask. This time she didn't put the flask away but left it out on the table.

Immolatus, whose hearing was excellent, smiled to himself. He grabbed hold of the lank and greasy hair of the bartender and jerked his head up off the counter.

"Slug! Wake up!" Immolatus banged the man's head several times upon the counter. "Listen to me! I have a question for you." He thumped the man's head a few more times.

The bartender winced, groaned, and opened bleary, bloodshot eyes. "Huh?"

"Where are the oldest buildings in town?"

Bang went the man's head on the counter.

"Where are they located?"

The bartender squinted, gazed up at Immolatus in drunken confusion. "Don't shout! Gods! My head hurts!

The oldest buildings are on the west side. Near the old temple . . ."

"Temple!" Immolatus said. "What temple? To what god?"

"HowshouldIknow?" the man mumbled.

"A fine specimen," Immolatus said irritably and lifted the man's head again.

"What are you doing?" Kit was on her feet.

"Humanity a favor!" Immolatus stated and, with a jerk of his hand, he snapped the man's neck.

"That was brilliant," Kitiara said, exasperated. "How are we supposed to find out anything from him now?"

"I don't need him." Immolatus headed for the door.

"But what do we do with the body?" Kit asked, hesitating. "Someone might have seen us. I don't want to be arrested for murder!"

"Leave it," said the dragon. He cast a scathing look back at the dead bartender, slumped over his bar. "No one's likely to notice the change."

"Ariakas, you owe me!" Kit muttered, trailing Immolatus. "You owe me big. I expect to be made a regimental commander after this!"

4

he streets grew narrower and more crooked, the crowds thinned. Kitiara and the dragon had entered the old part of Hope's End. Most of the original homes and dwellings had been torn down, their stone used to make the large warehouses and granaries that replaced them. By day, tradesmen came and went. By night, vermin—both four-legged and two-legged—were the primary occupants. On rare occasions, the lord mayor, in a fit of energy and civic pride, would order the sheriff and his men to descend on the warehouse district and evict those who sought refuge there, ferreting them out of the nooks and crannies where they lay hidden.

With the coming of war, most of the two-legged vermin had abandoned ship, fleeing to safer cities. Since the warehouses held nothing in them anymore, no tradesmen walked the streets or made deals on the street corners. This part of town, the west side, was empty and deserted, or so it appeared. Still, Kit kept a watchful eye out. She couldn't imagine what Immolatus hoped to find here, unless he had some notion that the dragons had stored their eggs in a warehouse.

The day was almost finished, the sun setting in a haze of smoke from the burned fields beyond the city walls. The shadows of the mountain fell across the city, bringing early night with them. Immolatus finally called a halt, but only, it seemed to Kit, because he'd run out of street.

The dragon appeared immensely pleased with himself however. "Ah, just as I expected."

The street ran headlong into a high crumbling granite wall, or so it appeared. Catching up with the dragon, Kitiara saw that she'd been mistaken. The street actually passed through the wall, in between two tall pillars. Rusted holes in the rock indicated that iron gates might have been used to control the flow of traffic in and out of the area. Looking through the entryway, Kitiara saw a courtyard and a building.

"What is this place?" Kitiara asked, regarding the building with a disparaging frown.

"A temple. A temple to the gods. Or perhaps I should say a temple to one god." Immolatus cast the building a look of pure loathing.

"Are you sure?" Kit said, comparing it unfavorably to the grand Temple of Leurkhisis. "It's so small and . . . shabby."

"Rather like the god himself." Immolatus sneered.

The temple was small. Thirty paces would take Kit from the front to the back. In the front, three broad steps led to a narrow porch under a roof supported by six slender columns. Two windows looked out upon a courtyard paved with broken flagstones. Chickweed and some sort of choking vine were growing through the cracks. Here and there, among the weeds, a few wild rosebushes still flourished, climbing up the wall surrounding the courtyard. The roses were tiny and white and caught the last rays of the sun, the blossoms seemed to almost glow in the twilight. The roses filled the air with a sweet, spicy scent, which the dragon found offensive, for he coughed and snorted and covered his nose and mouth with his sleeve.

The temple was made of granite, and had once been covered with marble on the outside. A few slabs of marble—yellow-stained and damaged—still remained. Most of the other marble slabs had been torn off, used elsewhere. The front doors were cast in gold, they gleamed in the sunlight. A frieze, carved around the sides of the building, was almost completely obliterated, scarred with deep gouges, as if it had been attacked by picks and hammers. What images it had once portrayed had been erased.

"Eminence, how do you know what god this temple was built to honor?" Kitiara asked. "I see no writing, no symbols, nothing to indicate the name of the god."

"I know," said Immolatus, and his voice grated.

Kitiara walked past the stone pillars into the courtyard to gain a better view. The golden doors were dented and battered. She wondered that the doors were still there at all, that they hadn't been melted down for their value. Admittedly gold wasn't worth much these days, not as much as the far more practical steel. No one ever marched to war with a sword made of gold. Still, if those doors were solid gold, they would be worth something. She would remember to tell Commander Kholos, advise him to take the doors with him when he left the city.

She could see a slight crack between the two golden doors, realized that they stood partially open. Kit had the strangest idea that she was being welcomed, invited to come inside. The idea was repugnant to her. She had the strong impression that something in there wanted something from her, was out to rob her of something precious. The temple had probably become a haunt for thieves.

"What was the god called, Eminence?" Kit asked.

The dragon opened his mouth to reply, then snapped it shut. "I won't foul my mouth by pronouncing his name."

Kit smiled derisively. "One would almost think you were afraid of this god, who obviously isn't around anymore."

"Don't underestimate him," Immolatus snarled. "He's sneaky. His name is Paladine. There! I've said it and I curse it!"

A gout of flame burst from his mouth, flared briefly on the broken flagstones of the empty courtyard, burned a few weeds, then flickered out.

Kit hoped to heaven no one had seen the tantrum. Red-robed wizards, even the greatest of them, are not known to be able to spit fire.

"Well, I've never heard of him," said Kit.

"You are a worm," said Immolatus.

Kit's hand clenched over the hilt of her sword. Dragon he might be, but he was in human form, and she guessed that it would take him a moment or two to change from clothes to scales. In that moment, she could strike him dead.

"Calm down, Kit," she remonstrated with herself. "Remember all the trouble it cost you to find the beast and bring him to Ariakas. Don't let him provoke you. He wants to lash out at something, and I don't blame him. This place is unnerving."

She was starting to have an active dislike for her surroundings. There was a serenity, a peacefulness about the temple and the grounds, which she found annoying. Kitiara was not one to waste time pondering the complexities of life. Life was meant to be lived, not contemplated.

She was reminded, suddenly, of Tanis. He would have liked this place, she thought disdainfully. He would have been content here, sitting on the cracked front steps, gazing up at the sky, asking questions of the stars, foolish questions to which there could be no answer. Why was there death in the world? What happened after death? Why did people suffer? Why was there evil? Why had the gods abandoned them?

As far as Kit was concerned, the world was the way the world was. Seize your part of it, make of that part what you could, leave the rest to take care of itself. Kit had no patience with Tanis's cobweb spinning, as she termed it. His image, coming to her unbidden and unwanted, further increased her irritation.

"Well, this has been a waste of time!" she stated. "Let's leave before Kholos starts flinging molten rocks over the wall."

"No," said Immolatus, glowering at the temple and gnawing his lip. "The eggs are there. They are inside."

"You're not serious!" Kitiara stared at him incredulously. "How big are these golden dragons? Are they as big as you?"

"Perhaps," said Immolatus disdainfully. He rolled his eyes, refused to look at her, gazed off into the haze-filled sunset. "I never paid them that much attention."

"Hunh," Kit grunted. "And you expect me to believe that a creature as big or bigger than you crawled into that building"—she jabbed a finger at it—"and laid eggs inside!" Her patience snapped. "I think you're playing me for a fool. You and Lord Ariakas and Queen Takhisis! I'm finished with the lot of you."

She turned away, started back down the dead-end street.

"If the pea that you term a brain weren't rattling around inside your skull, banging off the walls, and caroming into dark corners, the truth might occur to you," said Immolatus. "The eggs were laid in the mountains and then the entrance sealed up and a watch placed on them. The temple is the guardhouse, as it were. The fools thought they would be safe here, that they would escape our knowledge. Probably intended that the priests would remain to guard them. But the priests fled before the mobs, either that or they were killed. Now no one remains to guard the eggs. No one."

The dragon's reasoning was highly logical. Turning back to face him, Kitiara surreptitiously sheathed her sword, trusting he hadn't noticed she'd drawn it.

"All right, Lord. You enter the temple, find the eggs, count them, identify them, or do whatever it is you're supposed to do with them. I will stay here and keep watch."

"On the contrary," said Immolatus, "you will enter the temple and search for the eggs. I'm certain there must be a tunnel leading to hatching chambers. Once you have found it, follow the tunnel until you discover the second entrance in the mountains. Then report back to me."

"It is not my responsibility to search for the eggs, Eminence," Kitiara returned grimly. "I don't even know what dragon eggs look like. I don't 'sense' them or smell them or whatever it is you do. This is your assignment, given to you by Queen Takhisis."

"Her Majesty could not have foreseen that the eggs would be guarded by a Temple of Paladine." Immolatus cast the temple a baleful glance. His eyes, slits of red, slid back to Kit. "I cannot go. I cannot enter."

"You won't, you mean!" Kitiara was angry.

"No, I cannot," Immolatus said. He crossed his arms over his chest, hugging his elbows. "He won't let me," he added in sulking tones, like a child banished from a game of goblin ball.

"Who won't?" Kit demanded.

"Paladine."

"Paladine! The old god?" Kit was amazed. "I thought you said he was gone."

"I thought he was. Her Majesty assured me he was." Immolatus breathed a flicker of fire. "But now I'm not so certain. It wouldn't be the first time she has lied to me." He snapped his teeth viciously. "All I know is that I cannot enter that temple. If I tried, he would kill me."

"Oh, but he'll let *me* just walk right in!"

"You are only a human. He cares nothing about you, knows nothing of you. You should have no difficulty. And if you do find trouble, I'm certain you are capable of dealing with whatever you encounter. I've seen the way you handle your sword." Immolatus grinned at her discomfiture. "And now, uth Matar, you really should be on your way. As you keep reminding me, we haven't much time. I will meet you back at Commander Kholos's camp. Remember, find the chamber where the eggs are located and the entrance in the mountains. Mark down everything in this book."

He handed her a small leather-bound volume. "And don't dawdle. This wretched city upsets my digestion."

He walked away. Kitiara permitted herself a fond image of the tip of her blade protruding from beneath the dragon's breastbone, the hilt buried in his back. She stood in the broken courtyard, enjoying the vision for long moments after the dragon had departed. Various wild thoughts entered her head. She would leave, abandon Immolatus and her mission. The hell with Ariakas, the hell with the dragonarmy. She had done well enough without them, she didn't need them, any of them.

An aching in her hand, clenched over the hilt of her sword, brought her to her senses. She had but to look out over the walls to see the myriad campfires of the army of General Ariakas, campfires whose numbers were almost as great as the stars above. And this army was but a fraction of his might. Someday he would rule all of Ansalon and she intended to rule at his side. Or perhaps in his stead. One never knew. And she would not achieve these goals, any one of them, as an itinerant sell-sword.

Which meant that, god or no god, she had to go into that blasted temple, a place that seemed so welcoming and yet at the same time filled her with a strange, cold fear, a dread foreboding.

"Bah!" said Kitiara and walked quickly across the broken courtyard.

She climbed the two stairs leading to the battered golden doors, halted at the top to have a brief argument with herself concerning this unreasoning terror, which only seemed to grow worse the closer she came to the temple.

Kitiara peered inside the opening between the doors, stared into the darkness beyond. She watched and listened. She no longer believed that thieves might be using this temple as a hideout, not unless they were thieves made of sterner stuff than herself. But Something was inside that temple and whatever the Something was, it had scared away a red dragon, one of the most powerful creatures on Krynn.

She saw nothing, but that meant nothing. The deepest night was not so dark, the Dark Queen's heart was not so dark, as this abandoned temple. Berating herself for not bringing along a torch, Kit was startled past all amazement when silver light flared suddenly, dazzling and half-blinding her.

Drawing her sword from the scabbard, she fell back on the defensive. She held her ground, she did not leave, though a panicked voice—the same voice of unreasoning fear—cried out to her to abandon the mission and run away, run far away.

Just like the dragon.

He fled. A creature far more dangerous, far more deadly, a creature far stronger than I am, Kitiara thought. Why should I go where Immolatus will not? He is not my commander. He cannot order me. So I return to General Ariakas a failure. I can lay the blame on Immolatus. Ariakas will understand. It is the dragon's fault. . . .

Kitiara stood inside the golden doors, hesitating, wavering, listening gladly to the cowardly voice inside her and hating herself for actually giving serious consideration to its suggestions. Never before had she experienced fear like this. She had never imagined that anything could frighten her so much.

If she turned and walked away, every moment from this moment until the time of her death, she would see this place whenever she closed her eyes. She would relive her fear, relive her shame, relive her cowardice. She could not live with herself. Far better to end it right now.

Sword in hand, she took a step forward into the bright, silver light.

A barrier—invisible, wispy, thin as cobweb, yet strong, as though the web had been spun from strands of steel—stretched across her chest. She pushed against it, but found her way blocked. She could not pass.

A man's voice, low and resolute, spoke from the darkness. "Enter, friend, and welcome. But first lay down your weapon. Within these walls is a sanctuary of peace."

Kitiara's breath caught in her constricting throat, her sword hand shook. The barrier kept her out, and her first thought was one of relief. Angered, she retained hold on her sword, shoved against the barrier.

"I warn you," said the man, and his voice was not threatening, but filled with compassion, "that if you enter this holy place with the purpose of doing violence, you will start down a road that will lead to your own destruction. Lay down the weapon and enter in peace and you will be welcome."

"You must take me for a fool to think I would give up my only means of defense," Kitiara called out, trying to see the person speaking, unable to make him out against the bright light.

"You have nothing to fear inside this temple except what you yourself bring into it," the voice returned.

"And what I'm bringing into it is my sword," Kitiara said. She took a resolute step forward.

The bands pressed tight across her chest, as if they would cut into her flesh, but she did not yield. The pressure melted away with such swiftness that she was caught unsuspecting and stumbled forward into the temple, almost falling. Catlike, she regained her balance and looked swiftly about her, pivoting, holding her sword before her, prepared for an attack. She looked to the front, to either side, behind.

Nothing. No one. The silver light, which had blinded her outside the temple, was soft and diffused now that she was inside. The light illuminated all within; she could see every detail of the temple's interior in the eerie glow. Kitiara would have preferred the darkness. The light had no source that she could locate, it seemed to radiate from the walls.

The main room of the temple was rectangular in shape, devoid of decoration, and it was empty. No altar stood in front, no statue of the god, no braziers for incense, no chairs, no tables. No column cast a shadow in which an assassin could lurk. Nothing here was hidden. In the silver-white light, she could see everything.

Set in the eastern wall, the wall that butted up against the mountain, was another large door, a door made of silver. Immolatus had been right, curse him. This door must lead to the caverns within the mountain. She looked for a lock or a bolt, but saw none. The door had no handle, no means of opening. There must be a way, she had only to discover it. But she didn't want to leave an unknown enemy behind her.

"Where are you?" Kitiara demanded. The idea came to her that perhaps her enemy had absconded through the silver door. "Come out, you coward. Show yourself!"

"I stand here beside you," said the voice. "If you cannot see me, it is because you yourself are blind. Put down your sword and you will see my hand outstretched."

"Yes, with a dagger in it," Kitiara returned scornfully. "Ready to kill me once you have disarmed me."

"I repeat, friend, that whatever evil is here you have brought with you. Only the treacherous fear treachery."

Impatient at talking with empty air, Kitiara aimed at the sound of the voice, sliced her sword through what should have been the gut of her invisible enemy.

The blade met no resistance, but a paralyzing shock, as if the metal had come in contact with a lightning bolt, jolted through her sword arm. Her hand and fingers stung, a tingling sensation flashed from her palm up her arm. She gasped in pain, very nearly dropped the weapon.

"What have you done to me?" she cried angrily, clutching at the sword with both hands. "What magic do you use against me?"

"I have done nothing to you, friend. What you do, you do to yourself."

"This is some sort of spell! Coward wizard! Face me and fight!"

She whipped the blade through the air again, slashing and cutting.

The pain was like a streak of fire burning her arm. The hilt of the sword grew hot to the touch, hot as if it had come straight from the blacksmith's white-hot forge. Kitiara could not hold on to it. She flung the sword to the floor with a cry, nursed her burned hand.

"I tried to warn you, friend." The voice was sad and sorrowful. "You have taken the first steps upon the path of your own destruction. Leave now, and you may still avoid your doom."

"I am not your friend," Kitiara hissed through teeth gritted against the pain of the burn. A red and blistering welt in the shape of the sword hilt was visible on her palm. "All right, wizard. I've dropped the damn sword. Let me see you, at least!"

He stood before her. Not a wizard, as she had expected, but a Knight in silver armor, armor that was outdated and outmoded, heavy armor of a type worn about the time of the Cataclysm. The helm had no hinged visor, as did modern helms, but was made of one piece of metal and did not cover the mouth or the front of the neck.

Over his armor, the Knight wore a surcoat of white cloth on which was embroidered a kingfisher bird carrying a sword in one claw and a rose in the other. His body had a shimmering quality, was almost translucent.

For a moment Kitiara's courage failed her. Now she knew why Immolatus had not entered the temple. The temple would be guarded, he had said. What he had not said was that it would be guarded by the dead!

"I never believed in ghosts," Kit muttered to herself, "but then I never believed in dragons either. My bad luck both had to come true."

She could turn tail and run, probably should run. Unfortunately her feet were too busy shaking to do much in the way of fleeing.

"Pull yourself together, Kit!" she commanded. "It's a ghost now, but it used to be a man. And the man hasn't been born you can't handle. He was a Knight, a Solamnic. They're usually so bound up in honor that it's hard for them to take a crap. I don't suppose death would change that."

Kitiara tried to see the eyes of the spirit-knight, for an enemy's eyes will often give away his next point of attack. The Knight's eyes were not visible, however, concealed in the shadow cast by the overhanging helm. His voice sounded neither young nor old.

Forcing her stiff lips into a charming smile, Kit glanced around, located her sword lying on the floor. She could fight with her other hand, her uninjured hand, if need arose. A quick stoop, reach, grab, and she'd have her weapon again.

"A Knight!" Kitiara breathed a mock sigh of relief. She'd be damned if she was going to let this ghost know he had frightened her. "Am I glad to see you!"

She moved a step nearer the spirit, a move that she didn't want to make, but which brought her a step nearer her sword. "Listen to me, Sir Knight. Watch yourself! There is evil in this place."

"Indeed there is," said the Knight.

He did not move, but stood set and still. His fixed and unwavering attention was disconcerting.

"I guess whatever was in here has gone for the time being," Kit continued, favoring him with her crooked smile and an arch look. She was growing bolder. If the ghost meant to harm her, it would have done so before now. "You probably frightened it away. It will likely be back, however. We will fight it together, then, you and I. I will need my sword—"

"I will fight the evil with you," said the Knight. "But you do not need your sword."

"Damn it!" Kit began angrily and bit her lips to halt her hasty words.

She had to find a way to distract the spirit for only a few seconds, long enough for her to recover her sword.

"What are you doing here, Sir Knight?" Kit asked, quelling her anger, retrieving her smile. "I'm surprised that you're not out on the walls, defending your city against the invaders."

"Each of us is called upon to fight the darkness in his own way. The Temple of Paladine is my assigned post," said the Knight with solemn gravity. "The temple has been my post for two hundred years. I will not abandon it."

"Two hundred years!" Kit tried to laugh, coughed when the laugh caught in her throat. "Yeah, I guess it must seem that long, all by yourself in this godforsaken place. Or does someone share the watch with you?"

"No one shares my watch," the Knight replied. "I am alone."

"Some sort of punishment detail, I suppose," Kit said, glad to hear that the spirit had no more ghostly companions. "What's your name, Sir Knight? Perhaps I know your family. My father—" She was about to say her father had been a Solamnic Knight, then thought better of it. There was a possibility this spirit might not only know her father, but know her father's less than glorious history. "My people are from Solamnia," she amended.

"I am Nigel of Dinsmoor."

"Kitiara uth Matar." Kitiara extended her hand, shifted, twisted, dropped, made a grab for her sword.

A sword that was no longer there.

Kitiara stared at the empty place on the floor. She groped about with her hands until she realized how foolish and how frantic she must look. Slowly, she rose to her feet.

"Where is my weapon?" she demanded. "What have you done with it? I paid good steel for that sword! Give it back to me!"

"Your sword is not harmed. When you leave the temple, you will find it waiting for you."

"For any thief to steal!" Kit was fast losing her fear in her anger.

"No thief will touch it, I promise you that," said Sir Nigel. "You will also find there the knife you carried concealed in your boot."

"You are no Knight! No true Knight, at least," Kit cried, seething. "A Knight—dead or alive—would not resort to such knavery!"

"I have taken the weapons for your own good," Sir Nigel replied. "Should you try to continue to use them, far greater harm would come to you than you could do to anything else."

Baffled, thwarted, Kitiara glared in helpless frustration at this maddening ghost. She'd known few men who could stand against the fire of her displeasure, few men who could endure the scorching heat of her dark eyes. Tanis had been one of those few, and even he had come out singed on more than one occasion. Sir Nigel remained unmoved.

None of this was accomplishing the task at hand. Since anger would not work, she would try guile and charm, two weapons no one would ever take from her. She turned from the spirit, walked about the empty room, ostensibly admiring the architecture while she smoothed the bite marks from her lips, doused the fire in her eyes.

"Come, Sir Nigel," she said in wheedling tones, "we started off on the wrong foot and now we're in a hopeless tangle. I interrupted you in some pursuit of your own. You had every reason to be offended. As for my drawing a sword on you, you scared me half to death! I wasn't expecting anyone in here, you see. And there's something awful about this place," Kit added with rather more sincerity than she'd intended. She glanced about with a shudder that was not entirely faked. "It makes my flesh creep. The sooner I'm away from here the better."

She lowered her voice, moved closer to him. "I'll bet I know why you're here. Shall I make a guess? You're guarding a treasure, of course. It makes perfect sense."

"That is true," said Sir Nigel. "I am here to guard a treasure."

So that was it. Kitiara was amazed that she hadn't figured out the reason sooner. Immolatus had mentioned that the eggs would be guarded and so they were. But not by priests.

"And they've left you here all alone," said Kitiara with a sympathetic sigh. She frowned slightly. "Brave, but foolhardy, Sir Knight. I have heard tales of the commander of the enemy forces who now surround your city. Kholos is a hard man, a cruel man. Half-goblin, so they say. They also say that he can smell a steel piece at the bottom of a privy hole. He has two thousand men under his command. They will tear this temple down around your ears and there will be nothing even the dead can do to stop them."

"If these men are as cruel as you say, they will never find the treasure I guard," said Sir Nigel, and it seemed to Kit that he smiled.

"I'll bet I can find it," she said with an arch glance and a quirk of her eyebrow. "I'll bet that it's not hidden as well as you think. Let me look. If I manage to locate the treasure, you can move it to a better hiding place."

"All are free to search," said Sir Nigel. "It is not my place to stop you or anyone else from looking."

"So do you want me to look for the treasure or don't you?" Kitiara demanded impatiently, wishing for once this spirit would give her a straight answer. "And what do I do if I find it?"

"That depends entirely on you, friend," Sir Nigel replied.

He extended his arm, gestured toward the silver doors. The eerie light shone in the plate mail, glittered on his chain mail.

"I'll need a torch," she said.

"All who enter carry their own light within," Sir Nigel replied. "Unless they are truly benighted."

"You're the only one around here who's 'benighted,'" Kit said jocularly. "It's a joke. Knight. Benight—never mind."

Kit was reminded of Sturm Brightblade. This ghost was every bit as gullible and just as humorless. She couldn't believe he'd fallen for that treasure ploy. "I guess you'll be here when I get back?"

"I will be here," said the spirit.

Kitiara gave the silver doors an experimental shove, expecting resistance. To her astonishment, the doors opened easily, smoothly and silently.

Light flowed from the chamber in which she stood, washed around her and over her like in a gentle flood to illuminate a corridor before her, a corridor made of smooth white marble, which extended deeper into the mountain. She inspected the corridor closely, cocked her head for any sounds, sniffed the air. She heard nothing sinister, not even the skittering of mice. The only scent that came to her was—oddly—the scent of roses, old and faded. She saw nothing in the corridor except the white walls and the silver light. Yet fear gripped her, as she stood within the open doors, fear much like the fear she'd experienced on entering the temple, but worse, if that were possible.

She felt herself threatened, her back unprotected. She turned swiftly, hands raised to block an attack.

Sir Nigel was not there. No one was there. The temple was empty.

Kit should have felt relieved, yet still she stood trembling on the threshold, afraid to go beyond.

"Kitiara, you coward! I'm ashamed of you! Everything you want, everything you've worked for, lies before you. Succeed in this and General Ariakas will make your fortune. Fail and you will be nothing."

Kitiara walked into the darkness. The silver doors swung shut behind her, closed with a soft and whispered sigh.

5

The rest of the Mad Baron's army arrived outside the walls of Hope's End the morning following Commander Kholos's arrival. Smoke was still rising from the smoldering fields, burning the eyes and stinging the nose and making breathing difficult. The officers put the men to work immediately, throwing up breastworks and digging trenches, pitching tents, unloading the supply wagons.

Commander Morgon, resplendent in his ceremonial armor, mounted his horse, which had been curried and brushed to remove the dust of the road, and left the camp, riding to the camp of their allies in order to arrange a meeting between the baron and the commander of the armies of Good King Wilhelm. The commander returned in less than an hour.

The soldiers paused in the work, hoping that the commander would let fall some word indicative of his opinion of their allies. Commander Morgon said nothing to anyone, however. Those who had served with him longest said that he looked unusually grim. He reported directly to the baron.

Scrounger lurked around the stand of maple trees located near the baron's tent, gathering wild onions and trying his hardest to hear what was being said. Commander Morgon's voice was low anyway, he had a habit of speaking into his beard. Scrounger couldn't understand a word the man said. He might have gained something from the baron's answers had they been lengthy, but the baron's replies were nothing more enlightening than "yes," "no," and "Thank you, Commander. Have the officers meet me at sundown."

At this point one of the baron's bodyguards stumbled over the half-kender, crouched in a weed patch, and shooed him away. Scrounger returned to camp empty-eared, so to speak, and smelling strongly of onion.

That evening, around sundown, everyone stopped work to watch the baron and his entourage ride toward the allied camp. Outraged, the sergeants roared into action, storming through camp to remind each soldier that he had a job to do and that job didn't include standing around gawking.

Caramon and C Company took up positions about a half-mile from the city wall, joining the line of pickets already established by their allies. This line prevented anyone inside the city from leaving and, more important, prevented anyone from outside the city from entering. Hope's End was cut off from help, should any help be in the offing.

Accompanied by three of his staff officers and a bodyguard of ten mounted men, the baron rode behind the line of pickets, using them to screen his movements from those manning the city walls.

"Never give information to your enemy for free," was one of the baron's many martial adages. "Make him pay for it."

The commander of the city forces was almost certainly watching every movement of the enemy armies. He did not need to see that the commander of the army's left flank was not part of the main body of the army, that the baron was "hired help." Such knowledge might imply a weakness in the cohesiveness of the army, a weakness the enemy might try to use to his advantage.

Leaving his own picket lines, the baron advanced into those posted by his allies. At sight of him, the first sentry came to attention, saluting with upraised fist. From here on, every fifty yards, the sentries came to attention and saluted as the baron's entourage rode past. The sentries wore full battle armor, helmet, and shield, each bearing the royal crest of Good King Wilhelm. The armor was polished and shone in the hazy twilight. Each sentry carried at his side a small hunting horn, an innovation that intrigued the baron.

"Well-disciplined troops," he said, nodding appreciatively. "Respectful. Armor so clean I could eat off that man's breastplate, eh, Morgon?" He glanced at his senior staff officer, the commander who had arranged the meeting. "And I like that idea of the sentries carrying hunting horns. If there's an alarm, the whole countryside will hear them blasting away. Much better than shouting. We'll implement that ourselves."

"Yes, my lord," Morgon replied.

"They've been busy," the baron continued, pointing to a low breastworks made of dirt that already surrounded the encampment. "Look at that."

"I see it, my lord," Morgon returned.

Everywhere they looked, men were busy. No one was idle, the camp bustled with purposeful activity. No idlers hung about, breeding discontent. Soldiers hauled logs from the forest, timber that would be used to build siege towers and ladders. The blacksmith and his assistants were in their tent, forge fires burning brightly, hammering out dents in armor, pounding in rivets, turning out horseshoes for the cavalry. The smell of roast pig and beefsteak wafted through the camp. The baron and his men had been living on dry waybread and salt pork. The tempting odors made the mouth water.

The tents were arranged in an orderly manner, positioned so that each could catch the evening breeze. Arms were stacked neatly outside. The baron was loud in his approval.

"Look there, Morgon!" the baron said, indicating twenty soldiers wearing full battle gear lined up at attention beside a row of tents. "They have a standing ready-force like ours, except that theirs is at the full battle-ready. That's something else I think we should implement."

"Begging your lordship's pardon—that's not a standing ready-force," said Commander Morgon.

"It's not? What is it then?"

"Those men are on punishment detail, sir. They were standing there like that when I rode in this morning to arrange this meeting. There were thirty of them then. Ten must have fallen during the heat of the day."

"They just stand there?" The baron, astonished, shifted in the saddle to have a better view.

"Yes, my lord. According to the officer who escorted me, they're not allowed to eat, to rest, or drink water until their sentence time is served. That could be as long as three days. If a man collapses, he's carried off, revived and sent back out. His sentence starts over from that point."

"Good gods," the baron muttered. He continued staring until they passed out of range.

The baron and his officers halted just inside the entrance to the camp. The officers dismounted. The bodyguard remained on their horses.

"Give the men leave to stand down, Commander," the baron ordered.

"With my lord's permission, I think the men should stay mounted," Morgon returned.

"Is there something you want to tell me, Commander?" the baron demanded.

Morgon shook his head, avoided the baron's eyes. "No, sir. I just thought keeping the bodyguard ready to move out quickly would be prudent. In case Commander Kholos has urgent orders for us, my lord."

The baron stared hard at his commander but was unable to read anything from Morgon's expression except dutiful obedience. "Very well. Keep the men mounted. But see that they get some water."

An officer wearing armor covered by a tunic bearing the royal crest approached the waiting entourage and saluted. "Sir, my name is Master Vardash. I have been assigned to escort you to Commander Kholos."

The baron followed, accompanied by his officers. The entourage marched past rows of tents. Taking a right turn north of the blacksmith's works, the baron was looking over a stand of armor, approving the workmanship, when a cough from Morgon caused the baron to lift his head.

"What in the name of Kiri-Jolith is that?"

Hidden from the front of the camp by the large tent belonging to the blacksmith was a hastily constructed wooden gallows. Four bodies hung there. Three of the bodies had obviously been there since the day before—their eyes had been pecked out by carrion birds, one of whom was continuing his meal with the corpse's nose. One of the men was still alive, though he wouldn't be for long. As the baron watched, he saw the body jerk a couple of times, then quit moving.

"Deserters?" the baron asked Master Vardash.

"What, sir? Oh, that." Vardash cast the bodies an amused glance. "No, sir. Three of them thought they could get away with keeping some of the loot we took from the farmers for themselves. The fourth, there, the one who's still dancing, got caught with a young girl hidden in his tent. He said he felt sorry for her and was going to help her escape." Vardash smiled. "A likely story, wouldn't you agree, your lordship?"

His lordship had nothing to say.

"She is a pretty thing, I'll say that for him. She'll fetch a good price in San—That is"—Vardash appeared to recollect himself—"she will be handed over to the proper authorities in Vantal."

Commander Morgon cleared his throat loudly. The baron glanced at him, scratched at his beard, muttered beneath his breath, and marched on.

The command tent, marked by a large flag bearing the royal emblem of Good King Wilhelm, was flanked by a small section of six soldiers, obviously handpicked for the duty. Commander Morgon was a good six feet tall and these men towered over him. They dwarfed the short-statured baron. The guards wore armor that had obviously been specially designed, probably because no regulation armor would have fit over those hulking shoulders and bulging biceps.

These bodyguards did not wear the royal crest, the baron noted. They wore another crest, that of a coiled dragon, he thought, although he couldn't get a close look. Noting his gaze upon them, the guards very properly stiffened to attention, bringing their massive shields forward and thudding the butt end of the enormous spears they carried into the ground.

Dragons, the baron thought. A good symbol for a soldier, if rather quaint and old-fashioned.

Master Vardash announced the baron. A surly voice from within the command tent wanted to know what the devil this baron meant, interrupting him during supper. Master Vardash was apologetic, but reminded the commander that the meeting had been set for sunset. The commander gave ungracious permission for the baron to enter.

"Your sword, sir," said Master Vardash, barring the way.

"Yes, that's my sword." The baron put his hand on the hilt. "What about it?"

"I must ask you to entrust your sword to me, sir," said Vardash. "No one is allowed to enter the commander's presence carrying a weapon."

The baron was so outraged that for a minute he thought he was going to punch Master Vardash. Master Vardash apparently thought so as well, for he fell back a step, and put his hand to the hilt of his own sword.

"Our allies, my lord," said Commander Morgon softly.

The baron mastered his anger. Taking off his sword belt, he threw it in the direction of Master Vardash, who deftly caught it. "That's a valuable weapon," the baron growled. "It belonged to my father and his father before him. Take care of it."

"Thank you, sir. Your sword will be under my personal protection," the master said. "Perhaps your staff officers would be interested in seeing the rest of the camp."

"We've seen enough," said Commander Morgon dryly. "We will wait for you out here, my lord. Shout if you need us."

Grunting, the baron thrust aside the tent flap and stalked in.

He entered what he had supposed would be the usual command tent, furnished with a cot and a couple of camp-stools, a collapsible table covered with maps marked with the positions of the enemy. Instead, he thought for a moment he'd walked into Good King Wilhelm's front parlor. A fine rug, handwoven and embroidered, covered the ground. Elegant chairs, made of rare wood, surrounded an ornate table decorated with carved fruit and garlands. The table was loaded with food, not maps. Commander Kholos looked up from tearing apart a chicken.

" Well, you're here," Kholos said truculently by way of greeting. "Admire my furniture, do you? Perhaps you saw that manor house we burned down yesterday. If a house doesn't have walls, it doesn't need a table, does it?"

The commander chuckled and, thrusting his dirk—the handle crusted with dried blood—into half the chicken, he lifted it from his plate and popped it into his mouth, devoured it at one gulp, bones and all.

The baron mumbled an incoherent reply. He had been hungry when he'd entered, but at the sight of the commander, he lost his appetite. In some not too distant past, goblin and human had come together—one didn't want to speculate how—the result being Commander Kholos. The goblin part of his heritage was visible in his sallow, slightly green-tinged complexion, his underslung protruding lower jaw, his squinty eyes, overhung brow, and in his ruthless, brutal toughness. The human part could be seen in the cunning intelligence that burned in the squinty eyes with a pale and unnatural light, such as is given off by the decay of a loathsome swamp.

The baron could guess that the commander inspired as much fear in his own troops as he did in the enemy—perhaps more because the enemy had the good fortune of not being personally acquainted. The baron wondered why in the name of Kiri-Jolith any man would volunteer to fight under such a commander. Seeing the loot in the commander's tent and recalling Vardash's words—

quickly cut off—about some captive girl "fetching a price" somewhere, the baron guessed that so long as Kholos's troops could look forward to the spoils of war, they would endure his abuse.

The baron knew King Wilhelm. He couldn't imagine what had possessed the man to hire a commander like this. Yet he'd done so, apparently, and he was king and these were their allies, damn it all to the Abyss and back. The baron sorely regretted ever putting his signature to the contract.

"How many men have you brought?" the commander demanded. "Are they any good in a fight?"

Kholos did not invite the baron to be seated, he did not offer the baron food or drink. Grabbing a mug, the commander gulped noisily, slammed it down, splashing ale over the fine table, and wiped his mouth with the back of a hairy hand. Looking at the baron, the commander belched loudly.

"Well?" he demanded.

The baron drew himself to his full height. "My soldiers are the best in Ansalon. I assume that you knew that or you wouldn't have hired us."

The commander waved a chicken leg, used it to brush aside the baron's reputation. "I didn't hire you. I never heard of you. Now I'm stuck with you. We'll see what you can do tomorrow. I need to know what sort of a fight your rabble will put up. You and your men will attack the west wall at dawn."

"Very good," the baron said stiffly. "And where will you and your men be attacking, Commander?"

"We won't," Kholos returned, grinning. He chewed and talked at the same time, dribbling bits of the chicken mixed with saliva down his chin. "I'll be watching to see how your men perform under fire. My men have been well trained. I can't afford to have them ruined by a bunch of yelping curs who will roll over and piss themselves when the arrows start to fly."

The baron stood staring at the commander. His silence was an ominous cloud roiling black with astonishment and incredulity, lightning-charged with fury. Commander Morgon, waiting outside, would later say that he had never in his life heard anything—not even a thunderclap—louder than the baron's silence. Commander Morgon would also later report that he had his sword ready, for he assumed that the baron would kill the commander on the spot.

Kholos, seeing that the baron had nothing to say, forked another chicken.

The baron managed to throttle his desire to fork Kholos and said, speaking in a voice so unlike his own that Morgon would later swear he had no idea who was talking, "If we attack the city without support, you'll see nothing except my men dying, sir."

"Bah! The attack's just a feint. Testing the city's defenses, that's all. You can retreat if things get too hot for you." The commander took another swig of ale, belched again. "Report to me tomorrow at noon after the battle. We'll go over any improvements your men need to make then."

Kholos jerked a greasy thumb in dismissal and turned his complete attention to his meal. The meeting between allies was at an end.

The baron could not see the tent flap opening for the fiery red mist obscuring his vision. Fumbling his way out, nearly bringing down the tent in the process, he almost knocked over Vardash, who had stepped forward to assist him. The baron snatched his sword from the master, didn't take time to buckle it back on, but began walking.

"Let's get out of here," he said through gritted teeth. His officers fell into step behind, moving so rapidly that Vardash, who was supposed to escort them, had to jump to catch up.

The baron and his officers retraced their route, returned to their mounts and the bodyguard. It was now night. Despite the darkness, a company of soldiers was beginning a sword drill. Sergeants with bullwhips stood behind the ranks, waiting to correct any mistakes. The baron glanced at the punishment detail, counted eighteen men still standing. Two lay on the ground. No one paid any attention to them. One soldier, off on some errand of his own, actually stepped over the unmoving bodies. The baron quickened his pace.

The bodyguard was still mounted, ready to ride. Within minutes, the baron was out of the camp and heading back toward his own lines. He made the journey in silence, had nothing to say about the shining armor or noteworthy discipline of their gallant allies.

6

Light there was on the other side of the silver door, feeble and dim, but light enough for Kitiara to find her way. She advanced cautiously down the tunnel, fear walking with her. She kept expecting the spirit's bony fingers to clutch at her tunic, touch her shoulder, scrape across the back of her neck.

Kitiara was not imaginative. Even as a child, she'd laughed at stories that sent other children crying to their mamas. Assured by a playmate that monsters lived under her bed, Kitiara went after them with the fireplace poker. She was wont to say with a laugh that the only spirits she had ever encountered had been at the bottom of a wineskin. So much for that notion. The Knight wasn't the only ghost in the temple, unfortunately.

Figures in white robes walked alongside her, hastening on urgent errands or strolling slowly in meditative thought, figures that disappeared when she turned to confront them directly. Worse were the conversations, whispered echoes of long-silenced voices wisping through the corridor like smoke. At times she could almost make out distinct words, could almost catch what they were saying, but never quite. She had the impression they were talking about her, that they were saying something important. If they would only quit whispering, she could understand.

"What? What is it? What do you want?" Kitiara shouted out loud, deeply regretting the loss of her sword. "Who are you? Where are you?"

The voices whispered and murmured.

"If you've got something to say to me, come out and say it," Kitiara demanded grimly.

Apparently, the voices didn't, for they continued to whisper.

"Then shut the hell up!" Kitiara yelled and marched down the corridor.

The smooth marble floor gave way abruptly to stone. The man-made walls to the natural walls of a cavern. She walked a trail that was narrow and crooked, skirting large outcroppings of rocks that thrust up from the floor. Though rough, the path was not difficult to walk. In some places, it had been repaired or shored up to make walking easier.

She should have walked in darkness as dark as all the past ages of Krynn layered one on top of the other, for the only light to have ever penetrated this far beneath the mountain must have been the light of the sparks of Reorx's hammer. Yet down here the darkness had been banished. Light glistened on the wet stone, glinted when it touched veins of silver or of gold, illuminated columns of water-hewn rock that spiraled up to support a vast dome of sparkling crystalline formations.

The light was bright, dazzling, and try as she might, Kitiara could not locate the source. The light could not be coming from outside, for outside night had fallen.

"Stop fretting over it," Kit admonished herself. "Be grateful for the light. Otherwise it would take all night to traverse this path. There's an explanation for it. There has to be. Maybe molten lava, as in Sanction. Yes, that has to be the reason."

Never mind that this light wasn't red and garish as the flames that lit Sanction's smoke-filled skies. Never mind that this light was silver gray and cool and soft as moonlight. Never mind that there was no heat and no sign of a lava flow. Kitiara accepted her own explanation, and when that explanation became untenable—when she did not pass by any lava flows, nor did she come across any bubbling pools of magma, when the light continued to grow stronger and brighter the farther she traveled under the mountain—Kitiara ordered herself not to think about it anymore.

It seemed almost as if the white-robed figures had known she was coming and had gone out of their way to take her where she needed to go in the swiftest manner possible.

"Fools!" she said in her throat with a small, albeit nervous, chuckle and continued on.

The path wound about among the glittering stalagmites, carried her from one cavern room into another and always down, down deep into the mountain. The light never failed her, but led her on. When she was starting to feel thirsty and wished she'd thought to bring a waterskin, she came upon a clear, cold, rushing stream that looked as if it had been placed there for her convenience. But no sign of eggs, no sign of any cavern big enough to contain eggs or a dragon. The cavern ceiling was low. She could barely walk upright. A dragon could not have squeezed his little toe into this part of the cave.

She judged she had been walking about an hour and wondered how many leagues she had traveled. The path took her around a particularly large rock formation and brought her suddenly up against what appeared to be a sheer and impenetrable rock wall.

"This is more like it," Kit said, gratified and even relieved to find her way blocked. "I knew this was just too damn easy."

She searched for a way through the wall and eventually found a small archway that had been carved into the rock. A gate made of silver and gold blocked her way. In the center of the gate was wrought a rose, a sword, and a kingfisher. Looking through the gate, Kitiara saw a shadowed room, a room where the light dimmed as if in respect.

The room was a mausoleum.

A single sarcophagus stood in the center of the room. Kitiara could see the white marble of the tomb glimmer ghostly in the eerie light.

"Well, Kit, you've reached a dead end," she said, and laughed to herself at her little joke.

Not particularly wanting to disturb the rest of the dead, Kit set about looking for some other way around the wall. A half-hour's search left her hot and frustrated. It seemed impossible that there should be no more openings, no cracks through which she could squeeze. She muttered and swore and poked and kicked, now furious to find her way blocked. She would have to retrace her steps, look for some branching pathway that she must have missed.

Yet, she knew very well she had not missed anything. She had come to no crossroads. She had not once had to stop to decide which way she should take. The path led straight to this. A tomb.

She would have to examine it. If she couldn't find a way past it, she would be able to say to herself and to General Ariakas that she had done her duty. Immolatus probably wouldn't believe her, but if he doubted her word, he could jolly well come down here himself.

Kitiara entered the archway, came to stand before the gold and silver gates. No sign of a lock. The gate was fastened by a small bar, which could easily be lifted. She had only to reach out her hand.

Kitiara reached out her hand but did not touch the gate. She wanted to turn and run. Or, worse, she wanted to fall to the rock floor, curl up in a ball, and cry like a child.

"This is nonsense!" she said sternly, giving herself a mental shaking. "What's the matter with me? Am I afraid to walk past a graveyard in the night? Open that gate this instant, Kitiara uth Matar."

Cringing, as if she expected the metal to be white hot to the touch, she lifted the latch. The gate swung aside silently on well-oiled hinges. Not giving herself time to think, Kitiara walked boldly and defiantly into the mausoleum.

Nothing happened.

And when it didn't, she grinned in relief, laughed at her fears, and took a quick investigative look around.

The mausoleum was circular, small, domed. The sarcophagus stood in the center, the only object in the room. A frieze carved around the wall portrayed scenes of battle: knights carrying lances riding on the backs of dragons fighting other knights, dragons fighting each other. Kit paid little attention to the carvings. She had no interest in the past or in tales of past glory. She had yet to win her own glory and that was all that mattered.

Her search was rewarded. Directly opposite the gate stood another wrought-iron gate, a way out. She strode past the sarcophagus, glanced at the tomb out of curiosity.

Kitiara stopped, startled.

The corpse of Sir Nigel, the ghost she had encountered in the temple, was stretched out upon the top of the tomb.

Kit had trouble breathing, her fear squeezed the air from her lungs. She forced herself to stare at the tomb until her fear dissipated. She was not looking at a body dead these two hundred years. The Knight was carved of stone.

Her breathing coming easier, Kit walked boldly over to the tomb. Her mistake was a reasonable one. The helm was the same: old-fashioned, made of one piece just like the helm worn by the Knight. The armor was the same down to the last detail.

The tomb was open. The marble lid had been shoved aside.

"So that's how it got out," she muttered. "I wonder what happened to the body?"

Kit peered inside the tomb, searched the shadows. Solamnic Knights often buried weapons with their dead. She thought it possible that she might find a sword or at the very least a ceremonial dagger. Possible, but not probable. The tomb was stripped bare. Not so much as a leg bone, not so much as a finger left behind. Probably the body had crumbled to dust.

Kit shivered. "The sooner I get back to sunlight and fresh air the better. Now for the gate. Let's hope this leads me to where I want to go. . . ."

"You need go no farther," said a voice. "The treasure of which I spoke is here for you to find."

"Where are you?" Kitiara demanded. "Let me see you!"

She heard a whispered cry, caught a glimpse of movement out of the corner of her eye. Her hand reached instinctively for her sword and she muttered a curse as her fingers closed over air. Placing her back against the sarcophagus, she turned to confront whatever was in the mausoleum, ready to fight with fists, feet, and teeth, if necessary.

Nothing attacked her. Nothing threatened her. The movement came from a part of the circular room near the second door, the door leading out of the mausoleum. On the floor lay what appeared to be a body. Just when Kitiara had decided it was a dead body, it stirred, moaned in pain.

"Sir Nigel?" Kitiara hissed.

No answer.

Kit was exasperated. Just when it seemed she must be nearing the end of her search, she'd run into yet another obstacle.

"Look, I'm sorry," she advised the person, "but there's nothing I can do for you. I'm on an urgent errand and I don't have much time. I'll send someone back for you. . . ."

The person moaned again.

Kitiara headed resolutely toward the door. Halfway there, she recalled the Knight's words. The treasure was here. Perhaps this person had found it first. Kit veered from her path. Keeping a sharp lookout for attackers lurking in the shadows, thinking that this might be a trap, she moved swiftly to where the body lay huddled on the floor and knelt down beside it.

The body was that of a woman, Kit saw in astonishment. A woman dressed in black, skintight clothing, clothing meant to be worn beneath metal armor. She lay on her stomach, her face pressed against the stone floor. She had been in a horrific fight, by the look of her. Long bloody gashes had torn her clothes. Her black curly hair was matted with blood. A large pool of blood had formed beneath her stomach. Judging by that and the victim's ashen skin, Kit guessed that the woman was near death. Kit searched, but found no treasure. Disappointed, she started to rise to her feet, then paused, looked more closely at the dying woman.

Something about her seemed familiar.

Kit reached out her hand to brush aside the woman's hair, get a better look at the face. Her fingers touched . . .

Black curly hair cut short. The hair Kit was touching she'd touched many, many times before. The hair was her own.

Kitiara snatched her hand back. Her mouth went dry, breathing ceased. Terror stole her reason. She couldn't think, she couldn't move.

The hair was her own. The face was her own.

"I have always loved you, half-elf," the dying woman whispered.

The voice was her own. Kitiara looked upon herself, wounded, dying.

Kit jumped to her feet and fled. She hit the iron gate running, flung her weight against it, beat on it with her fists when it wouldn't open. Pain from bruised flesh brought her to her senses. The darkness that had blinded her cleared from her eyes. She saw that the gate had a handle and, with a sob of relief, she grabbed it and turned.

The catch clicked. She shoved open the gate, raced through it, slammed the gate shut behind her with all her strength. She leaned against the gate, too weak from fear to keep moving. Panting for air, she waited for her heartbeat to slow, the sweat to dry on her palms, her legs to stop shaking.

"That was me!" she gasped, shuddering. "That was me back there. And I was dying. Dying horribly, painfully . . . 'I have always loved you . . .' My voice! My words!" Kitiara buried her face in her hands, prey to such terror as she had never before known. "No! Please, no! I . . . I . . ."

Kit drew in a breath. "I am a fool!" She slumped against the door, shivering, a reaction to her fear. She gave herself a mental slap, intended to clear her mind of what had to be visions, fancies, a waking dream. . . .

"It wasn't real. It couldn't have been real." She sighed and swallowed, swallowed again. The moisture had returned to her mouth and with it the bitter aftertaste of terror. "I'm tired. I haven't slept well. When a person doesn't sleep, he starts to see things. Remember Harwood in the Plains of Dust, fighting goblins? Stayed awake three nights running, then went rampaging through the camp, screaming that snakes were crawling on his head."

Kitiara stood leaning against the gate, hugging her chill body, trying to banish the memory of the dream.

It had to be a dream. No other explanation.

"If I walked back in there," she told herself, "I'd find nothing. No body. Nothing. That's what I'd find. Nothing."

But she didn't walk back in there.

Kitiara drew a deep breath and, feeling the horror start to fade, she shook off the unreasoning fear and looked at her surroundings.

She stood inside a large cavern, an enormous cavern. A glow came from the far end of the cavern, a glow that might have been created by torchlight shining on mounds of silver and of gold.

"Come now, this is better," said Kitiara, cheering up immensely. "I think I may be getting somewhere."

She hurried in the direction of the shining light, glad to have a purpose, extremely glad to leave the ill-fated chamber behind her.

The cavern floor was smooth, the cavern itself commodious. Immolatus in dragon form could have fit himself in here and still accommodated two or three large red friends. If ever there was an ideal location for dragons to hide their eggs, this was it. Excited at the prospect, Kitiara broke into a run. The blood pumped through her body, brought warmth back to numb feet and hands.

She reached her destination, breathing hard, but feeling refreshed and renewed. And triumphant.

Nestled in an alcove in the cavern were hundreds of eggs. Enormous eggs. One egg was as tall as Kitiara or taller and so wide around that she might extend her arms and only embrace a small portion of the shell. Each egg radiated with a soft light. Some of the eggs shone with a golden light, some gleamed silver. There were a great many. Kitiara couldn't begin to count them, but counting them was what she was going to have to do. A task that would be tedious and boring. Still, she found herself looking forward to it.

Cataloging eggs and mapping their location for future reference would be drudge work, guaranteed to brush away the last vestiges of horror that webbed her mind. Just as she reached this satisfying conclusion, she felt a breath of air, fresh air, touch her cheek. She inhaled deeply.

A large tunnel, large enough for a dragon's body, led to the secret entrance for which Immolatus had been searching. An enormous hole in the side of the mountain, a hole completely hidden from the outside by a stand of fir trees. Pushing her way past the trees, Kitiara stepped out onto a large rock ledge. She looked up into the night sky, hazy with smoke, looked down on the doomed city of Hope's End. It must be about midnight. Time enough to complete her work and make her way down the mountainside to the camp of Commander Kholos.

Kitiara returned to the chamber of the eggs, which gave off light enough for her to see by, and went to work, thankful to have something to occupy her thoughts. Taking out the small leather-bound book Immolatus had given her, Kit searched until she found a bit of sandstone, which she could use like chalk.

First she drew a map of the location of the hidden entrance, making careful calculation of where it stood in relation to the city walls and landmarks, so that Commander Kholos could find this cavern without going through the temple. She had to wonder how he was going to cart the eggs down the mountainside, for the way was steep. But that wasn't her concern, thank the Dark Queen. Her task was finished.

Map completed, she stood up and walked into the chamber of the eggs, a chamber suffused in golden and silver light, the light of unborn dragons, whose souls played among the star fields and danced on the ethers.

What would happen to those souls who would never be born into this life? Kit shrugged. That was not her concern either.

She eyed the eggs, decided that it would be best to count them by rows in order not to lose track. Clambering onto a rock ledge that overlooked the chamber, Kitiara spread the book out on her lap.

"You discovered the treasure," said a voice behind her.

Kitiara closed the book hastily, covered it with her hand, and turned around. "Sir Nigel," she said. "So this is where you flitted off to. As for treasure, hah! I didn't find anything except these things, whatever they are. Eggs, I guess. Big, aren't they? Make a whopping big omelet. Big enough to feed an army. What sort of creature do you suppose laid them?"

"This is not the treasure," said the Knight. "The treasure was inside the mausoleum, a treasure left there by Paladine."

Kitiara managed a shaky grin. "Tell this Paladine that I prefer my treasure in rubies and emeralds."

"You have seen your death. A horrible one. You can yet change your fate, however," Sir Nigel continued. "That is why the future was revealed to you. You have the power to alter it. Leave your task here unfinished. Do so, and you will take the first step to stop what otherwise must be."

Kitiara was tired and she was hungry. The burn on her hand hurt, she didn't like being reminded of the horrible sight in that mausoleum. She had work to do and this blasted spirit was interrupting her.

She turned her back on him, hunkered over her book. "Hey, I thought I heard your god calling you. Maybe you better go answer."

Sir Nigel made no response. Kit looked over her shoulder, was relieved to find that he had gone.

Putting the ghost and his "treasure" out of her mind, she settled down to count eggs.

7

"Red! Pass the word for Red!"

Raistlin was in his tent, taking advantage of a few quiet moments in the late evening to continue his study of the book about Magius. Raistlin had read the book through once, but parts remained unclear—the handwriting of the chronicler was almost unreadable in places—and Raistlin was now going through the book line by line, making his own copy for future reference.

"Horkin wants you," said one of the soldiers, poking his head inside. "He's in the wizard tent."

"You sent for me, sir?" Raistlin said.

"That you, Red?" Horkin did not look up. He was engrossed in his work, heating a concoction in a small pot hung on a tripod over a charcoal brazier. He took a sniff, frowned, and stuck the tip of his little finger into the pot. Shaking his head, he stirred the mixture. "Not hot enough." He glared impatiently at the pot.

"You sent for me, sir," Raistlin said again.

Horkin nodded, still not looking at him. "I know it's late, Red, but I've a job for you. I think this one you might even like. More interesting than my socks."

He cast a sidelong glance at Raistlin, who flushed in embarrassment. True, he had been frustrated beyond measure at being made to perform menial tasks about camp, tasks that wouldn't have challenged a gully dwarf: washing linens to be used for bandages, cutting those same linens, sorting through bags of herbs and flowers, watching some foul brew simmer over the brazier. The last tug of the dwarf's beard had been darning Horkin's socks.

Horkin was no seamstress and when he discovered that Raistlin had a certain talent in this field—a talent gained during the lean days when he and his twin were orphaned, forced to live on their own—Horkin had given Raistlin the chore. Raistlin imagined that he had handled the onerous tasks with good grace. Apparently not.

"Commander Morgon tells me that there's a red-robed mage marching with the army of our allies. Morgon says he caught a glimpse of him walking through camp."

"Indeed, sir?" Raistlin was definitely interested.

"I thought you might enjoy going on a trading expedition, if you're not too tired."

"I'm not tired at all, sir." Raistlin accepted the assignment with far more enthusiasm than any he'd received thus far. "What do you want me to take to trade?"

Horkin rubbed his chin. "I've been considering. We've got those scrolls neither of us can read. Perhaps this mage can make something of them. Don't let on you don't know what's in 'em, though. If he thinks you can't read them, he'll pass them off as trash and we won't get a cracked amulet for them."

"I understand, sir," said Raistlin. His chagrin at being unable to read the scrolls ran deep.

"Speaking of amulets, I brought that box of stuff you sorted and labeled. Anything in there you think might be worth something?"

"You never know, sir," Raistlin replied. "Just because we don't consider an artifact valuable doesn't mean another wizard might not find a use for it. At any rate," he added with a sly smile, "I can hint to him that they're more than they are. I am your apprentice, after all. It's not likely you would trust me to handle such magical objects if I understood their true power."

"I knew you were the right man for the job," Horkin said, greatly delighted. "Throw in a couple of our healing ointments for good measure. And, don't show this around"—Horkin handed over a bag of coins—"but if he has something really valuable and he won't trade for it, you can pay in steel. Now, what are we in the market for?"

The two went over what magic they already possessed, determined what they lacked, debated over what might be useful and how much Raistlin would be willing to pay.

"Five steel for a scroll, ten for a potion, twenty for a spellbook, and twenty-five for an artifact. That's my limit," Horkin stated.

Raistlin argued that his master was out of touch with current market prices, but Horkin refused to budge. Raistlin could do nothing but agree, though he privately resolved to take along some of his own money, do his own bargaining if he found something of value priced beyond what Horkin was willing to give.

"Ah, it's done!" Horkin said, looking with satisfaction into the pot, whose contents were now bubbling. He wrapped the handle in cloth, lifted the pot from the heat and carefully poured the contents into a large crock. Stopping the crock with a cork, he wiped off the sides and placed the crock into a basket. He handed the basket to Raistlin. "There, take that to the Red Robe. It's a deal clincher if there ever was one."

"What is it, sir?" Raistlin asked, mystified. He had caught only a glimpse of the brew—some sort of cloudy liquid filled with whitish lumps. "A potion?"

"Chicken and dumplings for his dinner," said Horkin. "My own recipe. Give him a taste and he'll hand over his smalls if that's what you want." He gave the crock a fond pat. "There's not a wizard alive who won't succumb to my chicken and dumplings."

* * * * *

Loaded down with artifacts, scroll cases, and the crock of chicken and dumplings, along with numerous jars of ointments and unguents and a flask of honey wine to smooth the wizard's throat into saying "yes,"

Raistlin left the baron's camp and walked toward the camp of their ally. Horkin did not think to provide the young mage with an armed escort, although if he had heard Commander Morgon's full report about what he and the baron had seen and heard in the ally's camp that afternoon, he might have done so. As it was, Raistlin took only the Staff of Magius for light and his small, hidden knife for protection. After all, he thought, he was among friends.

His first encounter was with the line of pickets of the allied force. The soldiers regarded him with considerable suspicion, but by now Raistlin was accustomed to dark looks and knew how to handle the situation. He stated his errand truthfully, said he was visiting a fellow wizard interested in doing a little trading. At first the soldiers had no idea what he was talking about. A Red Robe? They didn't think so.

Then one recalled that a Red Robe had arrived in camp earlier that evening, appearing out of nowhere. A slimy fellow, no one liked him, the soldier said. They'd thought of slitting his throat, but there was something about him . . . The Red Robe insisted on meeting with Kholos and, such was the unease the wizard inspired, he'd been taken immediately to the commander. The next thing the soldiers knew, they were pitching a tent for the Red Robe and treating him as if he were the commander's long-lost brother-in-law. The soldiers passed Raistlin on through the lines, with only a cursory examination of what he carried—no one wanted to investigate a wizard's wares too closely. Several hinted broadly that if Raistlin would like to leave his basket and take the Red Robe back with him, it would be much appreciated.

Apparently, unlike the popular Horkin, this war wizard was not held in high regard by his fellow soldiers.

"But then, neither am I," Raistlin said to himself and continued on through the lines into the allied camp.

He saw the punishment detail, but he did not understand what was transpiring. Seeing men lying comatose on the ground, he assumed this was merely some sort of strange practice common among soldiers and walked by without a second glance. He did not see the corpses dangling from the gibbets, but, from what he'd seen of harsh military discipline, even that might not have surprised him.

He asked around for the tent of the war wizard. It was pointed out to him with reluctance and one man asked him outright if he was certain he wanted to have dealings with the wizard. All who spoke of him did so with surly looks behind which was a hint of fear. Raistlin's estimation of this Red Robe rose accordingly.

Raistlin eventually found the wizard's tent, positioned at a distance from all the other tents in the encampment. The tent was large and commodious.

Raistlin paused outside the tent, drew in a deep breath to calm his excitement and anticipation. He was about to meet a true war wizard, a fellow Red Robe, perhaps of high ranking. A wizard who might be in the market for an apprentice. Raistlin would not leave Horkin, not yet. He was bound by contract and honor to serve out his term with the baron. But here was a chance to make himself known and, perhaps, favorably impress the wizard. Who knew? This Red Robe might be so impressed that he would be willing to buy out Raistlin's contract, take him on immediately.

The young are made of dreams.

Peering through the slight part in the tent flap opening, Raistlin could catch just a glimpse of red by the light of a dip set in a bowl of perfumed oil. He heard the sound of what seemed hissing breath. He had regained his composure, was prepared to represent himself as cool and competent and professional. Raistlin shifted the basket with the chicken and dumplings onto the arm that was also holding the Staff of Magius and knocked on the tent post with his free hand.

"Is that you, worm?" came a deep voice from within the tent. "If so, quit shaking the tent and come inside and make your report. What did you find in that damn temple?"

Raistlin was in an extremely awkward situation. He had to admit that he was not the expected "worm" and, from that unpropitious start, go on to introduce himself. Worse, he felt his lungs starting to clog. He made a desperate attempt to clear his throat with a single, harsh cough, and decided to pretend he hadn't heard.

"Excuse me for disturbing you, Master," he called, thankful to feel the smothering sensation in his lungs recede. "My name is Raistlin Majere. I am a red-robed wizard connected with the army of Baron Ivor Langtree. I have with me various scrolls, magical artifacts, and potions. I've come to see if you might be interested in making a trade."

"Go to the Abyss."

Considerably taken aback by the rude remark, Raistlin stared at the tent post in speechless amazement. Whatever he had expected, it wasn't this.

He had never met the wizard, not even the powerful and puissant Par-Salian himself, who would pass up an opportunity to acquire new magic. Curiosity alone would have had any wizard of Raistlin's acquaintance barging out of that tent to rummage through the scroll cases and bag of artifacts. Perhaps the Red Robe wasn't in the market for trading. But, damn it, at the very least, the man should be interested to see what Raistlin had brought with him.

Raistlin risked peeping inside the tent, hoping to see the wizard. The Red Robe was leaning back in his chair, apparently, for he was lost in the shadows.

"Perhaps you did not understand me, Master," Raistlin said, speaking with the utmost respect. "I have brought with me many magical items, some of which are quite powerful, in hopes that you—"

He heard a sound as of a kettle boiling over, an angry rustling of robes and suddenly the tent flap jerked aside. A face—livid, with glaring red eyes—thrust out of the tent. Anger like a hot wind struck Raistlin, caused him to retreat a step.

"Leave me in peace," the Red Robe snarled, "or, by the Dark Queen, I'll send you to the Abyss myself—"

The Red Robe's glaring red eyes widened in shock. The furious oath died on his lips. The wizard glared, not at Raistlin, but at the staff in Raistlin's hands. As for Raistlin, he gazed intently at the wizard. Neither spoke a word, both were struck dumb, each seeing something he had not expected.

"Why are you staring at me!" the wizard demanded.

"I might ask the same question, sir!" Raistlin countered, shaken.

"I'm not staring at *you*, worm," Immolatus growled, and that was true enough. He had barely glanced at the human. The dragon's gaze was riveted upon the staff.

Immolatus's first dragonish impulse was simply to snatch the staff and incinerate the human. His fingers twitched, the words of the spell flared in his throat, burned on his tongue. He resisted the impulse, after a struggle. Killing the human would invite unwanted attention, require tedious explanations, and leave a blackened, greasy mark on the ground outside his tent. Most important in his decision to allow the human to live—at least temporarily—was the dragon's curiosity about the staff. One could not gain information from a greasy spot on the grass.

Immolatus realized, much to his ire, that in order to find out the answers to the questions boiling in his mind he would actually have to be—what was the word uth Matar was always using? "Diplomatic." He would have to be diplomatic in his dealings with the human. Difficult to manage when what Immolatus really wanted to do was to rip open the creature, yank out its brain, and pick through it with a sharpened foreclaw.

"You had better come inside," Immolatus muttered and he actually considered that a gracious invitation.

Raistlin remained where he was standing, outside the tent. He had grown accustomed to his accursed eyesight, to looking at the world through the spell-laden eyes, which saw all things as they were affected by time, saw youth wither, saw beauty brought to dust. Looking at this man, who was, perhaps, in his early forties, Raistlin should have seen the Red Robe wrinkled and elderly. What Raistlin saw was a blurred portrait, two faces instead of one, two faces in a botched painting, as if the artist had allowed all the colors to run together.

One face was the face of a human wizard. The other face was more difficult to see, but Raistlin had a fleeting impression of red, vibrant red, glittering red. There was something reptilian about the man, something reptilian about his second face.

Raistlin had the feeling that if he could just focus on that second face, he would see it clearly and understand what he saw. But every time he tried to concentrate, the second face flowed into the lines of the first.

Two faces, he noticed, yet both regarded him with a single pair of red-flame eyes. The man was dangerous, but then all wizards are dangerous.

Wary, cautious, Raistlin accepted the invitation to enter the tent for exactly the same reason that he'd been invited. Curiosity.

The Red Robe was tall and thin, his clothes rich and expensive. He walked to a small camp table, sat down in a folding chair and made an abrupt gesture at the table. His movements were both graceful and awkward at the same time, rather like the blurred double image of the face. Small movements—the flutter of the long fingers, for example, or the slight inclination of the head—were performed easily and with fluid motion. Larger movements—seating himself in the chair—were clumsy, as if he were unaccustomed to such motions and had to stop to think about what he was doing.

"Let's see what you've brought," Immolatus said.

Absorbed in trying to sort out this mystery, Raistlin did not respond. He stood and stared, clutching the basket and the scroll cases and the staff.

"Why in the Abyss do you look at me with those freakish eyes of yours?" Immolatus demanded irritably. "Have you come to deal or not? Let us see what you have." He tapped impatiently on the table with the long, sharp nail of a forefinger.

Actually there was only one artifact in the tent in which Immolatus was truly interested and that was the staff. But he needed to find out a few things about it first, most especially—how much did the human know about what he held? To look at him, not much. Certainly not like the first human Immolatus had met who had wielded that staff. Immolatus ground his teeth at the memory.

Raistlin lowered his gaze, ignored the insult about his eyes. He could have made a few choice remarks about this man's appearance had he chosen. He refrained. The wizard was his elder and his better, no question about that. Raistlin felt himself standing in the center of a veritable vortex of magical power. The magic whirled and crackled and sparked around him and all of that power emanated from this man. Raistlin had experienced nothing like this magical storm before, not even in the presence of the Head of the Conclave. He was humbled and consumed with envy and resolved to learn from this man or perish in the attempt.

In order to have both hands free to divest himself of the trade goods, Raistlin leaned the Staff of Magius against the small camp table.

Immolatus's hand snaked across the table toward it.

Raistlin saw the move and dropped the basket. He caught hold of the staff, stood clutching it close to his body.

"A fine walking staff," said Immolatus, baring his teeth in what he meant for a friendly, disarming smile. "How did you come by it?"

Raistlin had no intention of discussing the staff and so he pretended he had not heard. Keeping fast hold of the staff in one hand, he spread out the scrolls, the artifacts, unpacked the jars of potions, much like a peddler at a fair.

"We have several very interesting items, sir. Here is a scroll captured from a Black Robe whom we have reason to believe was of extremely high rank and here is—"

Immolatus thrust out his arm and swept all the objects—scrolls, potions, basket, and crock—off the table. "There is only one magical item I am interested in obtaining," he said, and his gaze went to the staff.

The scroll cases rolled under the table, the artifacts scattered in every direction. The crock crashed to the hard-packed ground and broke, splashing chicken broth on the hem of Raistlin's robes.

"This is one magical artifact which I have no intention of trading, sir," Raistlin said, holding on to the staff so tightly that the muscles of his hand and forearm began to ache with the strain. "Some of the rest of these are quite powerful—"

"Bah!" Immolatus seethed. He rose to his feet with a twist of his body, uncoiling, not standing. "I have more power in my little finger than is contained in any one of the paltry trinkets you have the temerity to try to palm off on me. Except the staff. I might possibly be interested in that staff. How did you come by it?"

It was on the tip of Raistlin's tongue to tell the truth, to say—with some pride—that the staff had been a gift from the great Par-Salian. His natural proclivity to secrecy stopped the words in his throat. Describing the staff as a gift from the Head of the Conclave would only invite more discussion, more questions, perhaps increase the value of the staff in this wizard's eyes. Raistlin wanted nothing more to do with this wizard, wanted to leave this strange man's presence as soon as possible.

"The staff has been in my family for generations," he said, edging backward toward the tent flap. "Thus, you see, sir, I am constrained by family tradition and honor not to part with it. Since it seems we cannot do business, sir, I bid you good day."

By accident, Raistlin said the right words, words that probably saved his life. Immolatus immediately jumped to the conclusion that Raistlin was a descendant of the powerful wizard Magius. Magius must have left a written account of the powers of the staff with his relations or at least handed down such an account by word of mouth. Now that Immolatus looked at the young man, he did seem to bear a certain family resemblance to Magius of accursed memory.

For it was Magius who had defeated the red dragon Immolatus. Magius and the magical power of that very staff had come very near slaying Immolatus, had wounded him grievously, wounds that, though healed, still pained him. Immolatus dreamed of that staff, its magic flaring, blinding, searing, killing, for long centuries. He would have traded all his lost treasure for that staff, to seize it, hold it, dote on it, use it to strike back at his enemies, use it to slay them as it had very nearly slain him. Use it to slay the descendant of Magius.

Immolatus could not battle the heir to the staff in this puny, human body. He considered changing back to his dragon form, decided against it. He would have his revenge upon all those who had wronged him—the gold dragons and the silver, his duplicitous queen, and now Magius. The dragon had waited years upon years for his revenge, a few more days were drops of water in the ocean of his waiting.

"You forget your wares, Peddler," Immolatus said, casting a scathing glance at the magical paraphernalia that lay scattered at his feet.

Raistlin was not about to start crawling on the ground, gathering up the scrolls and jars and rings, leaving himself vulnerable to attack.

"Keep them, sir. As you have said, they are of little value."

Raistlin made a slight bow to the wizard, a bow that was more than mere politeness, for he was able to use the bow as an excuse to depart the tent gracefully, without turning his back on the wizard.

Immolatus made no response, but watched Raistlin leave—or rather watched the staff leave—with red eyes whose gaze, like that of a crystal absorbing and focusing the energy of sun upon a straw, might have set the staff ablaze.

Raistlin walked from the tent and kept walking with a rapid pace, seeing nothing in his path and not even very certain of the direction he was taking. His one thought was to put as much distance as possible between himself and the fey man with the blurred face and lethal eyes.

Only when he was safely in sight of the bonfires of his own camp, the comforting sight of hundreds of well-armed soldiers, did Raistlin slow his pace. As thankful as he was to be back among friends, Raistlin pulled his hood over his head and took a circuitous route back to his tent. He did not want to talk to anyone, especially not Horkin.

Once safely hidden from view, Raistlin sank, exhausted, upon his bed. Sweat bathed his body, he felt dizzy and light-headed and sick to his stomach. Holding on to the staff, still afraid to let go, he stared down at his boots, wet with chicken broth.

The smell sickened him, brought back to Raistlin the terror of the encounter in the tent, the memory of the red-fire eyes of the wizard, the horror-filled, helpless knowledge that if the Red Robe had chosen, he could have taken the precious staff and Raistlin would have been powerless to prevent him.

Raistlin choked and retched. Months after, the very sight of a stewed chicken would fail to render him so nauseous that he would be forced to leave the table, making Caramon the one clear winner in the encounter.

Once the sickness passed and he felt more equal to the task, Raistlin went to make his report to Horkin. Raistlin pondered long over what to say. His first impulse was to lie about the incident, which made him appear a fool at best.

In the end, Raistlin decided to tell Horkin the truth, not from any noble aspirations, but because he could not think of a lie that would adequately explain the loss of their magewares. Where were kender when you needed them?

Horkin was astonished to see Raistlin return empty-handed. Astonishment gave way to glowering anger when Raistlin admitted calmly and steadily that he had fled the tent of the Red Robe, leaving the magewares behind.

"I think you better explain yourself, Red," Horkin said grimly.

Raistlin did explain, portraying the meeting in vivid detail. He described the Red Robe, described his own fear and the almost blind panic that had overtaken him when he was certain that the Red Robe was going to attack him to gain the staff. Raistlin kept to himself only one thing and that was the appearance of the two faces, merging and separating and merging again. He could never explain that, not even to himself.

Horkin listened to the tale with suspicion at first. He was truly disappointed in his apprentice, suspected that the young mage had sold the goods himself and was intent on keeping what he had earned, though—Horkin admitted—he found such a deed difficult to believe of a young man he'd come to grudgingly respect and even like a little. Horkin eyed Raistlin closely, well aware that this young man would have no compunction about lying if he thought a lie might be to his gain. But Horkin saw no lie here. Raistlin's complexion paled when he spoke of the encounter, a shudder shook the frail body, the shadow of remembered fear haunted his eyes.

The longer Raistlin talked—and once he had overcome his reluctance to speak of the matter, he talked with an almost feverish compulsion—the more Horkin came to believe the young man was telling the truth, strange as that truth might be.

"This wizard is powerful, you say." Horkin rubbed his chin, an action that apparently aided him in thinking, for he often resorted to it when puzzled.

Raistlin halted his pacing of the wizard tent. Though he was dead tired, he could not sit still, but walked the length and breadth of the small tent restlessly, leaning upon the staff, which he had resolved not to let out of his sight or his grasp.

"Powerful!" Raistlin exclaimed. "I have stood in the presence of the Head of the Conclave himself, the great Par-Salian, purportedly one of the most powerful arch-magis ever to have lived, and the magic I felt emanate from him was as a summer shower compared to a cy-clone in the presence of this man!"

"And a Red Robe, for all that."

Raistlin hesitated before replying. "Let me say, sir, that although this wizard wore red robes, I had the dis-tinct impression that they were not worn out of alle-giance to one of the gods of magic so much as they were . . . well"—he shrugged helplessly—"like his skin."

"Red eyes and orange-colored skin. He's an albino, maybe. I knew an albino once. A soldier when I first joined up with the baron. In C Company, I think it was. He—"

"Begging your pardon, sir." Raistlin cut off Horkin's reminiscences impatiently. "But what should we do?"

"Do? About what? The wizard?" Horkin shook his head. "Leave him alone, I should say. Sure, he stole our stuff, but, let's face it, Red, there was nothing there of any value except your staff, which he spotted right off, small blame to him. If you don't mind, though, I think I will mention the incident to the baron."

"Tell the baron that I ran away in a panic, sir?" Raistlin asked bitterly.

"Of course not, Red," Horkin replied gently. "Given the circumstances, it seems to me that you acted with good, plain common sense. No, I'll just mention to the baron that we think there's something a bit sinister about this wizard. Judging by what else I've heard of our allies, I doubt if his lordship will be much sur-prised," Horkin added dryly.

"There's a possibility that this wizard is a renegade, sir," Raistlin said.

"Aye, Red, there is," Horkin returned.

Renegade wizards did not follow the laws laid down by the Conclave of Wizards, laws designed to assure that powerful magicks would not be used recklessly or with abandon. Such laws were meant to protect not only the general populace but wizards themselves. A renegade wizard was a danger to every other wizard, and it was the avowed duty and responsibility of every wizard, who was a member of the Conclave to seek out renegades and either attempt to persuade them to join the Conclave or to destroy them if they refused.

"What do you intend to do about it, Red?" Horkin continued. "Challenge him? Call him out?"

"In other days I might have," Raistlin said with a slight smile, remembering the time he had challenged another renegade wizard, with almost disastrous results. "I have since learned my lesson. I am not such a fool as to go up against this man, who—as he said—has more magic in his little finger than I do in my entire body."

"Don't sell yourself short, Red," Horkin said. "You've got potential. You're young yet, that's all. Someday, you'll be a match for the best of them."

Raistlin regarded the master with astonishment. This was the first compliment Horkin had ever paid him and the chill of the young man's fear warmed with pleasure.

"Thank you, sir."

"Likely that day will be long in coming," Horkin continued cheerfully. "Seeing that you can't even cast a burning-hands spell now without setting your own clothes afire."

"I told you, sir, I was not feeling well that day—" Raistlin began.

Horkin grinned. "Just teasing, Red. Just teasing."

Raistlin was in no mood for Horkin's jollity. "If you will excuse me, sir, I am very tired. It must be well past midnight and from what I understand there is a battle to be fought tomorrow morning. With your permission, I will go to bed."

"It's all very strange," muttered Horkin to himself after his apprentice had departed. "This albino wizard. Like nothing I've encountered before and I've been pretty well all over this continent. But then it seems to me that Krynn itself is becoming a very strange place. A very strange place indeed."

Shaking his head, Horkin went off to drink a late night's toast to the world's strangeness with the baron.

8

The baron had said nothing to his troops about Commander Kholos and his insulting remarks. But the baron had not forbidden his bodyguards to talk of what they had seen and heard in the ally's camp. The commander's words about "yelping curs" spread among the mercenaries like a forest fire during the night, jumping from one knot of angry men to the next, starting blazes all over camp. The men began to say that they'd take the west wall, damn the commander's eyes, and not only that, they'd take the whole blasted city, too, before he'd finished his breakfast.

When word came that the flank company, under command of Master Senej, would have the honor of attacking in the morning, the rest of the soldiers regarded them with raw envy, while members of the lucky company busily polished their armor and tried to look nonchalant, as if this were all in a day's work.

"Raist!" Caramon burst like a gust of wind into his brother's tent. "Did you hear—"

"I am trying to sleep, Caramon," Raistlin said caustically. "Go away."

"But this is important. Raist, it's our squad that's—"

"You knocked over my staff," Raistlin observed.

"Sorry. I'll pick it—"

"Don't touch it!" Raistlin ordered. Rising from his bed, he retrieved the staff, moved it to stand by the head of his cot. "Now, what is it you want?" he asked wearily. "Make it quick. I am extremely tired."

Not even his brother's ill temper could destroy Caramon's pride and excitement. He seemed to fill the entire tent as he spoke, his good health and his powerful body swelling in the darkness, expanding to take up all the space, sucking away all the air, leaving his twin crushed and smothered.

"Our squad's been chosen to lead the assault tomorrow morning. 'First to fight,' that's what the master said. Are you coming with us, Raist? This'll be our first battle!"

Raistlin stared into the darkness. "If so, I have not yet received any orders."

"Oh, uh, that's too bad." Caramon was momentarily deflated. But excitement soon returned, swelling him again. "You will. I'm sure of it. Just think! Our first battle!"

Raistlin turned his head on the pillow, away from his brother.

Caramon felt suddenly that it was time to leave. "I got to sharpen my sword. I'll see you in the morning, Raist. G'night." He departed with as much noise and clamor as he had entered.

* * * * *

"Excuse me, sir," said Raistlin, standing outside Horkin's tent. "Are you asleep?"

There came a grumbling growl in response. "Yes."

"I'm sorry to wake you, sir." Raistlin slipped inside the tent where his master lay on a cot, blankets pulled up to his chin. "But I have just heard that my brother's company has been ordered to attack the west wall tomorrow morning. I thought perhaps you would like me to prepare some magicks—"

Horkin sat up, his eyes squinched shut against the light of the Staff of Magius. The mage did not sleep in his robes, which were folded neatly on top of his pack at the side of cot. He slept in what he termed his "altogether."

"Shut off that damn light, Red! What are you trying to do? Blind me? There, that's better. Now, what is this folderol you're singing me?"

Patiently Raistlin repeated himself. Quenching the light of his staff, he stood in the darkness of the tent, a darkness that smelled of stale sweat and crushed flowers.

"You woke me up to tell me that?" Horkin grumbled. Lying back down, he grabbed hold of the blanket, twitched it up over his shoulders. "We'll both need our sleep, Red. We'll have wounded tomorrow."

"Yes, sir," Raistlin said. "But about the battle—"

"The baron hasn't given me any orders about the battle tomorrow, Red. But then"—Horkin tended to be sarcastic when he was sleepy—"perhaps he gave them to you."

"No, sir," Raistlin said. "I just thought—"

"There you go, thinking again!" Horkin snorted. "Listen to me, Red. Tomorrow's fight is a feint, a skirmish. We're testing the city's defenses. And the last thing you want to do when you're testing the enemy is to show them everything you've got! We're the big finish, you and I, Red. The baron brings us mages in at the last act to the dismay and wonderment of all. Now go and let me get some sleep!"

Horkin pulled the blankets up over his head.

* * * * *

No one wanted to settle down to sleep that night. Everyone wanted to stay up and talk and boast of what deeds he would do tomorrow or complain bitterly that he was being left out or go offer advice and well-wishes to those fortunate enough to be in on the first assault. The sergeants let them talk it out, then went through the camp, ordering everyone to hit the hay, they'd need their rest for the morrow. Eventually, the camp quieted, though few actually slept.

Raistlin returned to his tent, where he was seized with an unusually severe fit of coughing. He spent most of the night attempting to breathe.

The baron lay in his tent thinking regretfully of all the things he might have said to flatten Commander Kholos.

Horkin, having been awakened by Raistlin, could not go back to sleep. He lay awake in bed, muttering imprecations on the head of his assistant and thinking about the upcoming assault. Horkin's usually cheerful face was grave. He sighed and with a muttered prayer to his drinking buddy, dear Luni, he fell asleep.

Scrounger lay awake staring into the darkness in fear and trembling because someone had told him that he was going to be left behind during the assault due to the fact that he was too short.

After Caramon had polished his armor until it was a wonder he didn't wear a hole in it, he rolled himself in his blanket, lay down, and thought, "You know, I might die tomorrow." He was pondering this eventuality and wondering how he felt about it when he woke to find it was morning.

* * * * *

The sky was pearl gray, covered with low-hanging clouds. And though it was not yet raining, everything in camp was wet. The air itself was damp and soggy, hot without the hint of a breeze. The company flag hung limp and listless on its standard. All sounds were muted in the thick air. The blacksmith's usually ringing blows sounded discordant and tinny.

Master Senej's company was up early. They fell into line in front of the mess tent.

"First to fight, first to breakfast!" Caramon said, grinning as he clapped Scrounger on the back. "I like this arrangement!"

During the nights leading up to the attack, the flank company had been out scouting, which meant that they were the last ones into camp and the last to line up for breakfast or what was left of breakfast after the rest of the troops had descended on it like gully dwarves.

Caramon, who had been subsisting on cold oatmeal for the past few days, eyed the rashers of sizzling bacon and fresh hot bread with immense satisfaction.

"Aren't you eating?" he asked Scrounger.

"No, Caramon, I'm not hungry. Do you really think what Damark said was true? Do you really think the sergeant won't let me—"

"Go on, fill your plate!" Caramon urged. "I'll eat what you don't want. He'll have some of those wheat cakes, too," Caramon told the cook.

Caramon settled down at the long plank table with two loaded plates. Scrounger sat beside him, chewing on his nails and casting pleading glances at the sergeant every time she walked past.

"Oh, hullo, Raist," Caramon said, looking up from his food to find his brother standing over him.

Raistlin was pale and wan, with dark smudges beneath his eyes. His robes were soaked with rain and his own sweat. The hand holding the staff trembled.

"You don't look good, Raist," Caramon said worriedly, rising to his feet, breakfast forgotten. "Do you feel all right?"

"No," Raistlin returned in a rasping voice. "I don't feel 'all right.' I never feel 'all right.' If you must know, I have been up all night. No, don't fuss over me! I am better now. I cannot stay long. I have my duties to attend to. Rolling bandages in the healing tent." He sounded bitter. "I just came by to wish you well."

Raistlin's thin fingers touched Caramon's forearm, startling him.

"Take care of yourself, my brother," Raistlin said quietly.

"Uh, sure. I will. Thanks, Raist," Caramon said, touched.

He started to add that his twin should also take care of himself, but by the time the words were out, Raistlin was gone.

"Gee, that was odd," said Scrounger as Caramon resumed his seat and his breakfast.

"Not really," Caramon said, smiling, elated. "We're brothers."

"I know. It's just that I . . ."

"You what?" Caramon looked up.

Scrounger had been about to say that he had never before known Raistlin to do or say anything the least bit brotherly and that it was odd for him to start now. But seeing Caramon's open face and his honest pleasure, the half-kender changed his mind.

"You want my eggs?"

Caramon grinned. "Hand 'em over."

He had no chance to finish his own eggs, however. The attack was set for early morning and before he was halfway through breakfast, the drums began to beat, calling the men of Flank Company to arms. As the soldiers were putting on their gear, a light rain began to fall. Water dribbled down metal helms into their eyes and seeped into their leather padding, causing it to chafe the skin. Beads of water formed in the men's beards, droplets hung off the men's noses. The soldiers wiped their eyes to see. Their hands fumbled on the wet metal of buckles. Leather straps proved recalcitrant in the damp. No amount of tugging would cause them to cinch properly. Swords slipped from wet hands.

Most strange and ominous, the rain caused the city walls to change color. The walls were formed of rock that was a light brown in color. The rain brought out a red tint in the rock, made the walls look as if they had been washed with a thin coating of blood. The soldiers cast dour glances at the west wall that was their objective and then looked glumly at the sky, hoping the sun would reappear.

Scrounger assisted Caramon to put on the leather armor, which was different from the armor the Flank Company usually wore. This armor was padded along the arms and the torso, then covered with strips of metal. The armor was heavy but provided much better protection than the lightweight leather armor the men wore during scouting missions. The men had borrowed the armor from A Company, along with the large shields they would be carrying into battle this day.

Scrounger was glum, kept blinking his eyes. The rumor he'd heard had proven true. He'd been ordered to stay behind while the rest of the company advanced for the attack. Scrounger had pleaded and even argued until Sergeant Nemiss lost patience with him. She brought forth one of the huge shields the soldiers would be carrying and tossed it to the half-kender. The shield knocked him flat.

"See there," she said. "You can't even lift it!"

The men laughed. Scrounger struggled out from under the heavy shield, still arguing. Sergeant Nemiss clapped him on the shoulder and told him he "was a game little fighting cock" and that "if he could find a big shield he could carry, he could come along." Then she ordered Scrounger to help the other soldiers with their armor.

He did as he was ordered, complaining and protesting the entire time that it wasn't fair. He had as much training as anyone. The others would think he was a coward. He didn't see why he couldn't use his old shield and so on. Suddenly, however, Scrounger's complaints ended.

Caramon felt badly for his friend, but he thought that the whining had really gone on long enough. He breathed a sigh of relief, thinking that Scrounger had finally acceptied his cruel fate. "I'll see you after we take that wall," said Caramon, putting on his helm.

"Good luck, Caramon," said Scrounger, holding out his hand with a smile.

Caramon stared hard at his friend. He'd seen that same sweet and innocent smile before on the face of another good friend, Tasslehoff Burrfoot. Caramon knew kender well enough to be highly suspicious. He couldn't imagine what Scrounger might be up to and before he could give the matter serious thought, Sergeant Nemiss called the company to attention.

Master Senej rode his horse to the front of the ranks. Dismounting, he made a quick but thorough inspection, tugging on armor to make sure it wasn't going to come loose, examining the points of the spears to make certain they were sharp. Inspection completed, he faced his troops. The entire camp had gathered to listen and to watch.

"We're going to test the western defenses today, men. We want to see if there are any surprises waiting for us in that city. The drill is simple. Close ranks as tight as possible, hold your shields high, and march in formation toward the wall. We'll take a hell of a beating from their archers, but most of the arrows will hit our shields.

"Our own archers will try to clear the wall as best they can, but don't think they're going to solve our problems. Having seen our archers at practice, I'm more worried about them hitting us than I am about them clearing the wall."

Archer Company began to jeer and boo. The Flank Company laughed. Tension eased, which was what the master intended. He knew that unless the enemy was completely incompetent, his men would be facing overwhelming odds. How overwhelming the odds and how skilled the enemy were two questions he was about to have answered. He did not mention the army of their allies, who had gathered to watch the assault. The hulking figure of their commander could be seen mounted on his battle horse a safe distance from the firing.

"Enough talk then!" Master Senej shouted. "As soon as we get the signal that the Archer Company is in place, we'll do our duty and be back in time for lunch." His gaze roamed the lines, fixed on Caramon. The master smiled and added, "We're first in line for lunch, too, Majere."

Caramon felt his face redden, but he was always ready to laugh at himself and he joined good-naturedly in the ribbing.

C Company marched to the front of the camp and assembled in tight formation, three ranks deep. Caramon stood in the last rank. Master Senej took his place in the front of the ranks. An aide led his horse away. The master was going to walk with his men. As the master raised his sword, Caramon felt a hand tugging the back of his armor. Twisting his head, he looked around and saw Scrounger crowding close behind him, nearly stepping on the big man's heels.

"The sergeant said I could come if I found a shield," Scrounger said. "I guess you're it, Caramon. I hope you don't mind."

Caramon didn't know whether he minded or not. He didn't have time to consider. Off to the right, a flag dipped and raised again. Archer Company was in place. The master raised his sword.

"Forward! Flank Company—first to fight!"

The company gave a cheer and began to march forward at a slow but steady pace, their flag bearer proudly taking the lead behind the master.

Back in camp, the trumpets and drums of the baron's signalers began to play a marching tune with a pounding beat making it easier for the men to keep in step. Left feet came down with the beat of the bass drum. The soldiers moved forward in unison, locked together with their shields and spears at the ready.

The music heightened Caramon's excitement. He looked at the men next to him, his comrades, and his heart swelled with pride. He had never felt so close to anyone before, not even to his twin, as to these men moving forward to face death together. The little flutter of fear that had bothered his stomach and gripped his bowels disappeared. He was invincible, nothing could harm him. Not this day.

A small creek crossed the field between the camp and the city wall that was their objective. The creek bed was dry in the summer, but the sides were fairly steep and it would take time to cross, particularly as the grass that covered the bank was slippery wet with the light rain. The company met the creek bed at an angle, the right flank of the company crossing before the left. Small gaps appeared in the line while the soldiers slowed to watch their footing, then the line reformed on the other side.

"Why haven't they fired at us?" Scrounger wondered. "Why are they waiting?"

Sergeant Nemiss, off to Caramon's left, barked, "Shut up and keep tight. They'll fire soon enough. Sooner than you're ready!"

A soft sibilant sound, unlike any sound Caramon had ever heard in his life—a hissing and a whirring and a swishing sound all combined—caused the hair to rise on the back of his neck.

The line's advance faltered. Everyone heard the ominous noise. Caramon looked up over his shield to see. The sky above him was dark with what he realized in astonishment was a deadly flight of hundreds of arrows.

"Keep your damned shield up!" the sergeant yelled.

Remembering his training, Caramon hastily lifted his shield over his head. Less than a second later, the shield vibrated and shook with the impact of arrows. Caramon was amazed at the force of the blows, as if someone were pounding on his shield with a war hammer.

And then it was over.

Caramon hesitated, cringing, waiting for another attack. When none came, he ventured to look at the front of his shield. Four arrows stuck out of it, their feathered shafts lodged solidly in the metal. Caramon gulped, thinking what those arrows would have done if they had struck him instead of the shield. Some of the soldiers were yanking the arrows from their shields, tossing them aside. Caramon twisted around to see how Scrounger had fared.

Scrounger looked up with a tremulous smile. "Whoo, boy!" was all he said.

Caramon glanced on either side, couldn't see anyone down. There were no holes in the line. The master looked back with a quick glance to see that the company was still with him.

"Forward, men!" he yelled.

The sibilant hissing came again, but this time, from their right flank. Archer Company was firing back. Arrows sped toward the city walls, flying over the heads of the Flank Company as they moved forward. Another flight of arrows launched from the city.

Caramon raised his shield. Arrows thunked home. He staggered from the impact, but continued moving forward. A ragged cry nearby caused him to jerk his head. A man in Caramon's line dropped to the ground, rocking back and forth in agony, screaming. An arrow had shattered his shinbone. A hole gaped in the line. The man behind the wounded man jumped over him and plugged the hole.

C Company continued to move. Caramon was angry and frustrated. He wanted to lash out, to attack something, but there was nothing to attack. He couldn't do a damn thing but walk forward and get shot at. Archer Company's return fire didn't seem to be having any effect. Yet another volley of arrows rained down from the sky.

The third volley struck. A man in front of Caramon fell backward, landed at Caramon's feet. The man didn't scream. He couldn't scream, Caramon saw, horrified. The man had taken an arrow through the throat. He clasped his hand over the terrible wound. Gurgling sounds came from his gaping mouth.

"Don't stop! Close up the line, damn you!" a veteran yelled and thwacked Caramon on the arm with his shield.

Caramon hopped sideways to avoid stepping on the wounded man. Slipping on the wet, bloody grass, he nearly lost his balance. Hands behind him grasped hold of his belt, helped him keep his feet. When the whirring sound came again, Caramon scrunched down to try to make himself as small as he could behind his shield.

And then, inexplicably, the arrows stopped. The company closed within a hundred and fifty yards of the objective. Perhaps Archer Company had cleared the wall. Perhaps the enemy had turned tail and fled. Caramon lifted his head cautiously to see. Then came a thud that Caramon felt more than heard, as of something heavy hitting the sodden ground. The thud was followed by a crack. Caramon looked around to see the nature of the odd sounds, watched two files of men cease to exist. One second there were six men to his right. The next, no one.

A large boulder rolled and bounded across the blood-stained grass, finally came to a halt. Fired from a catapult atop the city wall, the boulder had plowed into the line of men, and they were no longer men. They were nothing but blood and mangled flesh and splintered bone.

The screams of the wounded, the stench of blood and urine and excrement, for many of the dying soldiers could no longer control their bowels, caused Caramon to lose the breakfast he'd been so pleased to eat. Bending over, he purged his stomach. The sound of another volley was almost too much for him. He longed to run away, to flee this dreadful killing field. His training held him in place, training and the thought that if he ran he would be branded a coward, forever disgraced.

He crouched behind his shield. Twisting his head, he looked behind him, worried for Scrounger, but couldn't find his friend. Three men went down to his left, including the company standard-bearer. The company flag dropped forward into the grass. The entire line had stopped moving. Both the master and the sergeant were still advancing.

Suddenly there was Scrounger. Hopping over bodies of the dead and dying, he reached the standard-bearer and, braving a flight of arrows from the city walls, he picked up the flag and waved it proudly over his head with a defiant yell.

The rest of C Company joined the yell, but it was ragged. Both the sergeant and master turned their heads and saw the terrible destruction. Another volley of arrows and the thud of another boulder—this time falling short of the mark—spurred the master to action. His men had taken enough punishment.

"Fall back! Fall back in ranks! Keep your shields up!" the master yelled.

Caramon dashed over to protect Scrounger, covering his back with his shield. The half-kender paid no attention to the arrows that darted around him, but marched proudly, waving the flag in his hands. The company moved in orderly retreat, no panic, no breaking and running. If a man fell, the others moved in to close the line. Some stopped to help the wounded back to the camp. Archer Company sent volley after volley into the city walls, covering the retreat.

Scrounger carried the flag, Caramon held his shield so that it protected both of them. Fifty more paces, and the men began to relax. No more arrows came from the walls. The soldiers were finally out of range.

A hundred more paces and the master halted the company. He lowered his shield to the ground. The rest of the company did the same. Caramon felt the shield's weight fall from his arm. It must have weighed a hundred pounds, or so he felt. His arm trembled from the strain.

Scrounger, his face dead white, continued to hold the flag.

"You can put it down now," Caramon said to his friend.

"I can't let go," Scrounger said, his voice quivering. He stared at his hand as if it were a hand belonging to someone else. "I can't let go, Caramon!" He burst into tears.

Caramon reached out his hand to help loosen Scrounger's grasp. The big man saw his own hand covered with blood. Glancing down, he saw his breastplate smeared with blood and spatters of gore. He lowered his hand, did not touch Scrounger.

"All right. Listen here!" the master yelled. "The baron knows what he wanted to know. The city's defenses are more than adequate."

The men said nothing. They were exhausted, the spirit drained from them.

"You fought well. I'm proud of you. We lost good men out there today," Master Senej continued, "and I intend to go out there and bring back the bodies. We'll wait for nightfall."

A murmur of agreement came from the men.

Sergeant Nemiss dismissed the company. The men wandered back to their tents or went to the tents of the healers, to see how wounded comrades fared. Some of the new recruits, Caramon and Scrounger among them, remained standing in line, too dazed and shocked to leave.

The sergeant approached Scrounger. Reaching out her hand, she took the company standard from the half-kender's deathlike grip.

"You disobeyed orders, soldier," Sergeant Nemiss said, her voice stern.

"No, I didn't, sir," Scrounger said. "I found a shield." He pointed at Caramon. "One I could use."

Sergeant Nemiss grinned, shook her head. "If we measured men by their spirit, you'd be a giant. Speaking of giants, you did well yourself out there, Majere. I thought you'd be the first man hit. You make a great target."

"I don't remember much, sir," Caramon replied, bound to be honest, though it might lower him in her estimation. "If you want to know the truth, I was scared spitless." He hung his head. "I spent most of the battle hiding behind my shield."

"That's what kept you alive today, Majere," said the sergeant. "Looks like I might have taught you something after all."

The sergeant walked away, handing the standard to one of the veterans as she passed.

"You go on to lunch," Caramon said to his friend.

"I'm not very hungry. I think I'm going to go lie down."

"Lunch?" Scrounger stared at him. "It's not near time for lunch. It's only been half an hour since we ate breakfast."

Half an hour. It might have been half a year. Half a lifetime. A whole lifetime for some.

Tears welled up in Caramon's eyes. He turned his head quickly, so no one would notice.

9

lank Company recovered its dead under cover of darkness, buried them in darkness in a single grave so that the enemy would not be able to calculate how many men were lost. The baron spoke at the simple ceremony, citing each man by name and recounting some tale of his heroism, past and present. The common grave was covered with dirt and an honor guard was posted to keep off roving wolves. The baron gave C Company a barrel of dwarf spirits and bid them drink to the memory of their fallen comrades.

Caramon drank not only to their memory but also to the memories of those who had fallen since time began, or so it seemed to Scrounger, who had to practically drag the big man back to the tent. Caramon collapsed in a drunken stupor, falling face first into his cot with a thud that smashed the cot and caused the men in the tents on either side to wonder if the enemy was hurling more boulders at them.

Raistlin spent the night in the tent with the wounded, assisting Horkin with bandages and ointment. Most of the wounds were minor flesh wounds, with the exception of the soldier with the shattered leg. His comrades had carried him under a rain of arrows to the healing tent. Raistlin was privileged to witness his first battlefield amputation. He mixed a potion of mandrake root to be used to render the patient unconscious, added to that a sleep spell. The man's friends held his arms and shoulders to halt any involuntary movement.

Raistlin had spent hours with Weird Meggin, dissecting corpses under her tutelage to learn more about the marvels of the human body, and had not felt the least squeamish. He had practiced his healing skills among the plague-ravaged populace of Solace without blenching. He had volunteered to assist at the operation, had assured the leech that he was impervious to the sight of blood and would not fail at his post.

The blood—and there was an enormous quantity of it, Raistlin could not imagine that one body could hold so much—did not shake him. It was the sound of the saw blade, rasping and hacking through the bone just below the knee, that caused Raistlin to clench his teeth against the bile surging up from his stomach, caused him to close his eyes more than once to prevent himself from fainting.

He managed to make it through the operation, but when the leg was removed and carried off to be buried in the grave with the dead, Raistlin asked permission to leave the tent for a moment. The surgeon, looking at his assistant's deathly pale face, nodded his head curtly and told Raistlin to go get some sleep. The patient would manage well enough until morning.

Between mandrake and magic and loss of blood, the amputee was quiet. The other wounded were asleep. Raistlin returned to his tent, his body bathed in sweat, and sank down into his cot, an object of scorn and derision to one person at least. Himself.

* * * * *

The allies met again at noon, the baron once again riding over to confer with Commander Kholos. The commander was more respectful, if not more cordial. He permitted the baron to retain his sword and actually invited him to sit down while they discussed plans for the coming battle that would bring Hope's End to its knees.

Both men agreed that the city's defenses, as demonstrated yesterday, were formidable. A direct assault, even by the combined strength of both their armies, would most likely fail. Their forces would be decimated by the time they reached the walls. Kholos proposed settling in for a prolonged siege. Give the people of Hope's End a few months to deplete their food stores, a few more months of eating rats and watching their children die of starvation, and their enthusiasm for this rebellion would wane.

This plan was not acceptable to the baron, who had no intention of remaining in the commander's company for any longer than was absolutely necessary. The baron offered an alternative.

"I propose that we end this war quickly. Send a force inside the city, attack them from behind, and open the gate before they know what's hit them."

"Defeat them by treachery?" Kholos grinned. "I like it!"

"Yes, I thought you would," the baron said dryly.

"Whose force would we use to infiltrate behind enemy lines?" Kholos asked, frowning.

"I offer my men," the baron replied with dignity, having known that this question would be asked. "You have seen them in action. You cannot question their valor."

"Wait outside," said Kholos. "I have to think about this, discuss it with my officers."

Pacing outside the commander's tent, the baron overheard much of the conversation within. He flushed in anger and ground his teeth at Kholos's loud statement, "If the mercenaries are killed, we've lost nothing. We can always starve out the town later. If they succeed, we save ourselves a lot of time and trouble."

When he was invited back inside the commander's tent, the baron voluntarily handed over his sword to Kholos's aide, so as to not be tempted to use it.

"Very well, Baron," said Kholos. "We have decided to follow your plan. Your men will enter the city, attack from behind. At your signal, we will attack the gates from the front."

"I trust I may count upon you to storm the walls," the baron said, regarding the commander intently. "If your men do not draw off resistance, my people will be slaughtered."

"Yes, I'm aware of that," Kholos replied, picking his teeth with a bird bone. He grinned and winked. "I give you my word."

"Do you trust him, sir?" Commander Morgon asked, as they left Kholos's tent.

"Not as far as I can smell him," said the baron grimly.

"That would imply a considerable amount of trust, sir," said Morgon with a straight face.

"Ha! Ha!" The baron laughed boisterously and slapped his commander on the back. "A good one, Morgon. A very good one." He chuckled all the way back to camp.

* * * * *

"Sir," said Master Senej, "C Company volunteers for this duty. You owe us, sir," he added loudly. Every other company commander was making the same offer.

The baron cut them off, turned to Senej. "Explain yourself, Master."

"The men went out on a hopeless mission, sir," he said. "They were whipped. They had to turn tail in the face of the enemy and run for it."

"They knew there was that possibility when they went into battle," said the baron, frowning.

"Yes, sir." Master Senej stood his ground. "But they feel it, sir. Their heads are down, their rear ends dragging. That was the first time C Company has ever been defeated—"

"But, for the love of Kiri-Jolith, Master—" the baron began, exasperated.

"My lord, that was the first time anyone in this army has been defeated," Master Senej said, standing stiffly at attention. "The men want a chance to redeem their honor, sir."

The other commanders were silent. Though all were itching to take part in the action, they accepted the right of Major Senej to put forth his cause.

"Very well," the baron said. "Major Senej, C Company will enter the city. But this time I'm sending along a wizard. Master Horkin!"

"My lord!"

"You will go along on this mission."

"Begging your pardon, my lord, but I suggest that you send my assistant."

"Is the young man ready for an assignment this important, Horkin?" the baron asked gravely. "Majere seems awfully weak and sickly to me. I was going to suggest that he be mustered out."

"Red's stronger than he appears, my lord," said Horkin. "Stronger than he knows himself or such is my opinion. He's a better mage than I am." Horkin said this without rancor, simply stating a fact. "Where the lives of the men are at stake, I think you should use the best."

"Well, of course," said the baron, taken aback. "But you've had experience—"

"And how did I get that experience, my lord, if it wasn't for the experience," Horkin returned triumphantly. "Which he'll never get if you don't let him."

"I suppose that's true," the baron replied, though he still looked dubious. "You're in command of the wizardry. What I know about magic you could put in a rat's teacup. Major Senej, find Majere and tell him that he's now attached to your company. Report back to me for your orders."

"Yes, sir!" Major Senej said, saluting. "And thank you, my lord!"

* * * * *

"Raist, did you hear the news?" Caramon stood meekly outside the entrance to Raistlin's tent. The big man had a terrible headache, felt like gnomes were using his stomach for a boiler. What with the horror of the battle, the solemnity of the funeral, and the aftereffects of the wake, he was beginning to rethink his commitment to a life in the military. He tried to appear excited, however. For his brother's sake. "We're infiltrating the city and you're coming with us!"

"Yes, I heard," Raistlin called irritably, not looking up from the spellbook he had balanced on his knees. "Now go away and leave me alone, Caramon. I have all these spells to memorize before nightfall."

"This is what we always wanted, Raist," Caramon said, sounding wistful. "Isn't it?"

"Yes, Caramon, I suppose it is," Raistlin replied.

Caramon stood a moment longer, hoping to be asked inside, hoping to have a chance to talk about his fear, his shame, his longing to go back home. But Raistlin said nothing, gave no indication that he was aware of his twin's continued existence. Eventually, Caramon left.

After his brother had gone, Raistlin sat and stared at the spellbook. The letters ran higgledy-piggledy across the pages, the words slid from his brain as if they were greased. His brother and the others were going to be dependent on him to keep them alive. What a joke! But then, the gods were always playing jokes on him.

Raistlin went back despairingly to his studies, a coward so cowardly he dared not admit he was one.

10

Kitiara arrived in Kholos's camp the afternoon following the failed attack by the mercenaries on the city's wall. She was later than she'd thought she would be, knew that Immolatus would be seething with impatience. The secret opening in the mountain proved to be farther from camp than she had guessed, the way more difficult to travel.

She found the dragon sleeping soundly in his tent, heedless of the furious hammerings of the blacksmith, whose portable forge was nearby.

Kit could hear Immolatus's snore over the pounding of the smith's hammer. She barged into the dragon's tent without bothering to announce herself, tripped on something that rolled out from under her foot. Swearing roundly, she caught her balance, peered down at the object closely in the dim light.

A map case? She was about to pick it up when she saw that it was a scroll case, such as wizards use to carry their magic spells. Kit let the case lie. No telling what spells of protection might be laid upon it. Several other scroll cases lay scattered about, as well as numerous rings that had spilled out of a pouch and a broken crock of what had been, by the smell, chicken broth.

Here was a mystery. The scroll cases did not belong to Immolatus, nor did he appear to have any interest in them, since he left them lying on the ground. Kit guessed that some sort of meeting had occurred in her absence, though with whom she could not fathom. The scroll cases bespoke a wizard, the chicken broth a cook. Perhaps the camp cook was also a dabbler in magic. Kit hoped to the heavens that Immolatus had not insulted the cook. The food was bad enough as it was.

She stood glaring down at him, resenting the fact that he was here snug and cozy in his tent, taking a nap while she'd been out doing his dirty work. She took grim delight in waking him.

"Eminence." Kit shook him by the shoulder. "Immolatus."

He woke swiftly, eyes open, fully conscious, staring up at her with a fury and a loathing that was not directed so much at her but at the daily realization and bitter disappointment he experienced on waking to find himself imprisoned in human flesh. He glared up at her, his red eyes cold, hating her, despising her as he despised all her kind, regarding her as she herself might regard a bloated, swollen tick.

She moved her hand from his shoulder swiftly, took a step back. She had never known anyone rise from the depths of slumber to this level of awareness so quickly. There was something unnatural about it.

"I'm sorry to wake you, Eminence," she said, and that much was true. "But I thought you would like to know that I succeeded in completing our assignment." She really could not help adding a slight ironic emphasis to the plural. "I thought you might want to hear what I found."

Glancing about, she added offhandedly, "What happened, Eminence? What is all this stuff?"

Immolatus sat up on the bed. He slept in his red robes, never removed them, never washed them, never bathed. He gave off a disgusting odor, a musty smell of death and decay that reminded Kitiara of the dragon's dank lair.

"I had a most interesting encounter with a young mage," Immolatus replied.

Kitiara kicked aside a scroll case that was in her way and sat down. "He must have left in a hurry."

"Yes, he did not care to linger." Immolatus smiled unpleasantly, muttered, "He has something I want."

"Why didn't you just take it from him?" Kit asked impatiently.

She was truly not the least bit interested. The journey had been long. She was tired and irritable. She had important information to convey, if only the dragon would shut up long enough to hear it.

"A typical human response." Immolatus glowered. "There are subtleties involved that you would not understand. I will have the item, but in my own way and my own time. You will find a note on the table. I want you to take it to the young mage. He serves, I believe, with those we so quaintly term our allies."

Immolatus gestured to a scroll case lying on the table. The scroll had been removed. Apparently the message was inside.

Kit started to angrily retort that she was not Immolatus's errand boy. Fearing that this would provoke an argument, when all she wanted to do was to relay her information and go to bed, she swallowed the words.

"What is the mage's name, my lord?" Kitiara asked.

"Magius," returned Immolatus.

"Magius." She left the tent, hailed a passing soldier, and handed over the scroll case with orders to see that it was delivered.

"Well, uth Matar?" Immolatus said, on her return, "what of your mission? Was it successful? I gather it was not, since you are stalling, refusing to tell me."

In answer, Kitiara pulled the book from her belt and handed in to the dragon. "See for yourself, Eminence."

He accepted the proffered book eagerly, almost snatching it from her hand. "So you did find the eggs of the metallic dragons."

A low chuckle of malicious joy gurgled deep in his throat. He scanned the numbers covetously, as she explained her notation.

"I counted them by rows; there are quite a number of them. 'G' stands for 'gold' and 's' for silver, so that '11/34 eggs s' means that there are thirty-four silver dragon eggs in row number eleven."

"I am quite capable of understanding your scrawls, despite the fact that they look as if a hen has walked over the pages."

"I am glad my work pleases you, my lord," Kitiara said, too tired to care if he heard the sarcasm or not.

He did not hear her. He was intent upon studying her notes, muttering to himself, performing calculations, nodding, pleased, and emitting that sinister chuckle. When he turned the page and saw the map, a smirk contorted his features. He very nearly purred with delight.

"So this . . . this is the route to the secret entrance in the mountain." He eyed it, frowning. "It seems clear enough."

"It will be quite clear to Commander Kholos," Kitiara said, yawning. She held out her hand. "I'll take it to him now, Eminence, if you're finished with it."

Immolatus did not hand it back. He stared with intense concentration at the map. Kitiara had the impression that he was committing the map to memory.

"Are you going to the cave, Eminence?" Kitiara asked, startled and uneasy. "There's no reason for you to do so. I assure you that my figures are accurate. If you doubt me—"

"I do not doubt you, uth Matar," said the dragon pleasantly. He was in an extremely good humor. "At least not more than I would doubt any worm such as yourself."

"Then, Eminence," said Kitiara, giving him one of her most charming smiles, "you should not waste your time traveling to this cave. Our work is finished. Now would be an excellent time for us to depart. General Ariakas gave orders that we were to return to him with this information as quickly as possible."

"You are right, uth Matar," said Immolatus. "You should return to General Ariakas immediately."

"Eminence—"

The dragon was laughing at her. "I have no further need of your services, uth Matar. Go back to Ariakas and claim your reward. I am certain he will be most happy to provide it."

Immolatus rose from his bed, brushed past her, heading out of the tent. Kitiara caught hold of his arm.

"What are you going to do?" she demanded.

He gazed balefully at her. "Release your hold of me, worm."

"What are you going to do?" Kitiara knew the answer. What she didn't know was what in the name of all that was holy she was going to do about it.

"That is my business, uth Matar," he said. "Not yours. You have nothing to say in the matter."

"You're going to destroy the eggs."

He shrugged off her grasp, again started to leave the tent.

"Damn it!" Kitiara pursued him, seized hold of his arm, digging her nails into his flesh. "You know your orders—"

"My orders!" He rounded on her, furious, savage. "I do not take orders! Certainly not from some piddling human who sticks a horned helm on his head and calls himself a 'dragonlord'!

"Oh, yes." Immolatus bared his teeth in a scornful grin. "I have heard Ariakas term himself this. 'Dragonlord!' As if he or any other human had the right to link his puny might and his pitiful mortality with us! Not that I blame him. He thinks that by emulating us in this pathetic fashion, he can garner for himself some small portion of the respect and fear that all species on Krynn grant to us."

The dragon snorted, a gout of flame flickered in his nostrils. He hissed his words. "Like a child parading around in his father's armor, he will find the weight too heavy to bear, and he will fall, a victim to his own self-delusion!

"I am going to destroy the eggs," the dragon said with soft fury. "Do you dare to try to stop me?"

Kitiara was in dire peril, but, as she saw it, she didn't have much to lose.

"General Ariakas gave the order, that is true, Eminence," she said, boldly meeting the dragon's glaring eyes. "But we both know who it is who gives him his orders. Will you disobey your Queen?"

"In a heartbeat," said Immolatus with a snap of his teeth. "You think I fear her? Perhaps I would, if Takhisis were in this world. She isn't, you know. She's trapped in the Abyss. Oh, she can rant and rave and stamp her pretty little foot but she can't touch me. And therefore I will have my revenge. I will avenge myself on the foul golds and silvers who slaughtered my comrades and drove us into isolation and oblivion. I will destroy their young as they destroyed ours. I will destroy the evil temple of an accursed god. I will destroy the city in which the temple stands and then"—his tongue flicked, a flame licking blood—"I will destroy the descendant of Magius. My revenge on them all will be complete."

The red eyes flickered. "You should leave while you can, uth Matar. If I find that Kholos and his rabble stand in my way, I will destroy them, as well."

"Lord," Kit argued desperately, "Her Dark Majesty has plans for these eggs."

"So do I," said Immolatus. "Soon Krynn and its people will see the true might of dragons. They will know that we have returned to take up our proper sphere—rulership of the world."

Kitiara could not allow him to ruin Ariakas's plans, could not allow the dragon to flout the orders of the Dark Queen. Above all, she could not allow Immolatus to wreck her plans and hopes and ambitions.

She drew her sword as he talked, her motion swift and fluid. Had Immolatus been human, he would have found a foot of steel in his gut before he could draw his next breath.

He was not human. He was a dragon, a red dragon, one of the most powerful beings on Krynn. Flame enveloped Kitiara. The air sizzled and crackled around her, burned her lungs when she tried to draw breath enough to scream, searing her flesh. She fell to her knees and waited to die.

The flames abated suddenly. She was not hurt, she realized after a moment, except for the horrible memory of being burned alive. For the moment, that's all it was, a memory. A memory and a threat. She remained where she had fallen, dejected, defeated.

"Farewell, uth Matar," said Immolatus pleasantly. "Thank you for your help." He left with a smile, a mocking bow, and a snap of his teeth.

Kitiara watched him walk out of the tent, watched her career walk out the tent with him.

She remained in her crouched and fallen position until she was certain that he would not return. Painfully, stiffly, she leveraged herself to her feet, using the cot to assist her. Once up and moving about, Kitiara felt better.

She walked outside, drew in a deep breath. Smoke-polluted air was better than the fetid, dragon-tinged air inside that tent. She sought a secluded part of the camp, found it behind the gallows. No one came here if he could help it. The only drawback was the flies. Kit ignored them. Alone, unseen, Kitiara mulled over her predicament.

She could not—*must* not—allow Immolatus to proceed with his intentions. Kit cared nothing for the dragon eggs. She cared nothing for the city or its inhabitants. As for the temple, after her unpleasant experience, she would have gleefully helped Immolatus destroy it herself. But she could not indulge in personal revenge, nor could the dragon. There was too much at stake here, the prize for which they gambled was enormous. And now, instead of placing what they'd won on the final bet, the dragon was going to spend their winnings on dinner and a show. And what a show it would be! Kitiara stomped the ground in anger and frustration.

Soon everyone in Ansalon would know that dragons had returned. Ariakas's army was not yet ready to launch a full-scale assault. That much was obvious by simply looking around this camp. Kholos and his raw recruits would be dog's meat for Solamnic Knights or any other well-trained force. They would lose the war before it had even started, all because one arrogant and egotistical monster decided to spit in his Queen's eye.

"I cannot best him in a fight," Kitiara muttered, walking ten paces one direction, turning and walking ten paces back. "His magic is too powerful. He's proven that. But even the most powerful mage has a weak spot—right between the shoulder blades."

She drew her dagger from her boot, stood turning the blade in her hand, watching the sunlight glint off the sharp steel. Though "Sir Nigel" might have been a phony Knight, he was true to his promise. She had recovered both her sword and her knife from the cavern.

"Even dragons don't have eyes in the backs of their heads. And Immolatus thinks himself invincible, always a mistake."

Locating a knot on a tree about twenty paces from where she stood, Kit held the dagger by the blade, aimed, and threw. The blade flashed through the air, buried itself about a handsbreadth from the knothole.

Kit grimaced. "Always did pull to the right." Going to the tree, she yanked out the dagger, which was buried in the wood almost to the hilt. "That would have killed him," she reflected. "At least when he's in human form. It wouldn't have done much to a dragon."

The thought was daunting. If he changed form, she didn't stand a chance. A horrible qualm seized her—suppose he had changed form already! He might, since he obviously didn't give a damn about anyone seeing him. He might have decided to fly to the cavern. . . .

No, Kit reflected. Immolatus would remain in his disguise, at least until he reached the cave. For all he knew, the eggs might have a guardian. He had been in such a hurry, he never asked her about that. A guardian who wouldn't be concerned at the coming of a red-robed mage, but who would sound the alarm at the advent of a red dragon.

Immolatus would use his human form to sneak inside the cave. At least that's what she hoped he had the good sense to do. And at the thought of relying on the dragon's good sense, Kitiara shook her head and sighed.

But whether he did or he didn't, she didn't have much choice. She had to find a way to stop him or she would be nothing but an itinerant sell-sword for the rest of her days.

Like your father, said an unbidden voice inside her.

Ignoring the voice, angry with it, Kitiara replaced the dagger in her boot and set off on the trail of the dragon.

II

Master Senej was right. His company's morale lifted considerably on being told they had been chosen to infiltrate the city and undermine its defenses from the inside. The mission was dangerous, but after having been forced to endure the deadly fire from the walls without being able to strike back, the men welcomed the opportunity.

"This is what we've been trained for," Sergeant Nemiss told her assembled troops. "Secrecy, stealth. Right up our alley. Here's the plan.

"We scale the cliffs to the south of the city, cross over a ridge, and climb down the mountain. We enter the city on the side of the wall that butts up against the mountain. No one will be looking for us to come that way, so it should be minimally guarded.

"The baron's map shows that there is a warehouse district located near an old abandoned temple close to where we go over the wall. From what we hear, no one has goods to sell, so we should find the warehouse empty. The plan is to reach the city before dawn tomorrow, hole up in the warehouse during the day. Late the next night we launch our attack."

Sergeant Nemiss jerked a thumb in the direction of Raistlin, who stood on the outskirts of the crowd.

"The wizard Raistlin Majere will be marching with us."

"Hurrah!" yelled Caramon from his place in the ranks.

Raistlin flushed deeply and cast his brother an annoyed glance. He noted that the rest of the members of

C Company were not nearly so enthusiastic at the idea. Horkin's long years of service had endeared him to the men, who tended to regard his being a mage as a minor personality flaw that they, as friends, were more than willing to overlook. Raistlin's odd appearance, his sickly demeanor, and his tendency to remain aloof from the other soldiers combined to make them chary of his company.

The men muttered into their beards, but no one said anything aloud. Caramon was watching them and those few who had come into contact with his fists had a healthy respect for his ability to punish any insult, real or imagined, to his twin. Sergeant Nemiss was also watching them. She would not tolerate any "bellyaching" about orders. Thus Raistlin was accepted into Flank Company without a word of complaint. One man even offered to carry his gear for him, but Caramon took that upon himself.

Raistlin would carry his scrolls, his staff, and his magical components himself. He would have liked to have taken along a spellbook, for though he had finally been able to memorize the spells Horkin considered necessary to an operation of this kind, Raistlin would have felt more confident with several more hours of study. But Horkin said that the risk of the precious spellbook falling into enemy hands was too great.

"I can replace you, Red," he added jovially. "I can't replace that spellbook."

"As soon as night falls, we'll begin the march," Sergeant Nemiss continued. "We hope to be through the mountains, ready to enter the city around dawn. Our allies are supposed to mount a diversion to keep the eyes of the rebels fixed on the front of the wall, not the back."

Someone in line made a rude sound.

Sergeant Nemiss nodded. "Yeah, I know what you're thinking. I think the same, but there's not much we can do about it. Any questions?"

Someone wondered what happened if anyone was separated from the group.

"Right, that's a good one," the sergeant answered. "If any of you get separated, return to camp. Don't try to sneak into the city on your own. You could put the entire plan at risk. No more questions? You're dismissed. Meet back here at sunset."

The men returned to their tents to pack up their gear. They left their tents in place so that the enemy would think they were still sleeping in them. They took with them only short swords, dirks and knives. No shields, no mail, no long swords or spears. Two men skilled in archery carried two of the valued elven longbows and quivers of arrows. All wore leather armor, no mail or plate, deemed too heavy and cumbersome for mountain climbing and too noisy for stealth. Each man carried a coil of rope over his shoulder. They would find water on the trail and march with short rations.

The prospect dismayed Caramon, but he bore up under the blow by reminding himself of the hardships of war. Caramon was feeling much better at the prospect of action. Caught up in the excitement of the moment, he was able to banish the terrible memories of the attack on the wall. Never one to dwell on the past, Caramon looked forward confidently to the future. He accepted whatever came, did not waste time worrying over what might have been or what might be coming.

By contrast, Raistlin worried over what he considered his failure when confronting the renegade wizard, fretted that he did not have his spells letter-perfect, imagined every dire event that might occur to him, from tumbling down the side of the mountain to being captured and tortured by the enemy. By the time the company was ready to move out, he had worked himself into such a fever of dread that he feared he was too weak to make the trip. He considered pleading illness and was on his feet to report to Horkin when he heard a name being shouted through the camp.

"Magius! Pass the word for Magius."

Magius! A name that might have rung through Huma's camp hundreds of years ago, but had no place in this day and age. Then Raistlin remembered. He had given the name Magius to the wizard Immolatus. Ducking out of his tent, Raistlin called, "What do you want with Magius?"

"Why, do you know him?" a soldier asked. "I have a message for him."

"I know *of* him," Raistlin said. "Give me the message. I will see to it that it is delivered."

The soldier did not hesitate. The scroll case he was supposed to deliver was covered with strange-looking symbols that appeared to be magical. The sooner he was free of the thing, the better. He handed it over.

"Who sent this?" Raistlin asked.

"The wizard in the other camp," the soldier replied and left quickly, not anxious to stay around to see what the case contained.

Retreating to his tent, Raistlin shut the flap and tied it tightly. He inspected the scroll case with the greatest care, alive to the possibility that it might be rigged for his destruction. He sensed an aura of magic about the case, but that was only natural. The magic did not appear to be very strong, however. Still, it was wise not to take a chance.

Raistlin placed the scroll case on the ground, facing away from him. Drawing his small knife, he positioned the tip of the blade on the lid of the case. He worked the tip in between the lid and the case itself and slowly, carefully began to prize off the lid.

The tent was hot from the afternoon sun. His tension increased the heat tenfold. Sweat bathed his neck and breast. He continued grimly with his task. He almost had it, the lid was close to coming off, when the knife slipped from his wet hand, jarred the case. The lid suddenly popped loose, rolled away.

Raistlin scrambled backward, nearly overturning his cot, his heart lurching in fright.

Nothing happened. The lid wobbled over the uneven ground, came to rest at the edge of the tent.

Raistlin paused to wipe his forehead and calm his heartbeat, then reached out and gingerly lifted the scroll case. He peered cautiously inside.

A bit of parchment paper had been stuffed into the case. He could make out handwriting. He held the case to the light, tried to see if the words were ordinary or the words of a magical spell. He couldn't tell and finally, impatient and no longer mindful of the consequences, he snatched the paper from the case.

Magius the Younger. I truly enjoyed our conversation. I was sorry to see you leave. Perhaps I said something to offend you. If so, I want to apologize and also to return your things you inadvertently left behind. When the city falls to our might, I look forward to renewing our acquaintance. We can have a pleasant chat.

The message was signed, *Immolatus*.

"So this is what he thinks of me," Raistlin said bitterly. "He takes me for a simple-minded fool who would walk into a trap so blatantly obvious that a blind, deaf, and dumb gully dwarf would avoid it. No, my two-faced friend, as interesting as you are, I have no intention of remaking your acquaintance."

He crumpled the missive in his hand. On his way to join C Company, he flung it contemptuously into a campfire. All thoughts of refusing to go on this mission evaporated in the heat of the insult. He was so fired up for action now that if had he not been assigned to this mission, he would have volunteered for it. He took his place beside Caramon.

"Move out!" The word passed quietly down the line from man to man. "Move out!"

* * * * *

The sky was overcast. A light rain continued to fall. The damp soaked into everything—the bread was soggy, firewood wouldn't light. The soldiers complained of the wet. Sergeant Nemiss and Master Senej were both in good humor. Heavy clouds meant no moonlight or starlight this night.

C Company marched for three hours before they reached the cliffs that rose up behind the city of Hope's

End. The distance was not that great—a good brisk walk of less than an hour would have taken them to the same place had they traveled in a straight line. Master Senej wanted to make certain that no one in the city gained an inkling of their plan and, though it was not likely that even the sharpest-eyed scout on the wall could have seen them, C Company took a circuitous route, marching directly away from the city and then doubling back.

Advance scouts had been sent ahead to search for a suitable location for the company to begin their ascent. At first, the scouts couldn't find any place. They began to fear that they would have to report to Major Senej that he better think of a new plan. The problem was fording the Hope River, for which the city had been named, a deep, swift-flowing river that cut through a canyon at the bottom of the mountain. The river was dotted with mills, whose wheels still turned, creaking and groaning, though the mills themselves were abandoned, their contents looted. The scouts began to worry.

The sun had set and C Company was on its way by the time the scouts found a place to ford the river. Flowing down out of the mountain, the river split around an island of rock, forming two relatively shallow streams that merged together farther down and tumbled headlong into the canyon. Pleased and relieved, the scouts hastened back to the assigned meeting place to serve as guides to the ford.

The soldiers waded into the rushing water, holding their weapons high. Though the air was warm, the water, coming down out of the mountains, was frigid. Caramon offered to carry his twin, but Raistlin gave him a look that might have turned butter rancid. He girded his robes up around his waist and entered the stream.

He crossed slowly, testing each step, terrified of plunging into the icy current. He was not concerned so much with himself as with his magical scrolls. Though they were safely secured in scroll cases, which were tightly sealed, he could not afford to take the chance that even the tiniest drop of water should seep in, set the ink to running, spoil the magic. When at last he was safely across, he was chilled to the bone, shivering so with the cold that his teeth chattered in his head.

The rocks that formed the island also formed a natural bridge across the second stream. Raistlin would be spared having to enter the water again. His relief was short-lived. The climb over the rock bridge proved as difficult as wading through the water, if not quite as uncomfortable. Raistlin's legs and feet were numb from the cold. He couldn't feel his toes, the rock was slippery from the constant rain. Even the veterans lost their footing, muttering soft curses as they slipped and slithered in the darkness. More than one came perilously close to falling into the water below. Between Caramon and Scrounger, who proved extremely adept at rock climbing, they managed to assist Raistlin over the most difficult parts.

C Company finally reached the bottom of the cliffs, where the real work would begin. Breathing heavily, nursing cuts and bruises, the men eyed the dark immensity of the mountain in silence. The scouts pointed out a ledge far above. Beyond that ledge, they could see the top of the cliff.

Cross that ridge, said the scouts, and beyond lies the city wall.

"Majere, you're the strongest," said Sergeant Nemiss, handing him an iron grappling hook. "Throw that as high above the ledge as you can throw."

Caramon swung the heavy grappling hook twice round and then released, his powerful arms heaving the hook straight up. The hook made a graceful arc and came crashing back down a few seconds later, nearly smashing in the sergeant's skull. Sergeant Nemiss had to make a quick scramble to save herself.

"Sorry, sir," Caramon mumbled.

"Try it again, Majere," the sergeant ordered, this time from a safe distance.

Caramon threw again, this time taking care to launch the grappling hook at the mountain. The hook and rope sailed up at an angle. The hook clanged off a rock at the top and began to slide down the rock. At the last moment, it caught on a rock outcropping and snagged. Caramon pulled with all his might on the rope. The rope held.

"Tumbler, you're up first," the sergeant said. "Take more rope with you."

No one knew Tumbler's real name, including himself, for, he said, he had been called that as a child and now it came natural to him. He was from a family of circus folk, who had performed in fairs throughout Solamnia, including the royal circus in the lordcity of Palanthas. No one knew why he'd left the circus. He never spoke of it, though it was whispered that he'd lost his wife and partner in an accident during their rope-walking act and that he'd left the circus life, vowing never to return.

If this was true, his loss hadn't soured his disposition. He was jovial and friendly and was always willing to show off his skills in camp, to the admiration of his comrades. He could walk on his hands as easily as most men did on their feet. He could bend and twist his body into knots, cause his double-jointed fingers to stick out in strange directions, and climb any tree or wall in existence.

Reaching the ledge, Tumbler secured several more ropes and tossed them down to the waiting soldiers below. The men formed lines and, one by one, began the climb.

Raistlin watched and pondered. He had barely enough strength in his thin arms to lift a full wine cup, let alone pull himself bodily up a rope.

Caramon recognized this fact, as well. "How're you going to manage, Raist?" he asked in a whisper.

"You will carry me," Raistlin said matter-of-factly.

"Hunh?" Caramon eyed the rope, the distance he would have to climb, and looked at his twin in some dismay.

Though Raistlin was thin, he was a full-grown man and, in addition, he had with him his staff, his scroll cases, and his spell components.

"You will never notice my weight, Caramon," Raistlin said smoothly. "I will cast a spell on myself that will make me light as a chicken feather."

"Oh? Will you? That's fine then," Caramon said with unquestioning trust. He bent his back so that Raistlin could climb on. "Lock your hands around my neck. Is your staff secure?"

The Staff of Magius was secure, as were the scroll cases, fastened by leather thongs that ran around Raistlin's shoulders. Caramon began to climb the rope, pulling himself up hand over hand.

"Did you cast the spell, Raist?" he asked. "I didn't hear any magic words."

"I know my business, Caramon," Raistlin returned.

Caramon continued to climb, adrenaline pumping. He noticed very little extra weight.

"Raist! Your spell's working!!" he said over his shoulder. "I can barely feel you!"

"Shut up and pay attention to where you're going!" Raistlin returned, trying not to let his cursed imagination think of what would happen if Caramon lost his grip on the rope.

When they reached the ledge, Raistlin slid off his brother's back and sank down on the rock ledge, pressing his back against the cliff. He drew in a deep breath and almost immediately began to cough. Removing a small flask that hung from his belt, he sipped the special concoction that eased his breathing. His cough abated. He was already exhausted and the most difficult and dangerous part of the journey was yet to come.

"One more climb, men," said the sergeant, handing Caramon the grappling hook.

The top of the cliff was not as high above them as the ledge had been from the ground. Caramon threw the hook and secured the rope on the first try. Tumbler scrambled up the rope with ease, secured his ropes, sent them spiraling back down.

Raistlin once more climbed onto Caramon's back. This time, Caramon could definitely feel his brother's extra weight. The big man's arms began to ache with the strain. He barely had strength enough to pull them both up the cliff. Fortunately the distance they had to cover was shorter or he would have never made it.

"I don't think your spell was working that time, Raist," Caramon said, panting, wiping sweat and rainwater from his face. "Are you sure you cast it? I still didn't hear you say anything."

"You were fatigued, that's all," said Raistlin shortly.

The captain ordered a rest, and then they began marching toward the city. The terrain was rough, the going slow. The men labored up steep rock outcroppings, slid down into boulder-strewn depressions. The time was well past midnight, and the watch fires burning on the city walls did not seem to be appreciably closer. Master Senej was looking grim, when the scouts returned with welcome news.

"Sir, we found a path that runs right down into the city. Probably an old goatherd's trail."

The path cut through the rocks. It was well worn, but narrow. The men were forced to walk single file and even then some, like Caramon, had to edge along parts of it sideways in order to fit. They came to a halt in a rocky clearing to see the city directly below them. Enemy soldiers stood guard on the walls or gathered around the watch fires, talking in low voices, occasionally glancing out to where the bonfires of the besieging armies burned brightly.

The watch fires lit parts of the cliff face as bright as day. The men felt exposed on the rock ledge, even though they knew that someone standing down below would have to look very hard to see them. Moving quietly, keeping to the shadows, the soldiers continued to follow the path leading down into the city. They were within spitting distance of the walls, when Raistlin's worst fears were realized. He drew in a breath to find his air passages blocked. He struggled, trying to stifle his cough, but failed.

Master Senej halted, turned to glare.

"Stop that racket!" the sergeant hissed from her place in the front of the line.

"Stop that racket!" The word whispered from man to man, all of them looking angrily at Raistlin.

"He can't help it!" Caramon growled back, standing in front of his twin.

Raistlin fumbled at the flask, brought it to his mouth, gulped down the ill-tasting liquid. Sometimes the herbal concoction didn't work right away. Sometimes these coughing spells could last for hours. If so, he was certain the men would toss him off the cliff. Either the herbal tea helped him this time or his sheer force of will dampened the smothering ash that seemed to fill his lungs.

C Company continued on until the city's wall was almost directly beneath them. Master Senej sent the scouts ahead to reconnoiter. The soldiers flattened themselves against the cliff face, waited for the scouts to return. Raistlin took sips of his tea at intervals, was careful to keep his throat from drying out.

The scouts came back and this time their news was disappointing. The path led to a stream that entered the city through an aperture in the wall. The scouts had investigated the opening, hoping to be able to use it to enter themselves, but reported that it was so small not even Scrounger could squeak through. The only way into the city was over the wall. The men were almost level with a guard tower. A light burned brightly inside and they could see the silhouettes of at least three men moving back and forth in front of the arrow slits that served as windows.

"We'll have to jump for it, I guess," Master Senej said, eyeing the wall and the guard tower with a frown.

"We're likely going to have every guard in that tower on top of us, sir," said Sergeant Nemiss. "But I don't see any other way in."

Master Senej passed the word for the archers. Hearing the command, Raistlin left his position at the rear of the line.

"I need to reach the master," he said, and the men assisted him, hanging on to him as he edged his way along the narrow ledge.

"Cover us from up here until we can get down off the wall, then follow us in." The master was giving his orders to the bowmen. "Be accurate, that's all I have to say. Shoot to kill. The first scream and we're done for."

"No matter how accurate they are, their officers will find the bodies filled with arrows, sir," Raistlin said, climbing down to stand beside the archers. "They'll know we're in the city."

"Yes, but they won't know where we're hiding," the master argued.

"They'll start searching for us, sir. They'll have all day to find us."

"Do you have a better way, Wizard?" The master glowered.

"Yes, sir. My own way. I will see to it that we enter the city safely and secretly. No one will be the wiser."

The master and the sergeant were dubious. The only mage they trusted was Horkin and that was because he was more soldier than wizard. Neither of them liked Raistlin, they considered him weak and undisciplined. The coughing incident had only bolstered their bad opinion. But they had been ordered to take him and ordered to make use of him. The master and the sergeant exchanged glances.

"Well, I don't suppose we've got much to lose," Master Senej said ungraciously.

"Go ahead, Majere. You men"—Sergeant Nemiss glanced back at the archers—"keep your arrows nocked, just in case." She did not add that the first person they should shoot if the mage betrayed them was the mage himself, but that pretty much went without saying.

"How will you climb down there, Majere?" the sergeant asked.

A good question. The Staff of Magius possessed a spell that would allow the caster to float through the air light as a feather. Raistlin had read about the spell in the book on Magius he'd discovered in the Tower of High Sorcery. He'd tried practicing it a couple of times. The first resulted in a nasty fall from a rooftop. The second had been a success. He had never jumped from such a height, however. He was not certain how far the spell would carry him. This did not appear to be the time to experiment.

"I will climb down the same way I climbed up," he said, and the word was passed for Caramon.

Caramon secured a length of rope to a rock and tossed it over the edge.

"Wait!" Sergeant Nemiss held them.

One of the guards walking his beat on the wall passed right below them. They waited until he turned and began walking away.

Raistlin climbed onto his twin's broad back. Caramon grasped the rope with both hands, slid over the side, and began to rappel down the cliff face. They began their descent in shadow but soon passed into the light of the watch fires, reflecting off the cliff face.

The soldiers on the ledge held their collective breath. All it would take was one guard in the tower to look casually out of the arrow slits that served as windows and they would be discovered.

Raistlin looked over his shoulder at the wall and the tower. A guard's bulk blotted out the light in the narrow opening.

"Caramon, stop!" Raistlin breathed.

Caramon held in his position. He could not remain here long, supporting himself and his twin. His arms were already tired. They quivered from the strain. He and Raistlin would be ideal targets dangling helplessly from the rope. Raistlin waited for the man to cry out, but he left the window. No alarm followed. He had not seen them.

"Now!" Raistlin gasped.

Caramon began his descent again. The last few feet, his arms gave out. He slid down the rope, peeling most of the skin from his palms, and landed heavily on the wall. Raistlin slid from his back and scrambled for cover. He and Caramon ducked into the shadow of the wall, waited, cringing, certain that someone must have heard them.

The men inside the tower were talking loudly, arguing about something from the sound of it. They had not heard a thing. Raistlin peered down the length of the wall. The next guard tower was a good fifty yards distant. Nothing to worry about there.

"What do you want me to do?" Caramon whispered.

"Hand over your flask," Raistlin said softly.

"Flask?" Caramon tried to look innocent. "I don't—"

"Damn it, Caramon! Give me the flask of dwarf spirits you have stashed away in your pants. I know you carry it!"

Wordlessly, chagrined, Caramon dug the small pewter flask from beneath his armor and handed it to his twin.

"Wait for me here," Raistlin ordered.

"But, Raist, I—"

"Hush!" Raistlin hissed. "Do as I say!"

He left without further argument.

Not knowing what his brother intended and fearing to imperil him by disobeying, Caramon remained crouched in the shadows, his hand on the hilt of his short sword.

Raistlin crept silently along the wall until he reached the window of the guard tower. Inside, he could hear the guards talking. Raistlin paid no attention to anything they said. His entire concentration was focused on his spells. Kneeling beneath the slit in the wall, he drew forth a small box and slid open the lid. He called the words of the spell to mind, was gratified to note that the magic came to him immediately. His fear gone, he was amazed at his own calmness. He drew out a pinch of sand and tossed it in through the opening, spoke the words of magic.

The voices slid into incoherence, then silence. Something fell to the floor and broke with a loud crash. Raistlin cringed, waited a moment, just to make certain that the noise had not attracted attention. No one came to investigate. These guards were probably the only people in the tower. Cautiously Raistlin rose to his feet and looked inside.

Three men sprawled on a wooden table, deep in a magical slumber. The crash he'd heard was a mug, fallen from a nerveless hand. The arrow slit was too narrow for a man to enter. Raistlin uncorked the flask, tossed it into the room. The flask landed square on the table. The potent liquor sloshed over the table, dripped onto the floor. The place soon reeked of dwarf spirits.

Raistlin paused a moment to admire his handiwork. When the officer of the watch arrived, he would find three guards who had hoped to ease the monotony of their watch by a taste of spirits, only to imbibe a bit too much. Preferable to the officer finding three of his men had suddenly fallen sound asleep while on guard duty. Much preferable to the officer finding three guards with arrows sticking out of their backs.

When they wakened, the three would deny they had been drinking. No one will believe them. They would be punished for their dereliction in duty, perhaps even executed. Raistlin looked at them. One of the men was quite young, maybe not even seventeen. The other two were older, family men, perhaps, with wives at home, waiting, worrying . . .

Raistlin lowered himself from the window. These men were the enemy. He could not allow them to become people.

These three guards were settled for the night. The other guard had vanished into the shadows. Running soft-footed, Raistlin returned to his brother.

"All is well," he reported.

"What happened to the guards?" Caramon asked.

"No time for explanations!" Raistlin said. "Hurry! Bring the men down."

Caramon tugged three times on the rope.

A few moments later, the Tumbler shimmied down the rope, followed by the sergeant.

"The tower?" she asked.

"All is well, sir," Raistlin reported.

Sergeant Nemiss twitched an eyebrow. "Tumbler, go look," she said.

Angry words came to Raistlin's lips. He had sense enough to eat them, choke them back down. He stood in silence while the sergeant checked up on him.

"They're all taking a snooze, sir," Tumbler reported, grinning. He winked at Raistlin.

"Good," was all Sergeant Nemiss said, but she granted Raistlin a look of approval, then tugged on the rope. Scrounger slid down next, his grin wide and excited. The sergeant issued orders.

"Tumbler, find a good place to send the men over the wall. Scrounger, keep watch on that other tower."

The first signs of gray sky hinted that morning was very close. Tumbler peered over the edge of the far side of the wall. He returned to report that below them was an alleyway behind a large building, perhaps the very warehouse they were hoping to use for a hiding place.

"No one about, sir," he stated.

"There soon will be," the sergeant muttered. Her troops were still in shadows, but day was dawning with what seemed cruel rapidity. "Get the men down there fast." She glanced out in the direction of the besieging armies. "Where's that damn diversion we were promised?"

The men slid along the rope swiftly. Caramon remained at the wall, ready to assist the soldiers to make a silent landfall. He sent them across the ramparts. Tumbler tied a length of rope around one of the wall's crenellations, held the rope fast while the men slithered down the wall and ran down the alley. One of the men waved his arm and pointed at the building. Apparently they had found a way to enter.

"Sir!" Scrounger reported. "Someone's coming from the other tower! Walking this way!"

The sergeant swore. Most of the men had descended, but five still remained on the rock ledge, including Master Senej. And there was still no sound or sign of the promised attack from their allies.

"It's probably an officer," the sergeant said, "making his rounds. I'll go—" She drew her knife.

"I'll handle him, sir," Raistlin offered.

"Wizard! No—" the sergeant began.

But Raistlin was gone, keeping to the shadows, moving so silently he melded with the darkness.

The sergeant started to go after him.

"Begging your pardon, sir," Caramon said with dignity, laying a hand on the sergeant's arm, restraining her, "but Raist said he'd deal with the guard. He hasn't let you down yet."

A large wooden water barrel banded by rings of iron stood on the wall, kept there to put out fires should the enemy hurl flaming missiles. Raistlin crouched behind the water barrel, watched as the officer approached. He walked with his head down, deep in thought. He had only to lift his head and, if his eyesight was quite good, he would see the thin length of rope descending from the rock. All would be over.

"Master! Come quickly!"

The man's head snapped up. He did not look in front of him. He looked behind him, in the direction of the sound of the voice.

"Master! Make haste! The enemy!"

The officer hesitated, staring back at the tower he'd just left. Then, with perfect timing, the diversion came. Trumpets sounded, off-key and tinny, the sweetest music Raistlin had ever heard. The master-at-arms, now convinced of an imminent attack, turned and dashed back along the ramparts.

Raistlin smiled, pleased with himself. He hadn't used his ventriloquism skills in a long time, not since his days of working the local fairs. Good to know that he hadn't lost his talent.

By the time he returned, most of the company was over the wall and into the city. The sergeant had gone with them, along with Master Senej, leaving only Caramon and Tumbler.

A thought occurred to Caramon. "How will you get down?" he asked Tumbler.

"Same as you. The rope," Tumbler replied.

"But then, who's going to stay up here and untie the other end?" Caramon argued. "Someone has to, otherwise they'll know we're here!"

"A good point," said Tumbler solemnly. "Why don't

you stay up here and untie the rope after I'm down."

"Sure, I'll do that," Caramon said, then he frowned. "But how will I get down if I untie the rope?"

"That's a problem," said Tumbler, appearing concerned. "I don't suppose you can fly? No? Then I guess you'll have to let me worry about it."

Shaking his head, still concerned, Caramon climbed down the rope, his brother clinging to his twin's broad back. Tumbler waited until they were down, then he followed, shinnying down the rope with ease. Arriving at the bottom, he looked back up at the rope, which was tied firmly to the crenellation. Tumbler gave the rope a jerk. The knot came loose. The rope slithered down the wall and landed at his feet. Tumbler looked over at the two and winked.

"He said that knot was tight!" Caramon cried, aghast. "We could have been killed!"

"Come along, Caramon," Raistlin ordered irritably. His exhilaration was fading. The weakness that set in after his use of magic was starting to affect him. "You've wasted enough time proving to the world that you're a fool."

"But, Raist, I don't understand . . ."

Still talking, Caramon trailed after his twin.

Tumbler coiled the rope over his shoulder and hurried after them. He ducked into the warehouse just as the city woke in an uproar to prepare for the coming assault.

12

Once the warehouse was taken, secured, searched, and deemed as safe a hiding place as could possibly be found inside an enemy city under siege, the sergeant of C Company set the watch and told the rest to get some sleep. Raistlin was already deep in an exhausted slumber, worn out from the physical exertion and the rigors of his spell-casting.

Those keeping lookout tried hard to ignore the snoring of their comrades. The guards walked off their tiredness, pacing the length of the empty warehouse floor, pausing now and then to glance out the windows or exchange soft snatches of conversation. By the end of the watch, they were nodding at their posts, eyes closing and heads falling forward only to snap awake in sudden alertness at the sound of a footstep in the street or a rat in the rafters.

The morning passed without incident. Few people walked the streets in this part of town. The gate tax had shut down the markets, emptied the warehouses of their goods. The only civilians who ventured past were apparently on their way somewhere else, for they looked neither to the left nor to the right but continued on, their heads bowed with trouble. Once four guards marched into view, causing those on watch to lay their hands on their swords and prepare to wake their comrades. But the guards kept on going and the watch looked at each other, nodded, and grinned. The mage's tactics had apparently been successful. No one knew that the town's defense had been breached. No one knew they were here.

The rain ceased with the dawn. The midday sun rose high overhead. Raistlin slept as though he might never waken, his twin keeping watch over his brother. The rest of the men either continued their slumbers or lounged on the floor, glad of the chance to do nothing for a change, resting up for what was likely going to be a long and dangerous night.

Except Scrounger.

Scrounger was much more human than kender. The kender blood in him ran thin, but there were times when it would bubble up to the surface and break out all over him like a bad rash. The particular itch tormenting him at the moment was boredom. A bored kender is a dangerous kender, as anyone on Ansalon will tell you. A bored half-kender might be said to be only half as dangerous. However, those in the presence of a bored half-kender would do well to loosen their swords in their sheaths and be ready for trouble.

Scrounger'd had his fill of sleep; he needed little sleep as it was, and after four hours he was up and ready for action.

Action was a long way off, unfortunately. Scrounger whiled away an hour searching the warehouse from ceiling to cellar in hopes of finding something that might come in handy for bartering. Judging by the dust and chaff on the floor, the warehouse had been used as a granary. All Scrounger came across were some empty bags, the rats having done their own scrounging.

Returning empty-handed from his foraging, Scrounger attempted to engage Caramon in conversation, but was sharply and angrily "shushed!," told to keep his mouth shut so that he wouldn't wake Raistlin. It appeared to Scrounger that nothing short of a gnomic Steam-powered Screaming Window Washing device, such as he had seen once, when younger, would wake the mage.

Reminded of the device, Scrounger had been going to relate the interesting story to Caramon, all about how the device had not only failed to clean the windowpanes but had broken every one of them in the process. The owners of the windows had been furious and were about to set upon the gnomes, who, however, pointed out that the paneless windows now provided a perfectly clear and unobstructed view of the outdoors, which was all that the contract required. Proclaiming their machine a success, the gnomes left town. Another group of gnomes from the GlaziersGlassSpunandBlownMirrors- aSpecialtySevenYearsBadLuck Committee had arrived shortly after (they made it a policy to follow the win- dowwashers), but had been turned away at the border.

Caramon shushed Scrounger again, right at the inter- esting part where the gnomes set off their machine and the mayor's ears had started to bleed. The half-kender wandered off.

Scrounger made another desultory round of the ware- house, occasionally falling over a slumbering body lying unseen in the shadows, to be kicked and damned to the Abyss. In a sunlit corner, Master Senej and Sergeant Ne- miss were hunched over a map, plotting the night's at- tack. Here, at least, was something interesting. Scrounger stood near, peering down at the map.

"This is the main street leading to the north gate. Ac- cording to this map," the master was saying, "this build- ing standing right here will provide excellent cover for the men right up until the time they have to break out into the open to attack."

"And I'm saying, sir, that one of our spies told us this building burned down a month ago," Sergeant Nemiss argued. "You can't count on it being there. And if it's not there, we're in the open all the way from this block to the gate."

"There are trees here. . . ."

"They've been cut down, sir."

"According to your spy."

"I know you don't think much of him, sir, and I admit that he failed to warn us about the catapults, but—"

"Wait a minute, Sergeant." Aware of a shadow falling over the map, Master Senej looked up. "Can we help you, soldier?"

"I can go," Scrounger offered, ignoring the sarcasm. "I can go see if the house is still there and if the trees have been cut down. Please, sir. I really need to be doing something. I have this itching in my hands and my feet."

"Trenchfoot," the master said, frowning.

"Not trenchfoot, sir," said Sergeant Nemiss. "Kender. Half-kender, that is."

The master's frown darkened.

"I could be there and back in two shakes of a griffon's tail, sir," Scrounger pleaded.

"Out of the question," Master Senej said shortly. "The risk that you'd be noticed and caught is too great."

"But, sir—" Scrounger begged.

The master glowered. "Perhaps we should tie him up."

"You know, sir," Sergeant Nemiss said, "that's really not a bad idea."

"Tying him up?"

"No, sir. Sending him out to reconnoiter. The lives of the men might depend on whether that house is there or not. Scrounger's proven himself valuable before now."

The master eyed Scrounger, who, in order to inspire confidence, tried to look more human and less kender.

"I agree. It would help to know about that house. Very well," the master said, making up his mind. "But you're on your own, Scrounger. If you're caught, we can't imperil the mission to come rescue you."

"I fully understand that, sir," said Scrounger. "I won't be caught. I have a sort of way of blending in so that people never notice me or if they do they think that I'm—"

The master glared at him. "Shouldn't you be gone by now?"

"Yes, sir. Going now, sir."

Scrounger crept back to where Raistlin lay sleeping and Caramon lay watching his brother sleep.

"Caramon," Scrounger whispered, "I need to borrow that pouch."

"That's got our rations in it," Caramon protested. "What's left of 'em," he added gloomily.

"I know. I'll bring the food back. I promise. I might

even bring you more."

"But you've got a pouch!" Caramon protested.

"Staff . . ." Raistlin murmured in his sleep. "The staff is . . . mine . . . No!" He shouted the word, began to thrash about, arms flailing.

"Hush! Raist! Hush! It's all right," Caramon whispered. Holding his brother by the shoulders, he cast a sidelong glance in the direction of Sergeant Nemiss, who had looked over, glowering, at the commotion. "Your staff is here, Raist. Right here."

Caramon placed the staff beneath his brother's frantic hand. Raistlin grasped hold of the staff protectively, sighed, and sank back into sleep.

"He's going to get in trouble with the sergeant if he keeps yelling like that," Scrounger observed.

"I know. That's why I'm with him. He's quieter if I'm here." Caramon shook his head. "I don't know what's wrong. I've never seen him like this. He keeps thinking someone's trying to take the staff away from him."

Scrounger shrugged. Nothing Raistlin did or thought was of much interest to him. "C'mon. Hand over the pouch."

Caramon handed it over, watched as Scrounger looped Caramon's pouch over one shoulder, his own pouch over the other shoulder. "I really could use a couple more, but I guess this will have to do. Too bad they cut my hair. How does this look?"

Running his hands through his short hair, Scrounger caused it to stand on end, stick out every which way. He assumed a cheery, carefree smile.

"Say," said Caramon, astonished. "You look just like a kender. No offense," he added, knowing how sensitive his friend was on that point.

"None taken," said Scrounger, grinning. "That's what I wanted to hear, in fact. Be seein' you."

"Where are you going?" Caramon demanded.

"To reconnoiter," Scrounger said proudly.

* * * * *

In a walled human city where everyone knows everyone else and has known them for probably as long as they've been alive, any stranger entering town is certain to stand out, under the best of conditions. Now, with the city surrounded by enemy troops, everyone was on edge. Citizens went about their daily business armed to the teeth and ready for attack. Any stranger was set upon immediately, trussed up, and hauled off for interrogation. With the exception of kender.

The problem is not that kender all look alike to humans, but that the same kender never looks the same two times running. He has either switched clothes with a friend or snitched clothes from a friend or borrowed interesting-looking clothes left out to dry. He might have flowers in his hair one day and maple syrup in his hair the next. He might be wearing his shoes or your shoes or no shoes at all. Small wonder that most humans—especially upset, fearful, and worried humans—did not know whether they were seeing the same kender over a period of several days or several kender all attired in more or less the same outfit.

Thus, no one in Hope's End paid the slightest attention to Scrounger, beyond the instinctive reaction of clapping a protective hand over a purse.

Scrounger strolled down the main street of the walled city, admiring the tall houses crowded together side by side, houses made of plaster with dark wood supports. Lead-paned glass sparkled in the second-floor bay windows that bowed out over the street. Some of the buildings needed painting, however. Others were in a state of disrepair, which would not have been permitted had the owners had the means to fix the sagging eaves or replace the broken window.

The merchant shops he passed were boarded up, market stalls empty and falling down. Only the taverns were busy, that was where everyone went to hear the news. News that was, for the most part, not good.

The people Scrounger encountered were pale and downcast. If they paused to speak, their conversations were held in low and anxious voices. He loudly bid people a good day, but no one responded. Most just shook their heads and hurried on. The only cheerful people he saw in the entire city were two small boys, dirty and ragged, running through the streets, bashing each other with wooden swords.

"So these are the rebels," Scrounger said.

He passed by an open window where a thin young woman, who looked half-starved herself, was trying to nurse a fretful baby.

Scrounger brought to mind the sight of Borar taking the arrow in his throat. He pictured the smashed and battered bodies lying underneath the huge boulders and he was able to summon up a fair amount of hatred for these people. But since it was only the human part of Scrounger that could hate and that human part constituted only half of him, his hatred was considerably diluted. What hatred there was carried him up to the city gate, which was closed, barred and barricaded.

The spy had been partially right. The house in question had burned down, but the stands of tall trees beneath the wall, trees that were part of the city's defenses, would unwittingly help the city's attackers by supplying adequate cover for their assault.

Scrounger lingered near the wall, absorbing details of his surroundings, trying to anticipate the questions the master and sergeant were bound to put to him. This didn't take long. He supposed he should go back to the warehouse, but the thought of being cooped up in that building, watching Raistlin sleep, was too much for him to bear.

"The master would really like it if I could bring back some information on the enemy," Scrounger said to himself. "The enemy's all around me. Somewhere someone must be talking about what they plan to do."

A brief search produced a likely looking source. A group of people, a mix of soldiers and civilians, to judge by their dress, had gathered atop the city wall near a guard tower. One of the men, a large man, corpulent and well dressed, wore a heavy chain of gold around his neck. Such a chain as might denote a man of important standing.

Scrounger was just wishing most earnestly that he could be a mouse, skittering about their feet, when the sight of the trees against the wall gave him a better idea. He would not be a mouse, but a bird.

Selecting the tree that was tallest and nearest the group, Scrounger waited at the bottom, in the shadows, until he was quite certain the few passersby hadn't noticed him. He divested himself of his pouches, deposited them at the tree's base, and began climbing. Nimble and deft, he moved carefully from limb to limb, taking his time, studying out each hand- and foothold with care so as not to rustle the branches. So quiet was he that he startled a squirrel in her nest.

She scolded him roundly and flitted out of the hole in the tree, her young following her, tails twitching and voices raised in shrill alarm. The squirrels' turmoil provided excellent cover, permitting Scrounger to climb much closer than he'd hoped. He settled himself on a branch directly below the wall and concentrated on listening. A thrill went over him from head to toe when he heard one of the men refer to the man with the golden chain as "lord mayor."

"A council of war!" said Scrounger excitedly. "I've stumbled on a council of war!"

That was not precisely true, as he was soon to discover. The mayor had come up to view the results of the enemy's latest attack, an attack that had halted about mid-morning with the enemy retreating back to camp.

"That's two assaults we've driven off now," the mayor was saying in hopeful tones. "I think we stand a good chance of winning this war."

"Bah! Both of those were feints." The speaker was a elderly man, rough and grizzled. "Just drawing us out, testing our strength. They have a fair notion of it now, thanks to the numskull who gave the order to loose the catapult yesterday morning."

The lord mayor gave a deprecating cough, which was followed by silence. Then the elderly man spoke.

"You should face the facts, Lord mayor, Your Honor. We don't have a prayer of winning this fight."

More silence.

"Not a prayer," he continued after a moment. "I'm leading untrained men, for the most part. Oh, I've a few archers who can hit their mark but not many and they'll be cut down in the first major assault. Do you know what happened this morning, sir? I found three of my guard dead drunk on duty. Small blame to 'em. I'da been dead drunk myself last night if I could have laid hands on the wherewithall."

"What would you have us do?" the mayor asked, his voice breaking. He sounded on the verge of hysteria. "We tried to surrender! You heard what that . . . that fiend said!"

"Yeah, I heard him. And that's the one reason I wasn't dead drunk last night." The commander's voice tightened. "I'm hoping to live long enough to have my chance at him."

"It seems incredible to me," said the mayor, "but I could well believe that King Wilhelm wants us all dead. He had to know that imposing that outrageous tax on us would lead to open rebellion. He forced us to take this position, then he sent in his army to teach us a lesson. When we tried to make peace, his general gave us terms so impossible that no rational person could agree to them."

"You won't get any arguments from me on that, Your Honor."

"But why?" the mayor demanded helplessly. "Why is he doing this to us?"

"If the gods were around, they'd know. Since they're not, I have to assume that only King Wilhelm knows and he's gone potty, if what we hear is true. Perhaps he has new tenants for our homes. I'll tell you one thing, though. That's not the army of Blödehelm out there."

"It's not?" The mayor sounded astonished. "Then . . . what army is it?"

"I dunno. But I served a number of years in the army of Blödehelm and that ain't it. We were a homegrown army. We left our plows to pick up our swords, did a few hours march, fought our battle, and were back in our homes in time for supper. This army, now. This army's a fighting man's army. A professional army, not a bunch of farmers wearing their grandpappy's armor."

"But then . . . what does that mean?" The mayor sounded dazed, as if someone had struck him with a rock.

"It means that you're right, Your Honor," said the commander laconically. "The king—or someone—wants us all dead."

The commander bowed to the mayor, then walked away. The mayor muttered to himself, heaved a vast sigh, stood a moment or two longer on the wall, then descended.

Scrounger sat in his tree awhile longer himself, going over the conversation so that he could repeat it accurately. Once he had it memorized, he scrambled down out of the tree, retrieved his pouches, and emerged from the grove right under the nose of the lord mayor.

The lord mayor jumped and made a reflexive grab for his purse. "Get away!"

Scrounger was only too happy to take him up on his suggestion.

The mayor took a second look, shifted his bulk, and planted his substantial body squarely in front of the half-kender.

"Wait a minute! Do I know you?" The mayor regarded Scrounger intently.

"Oh, yes," Scrounger said cheerfully.

"How?" The mayor frowned.

"I've had the honor of appearing before you many times, Your mayorship." Scrounger gave a polite bow.

"Indeed?" The mayor was dubious.

"At the morning assize. You know. When they let us out of jail after we've all been arrested the night before and they take us before you and you make those really fine speeches—very affecting—about law and order and honesty being the best policy and all that."

"I see." The mayor still appeared puzzled.

"I've cut my hair," Scrounger offered. "Maybe that's why you don't recognize me. And I haven't been in jail in a long time. Your speeches," he swore solemnly, "helped me turn my life around."

"Well, I'm happy about that," the mayor said. "See that it continues. Good day to you."

He walked down the street, and mounted the steps of a very fine house, the finest house on the block.

"Whew!" Scrounger said, making certain he took a different street himself, not intending to give the mayor another look at him. "That was close. I can't believe he got down off the wall that fast! He moves pretty quick for a fat man, I'll say that for him."

* * * * *

"They tried to surrender?" Master Senej stared in blank astonishment. "You mean to tell me that we lost good men to a city that doesn't want to fight?"

"He must have heard wrong. You must have heard wrong," Sergeant Nemiss said to Scrounger. "What were the exact words?"

"'We tried to surrender,'" said Scrounger. "And there's more, sirs. Listen." He went on to relate the entire conversation verbatim.

"You know," said Master Senej, his brow furrowed, "I had the same thought about that army myself. I never fought with or for the army of Blödehelm, but I'd heard of them and they were just as that old man described—drop the plow to pick up the sword, drop the sword to go back to the plow."

"But if that's true, what does it all mean, sir?" Sergeant Nemiss asked, unconsciously echoing the lord mayor.

"It means that the enemy's raised his hand in surrender and we're about to lop off his head," said the master. "The baron won't like this, not one bit."

"What do we do, sir? The assault's set for tomorrow morning. Our orders are to attack the gates from behind. We can't go against orders."

The master pondered a moment, then made up his mind. "The baron should know what's going on. He has the reputation for being a just and honorable man. Think how his reputation and ours will suffer if it turns out that we're taking part in a cold-blooded butchery! No one would ever hire us again. He should at least have a chance to remand his orders or change them."

"I doubt we have time to send back a messenger, sir."

"It's only a little after midday now, sergeant. A man alone can move faster than an entire troop. If he cuts straight across country, he can be there in three hours. An hour to explain things to the baron. Three hours back. Allow an hour or two for mischance and he should be back here by sunset at the latest. The attack isn't scheduled until dawn. Who's your best man?"

"Tumbler," Sergeant Nemiss said. "Pass the word for Tumbler."

Tumbler appeared, disheveled from sleep and still yawning.

"We need you to take a message to the baron," said the master, and the tense tone of his voice jolted Tumbler to full wakefulness.

"Yes, sir," he said, straightening.

"You can't wait for darkness. You'll have to go now. The best route is probably back over the wall. We're dealing with a bunch of citizen soldiers, but take care all the same. No matter whether a trained man or an untrained one kills you, you're just as dead."

"I know the drill, sir. I'll get across," Tumbler said confidently.

"Take the most direct route to the camp. Report to the baron. This is what I want you to tell him. How's your memory?"

"Excellent, sir."

"Scrounger, tell him what you told us."

Scrounger repeated his story. Tumbler listened carefully, nodded once, said he had it. He was offered equipment, but he said all he needed was a rope and a knife, which were already in his possession. When the watch reported the street empty, Tumbler ducked out the door and vanished around the side of the warehouse.

"Nothing to do now but wait," said the master.

* * * * *

The hours of the afternoon crawled. The men passed the time playing at knight's jump, a game in which the player presses on the edges of a small metal counter with a larger counter, causing the smaller counter to "jump" into a cup. The person with the highest number of counters in the cup at the end of the game is the winner.

A very old game—it was said to have been a favorite of the legendary Knight, Huma—knight's jump was popular among the baron's men, who valued their handmade counters as highly as coins of the realm. Each soldier's counters were commissioned from the blacksmith, who made them from leftover scraps of metal; each was marked with his or her own special design. Variations of the game had developed. Sometimes the player was required not only to "jump" the counter into the cup but also to stack his counter neatly on top of the counter already in the cup.

The baron was a terror at knight's jump and it also proved to be a game at which Raistlin—with his highly developed manual dexterity—excelled. One of the few "frivolous" pursuits the usually serious-minded young man enjoyed, he played with a single-minded intensity and skill that casual players found extremely daunting, but which the experts were quick to recognize and approve. One poor sport insisted sourly that the mage must be using his magic to win, but Raistlin easily proved his detractor wrong to the satisfaction of his supporters, of which he had many. Not because they liked him, but because he made them money.

Raistlin's natural thrift and disinclination to wager his own hard-earned money kept him from joining in on the high-stakes games, but he soon found those who were glad to stake him for a share in the profits.

Caramon, with his big and clumsy hands, was a mediocre player at best. He enjoyed watching his twin, though he often annoyed Raistlin beyond measure with his well-meaning but ill-judged advice.

The only sound that could be heard all through the afternoon was the chink of counters rattling in the metal drinking cups and the occasional soft groan or muffled curse from the losers, murmured praise for the winner. The game ended with the setting of the sun and then only when it became too dark to adequately judge the distance needed for the jump. The men dispersed to eat their supper, munching on cold meat and hard bread, washed down with water. After that some slept, knowing that they had an early rising ahead of them. Others passed the time in storytelling or word games. Raistlin handed over his share of the winnings to Caramon for safekeeping, sipped cold tea, and slept peacefully, dreaming of counters and cups instead of sinister wizards.

Everyone knew of Tumbler's assignment by now, they knew the danger he ran. They followed him along his route in their minds, making calculations on the length of time it would take him to reach camp, arguing about whether he would stick to the main road or take a shortcut, speculating and even wagering money on the baron's answer.

As darkness neared, the soldiers looked at the door, peered out the windows, appeared hopeful when a footstep was heard in the otherwise deserted street, were downcast when the footsteps continued on. The time came and went by which Tumbler could have reasonably been expected to return. Master Senej and Sergeant Nemiss continued with their plans for the dawn attack.

And then one of the sentries called out softly and tensely, "Who goes there?"

"Kiri-Jolith and the kingfisher," was the password, correctly given, and a tired but grinning Tumbler slipped past the sentry.

"What did the baron say?" Major Senej demanded.

"Ask him yourself, sir," said Tumbler. With a jerk of his thumb, he indicated the baron, standing behind him.

The men stared, astonished.

"Attention!" Sergeant Nemiss called out, jumping to her feet. The men scrambed to obey. The baron waved his hand, ordered them to remain where they were.

"I'm going to get to the bottom of this barrel," he stated. "It may be clear water at the top but I've got the feeling there's sludge beneath. I don't like what I'm hearing about our so-called allies. I certainly didn't like what I saw of them."

"Yes, sir. What are your orders, sir?"

"I want to talk to someone in authority in this city. Maybe that commander—"

"That will be dangerous, sir."

"Damn it, I know it will be dangerous. I—"

"Begging your pardon, my lord." Scrounger popped up from beneath the baron's elbow. "But I know the house where the lord mayor lives. At least, I think it must be his house. It's the biggest and the finest on the block."

"Who are you?" the baron asked, unable to see the shadowy figure in the darkness.

"Scrounger, sir. I was the one who overhead the mayor talking and I watched him as he went down a street and turned into a house."

"Can you find your way back there?"

"Yes, sir," Scrounger replied.

"Good, let's go, then. It's not long until morning. Master Senej, you and Sergeant Nemiss stay with the troops. If we're not back by sunrise, go forward with the attack."

"Yes, my lord. Might I suggest, sir, that you take along a couple more men in case you run into trouble?"

"If I do run into trouble, Master, it won't much matter whether there are two of us or four of us, will it? Not if we're facing fifty angry citizens. And I don't want to go marching around town with an army rattling and clanking behind me."

"You don't need the army, sir," said the master stubbornly. "You should at least take the wizard Majere. He proved himself a real asset to us last night, my lord. Take him and his brother. Caramon Majere's a good fighter and big as a house. The two of them can't hurt, sir, and they could be a real help."

"Very well, Master. I like your suggestion. Pass the word for the Majeres."

"And, my lord," said Master Senej quietly, drawing the baron to one side, "if you don't like what His Honor the mayor has to say, he would always make a valuable hostage."

"My thoughts exactly, Master," the baron replied.

13

Though it was only a few hours after dark, the streets of Hope's End were deserted. Even the taverns had closed. People were in their homes, either finding refuge from their trouble in sleep or lying awake, staring into the darkness, awaiting the dawn with dread. Those who heard footsteps and who were actually curious enough or frightened enough to look out their windows saw only what appeared to be a patrol marching down the street.

"If we tiptoe and hug the shadows and look the part of spies sneaking around the city, we'll be taken for spies sneaking around the city. If we march straight down the middle of the road, not flaunting our presence but not hiding it either, chances are that in the darkness we'll be taken for the local militia making its rounds. We just have to hope," the baron added with characteristic calm, "that we don't run into the local militia making its rounds. Then there'll be trouble. Our cause is just. Kiri-Jolith will keep us out of harm's way."

Kiri-Jolith probably had little to do in those days, few prayers to answer. Perhaps he was as bored as the men forced to lie in wait in the warehouse, without even the mild distraction of a game of knight's jump to cheer their dull eternity. The baron's prayer, falling on his ears, might have come as a welcome change, an opportunity to be up and doing. The baron and his party encountered no living being on their swift march from the warehouse, not even a stray cat.

"That's the house I saw him enter, my lord," Scrounger whispered, pointing.

"Are you quite sure?" the baron asked. "You're looking at it from a different direction."

"Yes, I'm sure, sir. As you can see, it's the biggest house in the block and I remember that there was a stork's nest atop the chimney."

Solinari was almost full this night, shed his silver light down upon the city streets. The tall chimneys of the row of houses were lined up like soldiers. A stork's nest atop one was like a bristly hat.

"What if this isn't his house? It could be he was just visiting a friend," the baron suggested.

"He didn't knock on the door," Scrounger offered. "He just went right in as if he owned the place."

"And if it is not his house, my lord," Raistlin added, "then we will capture and interrogate some other prominent citizen. Whoever lives in this house is a person of wealth."

The baron agreed that this would suit him just as well. The small band left the street, circled around to an alley, which ran behind the row of houses. The houses looked much different from the back, but the house they wanted was easy to locate, due mainly to the nest on the chimney.

"I've heard that a stork's nest brings good luck to the house," Scrounger whispered.

"Let us hope that you're right in this instance, young man," the baron replied. "No lights in the house. The family must be in bed. I doubt they're out socializing. Who can pick this lock?" The baron looked at Scrounger, who shook his head.

"Sorry, sir. My mother tried to teach me. I just never took to it."

"I believe that I might be able to deal with the lock, my lord," Raistlin said quietly.

"You have a spell?"

"No, my lord," Raistlin returned. "In my school days, my master kept all his spellbooks in a locked case. Caramon, I'll need to borrow your knife."

Wooden stairs led to the back door. Raistlin glided up the stairs, taking care to keep from tripping on his robes. The others stood watch in the alley, looking in all directions, their hands on their weapons. The baron hadn't even begun to grow impatient when Raistlin motioned with his hand, pale white in the moonlight. The door stood open.

They entered the house quietly, or as quietly as possible with Caramon among them. His heavy footfalls caused the floorboards to creak ominously as he entered the kitchen and set the pots, hanging on hooks on a wall, to rattling.

"Quiet, Majere!" the baron whispered urgently. "You'll wake the whole house!"

"Sorry, my lord," Caramon returned in a smothered breath.

"You stay here to guard the exit," the baron ordered. "If someone comes, bash 'em on the head and tie 'em up. No killing if you can help it. But don't let anyone cry out, either. Scrounger, you stay with him. If there's trouble, don't shout. Come fetch me."

Caramon nodded and took up his post at the door. Scrounger settled himself on a stool nearby.

"Wizard, you're with me." The baron padded through the kitchen. Finding a door, he opened it, peered inside. "Unless I miss my guess, these stairs are the stairs the servants use to gain access to the upper levels. That's where we'll find the bedrooms. Do you see a candle anywhere?"

"We have no need, my lord. If you want light, I can provide it. *Shirak*," Raistlin said and the crystal atop his staff began to glow with a soft white radiance.

The servants' staircase was narrow and winding. Raistlin and the baron crept up the stairs single file, the baron leading the way, moving with feline stealth. Raistlin followed as best he could, terrified of accidentally treading on a squeaky stair or knocking his staff against the wall.

"The master bedroom will be on the second floor," the baron whispered, pausing before a door leading off the spiraling staircase, which continued upward. "Douse that light!"

"*Dulak!*" Raistlin said softly, and the light went out, leaving them in darkness.

He waited on the stairs as the baron opened the door slowly and cautiously. From his vantage point, Raistlin could see a moonlit hallway hung with tapestries. A heavy wooden door, ornately carved, stood directly across from them. The sounds of snoring, loud and sonorous, came from behind the door.

"I have a sleep spell ready to cast on him, my lord," Raistlin said.

"He's already asleep. We want him awake," the baron returned. "We can't question him if he's asleep."

"True, my lord," Raistlin conceded, chagrined.

"You have that spell of yours ready to cast on his wife," the baron continued. "Women are screamers and there's nothing rouses the household faster than a woman's scream. Enchant her before she has a chance to wake up. I'll deal with the mayor."

The baron left the doorway, crossed the hall. Raistlin came after him, the words to the spell burning on his tongue. The thought came to him that he had not coughed once on the entire journey and, of course, now that he had thought of it, a cough began to tickle his throat. Desperately he forced the cough down.

The baron placed his hand on the door handle, turned it softly, and pushed on the door. The mayor must employ good help, for the door hinges opened without a creak. Moonlight illuminated the room through a mullioned window. The baron soft-footed into the room, Raistlin keeping close behind.

A large bed, with bed curtains pulled closed, stood in the center of the room. The sound of snoring came from behind the curtains. The baron tiptoed across the floor, peeped through a crack in the bed curtain.

Fortunately for them, perhaps unfortunately for the lord mayor, he slept alone. One look convinced the baron that the man in the bed was the mayor. He fit Scrounger's description of a rotund, cheerful-faced man, now clad in a sleeping gown and a nightcap instead of his rich robes.

Flinging aside the curtains, the baron was on the slumbering man in a bound, clapped his hand over the snoring man's open mouth.

The mayor woke with a gasp muffled by the baron's hand. The mayor blinked at his captor with sleep-fuddled eyes.

"Make no sound!" the baron hissed. "We mean you no harm. Wizard, shut the door!"

Raistlin did as he was told, easing shut the door. He returned quickly, crossed over to the opposite side of the bed to be ready if needed.

The mayor stared at his captor in terror, shaking in fear so that the bed curtains swayed on their golden rings.

"Light," the baron ordered.

Raistlin spoke, and the crystal on the Staff of Magius gleamed brightly, revealing the baron's face.

"My name is Baron Ivor of Langtree," said the baron, still keeping his hand fast over the mayor's mouth. "Perhaps you've heard of me. That's my army out there, ready to attack your city the moment I give the order. I was hired by King Wilhelm to overthrow rebels who are said to be in control of the city. Are you understanding me?"

The mayor nodded his head. He still looked frightened half out of his wits, but he had stopped shaking.

"Good. I'll let you go in a moment, if you promise you won't yell for help. Are there servants in the house?"

The mayor shook his head. The baron snorted, obviously aware the man was lying. No one lived in a house this large without servants. He wondered whether to continue to press the issue or to carry on. He made a compromise.

"Wizard, watch the door. If anyone enters, cast your spell."

Raistlin opened the door a crack, placed himself so as to command a view of the hallway and also be able to see and hear what was transpiring in the bedroom.

The baron continued his one-way conversation. "I've seen some things and heard some things that have led me to question my reason for taking this assignment. I'm hoping you can help me. I want straight answers from you, Your Honor. That's all. I don't intend to harm you. Give me them and I'll leave as quickly as I've come. Do you agree?"

The mayor nodded his head tentatively. The tassel on his nightcap quivered.

"Play me false," said the baron, still not releasing the grip, "and I'll order my wizard to change you into a slug!"

Raistlin glowered at the mayor, looked stern and threatening, though he could no more have done the baron's bidding than he could have flown around the room. Thanks to the peculiar tint of his skin and the strange appearance of his eyes, he did look extremely intimidating, especially to a man who has just been violently roused from a sound sleep.

The mayor cast Raistlin a terrified glance and this time his nod was more emphatic.

Slowly, the baron moved his hand.

The mayor gulped and licked his lips, drew the bedclothes up to his chin as if they might protect him. His eyes went from the baron to Raistlin and back again. He was in a pitiable state and Raistlin wondered how they would ever get anything intelligent out of him.

"Good," said the baron. Looking around, he drew up a chair and, placing it beside the bed, sat down and faced the mayor, who appeared considerably astonished at this proceeding. "Now, tell me your story. From the beginning. Keep it short, though. We don't have much time. The attack is slated to start at dawn."

This news was not exactly conducive to putting the mayor at his ease. After many fits and false starts and beginning in the middle and having to backtrack, His Honor became immersed in the story of the wrongs inflicted on them by Good King Wilhelm. Forgetting his fear, he spoke passionately.

"We sent an ambassador to the king. He had the man disemboweled! We tried to surrender. The commander of the king's army said that 'we should line up our women' for him to take his pick!"

"You believed him?" the baron said, his dark brows drawn together in a heavy frown.

"Of course we believed him, my lord!" The mayor mopped his sweating forehead with the tassel of his nightcap. "What choice did we have? Besides"—he shuddered—"we heard the screams of those they took prisoner. We saw their homes and barns burning. Yes, we believed him."

Having met Kholos, the baron believed as well. He thought over all he'd heard, tugging on his black beard.

"Do *you* know what's going on, my lord?" the mayor asked meekly.

"No," the baron answered bluntly. "But I have the feeling that I have been duped. If you have heard of me, then you know that I am a man of honor. My ancestors were Knights of Solamnia and, though I am not, I still hold by the precepts of that noble order."

"You will call off the attack then?" the mayor asked with pathetic hopefulness.

"I don't know," said the baron, his head sunk in thought. "I signed a contract. I gave my word I would attack on the morrow. If I refuse and turn and flee the battle, I will be taken for an oath-breaker, probably a coward. No prospective employer will ask the circumstances. He will conclude that I am untrustworthy and refuse to work with me. If I attack, I will be taken for a man who slaughters innocents attempting to surrender! A fine spot I'm in!" he added angrily, rising to his feet. "Goblins to the left of me and ogres on the right."

"There aren't goblins and ogres out there, too, are there?" the mayor gasped, clutching at the blanket.

"A figure of speech," the baron muttered, pacing the room. "What is the hour, Wizard?"

Raistlin went to look out the window, saw the moon starting to wane. "Near midnight, my lord."

"I must make up my mind one way or the other and soon."

The baron marched the length of the bedroom one direction. Turning tightly on his heel in military fashion, as if he were on guard duty, he marched back the other, fighting his mental battle against the ogres of foul scheming on one flank and the goblins of dishonor on the other. To Raistlin the decision was an easy one—call off the attack and go home. He was not a Knight, however, with knightly notions of honor, however misguided. Nor was he responsible for an army, whose soldiers would expect to be paid as promised. Payment would not be forthcoming if the baron went back on the terms of the contract. A pretty dilemma and one Raistlin was thankful was not his own.

For the first time, he saw the burden of command, the isolation of the person in authority, the terrible loneliness of the commander. The lives of thousands of people hung in the balance of this decision. The lives of his men, for whom the baron was responsible, and now the lives of the people of this doomed city. The baron was the only one who could make this decision and he must make it immediately. Worse, he had to make it without being in full possession of the facts.

What had happened to King Wilhelm? Why was he intent on destroying this city and its inhabitants? Was it possible that the king had a good reason? Was this mayor telling the truth or, finding his city in a now untenable position, was this all a complete fabrication? The baron marched and Raistlin watched in silence, curious as to the outcome.

In the end, he was not to know it. The baron halted at a midpoint.

"I have made my decision," he said, his tone heavy. "Now tell me the truth, Your Honor. How many servants do you have in the house and where are they?"

"Two, my lord," the mayor said meekly. "A married couple, who have been with me a long, long time. You need fear nothing from them, sir. They both sleep soundly and would not waken if the city wall fell on them."

"Let's hope it doesn't come to that," the baron said gravely. "Wizard, find these servants and see to it that they continue to slumber."

"Yes, my lord," Raistlin said, as he was bound to say, though he was extremely loath to leave.

"After that, go tell my guards that I will be ready to depart shortly."

"He won't hurt them?" the mayor asked anxiously, referring to the servants.

"He won't hurt them," the baron replied.

The mayor was pale and unhappy, dismayed by the baron's dark and frowning expression and his ominous words. He supplied directions on where to find the servants. Raistlin lingered a moment longer, hoping the baron would give some hint as to his intentions. He waited so long that the baron glanced his way, frowning. Raistlin had no choice but to carry out the order or face an angry reprimand.

"These servants are probably fast asleep," Raistlin fumed as he ascended the stairs to the servants' quarters, a small room with a single gabled window located in the top part of the house, not far below the stork's nest. "Sending me to deal with them was just an excuse. The baron doesn't trust me, that's what it is. He has manufactured this fool's errand in order to get rid of me. He would have allowed Horkin to remain."

As it turned out, the baron's instincts were accurate. Perhaps he had heard some sound that had indicated the servants might be stirring. Raistlin opened the door to the bedroom to find the middle-aged retainer seated on the edge of the bed, tugging on his boots while his wife poked him in the back, saying frantically that she was certain someone was in the house.

Raistlin cast his spell just as the wife caught sight of him in the moonlight. Sleep closed her mouth over her scream. The husband dropped the other boot with a clunk and fell back on the bed. The spell would last a long time. Just to be safe, however, Raistlin locked the door and carried away the key, which he would afterward deposit on the kitchen table.

Somewhat mollified by the fact that there had indeed been danger of discovery, Raistlin returned to the kitchen, where he found Caramon keeping watch out the back window.

"Where's Scrounger?"

"He went to the front to make sure no one came in that way."

"I'll go fetch him. The baron says that he will be ready to leave shortly. You are to make certain the way is secure."

"Sure, Raist. What did he decide to do? Are we going to attack?"

"Does it matter one way or the other to us, my brother?" Raistlin asked indifferently. "We are being paid to obey orders, not question them."

"Yeah, I guess you're right," said Caramon. "Still, aren't you curious to know?"

"Not in the least," Raistlin said and left to retrieve Scrounger.

* * * * *

The baron gave no hint as to his intentions on their way back. The streets were empty. They took no chances but kept close to buildings, paused to look searchingly down side streets and alleyways before they passed them. They were about to cross the last street, the warehouse directly ahead of them, when Caramon, who had been walking in the lead, caught a glow of light from the corner of his eye and fell back against the side of an abandoned house.

"What is it?" the baron whispered.

"Light. Down at the end of the street," Caramon whispered. "It wasn't there when we left."

Motioning the others to remain in the shadows, the baron looked around the corner in the direction Caramon had indicated.

"I'll be blessed," he said softly, awed. "You have to come see this!"

The others stepped around him into the street. They halted, stared, struck by the sight, even to the point of forgetting that they were standing out in the open.

At the end of the street stood a building, a decaying, tumbledown building, that must have, at one time, been lovely. The remnants of graceful columns supported a roof decorated with carvings, whose images had been obliterated, either by time's blows or man's. The building was surrounded by a courtyard, its flagstones broken and overrun with weeds. Caramon would have walked right past this relic, taken no notice of it at all, had it not been for the moonlight.

Either by design or by accident, the building captured Solinari's moonbeams and held them within the stone, as a child captures fireflies in a jar, causing the building to shimmer with an argent radiance.

"I've never seen the like," said the baron in a voice that was hushed and reverent.

"Me neither," said Scrounger. "It's so beautiful it makes me hurt, right here." He laid his hand over his heart.

"Is it magic, Raist?" Caramon asked.

"Enchantment, surely." Raistlin spoke in a whisper, fearful that the sound of his voice might break the spell. "Enchantment," he repeated, "yet not magic."

"Huh?" Caramon was confused. "What other kind of magic is there?"

"Once there was the magic of the gods," Raistlin said.

"Of course!" the baron exclaimed. "That must be the Temple of Paladine. I saw it marked on the map. Probably one of the few temples to the old god left standing in all of Ansalon."

"The Temple of Paladine," Raistlin repeated. He glanced at Solinari, the silver moon. According to legend, the son of Paladine. "Yes, that would explain it."

"I must pay my respects before we depart," the baron said.

Recalling that they had urgent matters to decide before morning, he continued on his way to the warehouse.

Caramon and Scrounger followed. Raistlin trailed behind them all. When they came to the warehouse, he paused at the door for a last look at the wondrous sight. His gaze left the temple, again drawn to the silver moon, to Solinari.

The god of the silver moon had appeared to Raistlin before now; all three of the gods, Solinari, Lunitari, and Nuitari had honored the young mage with their attention. It was to Lunitari that Raistlin owed his primary allegiance, but a wizard who chooses to worship one of the siblings must in some part of his soul worship the other two.

Raistlin had always honored Solinari, though the young mage had the idea that the god of White Magic did not entirely approve of him. Gazing at the temple shining in the silver moonlight, Raistlin had the sudden impression that Solinari had lit the temple purposely, to call their attention to it as one might light a beacon fire. If that was true, did the light burn to warn them away from a perilous lee shore or was the light placed there to guide them through the storm?

"Raist?" Caramon's voice shattered his brother's reverie. "Say, guys, have you see my brother? He was right behind me . . . Oh, there you are. I was worried. Where have you been? Still looking at that old temple, huh? Gives you a kind of strange feeling inside, doesn't it?

"You know, Raist," Caramon added impulsively, "I'd like to go inside there, walk around. I know it's a temple to an old god who's not with us anymore, but I think if I went inside, I'd find the answer to my most important questions."

"I doubt seriously if the temple could tell you when your next meal is going to be," Raistlin said.

He did not know why, but he was always provoked beyond reason when Caramon spoke aloud what Raistlin had been thinking.

A cloud drifted across the moon, a piece of black cloth dropped over the silver orb. The temple disappeared, lost in the darkness. If it had ever known the answers to life's mysteries, the temple had long ago forgotten them.

"Hunh." Caramon grunted. "You better come inside, Raist. We're not supposed to be out here. Against orders."

"Thank you, Caramon, for reminding me of my duty," Raistlin returned, pushing past his twin.

"Sure, Raist," Caramon said cheerfully. "Any time."

In a corner of the warehouse, Master Senej and Sergeant Nemiss were meeting with the baron. They spoke in low tones. No one could hear what they said, not even Scrounger, who'd been caught lurking behind a barrel by an irritated Sergeant Nemiss and sent off to stand watch as punishment. The soldiers studied the faces of the three, searching in the shifting expressions for some sign of the baron's intentions.

"Whatever it is the baron's saying," Caramon said softly, "Master Senej doesn't look happy about it."

Master Senej was frowning and shaking his head. He was overheard to say, "don't trust" in loud and stern tones. Sergeant Nemiss was apparently not pleased, either, for she made an emphatic gesture with her hand, as if throwing away something. The baron listened to their arguments, appeared to consider them. Eventually, however, he shook his head. A slicing motion of his hand ended the debate.

"You have your orders, master," he said, for everyone in the warehouse to hear.

"Yes, sir," Master Senej replied.

"Tumbler," the sergeant called. "The baron's ready to leave now. You'll escort the baron back to camp."

"Yes, sir. Do I come back here, sir?"

"There won't be time before the attack," the sergeant said, her voice deliberately calm and even.

The men glanced at each other. The attack was going forward. Few said anything, either in pleasure or disappointment. They had come to fight, and fight was what they would do.

Tumbler saluted and gathered up his coil of rope.

He and the baron departed. Sergeant Nemiss and Major Senej conferred for a few moments longer, then the sergeant went to check the watch. The master lay down on the floor, pulled his hat over his face.

The men followed his example. Caramon was soon snoring loudly, so loudly that Sergeant Nemiss kicked him, told him to roll over and quit making such a racket; they could probably hear him in Solamnia.

Scrounger slept curled up in a tight, compact ball, rather like a dormouse, even to putting his hands over his eyes.

Raistlin, who had slept most of the day, was not tired. He sat with his back against the wall and recited his spells, over and over, until he had them fixed firmly in his mind.

The words of magic were still on his lips when sleep stole upon him, bringing him dreams of a temple bathed in silver moonlight.

14

Puny human body, my ass!" Kit muttered, on the trail of the dragon.

Having heard Immolatus complain bitterly about having to walk half a block from the inn to the tavern, Kitiara had figured she would catch up with him at the first creek where he'd stop to soak his aching feet. His track was easy to find—branches broken, bushes hacked to shreds, weeds trampled. The dragon was traveling at a pace that astonished Kit, left her far behind at the outset of the chase. Concentrating intently on his goal, Immolatus appeared to have forgotten he had taken human form. In his mind, he was barreling through the forest with lashing tail and crushing claws.

Already tired, Kit had to push herself to try to overtake him, for she wanted to catch him in the wilderness, before he reached the cavern where he could safely transform back to his old dragony self. And she had to catch him before night fell, for he could see in the dark and she could not.

Once Kit made up her mind to action, she set about her task resolutely, swiftly, with no second thoughts or hesitation. Self-doubt was a weakness, tiny cracks in the foundation that would someday bring down the wall; faulty links in the chain mail would allow the arrow to penetrate. Tanis had been afflicted with this weakness. He constantly questioned, constantly analyzed his own actions and reactions. Kit had found this habit of his particularly annoying, and had tried constantly to break him of it.

"When you decide to do a thing, do it!" she had scolded him. "Don't dither and blather and mull over it. Don't dive into the river and then flounder about wondering if you're going to sink. You *will* sink if you do that. Jump in and start swimming. And never look back to shore."

"I suppose it's the elf blood in me," Tanis had replied. "Elves never make any major decisions until they have thought the matter over for at least a year or two, gone round to all their friends and relatives and discussed the problem, done research, read tomes, consulted the sages."

"And what happens then?" Kit had demanded, still irritated.

"By then they've usually forgotten what it was they meant to do in the first place," he had replied, smiling.

She had laughed; he could always tease her out of a bad humor. She did not laugh now and she was sorry she'd thought about him again. The one time Tanis had made up his mind to act was the decision he'd made to leave her. Taking her own advice, she put him out of her mind and continued on.

Kit had one advantage over the dragon in that she knew where she was going. With her usual thoroughness and attention to detail, she'd drawn an excellent map, using landmarks as guideposts and keeping track of the distance by counting her paces. "Seventy paces from the lightning-struck oak to the bear's-head rock. Turn left on the deer path, cross the stream, travel up the cliff to the high ledge." Immolatus had studied the map, but he hadn't taken it with him. Probably because the dragon was not accustomed to using a map. You have little need to know trails over streams if you're flying far above those streams. Her thinking proved correct. She'd been following his trail for about three hours when she came across a place where had deviated from her directions. He had realized his mistake and doubled back, but he'd lost a considerable amount of time and Kit had gained it.

She traveled swiftly, but not carelessly. She kept silent as possible, watched her footing so that she did not step on a dry stick or crash noisily through the underbrush. She would see him long before he heard or saw her. She had transferred the knife from her boot to her belt, within easy reach. He would never know what hit him.

As for the dragon, he left a trail a blind gully dwarf could have followed: footprints in the mud, broken tree limbs, and once even a bit of red cloth, torn from his robes, caught in a bramble bush. Drawing near the mountains, entering the foothills, she found fewer signs of the dragon's passing, but that was to be expected on the hard, rock-strewn ground. Here were no twigs to bend, no mud in which to heedlessly place a booted foot. Still, she was certain she was on the right track. Immolatus was, after all, following her directions.

Shadows lengthened. Kit was footsore and tired, hungry and frustrated. She had only another hour of daylight left. The thought of giving up, of calling it quits, came to mind. Ambition dug his spurs into her flanks and drove her on.

The sun was setting. She followed the sheepherder's trail she had marked on her map, a trail that meandered up and down the rolling foothills. The sheep and their herders had fled to the safety of the city with the coming of war, but they had left their marks on the mountainside. She paused to rest from the heat in a small hut made snug with hay, drank from a waterskin dropped in the mad scramble to seek the shelter of the city walls. She was negotiating her way across a small, swift-rushing stream, taking care not to lose her footing. Instinct, or perhaps a smell or a sound, caused her to pause where she was, steady herself on the slippery rocks, look ahead instead of at her feet.

Immolatus stood not twenty paces from her, farther up the path that wound along the side of a steep cliff. His back was turned. Kit recalled the map, remembered that at this point, one had to leave the path behind, begin the ascent into the mountains. The trail would look tempting, compared to climbing up into rough and rocky terrain. The path was deceptive, looked as if it would lead the way the dragon wanted to go. Kit had seen from her vantage point atop the mountain that the sheep trail led, as one might expect, to a small grassy valley. Immolatus was trying to decide which route to take, trying to call the map to memory.

Caught out in the open, inwardly cursing, Kitiara clasped the knife's hilt and prepared a charming smile, ready to greet the dragon joyfully when he turned around to find her stalking him. She had her excuse prepared— urgent information from Commander Kholos about the disposition of the troops. She'd heard from the soldiers in camp that a mercenary force had sneaked into the city during the previous night, was planning to attack the city from the inside at dawn, while Kholos and his troops attacked from the outside. She thought the dragon should be informed of this important development, and so forth and so on.

Immolatus did not turn around.

Kitiara watched him warily, wondering if this was a trick. He must have heard her splashing through the creek; she did not see how he could have missed hearing her. She had been proceeding carefully, but her attention had of necessity been concentrated more on not falling in the water than on moving with silent stealth.

Immolatus remained standing with his head bowed, his back turned, studying his shoes or the trail or perhaps even taking a piss.

This was a lucky break obviously. Kit did not question her luck, prepared to take advantage of it. Queen Takhisis was going to go into battle minus one red dragon. Kit took hold of the knife's blade, balanced, aimed, and threw.

She was dead on her target. The knife passed right between Immolatus's shoulder blades. Passed through the shoulder blades and kept going, its steel blade catching the sunlight as its flight carried it beyond her sight. She heard steel hit rock with a small metallic clang, a scraping sound, and then nothing.

Kitiara stared, astounded, her brain scrabbling for purchase, trying to make sense of the senseless. She wasn't certain what had happened, but she knew she was in danger. She drew her sword, splashed through the creek, prepared to face Immolatus's fury. The damn dragon still didn't turn around, didn't move, didn't stir. Only when she came close to him, close enough to slice off his head, did Kit understand.

The moment she understood, the illusion of Immolatus standing on the trail disappeared.

A grating sound above her drew her attention. She looked up in time to see a boulder thundering down the hillside.

Kitiara fell to her stomach, pressing her body against the sun-warmed rock and covered her head with her hands. The boulder sailed past her, struck an outcropping of rock right below her and bounded into the creek with a splash. Another boulder followed. This one came closer. Immolatus missed again, but he could keep throwing rocks at her all day long. She had no where to go and sooner or later he'd hit his mark.

"Let him hit it then," Kit muttered.

Swiftly, she undid the straps holding the steel breastplate she wore, avoiding yet another boulder.

Craning her neck, she peered upward. The next boulder came thundering down. Kitiara drew in a deep breath and let it out in a scream, threw her breastplate directly into the boulder's path. The boulder caught the breastplate a glancing blow, sending it spinning into the creek, the steel flashing red by the light of the setting sun.

Dropping to her hands and knees, making herself as small as possible, Kit took advantage of the twilight, which would make it difficult for even the dragon to see if he had truly killed her. She used the noise of the falling boulder to cover the sound of her movements, scrambled into the brush alongside the path. She located a small crevice in the cliff face and wormed her way inside, scraping most of the skin off her thighs and her knees and her elbows, but safe for the moment from the dragon. Provided he had fallen for her ruse.

MARGARET WEIS AND DON PERRIN

Kitiara waited, her cheek pressed against the rock, panting for breath. No more boulders came hurtling down the mountainside, but that meant nothing. If he did not believe he'd killed her, he might very well come back to hunt her down. She listened for the sound of his pursuit, cursed her heart for beating so loudly.

She heard nothing and she began to breathe a bit easier. Yet she did not move. She remained hidden, just in case he was hanging about to watch. Time passed and Kitiara became convinced. The dragon must believe her to be dead. She would have been nothing more to him than a bright flash of armor on the mountain and he had seen that bright flash fall, heard her death cry. Arrogant as he was, Immolatus would easily convince himself that his clever little ruse had worked. He would wait a few moments to make certain, but, sure of himself and eager for his vengeance, he would not linger long, not with the smell of eggs in his nostrils.

"Still," Kitiara reminded herself ruefully, "I underestimated him once and nearly died for my mistake."

She would not do the same again.

Kitiara waited another few moments then, impatient, cramped and uncomfortable, she made up her mind that a fight would be preferable to being wedged between two slabs of rock. She slid cautiously out from her hiding place. Crouched on the trail, she peered upward, searching the shadows for a bit of red robe or a red wing tip or the glitter of a red scale.

Nothing. The mountainside was desolate, as far as she could see.

Seating herself on the trail, Kitiara examined her sword to make certain it had suffered no damage. Satisfied as to her weapon, she next looked for damage to herself. Cuts and bruises, that was about the extent of it. She dug a few sharp pieces of rock out of the palms of her hands, sucked blood from a deep cut on her knee, and wondered gloomily what to do next.

Give up, return to camp. That was the sensible course of action. To do so was to admit defeat and Kitiara had been defeated only once in her life and that was in love, not battle. Her own thoughts were bloody with vengeance. Up to now, she would have been content to merely stop Immolatus from destroying the eggs. Now she wanted him dead. She would make him pay for those few horrible moments she'd spent cowering in terror on the mountainside. She'd track the damn dragon through the mountains all night, if that was what it took to catch him.

Fortunately, Solinari would shine brightly tonight. And if Kit was very lucky or if Queen Takhisis was inclined to lend her aid, the dragon would manage to lose himself in the mountains during the night. He'd already started up the mountains the wrong way, to judge by the direction of the boulders.

If you make up your mind to do a thing, do it. Don't bother with the how and the why. Just do it.

Grimly, resolutely, Kitiara began her climb up the mountainside.

15

The night was a long one for Kitiara, slogging through the mountains. The night was also long for Immolatus. Kit's prayers were answered, he did manage to lose his way. Immolatus was tempted more than once to return to his dragon body with its glorious wings, wings that would carry him off this damnable mountain, wings that would carry him into the skies.

But Immolatus had the impression that the sneaky god Paladine had set spies on him, was watching for him. Immolatus imagined golden dragons lurking on the mountaintop, just waiting for him to change form to pounce upon him. Little as he liked to admit it, this human body was a useful disguise. If only it wasn't so weak. The dragon sat down for just a few moments to rest and woke later from a nap he'd never meant to take, to find that it was almost dawn.

The night was long for the men in the warehouse, who had finally been given their orders for the predawn attack and who, while not looking forward to the morning, would just as soon have it over.

The night was a short one for the lord mayor, who faced the coming dawn with extreme apprehension. The night was short for the people of Hope's End, well aware that this night might be their last. The night was extremely short for the baron, who had to reach his camp before the dawn.

The night was just another night for Commander Kholos, who snored all the way through it.

"You wanted to be wakened early, sir." Master Vardash entered the commander's tent, stood respectfully beside the bed, another prize from one of the manor houses, lugged along at considerable cost and inconvenience.

"What? What is it? What's going on?" Kholos blinked at his officer, who was lighting a lamp on the desk.

"It is nearly dawn, sir. You wanted me to waken you early. The city comes under assault today."

"Oh, yes." The commander yawned, scratched himself. "I suppose I had better get up then."

"Here is your ale, sir. The venison steaks are coming. The cook wants to know if you'll have potatoes or bread this morning."

"Both. And tell him to put some onions in those potatoes. I had an idea last night," Kholos added, seating himself on the bed and pulling on his boots. "Is that wizard Immolatus still around?"

"I suppose so, sir," Vardash answered slowly, trying to remember. "I haven't seen him recently, but then he keeps to himself."

"Eating our rations and not doing a damn thing to earn it. Well, I have work for him this morning. I was thinking that when the baron's men reach the wall—what's left of them after our archers are finished—the wizard could work some sort of magic, drop the wall on them. What do you think?"

"It's an awfully big wall, sir," suggested Vardash hesitantly.

"I know it's a big wall," Kholos returned peevishly, "but these wizards must have spells to handle that sort of thing. Or what use are they? Have the blasted wizard report to me. I'll ask him myself."

Kholos rose to his feet, naked except for his boots. Long, thick hair covered most of his body, except where his battle scars roped and slashed through the thick pelt. As he spoke, he scratched at himself again, captured a flea and crushed it between his thumb and forefinger.

Vardash dispatched a soldier to find the wizard. Breakfast arrived. The general devoured the still-bloody steaks, a loaf of bread, and quantities of potatoes and onions, all the while issuing orders in preparation for the day's battle. Though the sky was still dark, with dawn presaged by only a hint of pink along the horizon, the camp was up and doing. The men were eating breakfast, to judge by the noise coming from the mess tent.

The sky grew perceptibly brighter. A bird practiced a tentative call or two. His aide assisted Commander Kholos to dress and helped him on with his armor, which was heavy and massive. The aide had to ask Vardash for assistance with the commander's breastplate, which required two men to lift it. An ordinary human would have sunk to the ground beneath it. Commander Kholos gave a grunt, banged himself on the chest a few times to position the breastplate, adjusted his bracers, and pronounced himself ready.

A soldier arrived to say that the wizard was not in his tent, neither was Commander uth Matar. No one had seen either of them for some time now. One soldier said he had overheard uth Matar saying something to the wizard about the job being finished and returning to Sanction.

"Who gave them permission to return to Sanction?" Kholos demanded angrily. "They were supposed to bring me a map showing me where to find those blasted dragon eggs!"

"They were acting under Lord Ariakas's direct orders, sir," Vardash reminded him respectfully. "Perhaps the general changed his mind. Perhaps he intends to search for the eggs himself. To be honest, Commander, I think we are well rid of the wizard. I did not altogether trust him."

"I didn't plan on trusting him," Kholos returned irritably. "I just wanted him to knock down a single goddam wall. How hard can that be? Still and all, I guess you're right. Hand me my sword. And I'll take the battle-axe as well. We'll count on the archers to dispose of the baron's men. Do they have their orders, master? They know what to do?"

"Yes, sir. Their orders are to shoot them in the back, sir, the minute they've captured the gate. A far better plan than trusting to magic, if I may say so, sir."

"Perhaps you're right, Vardash. Between our archers and those in the city, the baron's army should be wiped out by—what time would you say, Vardash?"

"Noon, I should think, sir."

"Really? That late? I was thinking midmorning myself. A wager?"

"I would be delighted, sir," Vardash said without enthusiasm.

He never won a wager with Kholos, who, no matter what the outcome, conveniently remembered the terms of the bet as being favorable to himself. If the baron's men were still alive and kicking by noon, the commander would recall that he'd said noon himself and that it was Vardash who'd been overly optimistic and said midmorning.

Kholos was in a good humor. The city would most certainly fall into his hands this day. Tonight, he'd be sleeping in the lord mayor's bed, perhaps with the lord mayor's wife, if she wasn't a cow. If she was, he'd have his pick of the rest of the women of the town. He'd spend a day or two mopping up any resistance, selecting the choicest slaves, putting to death those who didn't make the cut, loading the wagons with loot, and then he'd set fire to the city. Once Hope's End was in ashes, he would start on the long, but triumphant road back to Sanction.

* * * * *

The mercenary camp was also up and at 'em this morning.

"Sir, you asked to be wakened before sunup," Commander Morgon started to say, then saw it wasn't necessary.

The baron was already awake. He had arrived back in camp just an hour earlier, lain down for a brief rest, and was now lying on his cot, mulling over his plans for the day. Swinging his legs over the side of the cot, he pulled on his tall leather boots. He was already wearing his breeches and shirt.

"Breakfast, sir?" Morgon asked.

The baron nodded. "Yes, have all the officers meet me in my command tent and have breakfast served there."

"Venison steaks and potatoes with onions, sir?" Morgon suggested with a grin.

The baron looked up, eyes narrowed. "What are you trying to do, Morgon, kill me before the enemy has a crack at me?"

"No, sir." Morgon laughed. "I've just returned from the camp of our gallant allies. That is Commander Kholos's favorite meal before a battle."

"I hope it gives him heartburn," said the baron grumpily. "I'll have the usual. Toast strips soaked in honey wine. And tell cook to mix up an egg in that. What did our gallant allies have to say for themselves?"

"The commander wishes us luck with our attack, and promises to support us on the way in."

The two exchanged glances.

"Very good, Morgon," the baron replied. "You have your orders. You know what to do."

"Yes, sir." Morgon saluted and departed.

The baron met with his officers, went over the plans for the assault on the gate.

"I'm not asking for questions, gentlemen," he said at the conclusion of the meeting. "I don't have the answers. Good luck to us all."

Four buglers, four drummers, a standard-bearer, several staff officers, five runners, and ten bodyguards formed the command group in the center of the infantry line.

"Uncase the standard," the baron ordered.

The standard-bearer pulled a lanyard attached to the top of the standard, caused the rolled flag to unfurl. The symbol of the bison fluttered above the army.

"Buglers—sound the call to arms!"

The four buglers blasted out notes in unison, repeating the short call three times. Morgon touched the baron's arm, pointed. Across the field, the first companies of Kholos's army were moving into position on the right flank.

When Kholos's heavy infantry had formed in the center of his line, the commander's standard went up, indicating he was in position.

The baron nodded. "Very well, lads. This is the big finish. Time to earn our pay. Or not," he muttered into his beard. He paused a moment, wondering if he'd made the right decision. Too late now if he hadn't. Shrugging, he sat up straight on his horse. "Buglers!" he shouted. "Sound Advance!"

A single note, held long and wailing, echoed back from the mountains. The note's end was punctuated by a boom from the four drummers, beating in unison, pounding out a continuous and slow cadence. The companies moved forward in battle line.

The baron looked down the left of the line. The polished breastplates shone in the newly risen morning sun. Sunlight glinted off spearpoints. The men carried spears and shields with short swords sheathed. The archers had taken up their positions to the far left of the line. They wore no breastplates, but carried large wooden shields that had spikes at the bottom tips. When the archers stopped to fire, they would plant the shields in the ground and fire from behind.

To the baron's right, a company of eight men carried a huge battering ram made of solid oak tipped with iron. Each man held a shield he would use to cover his head and body from attack while the ram battered the gates. More men marched alongside, ready to run in and take over a position if a man fell.

The men moved forward, rank upon rank. They could see soldiers crowding the top of the city's wall, but there was no answering fire. Not yet. The attackers were still out of range. The regiment neared the creek bed. The baron watched the tops of the battlements closely.

"Wait for it, wait for it." He issued the order to himself.

A flag flew up the flag post atop the wall, accompanied by the deadly hum of hundreds of loosed arrows.

"Now!" the baron yelled.

The buglers blew Charge, the drummers pounded a furious rhythm.

The men ran forward, fast enough to evade the first volley. Arrows thunked into the ground behind them. No one fell.

The men hauling the battering ram came within a hundred yards of the wall, heading straight for the gate.

The city loosed a second volley. Every man in the regiment ran harder, faster, trying to get ahead of the deadly rain of arrows. Again they outran them. None of the arrows hit, all fell behind the regiment's lines. The men cheered and jeered at the enemy.

The last hundred yards were a sprint. The line lost cohesion as everyone dashed toward the objective. The battering ram crew closed on the gate, came to a stop.

The men swung back once, then let the weight of the ram smack into the gate. The giant wooden structure resounded with a hollow boom. The gates flew open.

* * * * *

Across the field, Commander Kholos turned to his archers.

"Now! Now! They've breached the gates! Fire!"

A hundred archers fired into the mercenary's rear ranks. Before the first volley had hit home, a second was in the air.

The baron's troops had converged on the open gate, pushing to get through. A few soldiers fell, but not nearly as many as Kholos had hoped. Fuming, he turned to glare at his archers.

"Punishment detail for any man who misses a shot!" he yelled.

The archers reloaded, and fired two more volleys. But they were fast running out of targets.

"The fighting must have moved inside, sir," Vardash said. "The baron's men have breached the city's defenses. Should I send the archers forward? Apparently the fools haven't figured out that we're firing on them."

Kholos frowned. Something was wrong. He called for his spyglass, raised it to his eye, stared intently at the city gate. Snapping the glass shut, his goblinish face livid with fury, he turned to his signal drummers.

"Quickly! Sound Attack!"

Vardash turned. "Attack, sir? Now? I thought we were going to let the baron's men do the brunt of the fighting?"

Kholos struck Vardash a blow that crushed his jaw, sent him sprawling backward into the mud.

"You idiot!" Kholos howled, jumping over Vardash's unmoving body, racing forward to take his place at the head of the troops. "The bastards have tricked us! There *is* no fighting at the gate."

16

Kitiara pulled herself cautiously up the last rock ledge leading to the cavern's hidden entrance. She moved slowly, testing every hand- and foothold, taking care not to dislodge any rocks whose clattering fall might alert the dragon. Reaching the top, she crouched, sword in hand, looking and listening, thinking he might be lying in wait for her, to ambush her.

"The way is clear!" called a voice. "Come quickly. We don't have much time."

"Who is that?" Kit demanded, peering through the shadows cast by the tall pine trees that screened the entrance. The sun had just risen. Trumpet calls bounced off the rocks around her, the attack on the city of Hope's End had begun. "Sir Nigel? Or whatever the hell it is you're calling yourself?"

She found the spirit standing where she'd left it, inside the entrance to the cavern.

"I've been waiting for you," said Sir Nigel. "Hurry. We don't have much time."

"I take that to mean that you encountered the wizard." Kit entered the cavern. The dark cool shadows of the rock washed over her, chilling after the heat of her pursuit. Her skin prickled, she rubbed her arms.

"Yes, he passed by some time ago. You told him where to find the eggs," Sir Nigel said accusingly.

"Those were my orders," Kit returned. "I suppose even spirit-knights obey orders."

"But now you're here to stop him from destroying them."

"Those are my orders, too," Kit stated coldly and, walking past the ghost, she entered the cave, leaving the ghost to come or go as it chose.

The ghost entered with her and, once again, as when she had first entered the tunnel from the other direction, she found her way lighted.

No, she thought, it was not so much that her way was lighted, but that the darkness receded. When the spirit raised its hand, the darkness flowed away from it like the tide from the shoreline. Gold and silver scales, shed long ago, gleamed on the path, glittered on the walls. As long as Kitiara kept close to the ghostly Knight, she could find her way. Darkness flowed in behind them after the Knight had passed. If she lagged behind, even a pace or two, the darkness engulfed her.

"This spirit is just full of tricks," Kit muttered. She hurried to keep up. "Tell me how you knew I was coming back," she challenged him. "Or do all ghosts read minds."

"There is nothing very mystical in my knowledge," the Knight said, with a slight smile. "When Immolatus arrived in the cavern, he did not proceed straight to his goal, but stopped and waited, looking behind him, back the way he'd come. He waited until he caught sight of something and then he nodded to himself as if he'd expected to see what he saw. Following his line of sight, I observed you farther down the mountainside.

"Immolatus was not pleased," the Knight continued. "He growled and muttered, called you a nuisance, said he should have finished you when he had the chance. He hesitated and I thought he planned to stay and wait for you. He thought so himself, I believe, but then he glanced down the corridor, into the darkness, and his red eyes glowed.

"'First I'll have my revenge,'" he said and left.

Sir Nigel looked back at her, a measuring gaze.

"He is in dragon form now, Kitiara uth Matar."

Kit drew in a breath, tightened her grip on her sword. Logic dictated that Immolatus would change back. She'd expected nothing else, yet the knowledge that he'd actually done so was a blow to the pit of the stomach. Now that the ghost had mentioned it, she could feel the onset of the terrible debilitating fear that had come near to crippling her the first time she'd seen the dragon. The fear caused her palms to sweat and her mouth to go dry. She was angry at the Knight, angry at herself.

"Do you mean to tell me that you were lurking in that cavern all the time?" Kit demanded. "Why didn't you strike him? Stab him from behind before he had a chance to change his form! He obviously had no idea you were there!"

"Useless," Sir Nigel replied. "My sword has no bite."

Kit swore, beside herself with rage. "A fine guardian you make!" she sneered.

"I am the guardian of the eggs," the Knight replied. "Those are *my* orders."

"And how do you propose to guard them, Sir Undead? Say, 'Please, Master Dragon, go away and don't break the pretty eggs'?"

The Knight's face darkened or perhaps the light that flowed from him dimmed, because it seemed that the shadows closed in on them. "This is my geas," he said in a low voice. "I chose it myself, none laid it on me. But sometimes it is hard to bear. Soon, however, my watch will be over, for good or ill, and I will continue on my long-delayed journey. As for my plan, I will distract the dragon from the front. When his attention is concentrated on me, you will strike."

"Distract? What are you going to do? A little song and dance—"

"Hush!" Sir Nigel lifted his hand in warning. "We are close to the chamber!"

Kit knew well enough where she was. The corridor in which they stood made a turn. A short distance beyond, it opened into the huge chamber where the eggs were hidden. Kitiara stood just before that turn. Walk around the jutting rock wall to the right and she would walk into the chamber.

Walk into Immolatus.

Kitiara heard the dragon, heard his massive tail scraping over the rock, heard his stentorian breathing and the rumbling of the fire burning in his belly. She could smell him, smell the sulfur and the stench of reptile. The smell sickened her, her fear sickened her. She heard the dragon lash his tail against the rock. The corridor in which they stood shuddered. Her body went hot and then cold. Her palms were slippery, she had to continually adjust her grasp on the sword's hilt.

Immolatus was talking to the unborn of his enemies, haranguing them in the language of dragons, presumably. Kitiara couldn't understand a word.

"I must go now," Sir Nigel said and she felt his words as a breath on her cheek. She could hear nothing over the dragon's howls and grunts and taunting words that were like the cracking of bones. "Await my signal."

"Don't bother!" Kitiara snapped, angry, afraid. "Go back to your tomb. Maybe I'll join you."

Sir Nigel looked at her long and searchingly. "You truly do not understand anything you have seen or heard since you entered this temple?"

"I understand that I have to do this myself," Kit retorted. "That I can count on no one but myself! The way it's always been."

"Ah, that explains it." Sir Nigel raised his hand in salute. "Farewell, Kitiara uth Matar."

The light vanished and Kit was alone, alone in a darkness that was not as dark as she could have wished it, a darkness that was tinged with red, the fire of the dragon.

"He left me!" Kitiara said to herself, amazed. She had trusted she would be able to shame him into staying. "That bastard ghost really left me here to die! A pox on him, then. His soul to the Abyss."

Aware that she had to act now, while she was more angry than she was frightened, Kitiara wiped the wet palm of her sword hand upon her leather tunic, clenched her hand around the hilt, and strode through the fire-singed darkness.

* * * * *

Immolatus was enjoying himself. He had a right to indulge. He'd earned this moment, paid for it in blood, and he meant to make it last. Besides, he needed time to accustom himself to his dragon form again, revel in the return of his strength and power. He raked his front claws against the ceiling of the cavern, leaving great gouges in the stone. His hind claws dug into the rock, breaking it and tearing it. He would have liked to spread his wings, to stretch the muscles. Unfortunately the chamber, though large enough to accommodate him, was not large enough to accommodate his full wingspan. He made do with lashing his tail, feeling in satisfaction the very bones of the mountain tremble at his might.

Immolatus spoke to the unborn of his enemies, knowing that somewhere his enemies could hear him. They would sense his presence in the nest of their young. They would know what he intended and they would be powerless to stop him. He felt the parents' anguish, their helpless dread, and he laughed at them and mocked them and made ready to destroy their children.

He had planned to incinerate the unborn dragons; indeed, that is what he'd intended to do. The fire in his belly had very nearly gone out, having been nothing but a measly spark in his human form, a spark he had to constantly nurse to maintain. Needing time to stoke the fire, he determined that, in the beginning at least, he would crack the eggs with his claws and maybe even suck out the yokes of a dozen or so.

Anticipating the pleasure, he recited the catalog of his wrongs and gloated over his revenge, savoring every moment in order to relive it later in his hundred-year-long dreams.

Immolatus was enjoying himself so much that he paid little attention to the speck of light shining silver-white at his feet. He thought the light nothing more than one of the myriad silver scales left scattered about by his enemies. He shifted his head slightly, hoping the light would go away, for he found that it irritated him, like a bit of chaff caught in his eye.

The light remained. He could not rid himself of it and he was forced to pause in his recitative to deal with it. He looked at the light closely, though it hurt him to do so, and as he looked he saw it take form and shape. He recognized it.

One of Paladine's flunkies.

"A Solamnic Knight for me to kill!" Immolatus chuckled. "What joy! I could have wished for nothing more to increase my pleasure. Who says my Queen has abandoned me? No, she has given me this gift."

The Knight said no word. He drew his sword from its antique scabbard.

The dragon blinked, half-blinded. The silver light was a silver lance, stabbing through his eye. The pain was excruciating and growing worse.

"I would play with you longer, worm," Immolatus growled, "but I find that you begin to annoy me."

He made a swipe at the Knight with a slashing claw, intending to rip through the armor, impale him.

The Knight did not attack. Seeing certain death descending on him, he raised his sword, hilt-first, to heaven.

"Paladine, god of my order and of my soul," the Knight called out. "Witness that I have been faithful to my vow!"

Ridiculous Knights, Immolatus thought, his claw stabbing downward. Vowing, praying—even after their fickle god had abandoned them. Just as my Queen abandoned me, then returned to demand homage and service and worship, as if she deserved it!

Searing pain pierced the dragon's insides. His slashing blow went wild, missed its target. Furious, Immolatus turned to see what had hit him.

The worm. Uth Matar. That annoying, bloodsucking worm inflicted on him by that human excrement, Ariakas.

* * * * *

Kitiara had been both pleased and astonished to see the ghost reappear. The sight of the Knight lent her courage. Creeping around the dragon's left hind leg, she struck the dragon from behind, driving her sword with both hands deep into the dragon's flank. She aimed for a vital organ. Uncertain of dragon anatomy, she hoped to hit the heart, hoped for a quick kill. Her sword glanced off a scale. Her stab struck deep, but it struck a rib, nothing vital.

"Damn!" Kitiara yanked free the bloody sword and, guessing that her time was limited, made a desperate attempt to stab again.

* * * * *

Attacked from the front and on his flank, Immolatus returned his gaze to what he deemed the more dangerous foe, the accursed Solamnic. His lashing tail would deal with the worm. Quick as a whip snap, the dragon's tail curled and released. The tail hit Kitiara full in the chest, a blow that sent her tumbling, rolling head over heels back down the corridor. Her sword flew from her hand.

Immolatus would finish off this Knight, then he would finish off the worm.

"Requite my faith, my god," the Knight was yelling at the empty heavens. "Grant that I may fulfill my vow."

The Knight flung his sword into the air.

A stupid move, but one that was a popular among Knights. They were always hoping to poke out an eye. The blade blazed with silver fire. Immolatus made the standard defense, jerked his head up and back.

Sir Nigel had not aimed for the dragon's eye. The blade, blazing silver, soared high into the air, struck the ceiling of the cavern.

The sword that had no bite plunged deep into the rock.

The dragon laughed. He lowered his head, jaws snapping, intending to seize the Knight in his crushing jaws. His fangs opened and closed over nothing but air.

The Knight remained standing calmly, gazing upward, his hands raised in a salute or perhaps in prayer. Behind him, the eggs of gold and silver dragons lay nestled in a chamber of rock. Above him, the ceiling started to crack.

A large chunk of rock fell, struck Immolatus on the head. Another followed and another, and then a veritable cascade of rocks plunged down, threatening to bury the dragon. Sharp stones hit his body, wounding him, bruising him. One tore through a wing. Another crushed a toe.

Stunned by the blows raining down on him, Immolatus sought shelter. He retreated back down the corridor, trusting that its ceiling would hold, would not collapse around him. He crouched there as the ground shook beneath his feet. Dust and sharp shards filled the air, ricocheted off the cavern's wall. He couldn't see, could barely breathe.

And then the shaking ended. The avalanche ceased. The dust cleared.

Immolatus opened an eyelid cautiously, peered around. He was afraid to move, afraid that he would bring down the entire mountain.

The Solamnic Knight was gone, buried under a massive rockslide. Gone, too, were the eggs, their chamber sealed closed by tons of rocks and boulders. The unborn dragons were safely beyond Immolatus's reach.

Roaring his disappointment and outrage, he belched a blast of fire from his belly against the newly formed rock wall, but all that did was to superheat the granite, cause it to fuse together in a solid mass, impossible to shift. He scrabbled at the wall with a claw and, after much work, managed to dislodge a single small boulder, which rolled down the hill of rock and landed on the dragon's foot, hurting him.

He glared at the wall. Revenge might be sweet, but it was an awful lot of work. And then there was Her Dark Majesty. She would not be pleased at this turn of events, and though Immolatus might sneer at his goddess and dismiss her as fickle and capricious, deep inside him, he feared her wrath. If he had destroyed the eggs, he might have talked his way around her. No use crying over spilt yolks. Having disobeyed her orders and in so doing inadvertently sealed up the eggs where they would be safe until the day came when they hatched and their parents could come to free them. Immolatus had the feeling Her Majesty might be difficult.

He had a moment's fleeting hope that the eggs had all been smashed by the fall of the ceiling, but he knew Paladine well of old, knew that the Knight's prayer had been heard. The blow that had brought the ceiling down around the dragon's ears had not been struck by any mortal hand.

By some fluke, Immolatus himself had escaped the god's anger. He might not be so lucky the next time. As it was, he could feel the mountain continue to shake. It was time to go, before Paladine tried again. Immolatus turned to leave by the same way he had entered, only to find the corridor blocked, choked up with debris.

The dragon snarled in irritation. He was more annoyed than frightened. Dragons are accustomed to dwelling underground, their eyes can penetrate the darkness, their nostrils sniff out the tiniest whiff of air.

Immolatus smelled fresh air. He knew there was another opening somewhere. He recalled the map of the temple the worm had drawn for him, recalled another corridor leading up and out. A corridor that led into the accursed Temple of Paladine.

"If I do nothing else, I'll level that foul blot upon the landscape," Immolatus muttered, flame hissing through his teeth. "I'll burn it and then I'll burn this city. They'll smell the smoke of death in the Abyss and let my Queen or any other god try to touch me then! Just let them!"

Mumbling and grumbling his defiance, he sniffed the fresh air, located its source. Thrusting a clawed hand into the rubble blocking the way, rubble that was not very thick at this point, the dragon cleared it easily.

He found the corridor he'd remembered from the map. The corridor was open and clear, remained unaffected by the landslide. But it was a small corridor. A narrow corridor. A man-sized corridor.

Immolatus groaned and came near sinking under the weight of his severe disappointment. He would have to take that form again, that hated, heinous form, that weak and puny form, that human form. Fortunately, he would not have to traipse about in the flesh-bag too long, only long enough to traverse this corridor, which, if memory of the map served him correctly, was not very long.

He pronounced the words of magic, grinding them with his teeth, detesting every one of them, and the transfiguration occurred, painful and humiliating as usual. Immolatus the red-robed wizard stood in the midst of the ruin of the corridor. The fabric of his robe immediately stuck to a wound in his side, a wound that his dragon self had barely noticed, but a wound his human self was concerned to see was deep and bleeding freely.

Cursing the worm who had inflicted it, Immolatus wondered what had become of her. He glanced around the wreckage, saw no sign of her. He listened, but heard no sound, no moaning, no cries for help, and he assumed that she must be lying under half the mountain by now.

Good riddance, he thought and, pressing his hand against his side, each breath coming in a pain-filled gasp, he entered the corridor, cursing his weak human flesh with every step.

* * * * *

Kitiara waited until she no longer heard his footfalls and then waited to the count of a hundred after that. Certain that he had gone far enough that he would not hear her, she crawled out from beneath the rubble that had saved her life, protected her from the dragon's huge body.

Bruised, bleeding from countless cuts, covered with rock dust, exhausted by her fear and her exertions, Kit was fed up with this job. Her ambition was at the ebb. She would have traded the generalship of the dragonarmies for a mug of dwarf spirits and a hot bath. She would have walked away from this wretched place here and now, leaving the dragon to do his damnedest, had there been anywhere to walk. Unfortunately, the only way out was the dragon's way out. The path he walked was the path she would have to walk. Unless she wanted to remain down here in the dark, trapped inside an unstable mountain, she would have to deal with him.

"Sir Nigel?" she risked calling.

There was no answer. No help from that quarter. She had seen him buried beneath the mountain of rock. But his vow was fulfilled. He'd found a way to protect the eggs. A pity he hadn't killed the dragon in the process. It was up to her now. She was on her own. As usual.

She found her sword, partially buried in rubble. And she still had her knife. Immolatus had his magic—powerful, deadly magic. He was in his vulnerable human form, the path he walked was dark, his back was to her. His real back this time, not an illusion.

Kitiara drew her knife from the top of her booth, rubbed the grit from her eyes, spit the dust from her mouth. Entering the corridor, she padded soft-footed after the dragon.

Breaking ranks, the soldiers surged through the open city gates, carrying the battering ram with them. Once inside, temporarily out of danger, they came to a halt, breathless and seething with anger as word spread like flaming dwarf spirits that men in the rear ranks had dropped down dead, with black-fletched arrows in their backs. Some in the forward companies actually turned around, headed out the gate, prepared to go back to the field and claim vengeance.

Officers shouted, bullied, and tried to restore order, as the citizens of Hope's End watched warily from the walls. They had been told these hardened mercenaries brought salvation, but the first sight of them—howling for blood—left the civilians pale and shaking. The lord mayor was put in mind of the old saying—better the kender in front of you than the kender with his hand in your back pocket. He was clearly regretting that he'd ever opened the gates to these cold-eyed professionals, swearing terrible oaths of death on those who had betrayed them.

"Shut those gates!" the baron shouted from the back of his war-horse. The horse plunged and danced with excitement, nostrils flared, ears laid back, nipping at anyone who came too close. "Haul those wagons back in place! Archers, to the wall!

"Those bastards!" he yelled to Commander Morgon, who—greatly daring—had caught hold of the horse's bridle. "Did you see what they did? Fired at us when our backs were turned! By heavens, I'll find that Commander Kholos and cut out his liver! I'll have *it* with potatoes and onions!"

"Yes, my lord. I saw, sir." Commander Morgon calmed the horse, calmed the master at the same time. "You were right, Baron! I was wrong. I admit it freely."

"And don't think I'm ever going to let you forget it! Ha, ha, ha!" The baron roared his manic laugh, which just about finished the terror-stricken citizens. "By Kiri-Jolith," he added, glowering around him at the stamping, sword-clashing, swearing soldiers of his command, "these fools have gone berserk! I'll have order restored, Commander Morgon! Now!"

C Company had been responsible for clearing the barricades from the gates. The battering ram, pounding once on the gate, had been the signal for C Company to swing the gates wide open. Their two bowmen provided covering fire for their comrades, before retreating back inside the city in good order. C Company stood ready, poised for action, keeping themselves free of the tumult.

"Shut the gates!" Master Senej commanded, hearing the baron's order. "Keep everyone inside the city walls!"

The men of C Company acted swiftly to obey. Some sprang to the gates. Others shoved or struck with the flat of their blades those soldiers who had lost all reason and were trying to leave the city in order to revenge their fallen comrades.

"Stand there, Majere!" Sergeant Nemiss ordered, posting Caramon in the very center of the road, as the men worked to push the heavy wooden gates shut behind him. "Don't let anyone past!"

"Yes, sir." Caramon took up his position, unmindful of enemy arrows, which were flying through the slowly closing gate. His massive legs spread to maintain his balance, his arm muscles flexed. Those who tried to get past him were either hurled backward, plucked off their feet, or—as a last extremity—given a gentle buffet on the head intended to restore them to their senses.

The gates slammed shut. The flights of arrows ceased as the enemy paused to consider the unlooked-for situation and regroup.

"What now, sir?" Commander Morgon asked. "Do we stay here under siege?"

"That depends entirely on Kholos," said the baron. "If you were him, what would you do, Morgon?"

"I'd pull back my troops, establish my supply lines, and wait until everyone in the city starved to death, my lord," Morgon replied.

"Very good, Commander Morgon," said the baron. "What do you think Kholos will do?"

"Well, my lord, I think he's going to be madder than a wet wyvern. My guess is that he will throw everything he's got at us, try to breach the gates and cut us down where we stand."

"My thoughts precisely. I'm going up on the wall to take a look. Have the officers arrange their companies into column, center company leading, line companies to follow. You've got ten minutes and no more!"

Commander Morgon ran off, shouting for his officers. He issued orders quickly. Soon the drums were beating, the trumpets braying. Sergeants yelled, kicked, and shoved the men into position. Reassured by the familiar sounds that promised discipline and order, the soldiers settled down and reformed into ranks with alacrity.

"Do we put the barricades back in place, sir?" Master Senej asked.

Commander Morgon glanced up at the wall where the baron stood in conference with the lord mayor and the city's officers. Morgon shook his head. "No, Senej. I think I know what the baron has planned. Keep them ready just in case, though."

During the height of the confusion, Raistlin searched for Horkin. At first Raistlin was unable to find the master in the midst of the tumult and he began to be worried, especially when he heard of the casualties. The gates were swinging shut and Raistlin had begun to think that "dear Luni" had abandoned her drinking buddy, when he saw

Horkin come lurching through the gate, lending an arm to a fellow soldier with an arrow shaft stuck clean through his leg. The man's pain must have been intense, he could not put his foot to the ground without gasping and shuddering.

"I'm glad to find you, sir!" Raistlin said earnestly. He had not known until that moment how much he valued the bluff and gruff Horkin.

Raistlin added his arm to help share the burden of the wounded man. Between the two of them, they carried him to a quiet place beneath the trees, where more wounded had congregated. "I feared you were among the fallen. What happened out there?"

"Treachery, Red," said Horkin with a dark glance back out the gate. "Treachery and murder. We've been betrayed, there's no doubt about it. As to the why and wherefore, I know nothing." He cast Raistlin a shrewd glance. "It seems you might know more than I do, Red. The baron told me that you accompanied him to the mayor's dwelling last night. He said you proved quite useful."

"I gave an old couple probably the best night's rest they've had in years," Raistlin returned dryly, "and that was the extent of my service. As to what the baron and the mayor discussed, I have no more knowledge than yourself. He sent me from the room."

"Don't take it to heart, Red. That's the baron all over. The fewer who know a secret, the more likely to keep a secret, that's his motto. One reason he's lived so long. And now"—Horkin looked about him—"what are we to do with the wounded?"

"I was about to tell you, sir. I believe that I have found a place to shelter the wounded. Did you know that there is an old temple to Paladine in the city, sir?"

"A temple to Paladine? Here?" Horkin rubbed his chin.

"Yes, sir. It's a safe distance from the fighting. If we could commandeer a wagon, we could transport the wounded in that."

"And why do you think this old temple would be a good place to house our wounded?" Horkin asked.

"I saw the temple last night, sir. It seems, well . . ." Raistlin hesitated. "It seems a blessed place, sir."

"It might have been blessed once, Red," said Horkin with a sigh. "But not anymore."

"Who can tell, sir?" Raistlin said in a low voice. "You and I both know that one goddess has not left Krynn."

Horkin considered. "You say it's a safe distance from the fighting?"

"As safe as anything can be, sir," Raistlin replied.

"It must be old. Is it in ruins?"

"It has certainly been neglected, sir. We would need to investigate further, of course, but the building seems to be in fairly good shape."

"I suppose it can't hurt to go look at it," said Horkin. "And who knows? Even if Paladine is long gone, perhaps there's some residual holiness still hanging about. I just hope the roof is sound," he added, glancing skyward. "There'll be rain before nightfall. If the roof leaks, we'll find someplace else, blessing or no blessing. Go check your temple out, Red. I'll round up a wagon. Tell Sergeant Nemiss to give you an escort."

"I really don't need anyone, sir," Raistlin said.

After spending the night dreaming of the temple bathed in silver moonlight, Raistlin was now more convinced than ever that Solinari had drawn the mage's attention to the temple for a reason. Raistlin had no idea what that reason might be. He wanted to enter the temple alone, wanted to open himself to the will of the god. To do that, he needed to be attuned to whatever voice might choose to speak to him. He did not want some loud-mouthed clod stomping about, making crude remarks and offending whatever spirits might linger in the holy place.

"You'll probably want to take your brother with you," said Horkin.

"No, sir," Raistlin returned emphatically, this being the clod he'd had in mind. The temple was his discovery, belonged to him. He conveniently forgot the fact that it was Caramon who had first seen the temple. "I really don't need anyone—"

"You'll need a good fighter, Red," Horkin said crisply. "Never know what you might find lurking about in an old temple. I'll speak to Sergeant Nemiss. Perhaps she'll even let you have Scrounger."

Raistlin gave an inward groan.

* * * * *

The gray and lowering clouds, which had blanketed the city almost since the day the army had arrived, were blown to rags by a strong chill wind coming down from out of the mountain. The air temperature dropped precipitously, changing from early summer to late fall in a breath. Rain might fall tonight, as Horkin anticipated, but for now bright sunshine—so bright that it seemed newly minted—and crisp, fresh air lifted the hearts of those in the besieged city, although that hope dimmed somewhat when they looked over the walls to see the immense army of Commander Kholos marching to attack.

The baron laid out his plan. It was met by dismay from the lord mayor and his officers at first, but they were soon persuaded that this was Hope's End's last hope. The baron left to put his plan into action, as the first black-fletched arrows launched over the walls.

The refreshing wind dried the sweat on Caramon's body, and he filled his lungs with it, expanding his muscular chest with each huge breath, much to the admiration of several housewives, who peeped at him from behind closed shutters. Caramon had at first been devastated at having to miss the fighting, but the thought of finding shelter for his wounded comrades somewhat mollified him.

Scrounger was pleased with the assignment, figuring he would have been of little use in the upcoming battle anyway. He looked forward to investigating the temple and regaled them with stories of lost and forgotten treasure well known to lie hidden in such places.

"You don't suppose that someone might have thought to look for treasure in the last three hundred years or so," Raistlin said sarcastically.

He was in a bad mood. Everything irritated him, from the change in the weather to the company he was forced to keep. The wind caught at his robes, blew them around his ankles, nearly tripping him. The breeze was chill, set him shivering, and something in the air took him by the throat, made him cough so hard he had to lean against a building until he regained his strength.

"If there's treasure, there's bound to be a guard on the treasure," Scrounger said in a thrilled whisper. "You know what inhabits old temples, don't you? The undead! Skeletal warriors. Ghouls. Maybe even a demon or two . . ."

Caramon was starting to look uneasy. "Raist, maybe this isn't such a—"

"I promise to deal with any ghouls we meet, Caramon," Raistlin said in a croaking voice.

Behind them, they could hear the trumpets and the drums and a great shout, given by the men of the baron's army.

"That's the signal to attack!" Caramon said, halting and looking back over his shoulder.

"Which means that there will be more wounded," said Raistlin, with a jab of conscience.

Recalling the gravity of their mission, the three increased their pace. There was no further talk of undead or of treasure.

Arriving back at the warehouse, they followed the street that led to the temple and easily found the building.

"Is that the right place?" Caramon said, his brow wrinkled.

"It has to be!" Raistlin began to cough.

Last night, surrounded by darkness, the temple had seemed a place of awe and mystery. Viewed in the bright light of day, the temple was a disappointment. The columns supporting the roof were cracked. The roof itself sagged. The walls were stained and discolored, the courtyard drowning in weeds.

Worn out and aching from his coughing fit, chilled to the bone, Raistlin was beginning to regret ever having seen the temple, much less suggesting it as a refuge for the wounded. The building was far more shabby and decrepit than he had imagined. Recalling Horkin's injunction about the leaky roof, Raistlin doubted if there was a roof to the place at all. He could imagine this raw wind blowing a gale through the drafty ruins.

"It was a mistake to come here," he said.

"No, it wasn't, Raist," Caramon said stoutly. "There's a good feeling about this place. I like it. We'll have to make sure it's safe first, secure the perimeter." He'd heard Sergeant Nemiss use that expression and had been waiting for an opportunity to use it himself. "Secure the perimeter," he repeated with a relish.

"What perimeter? There is no perimeter!" Raistlin returned crossly. "There is nothing but a dilapidated old building and a weed-covered courtyard."

He was extremely disappointed and he couldn't understand why. What had he expected to find here? The gods?

"The building looks to be sturdy enough. Solid architecture. I think it must have been built by dwarves," Caramon stated with all the authority of one who knows absolutely nothing about the matter.

"It must be solid, to stand all these centuries." Scrounger added the voice of practicality.

"We should at least go check it out," Caramon urged.

Raistlin hesitated. Last night, Solinari had seemed to point the way, had urged his disciple to come to this once-holy place. But that had been at night, in the moonlight, a time when the mind—so stolid and trustworthy during the daylight hours—gives way to its dream-side and twists the dark shadows into all varieties of fanciful, frightful forms. Last night, the building had seemed so beautiful, safe, blessed. Today, there was something sinister about it.

He felt very strongly that he should turn away, leave in haste, and never come back.

"You can stay here in the street where it's safe, Raist," Caramon said with well-meaning solicitude. "Scrounger and I'll go take a look."

Raistlin shot his brother a glance that might have been one of the black-fletched arrows.

"Did I say 'safe'?" Caramon went red in the face, as red as if the arrow had pierced his forehead and drawn blood. "I meant 'warm.' That's what I meant to say, Raist. I didn't mean—"

"Come along, the two of you," Raistlin snapped. "I will take the lead."

Caramon opened his mouth to suggest that this was a rash course of action, that he—as the stronger and larger and better armed—should take the lead. At the sight of his brother's tightly drawn lips and glittering eyes, Caramon thought better of the notion and fell meekly into step behind.

The courtyard provided no cover. They would be in sight and range of anyone hiding inside the temple. Raistlin was disturbed to see that some of the chickweed growing up through the flagstones was trampled and broken. Someone else had walked across this courtyard and recently at that. The broken stems were still green, the leaves only starting to wither.

Raistlin pointed silently to the evidence that they might not be alone. Caramon put his hand to the hilt of his sword. Scrounger drew his knife. The three proceeded across the courtyard, eyes searching, ears pricked to catch the least sound. They heard nothing but the wind sweeping dead leaves into corners, saw nothing but the shadows of high, white clouds scuttle across the cracked flagstone. Drawing near the golden doors, Raistlin began to relax. If others had been here, they were gone now. The temple was deserted, he was certain.

But on reaching the steps leading up to the temple, Raistlin noted that the golden doors, which he had thought were closed, actually stood slightly ajar, as if someone inside had opened the doors a crack to peep out at them.

Seeing this, Caramon boldly took the lead, placing his body in front of his brother's. "Let us look inside, Raist."

Drawing his sword, he ran up the stairs, flattened himself with his back against the wall near the door. Scrounger dashed after him, took his place on the opposite side of the door, his knife in his hand.

"I don't hear anything," he said in a whisper.

"I don't see anything," Caramon returned. "It's dark as the Abyss in there."

He reached out his hand to press on the door, let in more light. As he did, the sun lifted above the city walls, a beam of sunshine struck the doors at the same time as did Caramon's fingers, making it seem as if his touch was the sun's touch. He burnished the gold, set it shining.

In that instant Raistlin, saw the temple not as it was, but as it had been. He gazed in wonder, awed and captivated. The cracks in the marble vanished. The patina of grime and dirt burned away in the light. The temple walls gleamed white. The frieze on the portico, obliterated in anger, was restored. In that frieze was a message, an answer, a solution. Raistlin stared at it. He needed only a few seconds to puzzle it out and he would understand. . . .

The world turned on its axis, the sun's dazzling rays were blocked by a guard tower on the wall. The tower's shadow fell across the golden doors. The vision vanished, the temple was as it had been—shabby, neglected, forgotten. Raistlin stared hard at the broken frieze, trying to fill in the missing pieces with the remnants of the vision, but he found he could not remember it, like a dream one loses on waking.

"I'm going inside," Caramon said. He returned his sword to its sheath.

"Unarmed?" Scrounger asked, amazed.

"It's not proper, taking a weapon in there," Caramon replied, his voice deep and solemn. "It's not . . ." He fumbled for a word. "Respectful."

"But there's nobody left to respect!" Scrounger argued.

"Caramon is right," Raistlin said firmly, to his brother's great astonishment. "We don't need weapons here. Put your sword away."

" 'Crazy as a kender,' they say," Scrounger muttered to himself. "Hah! Kender have nothing on these two!"

Having no desire to argue with the mage, however, Scrounger slid his knife back into his belt (though he kept his hand on the hilt) and accompanied the brothers inside.

Contrasted with the brightness of the reflected sunlight beating on the gold, the interior of the temple was so dark that for a few moments they could see nothing at all. But as their eyes became accustomed to the change, the darkness receded. The temple's interior seemed brighter than the bright day outside.

Fear vanished. No harm could come to them in this place. Raistlin felt the tightness in his chest ease, he breathed more deeply, less painfully. Solinari's promise held true, and Raistlin was more than a little ashamed of having doubted. The wounded could be made quite comfortable here. There was a purity to the air, a softness to the light that had healing qualities, of that he was convinced. The blessings of the old gods still lingered here, if the gods themselves were gone.

"This was a really good idea of yours, Raist," said Caramon.

"Thank you, my brother," Raistlin returned and, after a pause, he added, "I am sorry I was angry with you back there. I know you didn't mean it."

Caramon regarded his twin with amazed, marveling awe. He could not recall ever having heard his brother apologize to anyone for anything. He was about to reply when Scrounger motioned him to be quiet.

Scrounger pointed to a door, a silver door. "I think I heard something!" he whispered. "Behind that door!"

"Mice," said Caramon and, putting his hand on the door, he gave it a shove.

The door swung open silently, smoothly.

Fear flowed from the opening, a black, foul river of dread so strong, so palpable that Caramon felt it wash over him, try to drown him. He staggered backward, raising his hands as if he were sinking beneath turgid waves.

Raistlin tried to call out, tried to warn his brother to shut the door, but fear seized him by the throat and squeezed off his voice.

The dread rushed into the temple in a dark, crashing wave, submerging the kender part of Scrounger, leaving him a prey to human terror. "I . . . I never felt like this!" He whimpered, crouching back against the wall. "What's happening? I don't understand!"

Raistlin did not understand either. He had known fear. Any who take the deadly Test in the Tower of High Sorcery know fear. He had known the fear of pain, the fear of death, the fear of failure. He had never felt fear like this.

This was a fear that came from far away, a fear borne in the distant past, a fear felt by those very first people to walk upon this world. A primeval fear that looked up into the heavens and saw the fiery stars wheeling overhead, saw the sun, a bright and terrible orb of flame, hurtling down upon them. It was the fear of the noisome darkness, when neither stars nor moons were visible and the wood was wet and would not light and growls and snarls of unsatiated hunger came from the wilderness.

Raistlin wanted to flee, but the fear sucked the strength from his bones, left them soft and pliable as the bones of a newborn child. His brain shot jolts of fire to his muscles. His limbs trembled and jerked in panicked response. He clutched at his staff, and was astonished to see the crystal atop the staff—the crystal held by the dragon's claw—glowing with a strange light.

Raistlin had seen the staff glow before. He had only to say, "*Shirak*," and the crystal would light the darkness. But he had never seen it glow like this; a light that flared in anger, red around the edges, white at its heart, like the flame of the forge fire.

A Knight, clad in silver armor of ornate design appeared in the doorway. The Knight wore the symbol of a rose upon his tabard. He held his sword in his gloved hand. He removed the helm he wore and his eyes looked straight into Raistlin's heart and beyond that, into his soul.

"Magius," the Knight said, "I require your help to save that which must not perish from the world."

"I am not Magius," Raistlin answered, constrained by the Knight's noble aspect and mien to tell the truth.

"You bear his staff," said the Knight. "The fabled Staff of Magius."

"A gift," Raistlin said, lowering his head. Yet he could still feel the eyes of the Knight delving the depths of his being.

"Truly a valuable gift," said the Knight. "Are you worthy of it?"

"I . . . don't know," Raistlin replied in confusion.

"An honest answer," said the Knight, and he smiled. "Find out. Aid me in my cause."

"I am afraid!" Raistlin gasped, holding up his hand to ward off the terror. "I cannot do anything to help you or anyone!"

"Overcome your fear," said the Knight. "If you do not, you will walk in fear the rest of your life."

The light from the crystal blazed brilliant as a lightning bolt. Raistlin was forced to shut his eyes against the painful glare, lest it blind him. When he opened his eyes, the Knight was gone, as if he had never been.

The silver doors stood open and death lay beyond.

You had courage enough to pass the Test, said an inner voice.

"Courage enough to kill my own brother!" Raistlin answered.

Par-Salian and Antimodes and all the rest might view Raistlin with contempt, but they could never match the contempt with which he viewed himself. Bitter self-recrimination tagged always at his heels. Self-loathing was his constant shadow.

"Courage enough to kill Caramon when he came to rescue me, kill him as he stood before me, helpless, un-armed, disarmed by his love for me. That is my sort of courage," Raistlin said.

You will walk in fear the rest of your life.

"No," said Raistlin. "I won't."

Refusing to allow himself to think what he was doing, he lifted the Staff of Magius and, holding its shining light above him, he walked through the silver doors into darkness.

aramon had never experienced such fear. Not during that terrible and hopeless attack on the city, not when the arrows thudded into his shield, not when the boulders smashed into his comrades, changing them from living men into bloody pulp and bone slivers. His fear then had been gut-wrenching, but not debilitating. His training and his discipline had carried him through.

This fear was different. It didn't wrench the gut, it reduced the gut to water. It didn't galvanize the body to action, it wrung the body, left it limp as a bar rag. Caramon had one thought in his mind and that was to run as fast as he could away from this place, away from the unknown evil that flowed out of the silver door in a chill and sickening wave. He didn't know what was down there, he didn't want to know what was down there. Whatever it was, it was not meant for mortals to encounter.

Caramon watched with a horror that left him breathless and gasping, watched his brother cross that awful threshold.

"Raist, don't!" Caramon cried, but the cry came out a pitiful wail, like that of a frightened child.

If Raistlin heard him, he did not turn back.

Caramon wondered what dark force had seized hold of his brother, caused him to enter that place of certain death. In answer Caramon heard a voice, faint and distant, calling for aid. An armored Knight stood in the doorway. Reminded fondly of Sturm, Caramon would have been glad to go with the Knight but for this strange and horrible fear that had him groveling on the floor of the temple in a panic.

But that changed when Raistlin entered the darkness. Caramon had no choice but to go after him. Fear for his brother's life was like a fire in his brain and blood, burned away the sickening, unnameable fear. Sword drawn, he ran through the silver door into the corridor after his brother.

Left behind, Scrounger stared, disbelieving. His friend, his best friend, and his friend's twin, had just walked into death.

"Fools!" Scrounger pronounced them. "You're both crazy!"

His teeth chattered, he could barely speak. Pressed flat against the wall by his own terror, he tried to take a step toward that dark entrance, but his feet wouldn't obey what was admittedly a feeble command.

Where, oh, where was the kender side of him now that he needed it! All his life he had fought against that part of himself—slapped back the fingers that itched to touch, to handle, to take; fought against the wanderlust that tempted him to leave his honest work and go skipping down an untraveled road. Now, when his mother's kender fearlessness—a fearlessness that had nothing to do with courage and everything to do with curiosity— might have stood him in good stead, he searched for it and found it wanting.

His mother would have said it served him right.

Scrounger wasn't in the temple any longer. He was a little child standing with his mother outside a cave they'd stumbled across during one of their many rambles.

"Aren't you curious to know what's in there?" she asked him. "Don't you wonder what's inside? Maybe a dragon's treasure hoard. Maybe a sorcerer's workshop. Maybe a princess who needs rescuing. Don't you want to find out?"

"No," Scrounger wailed. "I don't want to go in! It's dark and horrible and it smells bad!"

"You're no child of mine," his mother said, not angrily, but fondly. She patted his head. She went into the cave, came dashing out about three minutes later with a giant bugbear in hot pursuit.

Scrounger remembered that moment, remembered the bugbear—the first one he'd ever seen and the last he ever wanted to see—remembered his mother haring out of that cave, her clothes in wild disorder, her pouches flapping open, spilling their contents, her face red with exertion, her grin wide. She caught Scrounger by the hand. They ran for their lives.

Fortunately the bugbear didn't have any staying power. It soon given up the chase. But Scrounger had determined in that moment that his mother was right. He was no child of hers and he didn't want to be.

"I know what I'll do," said Scrounger to himself, "I'll go back to the army. I'll get reinforcements!"

At that moment, a large hand reached out from the silver door, grabbed hold of Scrounger's shoulder, yanked him off his feet, and pulled him inside.

"Cripes, Caramon, you scared m-me half to death! What did you do that for?" Scrounger demanded when he could feel his heart start to beat again.

"Because I need your help to find Raist," Caramon said grimly. "You were running away!"

"I was g-going to g-get help," Scrounger said through the chattering of his teeth.

"You're not supposed to be scared." Caramon glared at the trembling Scrounger. "What kind of kender are you?"

"Half-kender," Scrounger retorted. "The smart half."

Now that he was here, he supposed he had to make the best of it. Anyway, he was too scared to go back alone.

"Is it all right with you if I draw my sword now? Or would that be disrespectful to whatever's down here that's going to murder us and chop up our bodies into little pieces and suck out our souls."

"I think drawing your sword would be a wise move," Caramon replied gravely.

They stood inside a tunnel that had been carved through the rock. The tunnel walls were smooth and formed an arch above them, the floor sloped slightly downward. The tunnel did not appear as dark once they'd entered it as it had seemed from outside. Sunlight reflecting off the silver door lit their way for a considerable distance, far longer than either would have imagined was possible. But there was no sign of Raistlin.

They kept going. The tunnel made a sharp curve. Coming around the corner, they saw, ahead of them, a shining light, brilliant as a star.

"Raist!" Caramon called softly.

The light wavered, halted. Raistlin turned and they could see his face, the skin glistening faintly gold in the light cast by the Staff of Magius. He beckoned. Caramon hurried ahead, Scrounger at his heels—close at his heels.

Raistlin's hand closed over his brother's arm, clasped Caramon warmly. "I'm glad you are here, my brother," he said earnestly.

"Well, I'm not glad to be here!" Caramon said in a low voice. He looked nervously to the left, to the right, ahead and behind. "I don't like this place and I think we should leave. Something down here doesn't want us down here. Remember what Scrounger said about ghouls? I tell you, Raist, I've never been so scared in my life. I only came to find you and the Knight."

"What Knight?" Scrounger demanded.

"So you saw him, too," Raistlin murmured.

"What Knight?" Scrounger persisted.

Raistlin did not answer immediately. When he did reply, he said only, "Come with me, both of you. There's something I want to show you."

"Raist, I don't think—" Caramon began.

The mountain shook. The tunnel shuddered, the floor trembled.

The three fell back against the tunnel walls, almost too

startled to be frightened. Rock dust sifted down on their heads, but before the realization came to them that they were in danger of being buried beneath the mountain, the shaking ceased.

"That does it," Caramon said. "We're getting out of here."

"A minor tremor. These mountains are subject to them, I believe. Did the Knight say anything to you?"

"He said he needed help. Look, Raist, I—" Caramon paused, regarded his brother anxiously. "Are you all right?"

Raistlin was choking on the rock dust, which had flown down his throat. He shook his head at the inanity of the question. "No, I'm not all right," he gasped when he could speak. "But I will be better in a moment."

"Let's leave," Caramon said. "You shouldn't be down here. The dust is bad for you."

"It's bad for me, too," said Scrounger.

They both stood there, waiting for Raistlin. When he could breathe, he looked back toward the silver door, then ahead. "Do what you want. But I am going to go on. We could not bring wounded into the temple without knowing that it is completely safe. Besides, I'm curious to know what lies ahead."

"Probably my poor mother's last words," Scrounger said gloomily.

Caramon shook his head, but he followed after his twin. Scrounger waited, still thinking he would take the mage up on his offer and run away. He waited until the comforting light of the mage's staff had almost vanished. Only when the darkness started to close over him did he race to catch up with the light.

The smooth tunnel walls gave way to natural rock. The path was uneven, more difficult to follow. It wound about among the stalagmites, led them from one cavern room into another and always down, down deep into the mountain. And then it ended, abruptly, in a cul-de-sac.

A wall of rock blocked their way.

"All this for nothing," said Caramon. "Well, at least we know it's safe. Let's go back."

Raistlin shone the light on the wall, soon discovered the alcove with the gate made of silver and gold. He looked through the gate into a small round chamber. Caramon peered over his shoulder. The chamber was empty except for a sarcophagus located in the very center of the oval room.

"Raist, this is a tomb," Caramon said uneasily.

"How very observant of you, Caramon," Raistlin returned.

Ignoring his brother's pleas, he pushed open the gate.

The light of the Staff of Magius shone with a bright silver radiance as he entered the chamber. He raised the staff so that the light fell on the sarcophagus, illuminated the stone figure carved on the top. Raistlin stood staring in silence.

"Look at this, my brother," he said at last, his voice soft, awed. "What do you see?"

"A tomb," said Caramon nervously.

He came to a standstill under the arch, his big body blocking the way. Behind him, Scrounger had no intention of being left alone in the tunnel. He shoved his way past the big man, wormed his way inside.

"Look at the tomb, Caramon," Raistlin persisted. "What do you see?"

"A Knight, I guess. It's hard to tell. There's so much dust." Caramon averted his eyes. He had just noticed that the lid of the sarcophagus was open. "Raist, we shouldn't be here! It's not right!"

Raistlin paid no heed to his brother. Approaching the sarcophagus, he peered inside the open lid. He stopped, stared, drew back slightly.

"I knew it!" Caramon gripped his sword so hard his hand ached.

Raistlin beckoned. "Come here, my brother. You should see this."

"No, I shouldn't," Caramon said firmly, shaking his head.

"I said come look at this, Caramon!" Raistlin's voice rasped.

Shambling, reluctant, Caramon edged his way forward. Scrounger came with him, holding on to his sword with one hand and Caramon's belt loop with the other.

Caramon sneaked a quick look inside the tomb, looked quickly away before he had a chance to see anything horrible, like a moldy skeleton with bits of flesh hanging off the bones. Startled by what he saw, he looked back.

"The Knight!" Caramon breathed. "The Knight who called to me!"

A body lay in the tomb, a body clad in ancient armor that gleamed in the light of the Staff of Magius, a soft light shed down upon the Knight with loving grace. The Knight wore a helm made in a style that had been popular before the Cataclysm. He wore a tabard over his armor. The tabard's fabric was old, yellowed; the embroidered satin rose that adorned it was worn and faded. The Knight clasped the hilt of a sword in his hands. Dried rose petals surrounded the Knight's body, lay scattered over the tabard and the shining sword. A sweet fragrance of roses lingered in the air.

"I thought I recognized the carven figure on the tomb," Raistlin said thoughtfully. "The armor, the tabard, the helm—all exactly like those worn by the Knight who came to ask us to aid him. A Knight who has been dead perhaps hundreds of years!"

"Don't say things like that," Scrounger pleaded, his voice a squeak. "This place is spooky enough as it is! Wouldn't this be a good time to go?"

Looking at the Knight lying in his tomb, Caramon was again reminded of his friend Sturm. The reminder was not a happy one. Caramon hoped it wasn't an omen.

He began to brush away some of the dust from the still, stone figure carved upon the lid.

Raistlin stood gazing upon the Knight, resting in a peace and tranquillity that the young mage, who suffered the constant burning in his lungs and the more painful burning of his own ambitions, momentarily envied.

"Look at this, Raist!" Caramon marveled. "There's an inscription."

Brushing aside the dust, he uncovered a small plaque made of bronze that had been set into the stone above the knight's heart.

"I can't read it," Caramon said, twisting his head at an odd angle to see.

"It's in Solamnic," Raistlin said, recognizing immediately the language he'd been wrestling for months, ever since receiving the book describing the Staff of Magius. "It says—" He brushed aside more dust and read aloud.

" 'Here lies one who died defending the Temple of Paladine and its servants from the faithless and the forlorn. By the Knight's last request, made with his dying breath, we bury him in this chamber so that he may continue to stand watch over the precious treasure, which it is our duty and our privilege to guard. Paladine grant him rest when his duty is fulfilled.' "

All three looked at one another. All three repeated the same word at the same time.

"Treasure!"

Caramon looked about the chamber as if he expected to see chests spilling out coins and jewels. "Scrounger was right! Does it say where the treasure is, Raist?"

Raistlin continued to brush away dust, but there was nothing more to be read.

"It's funny, but I'm not the least bit scared anymore," Scrounger announced. "I wouldn't mind exploring."

"It wouldn't hurt to look around," said Caramon, bending down to try to peer underneath the tomb. He was disappointed to find it set solidly into the cavern floor. "What do you say, Raist?"

Raistlin was sorely tempted. The strange and unreasoning fear he'd experienced was gone. He had a responsibility to the wounded, but as he had said before, he had a responsibility to make certain that the temple was safe. If he happened to come across a treasure chest while doing so, no one could fault him.

"What would you do if you found a treasure, Caramon?" Scrounger asked.

"I'd buy an inn," Caramon said.

"You'd be your own best customer." Scrounger laughed.

I would do only good, if a treasure came into my possession, Raistlin thought. I would move to Palanthas and purchase the largest house in the city. I would have servants to wait on me and to work in my laboratory, which would be the largest and finest money could buy. I would purchase every spellbook in every mageware shop from here to Northern Ergoth. I would start a library that would rival the library in the Tower of High Sorcery. I would buy magical artifacts and magical gems and wands and potions and scrolls.

He saw himself rich, powerful, beloved, feared. Saw himself quite clearly. He stood in a tower, dark, foreboding, surrounded by death. He wore black robes, around his neck, a pendant of green stone streaked with blood. . . .

"Look what I found!" Scrounger called out excitedly, pointing. "Another gate!"

Raistlin only half-heard him. The image of himself was slow to dissolve. When it finally faded away, it left a disquieting feeling behind.

Scrounger stood beside a wrought iron gate, his face pressed against the bars, staring into the darkness beyond.

"It leads into another tunnel," he reported. "Maybe it's the tunnel where the treasure is!"

"We've found it, Raist!" Caramon said exultantly, crowding behind Scrounger, looking out over his head. "I know we've found it! Bring your light over here!"

"I don't suppose it would hurt to take a look," Raistlin said. "Move away from there. Give me room to see what I'm doing. Don't touch the gate, Caramon! It might be magically trapped. Let me look at it."

Caramon and Scrounger dutifully stepped back.

Raistlin approached the gate. He could sense magical power, immense magical power. But not from the gate.

The power lay beyond. Magical artifacts, perhaps. Artifacts from hundreds of years ago, before the Cataclysm. Lying undisturbed all this time, waiting . . . waiting . . .

He turned the handle. The iron gate creaked open. Raistlin took one step into the darkness beyond only to find a shadowy form blocking his way.

"*Shirak.*" He lifted the staff to see what it was.

The staff's white light gleamed red in the burning eyes of Immolatus.

19

The wizard's eyes burned red, fed from the fire of hatred and frustration that still roared in his belly and that could find no outlet in this accursed body. The heat of the flames radiated from his flesh. He had lost considerable blood from the wound in his side. Each breath he drew was agony. His head ached and throbbed. These weaknesses, a plague to his weak human form, would disappear once he regained his splendid, strong, and powerful dragon form. Once he was out of this accursed building. He would make them pay, make them all pay. . . .

Finding his way blocked, Immolatus lifted his gaze and focused on a bright light, which pierced his aching eyes like a steel lance. He glared at the light, furious, and then he saw its source.

"The Staff of Magius!" Immolatus cried with a grinding glee. "I'll have something from this misadventure, after all."

Reaching out his hand, the dragon plucked the staff from Raistlin's grasp, and with the other hand, he struck the young man a blow that sent him sprawling to the stone floor.

* * * * *

Kitiara had trailed Immolatus through the cavern's corridors. When he stopped at the entrance to the burial chamber, Kitiara crept forward, sword drawn, planning to attack the wizard in the burial chamber, where she had room to swing her sword.

Unexpectedly, Immolatus stopped before entering the gate, shouting something about a staff. He sounded pleased, exultant, as if he'd just stumbled across a long-lost companion. Fearful that the dragon had found a friend and that he might yet escape her, Kitiara looked past Immolatus's shoulder to see what new foe she might face.

Caramon!

Paralyzed with amazement, Kitiara at first doubted her senses. Caramon was safely back in Solace, not wandering about caverns in Hope's End. But there was no mistaking those massive shoulders, the ham-fisted hands, the curly hair, and that gaping expression of dumbfounded astonishment.

Caramon! Here! She was so lost in startlement that she barely paid attention to his companions—a red-robed wizard and a kenderish-looking fellow. Kit paid little attention to them. The sight of her brother, wearing the armor of the baron—the enemy no less—brought such confused thoughts to her that she lowered her sword and retreated a safe distance back down the corridor to consider how to deal with this bizarre situation.

One thought was uppermost in her mind: now was *not* the time for a family reunion.

* * * * *

The blow of the wizard's hand struck Raistlin squarely on the breastbone. Stunned at the sight of Immolatus springing up out of the darkness, Raistlin could not react fast enough to save himself. He went down as if felled by a thunderbolt, struck his head when he landed—sprawled and gasping for breath—on the cavern floor. Pain lanced through his skull. He came near to blacking out.

Looking up blearily from the floor, Raistlin saw Immolatus holding the Staff of Magius, gloating over his prize.

Raistlin's most precious possession, his most valued treasure, the symbol of his achievement, his triumph over sickness and suffering, his reward for long and torturous hours of study, his victory over himself—this was the prize Immolatus had taken from him.

The loss of the staff banished pain, banished amazement, banished any fear he held for his life, any value placed on that life.

With a snarl of fury, Raistlin leapt to his feet, heedless of the pain and the blue and yellow stars that shot through his vision, half-blinding him. He attacked Immolatus with a courage and strength and ferocity that astounded his brother, already astounded by the sight of the strange Red Robe who had burst upon them so suddenly.

Raistlin did not fight his desperate battle alone. The Staff of Magius aided him. Created by an archmage of immense power, brought into being with one intent—to aid in the fight against Queen Takhisis—the staff and its master had fought her evil wyrms during the last Dragon War.

The staff had never known its master's fate. The staff knew that Magius was dead only when they came to bring the staff to be laid to rest on his funeral pyre. History never recorded the name of the White Robe who saved the staff. Some say that it was Solinari himself, come down from the heavens, who plucked the staff from the flames. Certainly it was someone who had the foresight and the wisdom to know that although the Queen might be defeated now, dark wings would once again blot out Krynn's sun.

The Staff of Magius penetrated Immolatus's disguise. The staff knew that a dragon, a red dragon, a minion of Queen Takhisis, had laid covetous hands upon it. The staff unleashed its anger, an anger pent up for hundreds of years. The staff waited until Immolatus had a good, solid grip on it, then let loose its magic.

An explosion of white light erupted from the staff. A blast rocked the burial chamber. Caramon was staring directly at the staff when its anger flared. The light seared his eyes. He fell back in agony, clapping his hands over his face. A black hole ringed round with purple fire obscured his vision, left him blind as a child in the womb. Warm blood splattered his face and hands. He heard a horrible, rising scream.

"Raist!" he cried, ragged and fearful, trying desperately to see. "Raist!"

The blast knocked Scrounger to the cavern floor, rattled his wits in his head. He lay staring up dazedly at the ceiling, wondering how a lightning bolt had managed to strike this far underground.

Raistlin had sensed the staff's fury, realized it was about to unleash its magical rage. Averting his eyes, he flung up his arm to protect his face. The force of the explosion sent him staggering back against the tomb, where, it seemed, he felt a firm hand support and steady him, keep him from falling. Raistlin thought the comforting touch belonged to his twin. Raistlin would later come to realize that Caramon, blind and helpless, was halfway across the burial chamber at the time.

Immolatus screamed. Pain such as he had known only once before—pain inflicted by the magical dragonlance—flared up his arm, spread like searing flame throughout his body. The dragon let go of the staff. He had no choice. He no longer had a hand.

Drenched with his own blood, cut by the shards of his own broken bones, Immolatus had never been so furious in his life. Though grievous, the dragon's wounds were not mortal. He had one desire and that was to kill these wretched beings who had inflicted such horrible damage on him. He released himself from the spell that bound him to human form. When he had regained his own body, he would incinerate these gnats, these worms with their infernal stinging bite.

Raistlin's enchanted gaze saw the dragon in midtransformation, he saw the wizard's human body shriveling, saw something red, glittering, monstrously evil rising from it. What that being was, he had no idea. Raistlin had one thought now and that was to retrieve his staff, which lay on the floor, its crystal blazing fiercely. He knelt, seized the staff. Using all his strength, strength he did not know he possessed, drawing on his fear and his terror and his pain, he swung the staff at Immolatus, smote him on the chest.

The staff's own magical fury added impetus to Raistlin's strike. Their combined force was like a lightning strike.

The blow lifted Immolatus, propelled him backward through the iron gate, flung him, half in and half out of his dragon form, clear of the burial chamber into the narrow tunnel. Immolatus smashed up against the rock wall of the corridor. Bones cracked and snapped, but they were the bones of his feeble human form and he could knit them back together with a single word of magic.

Immolatus lay a moment in the tunnel, in the darkness, reveling in the sensation of his strength, his power, his immenseness returning. His jaws grew and elongated, his teeth snapped with anticipation of crunching human bone, the muscles of his body rippled pleasantly beneath the newly forming scales that were soft now but would soon be hard as diamond. The fire burned in his belly, gurgled in his throat. He was growing too big for the corridor, but that didn't matter. He would rise up, cleave through the rock, raise the mountain, and drop it on the bodies of those who had dared insult him. He needed only a few more moments. . . .

A voice, a woman's voice, cold and biting as steel, pierced his head. "You have disobeyed me for the last time."

Kitiara's sword caught the light of the Staff of Magius and shone silver in that light.

Wounded, weakened by loss of blood and his spellcasting, dazzled by the flaring light, Immolatus looked into that light and thought he saw his Queen.

Furious, vengeful, implacable. She stood over him and pronounced his doom.

The sword drove into his back, severed his spine.

Immolatus gave a horrific cry of anger and malice, he jerked and twitched spasmodically, no longer in control of his own body. He glared at his destroyer and though he saw her through a blood-dimmed mist, he recognized Kitiara.

"I will not die . . . a human!" Immolatus hissed. "This will be my tomb. But I will see to it that it is yours, as well, worm!"

Kitiara wrenched her sword free of the body, stumbled backward. In his death throes, the dying dragon was continuing to revert to his original form. The transformation was almost complete, his body—a body far too big for the narrow cavern corridor in which she stood—continued to expand.

Immolatus twisted and writhed, his massive tail thrashed about, struck the rock wall, time and again. Wings flapped wildly, his clawed feet scrabbled and scraped against the tunnel walls. The ceiling cracked, supporting timbers creaked and sagged. The mountain shuddered, the floor shook.

"Raist!" Caramon's frantic voice. "Where are you? I . . . I can't see! What's happening?"

"I am here, my brother. Here. I have hold of you! Stop flailing about! Take my hand! Scrounger, help me with him! Back out the way we came! Quickly!"

Kitiara made a convulsive leap for the wrought iron gate. She stumbled into the burial chamber in time to see a flutter of red robe, a flickering light that came from a crystal atop a staff. The iron gate swung shut. The tunnel behind her gave way with a crash. Kitiara staggered toward the tomb of the Knight, hoping against hope that the burial chamber was strong enough to withstand the fury of a vindictive goddess.

Rocks fell down around her. She grabbed hold of the tomb, clung to it as the floor shook.

"I helped you, Sir Phantom!" she cried. "Now it's your turn!"

She crouched by the tomb, keeping her hand on the marble. Rocks fell, but not near her. They fell on the place where she'd seen the body, the body of herself. Nothing there now but crumbled stone. Kitiara shut her eyes against the grit and the dust and pressed herself close against the tomb with more fondness than she had ever pressed against the body of any lover.

Eventually the rumbling ceased, the dust settled.

Kitiara stirred, opened her eyes, blinked away the grime, and dared to draw a breath. Dust flew into her mouth, she began to cough. The darkness was absolute. She could see nothing, not even her hand in front of her face. Hands outstretched, she grabbed hold of the top of the tomb, felt the marble, smooth and cold. She pulled herself to her feet and stood leaning against the sarcophagus for support.

A faint light, softly gleaming, began to shine. Kit looked for the source, saw that the light came from the tomb. The sarcophogus was no longer empty, as it had been when she'd first seen it. It held a corpse. Kitiara looked on face of the corpse, a face at peace, a face victorious.

"Thanks, Sir Nigel," said Kit. "I guess we're even."

She looked around, took stock of her situation. The cavern was filled with fallen rock, but she could see no cracks in the ceiling or the floor, no holes in the walls. She looked back at the iron gate that led to the tunnel into the mountains. Beyond the iron gate was a wall of rock. The dragon's body lay buried beneath a cairn, flung down on him by his Queen. That way was blocked. But the way in, through the other silver and gold gate, was open and relatively clear of debris.

"Be seeing you," she said to the Knight and started to leave.

A force held her, a force not of this world.

Kitiara's hand, her sword hand, froze to the marble as if she had placed wet fingers on a block of ice. Fear twisted her stomach. She might wrench her hand free, but she would leave her flesh and her blood behind. For one horrible moment she thought that was to be the price she would have to pay, and then she realized, suddenly, that she might escape with a lesser cost.

She reached for her belt with her other hand, fumbled with numb fingers until she located the book containing the map that led to the egg chamber. She shook so she could barely hold the small volume. Wanting only to be rid of it, she flung the book into the open tomb.

"There!" she said bitterly. "Satisfied?"

The force released her. She snatched her hand from the tomb, rubbed her chill fingers, massaged life into them.

The burial chamber might be a safe haven, but Kitiara had seen all of it she wanted. She left by the silver and gold gate, taking the same route her brothers had taken, and kept walking until she had left the burial chamber and Sir Nigel far behind.

The sound of voices brought her to a halt. Up ahead, she could hear her brothers' voices and their footfalls echoing along the corridor. She could have caught up with them, but Kit decided she didn't want to see them. She didn't want to have to answer their questions, didn't want to have to make up a story to explain why she was here and what she was doing. Above all, she didn't want to join them in reminiscences about the days gone by, past times, old friends—especially old friends. She would wait here in the corridor until she was certain they were long gone, then she would sneak out.

Kitiara leaned back against the rocks, made herself as comfortable as she could. She wasn't bothered by the darkness. She found it soothing after that eerie and un-natural light in the Knight's tomb. Resting, she considered her future. She would return to Lord Ariakas. True, she had failed in her mission to steal the dragon eggs, but she could lay the fault for that failure squarely on the dragon. Since sending the dragon to find the eggs had been Lord Ariakas's idea, he had no one but himself to blame. She would be the one who had salvaged this mission, had seen to it that the dragon paid for his crime of disobedience, had taken care that the body of the slain beast was buried where no one would ever be the wiser.

"I'll have my promotion," Kitiara reflected, stretching out her legs. "And this will be just the beginning. I'll make myself indispensable to Ariakas, in more ways than one." She smiled to herself in the darkness. "The two of us will have the power to rule Krynn. In Her Majesty's name, of course," Kit added with an apprehensive glance into the darkness around her. She had witnessed the Queen's wrath, had come to respect it.

She had witnessed another power that day, the power of love, of self-sacrifice, of honor and resolve. She made nothing of that, however. Any feeling of respect she might have held for the Knight had vanished in resentment that he had bested her at the tomb. Her hand still hurt.

Exhausted by her efforts, Kitiara rested, half-dozed. She could no longer hear her brothers' voices. They had probably reached the entrance by now. She'd give them time enough to completely vacate the premises, then she would follow and leave this ill-fated temple.

She found herself thinking of her brothers. She had been disturbed at seeing them, at first. The twins brought back memories of a life and time she'd outgrown, memories of people she didn't want to remember. But now that they were gone and she was not ever likely to see them again, Kit was glad she'd had this opportunity to see how they had turned out.

Caramon was a warrior now, it seemed, and though he had not accorded himself with any particular distinction in this magical fight, Kitiara could well believe that in ordinary battles, he would prove himself a good and effective soldier. As for Raistlin, she didn't know what to make of him. She would never have recognized him had it not been for his voice, and even that had grown weaker than she remembered. But he was a wizard now, apparently, and he had fought Immolatus with a ferocity and courage she found extremely gratifying.

"Just as I planned," she said to herself. "They've both turned out just as I hoped."

Kitiara felt an almost maternal pride in her boys as she sat in the darkness, cleaning the dragon's blood from her sword, waiting for an opportunity to escape this accursed temple, leave the unlucky city of Hope's End.

* * * * *

"Raist! There's light ahead, isn't there?" Caramon said hoarsely, his voice raw with fear. "I think I can see it, though it's awfully dim."

"Yes, Caramon, there is light," Raistlin replied. "We are back in the temple. The light you see is sunlight." He did not add that it was bright sunlight.

"I'll be able to see again, won't I, Raist?" Caramon asked anxiously. "You'll be able to heal me, won't you?"

Raistlin didn't answer immediately and Caramon turned his sightless eyes in the direction of his brother. Scrounger, staggering beneath Caramon's weight, looked hopefully at Raistlin, as well.

"He *will* be all right, won't he?" the half-kender asked in trepidation.

"Certainly," Raistlin said. "The condition is only a temporary one."

He hoped to heaven that his diagnosis was true. If the damage was permanent, it was beyond his ability to heal, beyond anyone's ability to heal in this day and age when no clerics walked the land.

Raistlin recalled one of Weird Meggin's patients, a man who had stared too long into the sun during a solar eclipse. She had tried treating him with poultices and salves to no avail. His sight had been irrevocably lost. Raistlin did not mention this to Caramon, however.

"Raist," Caramon persisted anxiously. "*When* do you think this will go away. When do you think I'll be able to see—"

"Raistlin," Scrounger said at the same time. "Who was that ugly old wizard? It seemed like he knew you."

Raistlin did not want to tell Caramon the truth, did not want to say the words, "Maybe never." Raistlin feared that even the blind Caramon must eventually see through a comforting lie. Raistlin was thankful to Scrounger for changing the subject and answered the half-kender with a cordiality that both astonished and pleased him.

"His name was Immolatus. I met him in the enemy's camp," Raistlin replied. "Master Horkin sent me there to trade magical goods, but the wizard wanted none of what we had to offer. He wanted only thing—my staff."

He paused a moment, thinking how to phrase the next question, wondering even if he should ask it. His need to know was strong, overcame his natural reticence.

"Scrounger, Caramon, I want to ask you both something." He hesitated another moment, then said, "What did you see when you looked at the wizard?"

"A wizard?" said Caramon cautiously, afraid that this might be a trick question.

"I saw a wizard," said Scrounger. "A wizard in red robes like yours, only they were more of a fiery red now that I think about it."

"Why, Raist?" Caramon asked with disquieting astuteness. "What did *you* see when you looked at him?"

Raistlin thought back to the red-scaled monstrosity that for an instant had shimmered in his cursed vision. He tried to put shape and form to it, but nothing emerged. The Staff of Magius had struck at that moment, cast the wizard into darkness, a darkness that had come crashing down on top of him.

"I saw a wizard, Caramon," he said. His voice hardened. "A wizard who wanted to steal my staff from me."

"Then why did you ask the question?" Scrounger started to ask, but was silenced by a baleful glance.

"That magic spell you cast was really something, Raist," Caramon said, after a moment. "How did you do it?"

"You would not understand if I told you, Caramon," Raisltin said irritably. "Now, no more talking. It's bad for you."

Scrounger demanded to know how talking could be bad for Caramon's eyesight, but Raistlin didn't hear him or, if he did, he pretended that he didn't. He was thinking about the magic.

Ever since he had been given the Staff of Magius, Raistlin had been acutely aware of the life within the staff, magical sentience given to it by its creator. He had experienced a vague feeling of inadequacy, as if the staff were comparing him to its creator and finding him lacking. He remembered the terrible fear when Immolatus took the staff from him, the fear that the staff had left Raistlin of its own accord, leapt gladly into the hand of a wizard of more skill and power.

Raistlin had been overjoyed and relieved when the staff joined him in the battle. After the initial shock of the explosion, which he had sensed coming, but which he had not commanded, he and the staff had acted as a team. He had the feeling that the staff was pleased with itself and that it was also pleased with him. Odd to think, but he felt that he had earned the staff's respect.

His hand tightened lovingly on the staff as he emerged from the silver doors into the welcome light of the sun streaming in through the windows of the abandoned temple.

The sun shone warm on Caramon's face and he smiled. His vision was returning. He was certain of it, he said. He could see the sunlight and he swore he could see shadowy images of his brother and Scrounger.

"That is well, my brother," Raistlin said. "Keep your eyes closed, however. The sunlight is too strong and might do them more injury. Sit down here for a moment while I make a bandage."

He cut a strip of cloth from the hem of his robe and tied it gently around it Caramon's eyes. Caramon protested at first, but Raistlin was firm and, accustomed to obeying his brother, Caramon submitted to being blindfolded. He trusted his brother's diagnosis, accepted that his vision would return. Fretting and worrying would do him no good, and so he sat with his back against the sun-warmed stone, basked in the light shining on his face, and wondered how the attack was proceeding and if they'd set up the mess tent.

"Can you walk, Caramon?" Raistlin asked.

There had been no more tremors, but he had no idea if the temple had suffered any structural damage. Until someone who knew something about such matters came to look at it, he did not trust to its safety.

This holy place does appear to exert a healthful influence, Raistlin thought, watching color return to his brother's wan face. His pulse was strong and he stated stoutly that he was well enough to run up good old Heave-Gut hill. He gave it as his opinion that he was completely cured and if Raistlin would just take off this damn rag . . .

Raistlin said firmly that the rag must stay. He and Scrounger assisted Caramon to stand. Caramon walked under his own power, accepting his brother's hand on his arm to guide him.

The three left the temple to the sunshine and the silver moonlight, to the dead and to the living and the dragons, sleeping safely in their leathery shells, their spirits roaming the stars, waiting to be born.

20

ere they come!" the sergeant of the archers of Hope's End yelled from the wall. As if in witness to the truth of his words, the man standing next to him dropped down dead, an arrow through his helmet.

The baron's men stood at the ready behind the gates. One moment there had been confusion, yelling and shouting. The next, disciplined silence. All eyes were on the officers, whose eyes were on the baron, standing atop the wall, looking out at the enemy, an enemy whose numbers seemed to grow alarmingly. Even counting the forces of the city, the baron was outnumbered almost two to one. And these were fresh troops, well armed, with an able, if loathsome, commander.

Under heavy covering fire, the enemy's engineers were running across the ground, hauling siege ladders and battering rams. The ranks of the infantry were four deep and marched to the sound of booming drums. Even as he watched death flow toward him across the bloody ground, the baron admired the precise discipline, the men keeping their formation even when arrows from the wall hit their first ranks.

Looking at the size and might of the forces arrayed against him, the baron was confirmed in his thinking. No matter what others might say, the action he intended was not the rash act of a madman. It was the only way to save this city, save his own forces. If they remained here, hiding behind the walls, the great numbers of the enemy would swarm over them like ants on a carcass.

The baron turned to look to his own men. They were lined up by company along the road. Each company was eight men across and as many as twenty men deep. There was no talking in the ranks, no foolery. The men were in grim and deadly earnest. The baron looked down at them, and he was proud of them.

"Soldiers of the Army of the Mad Baron!" he yelled from the wall. The men looked up at him, answered with a cheer. "This is the end!" he continued. "We are victorious this day or we are dead." He pointed a jabbing finger out over the wall. "When you set eyes upon the enemy, remember that they *shot our dead in the back!*"

A roar of anger rumbled through the troops.

"It is time to take our revenge!"

The roar of anger swelled to a cheer for the baron.

"Good luck to us," he said to the city's commander and to the lord mayor, shaking each by the hand.

The lord mayor was ashen in color. Sweat rolled down his face, despite the cool wind that had recently surged out of the mountains. He was a political figure, he could have sought refuge in his own home, and few would have thought worse of him. But he was grimly determined to stick to his post, though he cringed and shook at every trumpet blast.

"Good luck to you, Mad Lad," said the elderly commander to the baron and ducked just in time to avoid an arrow. "Confound it," the old man muttered, with a sour look for the arrow that lay spent at his feet. "Let me at least live long enough to see this sight. Win or lose, it's going to be glorious."

The baron left the wall, ran nimbly down the stairs and back to street level. He took his place on foot at the front of his army, drew his sword, and raised it high. The sun's bright rays flashed along the blade. He held the sword poised, waiting.

The gate boomed and shuddered. The first of the battering rams had arrived. Before the enemy could hit the gate a second time, the baron gave the signal.

The gates to the city of Hope's End swung open.

The attackers cheered, thinking they had breached the defenses.

The baron let fall his sword. Trumpets sounded, drums rolled. "Attack!" the baron yelled and ran forward through the open gates, straight into the ranks of the enemy. Behind him came Center Company, the most experienced veterans in the army, the most heavily armored and armed. With a savage yell, they thundered through the gates, wielding swords and battle-axes.

Caught completely by surprise, the soldiers manning the battering ram dropped the oak log, fumbled for their swords. The baron hit their leader squarely in the chest with his sword, drove the weapon clean through the man's body so that it emerged covered with blood from his back. The baron yanked free his weapon, parried a vicious chop from another of the enemy, who was attacking him on his flank, thrust the sword into the man's rib cage.

He tried to recover the sword, only to find his weapon fouled in the man's ribs. He couldn't pull the sword free. Fighting and death were all around him. His men were shouting and screaming with rage, blood spattered on them all like rain. The baron placed his foot on the body, held it down and yanked free his sword. He was ready to face the next enemy soldier, only to find there were none. The battering ram lay in front of the gates, surrounded by the dead bodies of those who had wielded it.

Now began the real battle.

The baron looked for his standard-bearer, found the man right beside him.

"Forward!" he yelled and began the advance, his standard snapping in the cold wind.

Center Company continued their advance on the run, yelling their battle cries, brandishing weapons stained with blood. Arrows from Archer Company, manning the walls, buzzed over their heads and fell among the enemy like vicious wasps, decimating the enemy's front ranks. For many of the enemy soldiers, this was their first combat. And this was nothing like training. Their comrades were dying around them. An army of savage, screaming monsters hurtled toward them. The front ranks of the enemy halted, the soldiers wavered. Officers plied their whips, shouted for the lines to hold.

Center Company, led by the baron, hit the front ranks of the enemy with an armor-plated crash that could be heard on the walls. They stabbed and sliced and chopped, showing no mercy, giving no quarter. They had seen the bodies of their comrades lying before the gate, the black-feathered arrows in their backs. They had one thought and that was to kill those who had used them so treacherously.

The front ranks of the enemy collapsed under the fury of the charge. Those who stood their ground paid for their courage with their lives. A few fell back fighting. Many more flung down their shields and, heedless of the whips, broke and ran.

Center Company kept going, plowing through the enemy's lines, leaving a bloody furrow behind. Other companies came behind Center Company, fighting those of the enemy who, driven by the whips of their officers, came surging in to fill the great gaping hole left by the onslaught of the baron and his company.

"There's our objective!" the baron shouted and pointed to a small rise, where stood Commander Kholos.

Kholos had laughed loudly and derisively at the sight of the baron's men pouring out of the gate, leaving the safety of the city behind in a mad charge. He waited confidently for his men to overwhelm the baron's forces, crush them, annihilate them. He heard the crash as the two armies came together, he waited for the baron's standard to fall.

The standard did not fall. The standard advanced. It was Kholos's men who were running now, running in the wrong direction.

"Shoot those cowards!" Kholos roared in fury to his archers. Foam flecked his mouth. He pointed at his own fleeing troops.

"Commander!" Master Vardash, his face swollen from

his commander's blow, came running up to report. "The enemy has broken through the lines!"

"My horse!" Kholos yelled.

Other officers were shouting for their horses, but before the squires could bring forward the horses, Center Company and the baron smashed into the knot of men and their bodyguards. Master Vardash fell in the first onslaught, his face now a mask of blood.

"Kholos is mine!" the baron yelled and pushed and shoved his way through the press of heaving, struggling bodies to reach the commander who had insulted him and murdered his men.

Kholos held his ground and it seemed that he alone might yet turn the tide of battle. Heavily armored, he scorned to use a shield, fought with two weapons, a longsword in one hand and a dirk in the other. He thrust and slashed, seeming to use very little effort. Three men fell to the ground before him, one with his skull cleaved in two, another decapitated, the third from a dirk stab to the heart.

So formidable was Kholos that Center Company's advance faltered. The most experienced of the veterans fell back before him. The baron halted, shocked at the sight of that goblinish face twisted into a horrible smile, a smile made hideous with battle-lust and the delight in killing.

"You betrayed us!" the baron roared. "By Kiri-Jolith, I swear that I'll nail your head to my tent post this night! And spit on it in the morning!"

"Mercenary scum." Trampling bodies beneath his feet, Kholos strode forward. "I challenge you to single combat! A fight to the death! If you've the stomach for it, you cheap sell-sword."

The baron's face split into a grin. "I accept!" he yelled. Glancing behind him, he shouted, "You men know what to do!"

"Yes, sir," Commander Morgon bellowed.

The baron marched forward to meet his foe. His men held back, watching grimly.

Kholos swung a vicious blow with his longsword, but he was used to fighting taller enemies. The sword whistled clean over the head of the baron, who crouched low and made a running dive for Kholos's knees. The move took Kholos completely by surprise. The baron barreled into Kholos, took him down to the ground.

"Now!" shouted Commander Morgon.

The soldiers of Center Company rushed forward, leapt on top of the fallen commander, swords slashing and stabbing.

The baron crawled out from under the crush.

"Are you hurt, my lord?" Commander Morgon asked, assisting the baron to stand.

"I don't think so," said the baron. "I think this is mostly his blood. I can't believe that bastard thought I'd actually fight him in honorable combat! Ha, ha, ha!"

Morgon waded back into the fray, grabbed hold of his soldiers, pulled them back.

"All right, boys! Fun's over. I think the bastard's dead."

The men gradually fell back, breathing hard, bloody but grinning. The baron walked over to look at the body of the commander, weltering in his own blood, his eyes staring skyward, a look of utter surprise on his yellow, goblin face.

The baron nodded in grim satisfaction, then turned, his sword in his hand. "Our work's not done yet, men—" he began.

"I'm not so sure of that, my lord," said Commander Morgon. "Look at that, will you, sir?"

The baron looked around the field. The officers of Kholos's command staff who were not dead or wounded were on their knees, hands raised in surrender. The rest of the enemy was fleeing the field, running for the shelter of the woods, the baron's men in pursuit.

"It's a rout, sir!" said Morgon.

The baron frowned. Caught up in their own battle-lust, his troops had broken ranks, were scattered all over the field. The enemy was on the run now, but it would take only one courageous and level-headed officer to halt the rout, regroup his men, and turn defeat into victory.

"The bugler?" The baron looked around. "Where in the name of Kiri-Jolith is my goddamned bugler?"

"I think he was killed, my lord," said Morgon.

The sight of sunshine gleaming off brass caught the baron's eye. Among the enemy officers stood a boy, shivering and frightened, a bugle clutched in his white-knuckled hand.

"Bring me that boy!" the baron commanded.

Commander Morgon grabbed hold of the boy, dragged him forward. The boy fell to his knees in abject terror.

"Stand up and look at me, blast you. Do you know 'A Posey from Abanasinia'?" the baron demanded.

The boy slowly and fearfully regained his feet, stared at the baron in blank astonishment.

"Do you know it, boy?" the baron roared. "Or don't you?"

The boy gave a trembling nod. The tune was a common one.

"Good!" The baron smiled. "Sound the first chorus, and I'll let you go."

The boy shivered, panicked, confused.

"It's all right, son," the baron said, his voice softening. He placed his hand on the boy's shoulder. "My regiment uses that tune as Recall. Go ahead and blow it."

Reassured, the boy brought his instrument to his lips. The first note was a failure. The baron winced. Gamely, the boy licked his lips and tried again. The clear sounds of the call cut across the sounds of battle and pursuit.

"Good, boy, good!" the baron said with approval. "Repeat it, and keep repeating it!"

The boy did as he was told. The familiar call brought the men to their senses. They broke off the attack, looked around for their officers, began to reform into ranks.

"March them back to the city, Morgon," the baron ordered. "Pick up any of our wounded on the way."

He cast a grim glance in the direction of the enemy encampment. "We may have to do this all over again tomorrow."

"I doubt it, my lord," said Morgon. "Their officers are either dead or our prisoners. The soldiers will wait for nightfall, then break camp and head for home. There won't be a tent standing there by morning."

"A wager on that, Morgon?"

"A wager, my lord."

The two clasped hands. "This is one bet I hope I lose," said the baron.

Morgon ran off to organize the withdrawal. The baron was about to follow, realized that the trumpet was still blowing raucously and desperately.

"Very good, son," the baron said. "You can stop blowing now."

The boy lowered his trumpet hesitantly to his side.

The baron nodded, waved his hand. "Run along, lad. I said I'd let you go. You're free. No one will hurt you."

The boy didn't move. He stood staring at the baron, wide-eyed.

The baron, shrugging, started to walk away.

"Sir, sir!" the boy called. "Can I join *your* army?"

The baron stopped, looked back. "How old are you, boy?"

"Eighteen, sir," he answered.

"You mean thirteen, don't you?"

The boy hung his head.

"You're too young for a life like this, son. You've seen too much death already. Go home to your ma. Likely she's worried sick about you."

The boy didn't budge.

The baron shook his head, resumed walking. He heard footsteps patter along behind him. He sighed again, but did not turn around.

"My lord, are you all right?" Master Senej asked.

"Dead tired," the baron answered. "And I hurt all over. But otherwise unharmed, praise be to my god." He glanced behind him, motioned the officer to come near.

"Can you use some help, Senej?"

The master nodded. "Yes, my lord. We've got a lot of wounded, not to mention all these prisoners. I could definitely use another hand."

The baron jerked his thumb back at the boy. "You've got one. Go with Master Senej, boy. Do as you're told."

"Yes, my lord!" The boy smiled tremulously. "Thank you, my lord."

Shaking his head, the baron trudged across the field, heading back to the city of Hope's End, whose bells were ringing in wild triumph.

21

A glorious fight, Red!" Horkin said, gleefully rubbing his hands, which were black with flash powder. He came through the gates with the first of the wounded, to find his apprentice waiting for him. "You should have been there."

Horkin gazed intently at Raistlin. "I take that back. Looks like you saw some action yourself, Red. What happened?"

"Do we really have time to waste on this, sir?" Raistlin asked. "With all these wounded to care for? I found the temple. I think it would be an excellent shelter, but I'd like you to take a look at it."

"Perhaps you're right," said Horkin, giving Raistlin a searching glance.

"This way, sir," said Raistlin and turned away.

Raistlin explained that the temple had been shaken by tremors, nothing unusual for this region, according to the citizens. Horkin examined the temple, studied the pillars and the walls and finally deemed it sound. All that was needed now was a source for water. A search revealed a well of clear, cold springwater at the rear of the temple. Horkin gave orders that the wounded should be brought to this restful place.

The wagons bearing the wounded trundled through the streets. The grateful citizens crowded around with offers of blankets, food, bedding, medicines. Soon blankets covered the temple floor in neat and even rows. The surgeon plied his tools. Raistlin and Horkin and skilled healers from the city worked among the men, doing what they could to ease their pain and make them comfortable.

No miracles of healing occurred in the temple. Some of the soldiers died, others lived, but it did seem to Horkin's mind that those who died were more at peace and that the wounded who survived healed much more rapidly and completely than could have been expected.

The first order of business for the baron was to visit the wounded. He came as he was, fresh from the battlefield—grimy, bloody, some of the blood his own, most of it his enemy's. Though he was near to falling with exhaustion, he did not show it. He did not rush his visit, but took time to say a few words to each one of the casualities. He called all the soldiers by name, recalled his courage in the field. He seemed to have personally witnessed each valorous act. He promised the dying he would support their families. Raistlin would afterward learn that this was a vow the baron held sacred.

His visit to the wounded concluded, the baron paused to chat with Horkin and Raistlin about the temple they had discovered. The baron was intrigued to hear that a tomb of a Solamnic Knight lay in a burial chamber beneath the cavern. Raistlin described most of their experience in detail, keeping to himself certain facts that were really no one else's business. The baron listened attentively, frowned when he heard that the lid of the Knight's sarcophagus had been opened.

"That must be attended to," he said. "Robbers may have already tried to loot the tomb. This gallant Knight should be allowed to continue his slumber in peace. You have no notion of what this treasure is, do you, Majere?"

"The inscription made no mention of it, sir," Raistlin answered. "My guess is that whatever it was, it now lies beneath tons of rock. The tunnel that leads out from the burial chamber is completely impassable."

"I see." The baron eyed Raistlin closely.

Raistlin returned the baron's gaze steadily and it was

the baron who shifted his eyes away from the stare of the strange hourglass pupils. Continuing his rounds of the wounded, the baron came to the cot where Caramon fretted and fidgeted, an extremely uncooperative patient. He wasn't hurt, he maintained. Nothing wrong with him. He wanted to be up and around and doing. He wanted a proper meal, not some water they'd dragged a chicken through and called it soup. His vision was fine, or rather it would be if they'd just take off this confounded rag. Scrounger remained with the patient, trying to distract him with stories and reminding him twenty times a half-hour not to rub his eyes.

Though busy with his other patients, Raistlin kept watch on the baron's movements through the temple and when the baron came to his twin, Raistlin hastened over to be present during this conversation.

"Caramon Majere!" the baron said, shaking his hand. "What happened to you? I don't recall seeing you in the battle."

"Baron?" Caramon brightened. "Hullo, sir! I'm sorry I missed the fighting. I heard it was a glorious victory. I was here, sir. We—"

Raistlin laid a hand on his brother's shoulder and, when the baron wasn't looking, gave Caramon a hard pinch with his fingers.

"Ouch!" Caramon yelped. "What—"

"There, there," said Raistlin soothingly, adding in an undertone, "He has these momentary flashes of pain, my lord. As for what happened to him, he was with me, exploring the temple. We were caught in the tunnels when the quake hit. Rock dust flew in Caramon's eyes, blinding him. The blindness is temporary. He needs rest, that is all."

Raistlin's fingers, digging into Caramon's flesh, warned him to keep silent. A piercing glance at Scrounger caused the half-kender, who had opened his mouth, to shut it again.

"Excellent! Glad to hear it!" the baron said heartily. "You're a good soldier, Majere. I'd hate to lose you."

"Really, sir?" Caramon asked. "Thank you, sir."

"You rest like they tell you," the baron added. "You're under the healer's orders now. I want you back on the line as soon as you're fit."

"I will, sir. Thank you, sir," Caramon said again, smiling proudly. "Raist," he whispered, when he heard the baron's heavy boots move away, "why didn't you tell him what really happened? Why didn't you tell him you fought the enemy wizard and beat him?"

"Yes, why?" Scrounger asked eagerly, leaning across Caramon.

The answer: because it was in Raistlin's nature to be secretive, because he didn't want Horkin asking prying questions, because he didn't want Horkin or anyone else finding out about the amazing power of the staff, a power Raistlin had no idea how to use himself at the moment. All these reasons he could have given his brother and the half-kender, but he knew they wouldn't understand.

Sitting down by his brother's side, Raistlin motioned Scrounger to come close. "We didn't exactly cover ourselves in glory," Raistlin told them dryly. "Our orders were to inspect the temple and return to report. Instead, we were about to set off in search of treasure."

"That's true," said Caramon, his face flushing.

"You wouldn't want the baron to be disappointed in you," Raistlin continued.

"No, of course not," Caramon said.

"Me neither," Scrounger said, chagrined.

"Then we will keep the truth to ourselves. We hurt no one by doing so." Raistlin rose to his feet, prepared to return to his duties.

Scrounger plucked the sleeve of Raistlin's robe.

"Yes, what do you want?" Raistlin glowered.

"What's the real reason you don't want us to tell?" Scrounger asked in an undertone.

Raistlin made a show of glancing about to see if anyone was listening. He bent down, whispered in Scrounger's ear. "The treasure."

Scrounger's eyes opened wide. "I knew it! We're going back for it!"

"Someday, perhaps," Raistlin said softly. "Don't tell a soul!"

"I won't! I promise! This is so exciting," Scrounger said and winked several times in a manner calculated to arouse instant suspicion in anyone who happened to be watching.

Raistlin went about his duties, satisfied that his brother would keep silent out of shame and that Scrounger would keep silent out of hope. Raistlin would have never trusted a true kender with this secret, but in Scrounger's case, the mage guessed that the human side would see to it that the kender side kept its mouth shut.

Someday, Raistlin did intend to return. Perhaps the treasure was buried. Perhaps it was not.

"If I could find out what the treasure was," Raistlin said to himself, deftly wrapping a bandage around a soldier's lacerated leg, "I might have some idea of where to start looking for it."

He spoke with several of the city's inhabitants, asked subtle questions concerning the possibility of a treasure buried in the mountains.

The residents smiled, shook their heads, and said that he must have been taken in by some traveling peddler. Hope's End was a prosperous town, but certainly not a wealthy one. They knew of no treasure.

Raistlin could almost believe that the people of Hope's End were conspiring to keep the treasure from him, except that they were so damn complacent about it, so smiling in their denials, so amused by the entire notion. He began to think that perhaps they were right, that this was all a kender tale.

He went to his bed that night in an extremely bad mood, a mood not helped by the fact that he was troubled by fearful dreams in which he was being attacked by some immense, awful creature, a creature he could not see because a bright silver light had struck him blind.

* * * * *

The next day, the baron held a ceremony to clean the tomb of the fallen rocks and dust, replace the lid of the sarcophagus over the dead Knight. The baron's commanders accompanied him and, because they had discovered the Knight's tomb, Raistlin and Caramon and Scrounger were invited to be part of the honor guard.

Caramon wanted to remove the bandage. He could see fine, he said, except for a little blurriness. Raistlin was adamant. The bandage must stay. Caramon would have continued the argument, but the baron himself offered Caramon an arm in support, a great honor for the young soldier. Flushed with pleasure and embarrassment, Caramon accepted the baron's guidance, walked proudly if haltingly at the baron's side.

The baron and the honor guard, carrying torches, entered the burial chamber with grave and solemn aspect, silent and respectful. The baron took his place at the head of the carved Knight. The company commanders ranged themselves around the tomb. They stood with hands clasped before them, heads bowed, some praying to Kiri-Jolith, others thinking somber thoughts, reflecting on their own mortality. Raistlin took his place at the head of the sarcophagus, keeping close to his brother. Glancing inside the tomb, Raistlin was momentarily paralyzed with astonishment.

Inside the tomb was a leather-bound book.

Raistlin thought back to yesterday, tried to recall if the book had been there or not. He didn't remember seeing it, but the chamber had been dark yesterday, with only his staff for light. The book was pressed against the side of the marble casket. He might have easily overlooked the book in the shadows.

The thought came to Raistlin that this book contained information about the treasure, perhaps revealed its hiding place. He trembled with desire. He needed that book and, even as he stood gazing at it, the baron had ceased his prayers, was ordering his commanders to prepare to slide the lid of the sarcophagus back in place.

"I beg one moment, sir," Raistlin said, his voice half-stifled by his excitement and his fear that someone else would see the book and announce the fact. "I would do honor to the Knight."

The baron raised his eyebrows, probably wondering why a wizard should honor a Solamnic Knight, but he nodded that Raistlin was to proceed.

Reaching into one of his pouches, Raistlin drew out a handful of rose petals. He opened his palm, so that all could see what he held. The baron smiled and nodded.

"Most appropriate," he said, and looked upon Raistlin with approval and new respect.

Raistlin lowered his hand into the tomb, to scatter the rose petals over the body of the Knight. When he withdrew his arm, he managed that the capacious sleeve of his red robe covered his hand, concealed his fingers, which had deftly taken hold of the slim leather volume. Keeping the precious book hidden in his sleeve, Raistlin stepped back from the tomb and stood with his head bowed.

The baron looked to Commander Morgon, who ordered the officers to place their hands on the tomb's covering. At a second command, the officers lifted the heavy lid. The baron came to attention, raised his hand in the Solamnic Knight's salute.

"Kiri-Jolith be with him," the baron said.

At another command from Morgon, the officers slid the marble top into place. The lid settled upon the sarcophagus with a soft sigh that bore with it the fragrance of dried rose petals.

22

Raistlin had his duties to attend to before he could take time to examine his prize. He secreted the book beneath Caramon's mattress, not telling him of it, returning at every opportunity to make certain the book was still there, had not been discovered. Caramon was touched to find his brother so unusually attentive.

Raistlin or Horkin usually sat up during the night with the patients, not keeping broad awake, like those on guard duty, but dozing in a chair, starting up at the sound of a moan of pain, assisting a patient to answer nature's call. That night, Raistlin volunteered to take the first watch. The weary Horkin didn't argue, but lay down on his own cot and was soon adding his snores to the cacophony of snores, grunts, groans, coughs, and wheezes of the rest.

Raistlin made his rounds, dispensing doses of poppy syrup to those who were in pain, bathing the foreheads of the feverish, adding more blankets to those who chilled. His touch was gentle and his voice held a sympathy in which the wounded could believe. Not like the sympathy of the healthy, the robust, however well meaning.

"I know what it is to suffer," Raistlin seemed to say. "I know what it is to feel pain."

His fellow soldiers, who had never had much use for him, who had called him names behind his back and occasionally to his face (if his brother weren't around), now begged him to stay by their beds "just a moment more," gripped his arm when the pain was the worst, asked him to write letters to wives and loved ones. Raistlin would sit and he would write and he would tell stories to take their minds off their pain. After they were healed, those who had never liked him before he nursed them found that they didn't like him any better afterward, the difference being that now they would knock the head off anyone who said a bad word against him.

When the last patient had finally succumbed to the poppy juice and drifted off to sleep, Raistlin was free to examine his book. He slid it out from its hiding place carefully, although he did not particularly fear waking Caramon, who generally slept the deep sleep ascribed to dogs and the virtuous. Book in hand, concealed in the folds of his sleeves, Raistlin cast a sharp glance at Horkin. The mage slept lightly when he had wounded to tend, the slightest moan or restless tossing would wake him. As it was, he did open one eye, peered sleepily at Raistlin.

"All is well, Master," Raistlin said softly. "Go back to sleep."

Horkin smiled, rolled over, and was soon snoring lustily. Raistlin watched his superior a moment longer, determined at last that the man must be asleep. No one could fake such obstreperous snores, not without half-strangling himself.

Horkin had built a fire in a brazier placed at the front of the temple where an altar might be found. He had not done so out of reverence, although he had taken care to be extremely respectful, but to warm the building against the night's chill. Raistlin drew his chair close to the brazier of charcoal, which burned with a yellow-blue light. He'd added some sage and dried lavender to the fire to try to mask the smell of blood, urine, and vomit that was all-pervasive in the sick chamber, a smell he himself no longer noticed. Settling by the blaze, he cast a sharp look around the room. Everyone was asleep.

Raistlin breathed in a deep sigh, leaned the Staff of Magius against the wall, and examined his prize.

The book was made of sheets of parchment bound and stitched together. A leather cover shielded it from the elements. He found no markings on the outside, it was unlike a spellbook in that regard. It was an ordinary book of the type used by the quartermaster to mark down how many barrels of ale were drunk, how many casks of salt pork were left, how many baskets of apples he had remaining. Raistlin frowned, this was not a propitious omen.

His spirits improved immensely when he opened the book to find a hand-drawn map on one page and some scrawled letters and numbers on another. This looked much more promising. He glanced hurriedly at the numerals, saw only that they were probably keeping count of something. Jewels? Money? Almost certainly. Now he was getting somewhere! He left the notation, went back to the map.

The map had been drawn in haste, with the book resting on an uneven surface—as if the mapper had steadied it on a rock or perhaps his knee. Raistlin spent several moments puzzling out the crude drawings and the even cruder notations. At last he determined that he held in his hands a map showing a path that led to a hidden entrance into a mountain.

Raistlin pored over the map, studying every detail, and came at last to the unwanted and frustrated conclusion that the map was worthless to him. The mapper had drawn a clear trail that would be easy to follow once one found the trail's starting point. The mapper had marked the trail's starting point—a stand of three pines—but had not given any indication of where these pines might be found in relation to the mountain. Were they on the north, the south? Were they halfway up the mountainside, in the foothills?

One could presumably search the entire mountain for a stand of three pine trees, but that might take a lifetime. The mapper knew where to find the stand of pines. The mapper could return to the stand without difficulty, therefore the mapper had seen no need to add the route to the stands. A wise precaution in case the map fell into the wrong hands. The map was intended to refresh the mapper's memory when he came to claim the treasure.

Raistlin stared at the map gloomily, willing it to tell him something more, stared at it until the red lines began to swim in his vision. Irritably he flipped the page, returned to the notations, hoping that perhaps they would provide some clue.

He studied them, intrigued, baffled, so intent upon his work that he did not hear footsteps approaching. He did not know someone was standing behind him until the person's shadow fell across the book.

Raistlin started, covered the book with the sleeve of his robe, and sprang to his feet.

Caramon backed up a step, raised his hands as if to ward off a blow. "Uh, sorry, Raist! I didn't mean to startle you."

"What are you doing sneaking up on me like that!" Raistlin demanded.

"I thought you might be asleep," Caramon replied meekly. "I didn't want to wake you."

"I wasn't asleep," Raistlin retorted. He sat back down, calmed his racing heart, half dizzy with the sudden rush of blood and adrenaline.

"You're studying your spells. I'll leave you alone." Caramon started to tiptoe away.

"No, wait," Raistlin said. "Come here. I want you to look at something. By the way, who told you you could take off the bandage?"

"No one. But I can see fine, Raist. Even the blurriness is gone. And I'm sick of broth. That's all they feed a guy around here. There's nothing wrong with my stomach."

"That much is obvious," Raistlin said with a disparaging glance at his twin's rotund belly.

Caramon sat down on the floor beside his brother. "What have you got there?" he asked, eyeing the book with suspicion. He knew from sad experience that books his brother read were likely to be incomprehensible at best, downright dangerous at worst.

"I found this book in the Knight's tomb today," Raistlin said in a smothered whisper.

Caramon's eyes widened, rounded. "You took it? From a tomb?"

"Don't look at me like that, Caramon," Raistlin snapped. "I am not a grave robber! I think it was placed there on purpose. For me to find."

"The Knight wanted us to have it," Caramon said in excitement. "It's about the treasure, isn't it! He wants us to find it—"

"If he does, he's making it damn difficult," Raistlin remarked coldly. "Here, I want you to look at this word. Tell me what it says."

Raistlin opened the book to the page of notations. Caramon looked obediently at the word. There wasn't much doubt.

"Eggs," he said promptly.

"Are you certain?" Raistlin persisted.

"*E-g-g-s.* Eggs. Yep, I'm sure."

Raistlin sighed deeply.

Caramon gazed at him in sudden, stunned comprehension. "You're not saying that the treasure is . . . is . . ."

"I don't know what the treasure is," Raistlin said gloomily. "Nor, I'm thinking, did the person who wrote this down in the book. It appears that the Knight has given us his grocery list!"

"Let me see that!" Caramon took the book from his twin, stared at it, pondered it, even tried turning it upside down. "These figures—where it says, '25 g. and 50 s.' That could be twenty-five gold and fifty silver," he argued hopefully.

"Or twenty-five grapes and fifty sausages," Raistlin returned sarcastically.

"But there's a map—"

"—which is completely useless. Even if we knew where to find the starting point, which we don't, the trail leads into tunnels in the mountain, tunnels we saw collapse."

He held out his hand for the book.

Caramon was still staring at it. "You know, Raist, this handwriting looks familiar."

Raistlin snorted. "Give me back the book."

"It does, Raist! I swear!" Caramon's brow furrowed, an aid to his mental process. "I've seen this writing before."

"And you said your eyesight was improved. Go back to bed. And put that bandage on."

"But, Raist—"

"Go to bed, Caramon," Raistlin ordered irritably. "I'm tired and my head aches. I'll wake you in time to breakfast in the mess tent."

"Will you? That'll be great, Raist, thanks." Caramon cast one last lingering and puzzled glance at the book, then handed it back to his brother. His twin knew best, after all.

Raistlin made his rounds. Finding that everyone was slumbering more or less peacefully, he left to use the privies that were located in a small outbuilding behind the temple. On his return, he tossed the leather book onto the rubbish heap, set for tomorrow's burning.

Entering the temple, Raistlin found Horkin wide awake, warming his hands by the glowing fire. The elder mage's eyes were bright, quizzical in the firelight.

"You know, Red," Horkin said companionably, rubbing his hands in the comfortable warmth, "that red-robed wizard you talked about wasn't in the battle. I know because I was on the watch for him. A powerful war wizard, from what you said. He might have made a difference in that fight. We might not have won if he'd been there, and that's a fact. Strange, that Commander Kholos had a powerful war wizard on his side and didn't use him in the final conflict. Very strange, that, Red."

Horkin shook his head. He shifted his eyes from the blaze to look directly at Raistlin. "You wouldn't happen to know why that wizard wasn't there, would you, Red?"

He wasn't there because I was fighting him, Raistlin could have said with blushing modesty. I defeated him. I don't consider myself a hero. But if you insist on presenting me with that medal . . .

The Staff of Magius stood against the altar. Raistlin reached out his hand to touch the staff, to feel the life inside the wood, magical life, warm and responsive to him now.

"I have no idea what could have happened to the wizard, Master Horkin," Raistlin said.

"You weren't in the battle, Red," said Horkin. "And that wizard wasn't in the battle. Seems odd, that it does."

"A coincidence, nothing more, sir," Raistlin replied.

"Humpf." Horkin shook his head. Shrugging away his questions, he changed the subject. "Well, Red, you survived your first battle and I don't mind telling you that you handled yourself well. For one, you didn't get yourself killed, and that's a plus. For two, you kept me from getting myself killed, and that's a bigger plus. You're a skilled healer, and who knows but that someday, with the proper training, you'll be a skilled mage."

Horkin winked and Raistlin wisely chose not to be offended.

"Thank you, sir," he said, with a smile. "Your praise means a great deal to me."

"You deserve it, Red. What I guess I'm saying in my clumsy way is that I'm going to put you up for promotion. I'm going to recommend that you be made Master's Assistant. With an increase in pay, of course. That is, if you intend to stick with us."

Promotion! Raistlin was amazed. Horkin rarely had a good word to say to him. Raistlin would not have been surprised to have been paid off and dismissed.

He was beginning to understand his superior officer a bit better now, however. Quick to tell him what he was doing wrong, Horkin would never praise him for doing right. But he wouldn't forget what Raistlin had done either.

"Thank you for your faith in me, Master," Raistlin said. "I was thinking of leaving the army. I have been thinking lately that it is wrong for one man to be paid for killing another, for taking another's life."

"We did some good here, Red," Horkin said. "We saved the people in this city from slavery and death. We were on the side of right."

"But we started out on the side of wrong," Raistlin countered.

"We switched to the correct side in time, though," Horkin said comfortably.

"By chance, by happenstance!" Raistlin shook his head.

"Nothing ever happens by chance, Raistlin," Horkin said quietly. "Everything happens for a reason. Your brain may not know the reason. Your brain may never figure it out. But your heart knows. Your heart always knows.

"Now," he added kindly, "go get some sleep."

Raistlin went to his bed, but not to sleep. He thought about Horkin's words, thought about all that had happened to him. And then it occurred to him, hearing Horkin's words again in his head, that the mage had called him by name. Raistlin. Not Red.

Rising from his bed, Raistlin walked back outside. Solinari was full and bright, shining on the town as if he were pleased with the outcome. Raistlin searched the rubbish heap in the moonlight, found the book lying where he had tossed it.

"*Everything happens for a reason,*" Raistlin repeated, opening the book. He looked at the worthless map, its red lines stark and clear in the silver moonlight. Perhaps I'll never know what that reason is. But if I can make nothing out of this book, maybe others can.

Returning to his bed, he did not lie down, but sat up the rest of the night, writing a letter detailing his encounters—both encounters—with Immolatus. When the missive was complete, he folded the letter over the small book, recited an incantation over both book and letter, and wrapped it up in a parcel addressed to *Parsalian, Head of the Conclave, Tower of High Sorcery, Wayreth.*

The next morning, he would ask if the baron had any messengers riding in the direction of Flotsam. He placed another spell upon the package, to keep it safe from prying eyes, then wrote on the outside, "Antimodes of Flotsam" along with the name of the street where his mentor resided. By the time Raistlin was finished, night had departed. The sun's rays crept softly into the temple to gently waken the sleeping.

Caramon was the first one up.

"Come with me, Raist," he said. "You should eat something."

Raistlin was surprised to find that he was hungry, unusually hungry. He and his twin left the temple, were on their way to the mess tent, when they were joined by Horkin.

"You don't mind if I tag along, do you, Red?" Horkin asked. "The wounded are getting along so well I figured I'd have a proper breakfast this morning myself. I hear cook's preparing a special treat. Besides, we have something to celebrate. Your brother's been promoted, Majere."

"Have you? That's great!" Caramon paused, the implication of this suddenly occurring to him. "Does this mean that we're staying with the baron's army?"

"We're staying," Raistlin said.

"Hurrah!" Caramon gave a shout that woke up half the town. "There goes Scrounger. Wait till he hears. Scrounger!" Caramon bellowed, waking the other half of the town. "Scrounger, hey! Come here!"

Scrounger was pleased to hear of Raistlin's promotion, especially pleased when he heard this meant that the twins would be staying with the army.

"What *are* we having for breakfast?" Caramon asked. "You said it was special, sir?"

"A gift from the grateful people of Hope's End," said Horkin, adding, with a suspicious quiver in his voice, "a real treasure, you might say."

"What do you mean, sir?" Raistlin asked, casting the mage a sharp glance.

"Eggs," said Horkin with a grin and a wink.

23

For you, Archmagus," said an apprentice, standing deferentially in the door leading to Par-Salian's study. "Just arrived by messenger from Flotsam." He placed a parcel on the table and departed with a bow.

Par-Salian picked up the parcel, studied it curiously. It was addressed to Antimodes, he had apparently forwarded it on. Par-Salian examined the handwriting on the address: quick, eager, impatient strokes, overlarge capital letters—flaunting creativity, a nervous curl to the tail of an *s* A leftward slant and sharpness to the letters that was like a line of a lance. An image formed in his mind of the writer and he was not surprised to find, on opening the letter inside, that it had been written by young Raistlin Majere.

Par-Salian sat down and read with interest, astonishment, and wonder the forthright, bald, and unimpassioned account of the meetings between Raistlin and a wizard described as a renegade, a wizard who called himself Immolatus.

Immolatus. The name was familiar. Par-Salian finished his perusal of the missive, read it over twice more, then turned his attention to the small leatherbound book. He understood its secrets immediately. Not surprising. The mages who resided in the Tower often saw Par-Salian standing in the window, bathed in silver moonlight, his lips moving in a one-sided conversation. All knew he communed directly with Solinari.

Par-Salian's heart lurched, his hands chilled and trembled as he realized the terrible danger, the awful tragedy that had very nearly occurred, a tragedy they had escaped through the valor of a dead Knight, the inadvertent courage of a young wizard, and the long-nurtured vengeance of a stick of wood.

Par-Salian believed, as did Horkin and with perhaps better cause, that everything happens for a reason. Still, he found this account amazing, astounding, terrifying.

There was no doubt in his mind that whoever had ordered that attack on the city of Hope's End had known about the treasure beneath the mountain, had chosen that city to attack in order to win the treasure. But for what reason, what dark purpose, Par-Salian could not guess. Destruction of the eggs was the most likely, but there were arguments against that. Why go to the trouble to attack and take a walled city with an army when a few hardened men with pickaxes could do the job just as well?

A month had passed since young Majere had written this letter and it had reached Wayreth. In that time, word had come to Par-Salian that the king of Blödehelm, King Wilhelm, had been discovered in his own dungeon, having been made prisoner by strange and sinister people, who had run the business of the kingdom in his name. Par-Salian heard the story of how these same people had fled on the arrival of Baron Ivor of Langtree and his army, who marched into Vantal and laid siege to the castle. It was the baron himself who had freed the unfortunate king. Par-Salian had not given much thought to the story then. Now he viewed it with alarm.

Forces were at work in the world, dark forces. They had no face yet, but he could give them a name. Which reminded him. Immolatus. That name was undoubtedly familiar. Opening a secret compartment in a secret drawer, he drew forth the book he had been reading when Raistlin Majere left these very walls.

When Par-Salian read a book, he did not simply remember the gist of its contents, he remembered each and every page, the written text lithographed onto the stone tablet of his mind. He had only to turn through the pages of a thousand, thousand texts cataloged in his brain until he found the one he wanted. He turned immediately to the page he recalled and there it was.

The lists of the enemy arrayed against Huma were formidable, comprised of Her Dark Majesty's strongest, most powerful, cruel, and terrible dragons. Included in their ranks were Thunderstrike the Great Blue, Werewrym the Black, Icekill the White, and Her Majesty's favorite, the red known as Immolatus. . . ."

"Immolatus," said Par-Salian and he sighed and shuddered. "So it has started. Thus we begin the long journey into darkness."

He looked back at the letter written in that quick, nervous, bold, and hungry hand, signed at the bottom:

Raistlin Majere, Magus.

Par-Salian picked up the letter. Speaking a word of magic, he caused it to be consumed by fire.

"At least," he said, "we do not walk alone."